GRADARIUS

ROMAN EQUESTRIAN II

A·M·SWINK

HISTORIUM PRESS

FIRST EDITION
COPYRIGHT © 2025 A.M. SWINK

This book contains mature themes and subjects which may be distressing for some readers. Please visit the author's website to view content warnings.

For information, contact:

historiumpublisher@gmail.com

www.amswink.com

www.historiumpress.com/a-m-swink

Hardcover ISBN 978-1-964700-55-7

Paperback ISBN 978-1-964700-56-4

Ebook ISBN 978-1-964700-57-1

Library of Congress Cataloging-in-Publication Data on file

A HISTORIUM PRESS NOVEL

www.historiumpress.com
Cover by White Rabbit Arts at
The Historical Fiction Company

FOR LAURA,
WHO BATTLES ADVERSITY WITH
AN ADMIRABLE STRENGTH

TABLE OF CONTENTS

BRITANNIA
MID-1ST CENTURY C.E.

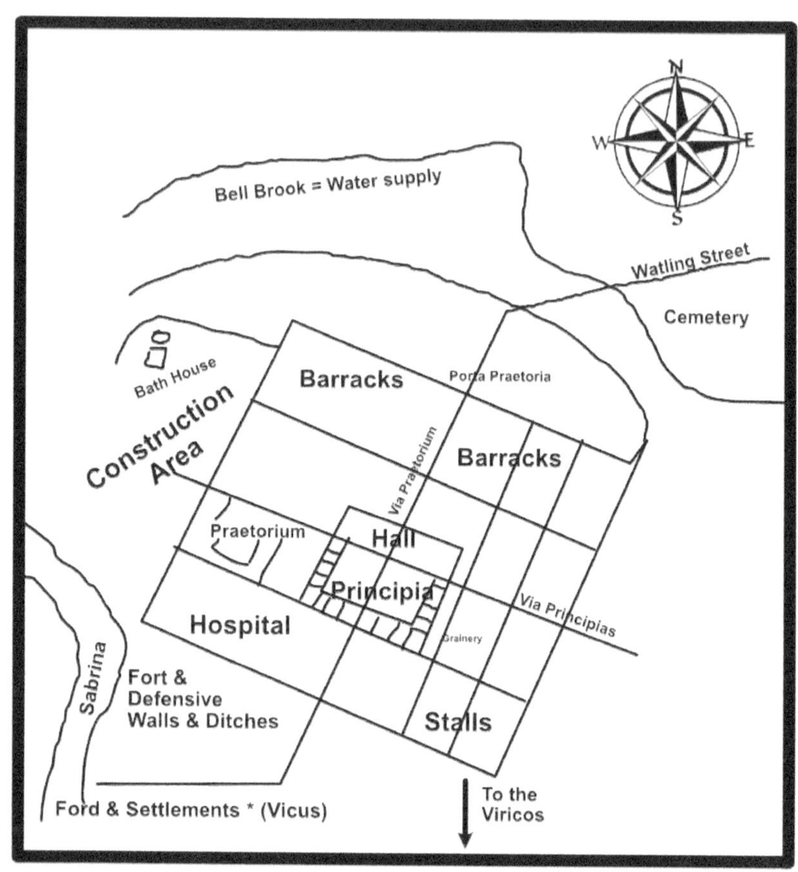

VIRCONIUM CA. AD 57-85

Dramatis Personae

A star (*) denotes a historical figure

<u>Romans</u>

Leucus Decimus Maximus: Primus Pilus, Legio XIIII Gemina

Publius Tullius Servius: Optio to Centurion Decimus

Marcus Afranius Regulus: Legate, Legio XIIII Gemina

Paulus Junius Fortunatus: Second Spear, Legio XIIII Gemina

Gaius Octavius Corvus: Camp Prefect, Legio XIIII Gemina

Sextus Cincinnatus: Tribunis Laticlavius, Legio XIIII Gemina

Lucius: Freedman of Tribune Cincinnatus; a trader

*Tiberius Claudius Tirintius: Decurion, 1st Thracian Cavalry

*Titus Flaminius: Aquilifer, Legio XIIII Gemina

Bellius Plancus: Signifer, 1st Cohort, Legio XIIII Gemina

Appius Rufinius Persius: Centurion, 5th century, 1st Cohort, Legio XIIII Gemina

*Gaius Suetonius Paulinus: Imperial Governor of Britannia

*Catus Decianus: Imperial Procurator of Britannia

Vulso: Legionary, 1st Century, 1st Cohort, Legio XIIII Gemina

Unimanus: Legionary, 1st Century, 1st Cohort, Legio XIIII Gemina

Catallus: Legionary aide to Legate Regulus

Nicomedes: Personal slave of Optio Servius; a Greek

*Titus Flavius Vespasianus: Young tribune attached to Governor Paulinus's staff

Afrania Regula:	Legate Regulus's eldest daughter
Aemilia Regula:	Legate Regulus's younger daughter
Hilaria:	Attendant to Legate Regulus's daughters; a Gaul
Gaius:	Hilaria's lively son
Fabia:	A Roman woman from Glevum
Aquila:	Personal mount of Centurion Decimus
Nero:	Personal mount of Optio Servius
Tor:	British hound; personal pet of Centurion Decimus

Britons

Luciana/Luigsech:	Cornovii slave to Centurion Decimus
Gwenfrewi:	Queen of the Cornovii Tribe; a prisoner
Morcant:	Chieftain of the Silure Tribe
Saibh:	Warrior of the Silure Tribe
Taraghlan:	Itinerant Druid; currently residing with the Silures
Muireach:	Chieftain of the Ordovice Tribe
*Prasutagus:	Chieftain of the Iceni Tribe
*Boudicca:	Queen of the Iceni Tribe; wife of Prasutagus
Emer:	Eldest daughter of Prasutagus and Boudicca
Rioghnach:	Younger daughter of Prasutagus and Boudicca
Catraoine:	Cornovii Woman; friend of Gwenfrewi

Trenus:	Cornovii Child; Catraoine's youngest son
Belena:	Close Friend and Personal Mount of Luciana

In the Vicus

Cassia:	Prostitute; Decimus's Oldest Friend; A Gaul
Metellus:	Proprietor of The Aurochs; an ex-legionary
Metella:	Daughter of Metellus
Porcius:	Legionary tonsor; a Greek
Antiope:	Practitioner of magicks; a Greek
Gale:	Weasel; familiar of Antiope

Pronunciation Guide

Acidinus	ah-KID-ih-noos
Aedicus	AI-dih-koos
Aeschylus	EH-skuh-luhs
Agamemnon	aga-MEM-nun
Amyntas	AH-meen-tas
Antedios	ahn-TEH-dyos
Antiope	an-TIE-oh-pee
Aquila	ah-KEE-lah
Aristides	ah-riz-TIE-deez
Awen	OW-when
Bakari	buh-kah-ree
Banna	BAHN-nuh
Belena	buh-leh-nuh
Belgae	BEL-gih
Brigantes	bre-GAN-tez
Caecus	KAI-koos
Camulodunum	KAH-moo-lawd-oo-num
Caratacus	kah-RAT-uh-kuz
Cartimandua	kar-tih-man-DOO-ah
Catraoine	cuh-trow-in
Catuvellauni	kat-oh-well-AHN-ee
Cernunnos	kair-NUH-nohs
Charis	KAER-his
Cornovii	kor-noh-wee
Cruscellio	kroo-KELL-io
Danu	DA-noo
Deceangli	deck-anh-lee
Demetae	deh-MEE-tay
Deoiridh	DJOHrd-ee
Diarmait	DER-mut
Dobunni	DOO-buhn-nee
Duros	DOO-rohs
Eaden	AY-den

Earrach	AH-ruh
Eisu	ay-shuh
Emer	EE-mur
Epona	uh-POH-nuh
Esus	EH-sus
Fearghas	fur-ghas
Gaesatae	guh-say-ree
Gemina	GEH-mih-nuh
Germania	GUR-man-ya (hard G)
Geta	GEH-tuh
Giamos	GHYAY-mohs (gh guttural)
Gnaeus	nyay-us
Gruffydd	GRIF-IDH
Guoy	GOO-ee
Gwenfrewi	GWEHNVReh-Wiy
Horace	ho-RAH-kay
Iceni	ai-SEE-nai
Io	ee-oh
Laodice	lay-OH-dis-ee
Lugh	LOO
Luigsech	LEE-sak
Manduessedum	MAHN-doo-ess-eh-dum
Mandusedos	MAHN-doo-see-dohs
Misenum	my-SAY-num
Morcant	MOR-CAHNT
Mordag	MOOR-dahk
Muireach	MYOOR-ock (ch guttural)
Nicomedes	NEE-koh-meh-dez
Ocelus	oh-SEH-luhs
Ordovices	or-doh-veh-suz
Osgar	OZ-GAHR
Phaedrus	FAY-druz
Philonikos	fee-LOH-nih-kos
Philosir	fee-loh-seer
Porcius	POR-kee-us
Prasutagus	prah-SOO-tah-gus
Regni	reg-NEE
Rioghnach	ree-uh-NUCK (ch guttural)

Saibh	SIVE (rhymes with 'five')
Samhain	SAW-when
Samos	SAW-mohs
Seanus	SHAY-nus
Sidhe	SHEE
Silures	SEE-lurh-ez
Suliac	SOO-lee-ack
Taraghlan	TAH-ruh-GHLAHN (gh guttural)
Taranis	TERR-ah-nis
Teutates	too-TAH-tez
Theophrastus	thee-oh-FRAH-stuhs
Tiernan	TEER-nan
Tirintius	TYE-ren-tee-us
Titianus	tee-SEE-ai-noos
Togodumnus	tah-guh-DUM-noos
Trinovantes	trih-noh-WHAN-tez
Unimanus	oo-nee-MAH-noos
Venutius	whe-NOO-tee-us
Viricio	weer-EE-kee-oh
Viricos	where-ih-kos
Viroconium	wee-roh-cohn-ee-um

PART ONE
GIAMOS

I

'Queen Gwenfrewi?'

B linking in the damp gloom of her prison, Gwenfrewi slowly turned towards the voice. 'Yes, little one. What is it?'

She could just make out the pair of eyes belonging to her friend Catraoine's youngest son. The darkness of the chamber enveloped the child's scrawny frame in shadow, obscuring the evidence of his deprivation. 'Have the soldiers forgotten about us? No one's been by to throw any breakfast.'

She hummed absently, lifting her head to listen. The faint rumble of fort activity had stilled; no forges roared, no boots crunched past in the snow, no horses could be heard whinnying outside their stables. She sighed. 'I don't know where they've gone, child. The ways of the Romans are mysterious to me.'

'You…you don't think…they left us here? To…?'

Gwenfrewi unfolded her arms, revealing the ragged remnants of the dress she'd been wearing upon her capture more than five moons ago. She beckoned to the boy. Catraoine's child clambered into her bony embrace and tucked himself tightly against her, shuddering against the dank, cool air.

She ran her hand over the child's long, matted tresses and slowly shook her head. 'No. They haven't abandoned the fort. They never leave this place once the snows come. Remember your previous winter? When the Romans left us all alone long enough to tend our own hearths during the dark months?'

The boy nodded. 'Eisu let me lead our pony through the forest when he collected firewood. Mother had stew ready for us when we came back. And then I rode on Duros's shoulders to the grove for the sacrifice and big pork feast.' He buried his head deeper in the crook of Gwenfrewi's shoulder. His voice grew smaller. 'They're both gone now.'

Gwenfrewi paled and clutched the child tighter to her. She remembered the brother, Duros, finally succumbing to a lingering fever only a moon or so ago. She shuddered to think what the soldiers might have done to the boy's body when they'd removed it from the cell. She wasn't sure if the boy's fate had been any better or worse than that of Catraoine's eldest, Eisu, nearly a man himself facing his twelfth winter when the Romans dragged him out of the chamber for use in one of their rites. Gwenfrewi would never forget the torture of hearing the boy's distant cries throughout the day. At long last, he'd fallen silent. The prisoners hadn't seen or heard him since.

'It's my fault,' the boy sniffled, stiffening in Gwenfrewi's arms. 'I'm the one…that got everyone sick.'

'Hush.' Gwenfrewi patted his back and caught the glints of more pairs of exhausted, jaded eyes in the darkness. 'It was bound to happen to one of us sooner or later in this place.'

His shoulders shook. 'B-but…'

'Trenus!' Catraoine lifted her head from her slumber beside Gwenfrewi. She turned reproachful eyes on her son, her sagging bulk cutting into Gwenfrewi's shoulder. 'Don't be burdening your queen with your tears again.'

'I don't mind, dear.' Gwenfrewi cradled the boy's head and placed a kiss on his crown. 'Being able to cry after all we've been through shows an admirable strength.'

Catraoine hmphed. 'Rather he didn't waste what little he's got.' She fell into silence as the women listened to the boy's whimpers. 'Danu knows he's got enough for the lot of us,' she sighed. 'I haven't any tears left.'

Gwenfrewi reached out, taking her friend's hand. She squeezed Catraoine's fingers, grimacing at the feel of her limp, drooping folds of skin. 'No woman should have to face what you've endured in here. To lose one's children is to lose a part of oneself.'

Catraoine turned towards her. 'You would know, too, wouldn't you? At least I've still got him and the others.' She nodded at Trenus. 'But you…'

Gwenfrewi closed her eyes. 'Tiernan lives. I would know, deep in my bones, if he didn't. He doesn't walk among his ancestor's shades. How he fares, I know not. As for Luigsech, she-,'

'May as well be dead.' Catraoine leaned back, gazing down at her hands. 'I find it hard to believe she'd leave us like this, with no word since the night she promised to break us out and never came.'

'Catraoine, we don't know why she hasn't sent word or kept her promise. We mustn't be hasty when it comes to judging her plans.'

'Mustn't be hasty? *She* wasn't hasty enough for Eisu and Duros! It's too late for them, just as it may be too late for us if she ever remembers to act!'

Gwenfrewi turned away. She drew a long, patient sigh. 'Her plan was doomed to fail. For all we know, the Roman learned of it and did away with her. Although my bones tell me she, too, lives.'

She tipped her head back and gazed into the darkness of their too-small prison. 'I believe that the gods have a hand in this. We must trust to their wisdom and wait.' She lifted her free hand to her breast, touching the bare place where her wheel pendant had formerly hung for years. Her fingers danced on the air, yearning for the familiar feel of the rough bronze spokes beneath them. 'Who knows what more they may demand of her? Of us?'

Catraoine opened her mouth to reply but stopped short. A low murmur of distant voices had broken the morning silence. Trenus gasped and ceased his sobs. All within the cell stilled. Slurred, melodious words became louder until the door to the fort's cells swung open overhead, revealing two staggering soldiers carrying a third between them. They sang off-key in their unintelligible tongue as they hurled their insensible comrade into one of the smaller cells beside theirs.

'Io, Saturnalia!' One dumped a tin pitcher of wine over the unconscious man's head while the other, giggling, shut and locked the door.

Trenus slipped off Gwenfrewi's lap and retreated into the further recesses of the cell. The two women watched pensively as the soldiers above their heads conversed. Suddenly, they both howled, slapping each other's shoulders.

'Aren't they a jolly pair?' Catraoine growled.

The Romans stilled, finally feeling the intent gaze of the prisoners. Gwenfrewi scowled and lifted her nose at the cruel smirks that curled across their faces. One pointed to them and barked something to his companion. His comrade, staggering, thrust his hips suggestively.

'Gwenfrewi,' Catraoine whispered, eyes locked upon the guards. 'What are they saying?'

She shook her head. 'I know not the Roman tongue. Only Luigsech…'

The mimer cried out when his comrade shoved him against the wall. He gestured towards the prisoners, a plaintive tone to his words. The other soldier nodded and replied, tapping a finger against the man's chest. In response, the legionary kicked the empty pitcher across the wooden floor, where it clattered loudly into a far wall. He yelled in response, the only word of which Gwenfrewi could pick out was *'Brittunculi,'* a name she'd grown too familiar with.

In response to the soldier's outburst, his companion grinned and spread his arms wide. Though she couldn't understand his words, Gwenfrewi didn't like the tone of his voice. As the two men approached the grate of their cell, Gwenfrewi flinched. She watched in growing alarm as the men hitched up the skirts of their tunics and pulled down their braccae. 'Get back, Catraoine.'

Her companion groaned. 'Haven't the energy, love.' She gazed around at the other women and children sprawled listlessly about their confines. 'None of us have.'

Gwenfrewi sighed, feeling her body losing its own fight with her sense of self-preservation. She turned her head just in time to feel twin streaks of urine splash against her brow. 'Avert your gaze, then.'

The soldiers cackled, waggling their penises through the bars to hit every one of the starving Britons. 'Io, Saturnalia! Io, Saturnalia!'

Luciana closed her eyes, suppressing her own sigh in response to the girlish giggles on either side of her. Afrania Regula, the legate's eldest daughter, finally managed to spear a pin through Luciana's wayward coil of hair.

'That should do it!' Afrania stepped back and examined her handiwork. 'Prettier than the empress's woman, Claudia Acte herself!'

'The new tribune says that she's gone blonde, but everyone in the imperial court knows it's a wig.' Afrania's sister Aemilia handed Luciana a bronze hand mirror, smiling. 'She could only wish hers was so genuine!'

Luciana held the mirror at arm's length, examining her reflection. Regulus's girls had made themselves her willing attendants as a Saturnalia gift, dressing her as a stately Roman woman for the legate's Saturnalia feast in his Londinium residence. The girls had marvelled over the length of Luciana's tresses, freeing her assorted braids and brushing her hair to a soft sheen before struggling to pin it on top of her head. Parted in the middle and drawn above her ears, Luciana's curled locks were secured to her crown in loops by dozens of bone and iron pins. Stray wisps had escaped the girl's clutches, hovering here and there about their slovenly handiwork. Her Aegyptian emerald pendant earrings hung from her lobes at either side.

'Thank you, girls.' Luciana set the mirror aside and held up a hand in refusal when Aemilia extended a jewelled clasp.

'Are you sure you don't want to borrow one of my necklaces tonight? It'd look a sight better than that frightful thing.' Amelia nodded towards the wheel pendant hung from its leather thong about Luciana's neck.

Her hand fluttered to the charm and felt the lumpy bronze burn her fingers as they brushed against it. *Failure. Betrayal. Surrender.* She frowned, feeling her chest constrict. *You're no better than Cartimandua, you little Roman bootlicker.*

Her eyes flickered to the reflective glass resting on the table before her. *Look at what you've become.*

'Luciana?'

Aemilia's tentative voice broke through her reverie. She forced a smile across her lips. 'Sorry, I…I am sure.' She tucked the pendant inside the neck of her lilac-coloured gown. 'I'll keep it hidden, if that will please you.' She fingered the pinned straps of the tunica. 'The dress is lovely, as it is.'

Afrania nodded. 'It's the closest thing we non-imperials can get to purple. Shame, it is a fetching colour.' She beamed as Luciana stood and turned to face them. 'Io, Saturnalia!'

Luciana allowed the sisters to gently embrace her, smiling softly. The legate's daughters had hardly left her side since she and Decimus had arrived with Regulus in Londinium. The opportunity to spend the holidays away from the fort and Nicomedes's relentless questions had been a welcome one, though she seemed to have traded one inquisitor for two. The girls, fascinated by the first Briton they could speak to and observe closely, had left her with little time for much else, including Decimus. She supposed, however, that it could be worse; she and the centurion were, after all, guests of the legate and the girls' curiosity made her feel far more welcome than their mother's frosty distance.

Luciana's face fell. It was just as well she hadn't spent much time with Decimus. Since arriving in Londinium, his behaviour had turned rather cold. A dark cloud seemed to hang about him, putting him in the foulest of moods. On the day of the governor's Saturnalia banquet, he'd said nothing but a few snapped monosyllables all day. Luciana had never felt more relieved to disappear into the kitchens for a day, glad that the 'citizens only' invite list prevented her attendance.

Tor, Decimus's adopted British hound, roused himself from the corner of the chamber and wandered over, wagging his curly tail. Luciana gave his tawny hide a vigorous rub. *You're as out of place as I am, poor fellow.*

'Come.' Each girl took one of her arms and tugged her away from the dog. 'We mustn't keep dinner waiting! Mother's been hard at it all day!'

Luciana grimaced. Her hand flew to the wheel pendant tucked against her skin. The thought of feasting while her people starved back in Viroconium rankled with her. Before she'd left the fort, she'd arranged with Nicomedes to try to scrounge scraps of the fort's Saturnalia feast and pass them to the British prisoners. But Nicomedes was just a boy. What if he were caught? What if her people starved over the holiday after all, and her plans had only made things worse?

'Put that thing away!' Aemilia swatted Luciana's hand. She released the wheel, tucking it back inside her dress. 'Come on! Now that we're ready, there's nothing keeping us!'

'Wait.' Luciana's brow furrowed. 'You aren't going to dress for the party yourselves?'

The girls shared a knowing look, bursting into laughter. Afrania gestured to her plain, homespun tunic. 'We *are* dressed, silly!'

'It's Saturnalia! Today, we are the slaves, and you are the masters.' Aemilia patted her dark braids, wound around her head and neatly pinned in place. 'We get to serve you and the staff and then eat in the kitchen.'

'But…why? Don't you mind?'

'Not at all! It's so different from every other night, it's great fun!' Afrania turned to the door. 'Now, come on!'

The girls stopped short and squealed when their bedroom door flew open. At the doorstep, their nurse's seven-year-old son swung a wooden staff in their direction. His bright blue tunic, offset with gold braid, hung loosely about his tiny frame and a beribboned fir crown perched atop his head.

'The Lord of Misrule commands you attend me!' He growled in as menacing a voice as his high register could muster.

'Gaius!' The sisters shrieked, stepping back as Tor bounded up to the boy, barking a warning. 'You naughty boy! How dare you enter a ladies' chamber?'

'I'm not Gaius! I'm the Lord of Misrule and I can do as I please!' He ducked to evade the dog's advance and darted into the room, waving his arms about. Tor wheeled as quickly as his stiff legs enabled him to, chasing Gaius. The girls rushed out the door and down the creaking wooden staircase, bustling Luciana between them.

'Oi! Lord of Misrule! Your servants await you in the triclinium!' The boy's mother, a buxom woman by the name of Hilaria reached out to tweak his ear as he raced past her. She turned to the breathless women and shook her head. 'I told Dominus not to give Gaius the bean. I knew that power would go right to the little devil's head.'

Luciana nodded in sympathy, her smile broadening at the sight of the woman. A Gaul with dark auburn hair and a gruff, commanding voice that frightened the legate's daughters into obedience, Hilaria had immediately warmed to Luciana upon meeting her. Their long conversations at the kitchen table had revealed much about the woman's childhood in Lugdunum, which didn't sound totally dissimilar to Luciana's formative years in Londinium. Hilaria confessed she felt more at home in Britannia than she previously had living with the legate's household in Rome. And her discreetly whispered words of advice had saved her on more than one occasion from committing grave social errors in front of the legate.

'Io, Saturnalia, Luciana.' Clad in a sparkling array of gems and a dark green tunica, her dark red curls lying in neatly arranged rows about her head, the freedwoman extended a bottle towards her. 'A gift from the lady of the house.'

Luciana took the generously sized vessel of sweet almond bath oil and tentatively lifted her gaze over Hilaria's shoulder. Legate Regulus's wife, pale and austere in a white frock, inclined her head and sneered back at her.

'Y-you must tell the lady I thank her and wish the blessings of the season upon her.' Luciana handed the jar to Aemilia, who swiftly ran it back upstairs. She smiled at Hilaria. 'Io, Saturnalia.'

'Now you're getting the hang of it.' Hilaria took her arm. The pair made their way along the corridor to the legate's indoor dining hall. Tor followed, head lowered. 'It's such fun, isn't it? We barbarians have nothing like it.'

'Well, I'm not sure about that.'

Hilaria squeezed her forearm. 'Ah, love. I miss the bonfires and pig roast, make no mistake. But times like these remind me that the Roman ways aren't all bad.'

'Aren't they?'

Luciana saw the woman's face crane towards her rapidly misting eyes. She halted them both before they reached the triclinium and turned to face her. 'What's the matter, dear?'

'It…' She averted her gaze, wiping her eyes. 'It's nothing. Ignore me.'

'Thinking of those who aren't here?'

A short laugh escaped her pressed lips. 'You could say that.'

'It's hard not to remember loved ones at midwinter.' Hilaria pulled her into a brief, no-nonsense embrace. 'It's why I find it best to focus upon the ones we have near.' She grimaced at the sound of her son's raised voice in the room beyond. 'Why else would we be here?'

'I'm beginning to wonder that myself,' Luciana muttered.

'You'll see, my British friend. Saturnalia is a time of joy.' Hilaria raised her head and swept Luciana towards the doorway.

'I highly doubt the Romans are capable of true…' Luciana's voice trailed off as they paused at the triclinium's entrance. Decimus, straightening from wiping clean the door porter's feet, turned and met her gaze. His bright hazel eyes lit up appreciatively beneath the felt Phrygian cap he wore to match his regulation scarlet tunic. The silver streaking his dark beard shimmered in the warm lamplight. Morose doubt receded in the wake of his small smile that reached up to crinkle the corners of his eyes. She squared her shoulders, basking in his worshipful stare.

'You've changed your tune.' Hilaria winked before taking Legate Regulus's proffered hand. He led her off to the dining couch at the right of her child, seated imperiously in the place reserved for honoured guests.

Luciana tossed her head, allowing the golden fringe of her earrings to dance about in the light of the bracketed lamps ringing the hall. She pretended not to notice Decimus's gradual approach, feigning surprise as he gently took her fingers in his and bowed low over her hand.

'This way, my lady,' he murmured, meeting her gaze.

Giddy tears sprang to Luciana's eyes. She managed a choking laugh. 'Just when I think I have you figured out…'

Dazed, she followed him to the couch across from Hilaria. As she sat upon the cushioned bench, Decimus crouched before her and slowly removed her sandals. He ran a newly damp cloth over her feet with deliberate care, cradling her heels within his palm. Luciana shuddered at the warmth emanating from her lover's grasp.

'Come, Maximus,' Regulus grunted as he passed behind the couch. 'The sooner we get to serving, the sooner we can eat ourselves.'

Decimus reluctantly relinquished his hold, allowing her to tuck her feet up within the folds of her gown. 'Io Saturnalia, my love.'

Luciana rewarded him with a promising smile.

II

Cassia poured the libation over the base of Cook's grave, her face stony. A simple wooden marker, incised crookedly by the wolf den's half-literate door guard, protruded from the frozen ground at an angle. Its stance mocked her, accusing her of its very existence.

She adjusted the palla draped over her head when she felt it slip and held her palms out in supplication. 'To the spirits of the departed: accept this sacrifice and heed my vow.'

She picked up a whetted blade and gutted the carcass of a small hare she'd purloined from the brothel's larder. Wincing, she cracked the creature's delicate ribs and plunged her hands deeper to saw out the heart. With a cry of triumph, she lifted the small organ high and tossed it into the embers of a smouldering cook fire to her left.

Smiling, she stretched her red palms to the sky. 'Accept my sacrifice. See my hands, soaked with the blood of the lives I've taken.' Showing her palms to the marker, she struggled to slow her racing, laboured breaths. She couldn't look at it without seeing Cook lying on the kitchen floor, throat cut by Morcant of the Silures. If only she'd arranged the swap of the tribune's letter to Morcant for the payment herself, instead of entrusting it to Cook. The woman hadn't deserved this fate. 'I killed you, Cook. Just as surely as I killed Cato.'

Invoking his name immediately brought her brother's freckled visage to mind. Sullen Cato, dissatisfied Cato, who'd only come to Britannia because Cassia had pressed him into Decimus's care as his personal slave. Cato, who'd resented his slave status, while Cassia, selfishly saving her own funds, couldn't buy his freedom. Cato, whose needs she had met merely by swapping a cruel master for a milder one. Cato, who'd found his end atop a hillfort visible from the cemetery. If she hadn't given Morcant the information he needed to frame the Cornovii tribe, the battle in which he'd lost his life wouldn't have happened. Cassia winced, squeezing her eyes shut. 'I shall never be free of your shades. They…forever…haunt…me.' She smeared her gory hands over her chest as sobs wracked her body.

She slowly collapsed on the ground, hunched over the stinking, gored hare. The stench of death filled her nostrils, her lungs, her being. Pluto enveloped her, tightening his firm embrace. 'I am yours, lord of Hades…I am your…h-handmaiden,' she mumbled.

The wounds scabbing her heart tore away and she dug her fingers into the dirt. 'Why?! Why in Jupiter's name must you punish me so?!'

'You know.'

Cassia gasped and lifted her head. There, standing opposite Cook's marker, hovering between two marble monuments erected by the legion, stood a squat, olive-hued woman with flinty dark eyes. Her grey, straw-like hair fell loose about her shoulders, as though she were a professional mourner. A dull, oft-mended tunic hung about her broad shoulders, obscured by a dark cloak fastened at the shoulder by a brilliant golden fibula in the shape of a snake eating its tail. In contrast to her weathered, threadbare form, her face shone taut and youthful, free of the lines scored into her hands.

Cassia pulled herself to a sitting position and shook her head as the woman knelt beside her. 'It was so long ago, Antiope. So, so long ago…'

'And yet it continues to rule your choices.' The woman drew soothing lines along Cassia's back with pointed fingernails. 'If your vow is sincere…'

'I know! I know!' Cassia cried, shaking her head. 'I know, I know…'

Antiope stilled and drew back, her silence expectant.

Cassia lifted her head, addressing the heavens. 'Hear me! I forsake him! I forsake…my…my child!'

Her eyes widened as soon as the words left her mouth. Her child. The child she'd never given voice to, yet had occupied her heart and mind ever since his birth nearly two decades ago. The child she'd had to sell back into the slavery she'd escaped. The child she hadn't seen since his infancy. The child she'd wanted to find so desperately, she'd sold military secrets to Decimus's enemies. The child who seemed continually out of reach, despite her attempts to accrue the pay for an informer to track him down. The child who'd indirectly brought about the deaths of her brother and now Cook. The child she'd refused to abort, choosing instead to bear him in secret…because he was Decimus's son.

The memory of his pinched, red face, of his piercing cry, of his soft hands and feet, had grown hazy over time. She had tried to cling to her only memory of him, but it grew less sharp, less detailed every year. Would she even recognise him if she met him again? She hadn't had the strength to sell him herself, instead sending a girl off with instructions to get a good price. The money from the sale had paid her way back to the frontier, back into Charis's employ, back to Decimus's side. She hadn't wanted their son to grow up in the backrooms of a lupanar. He'd deserved better than what she could give him then. But she'd resolved to one day buy their child back. As the years passed with that goal unfulfilled, she'd resorted to desperate measures. And now…was her goal truly worth the lives it had already claimed?

She closed her eyes as an icy pang sliced through her. She could never face him now that she'd become a murderess. She'd never be able to look at him without seeing Cato's and Cook's doleful eyes. Their shades would never let go of her…unless she first let go of him.

You never deserved him, anyway.

She threw off her toga and tugged down her tunic, freeing her breasts to the biting December air. The tears flowed freely down her face, erupting from the riven hole deep within her soul. 'I have no children!' She smeared her hands across her breastbone. 'I have no claimants upon my life! Upon my love! Upon my duty!'

Her head drooped and she slumped before the grave, shattered. 'I purge him from my heart and dedicate myself anew to your purposes.'

She heard Antiope rummaging in the hare's entrails. Her conflicted heart had led her to the seer's door only a few weeks ago. Antiope was revered and feared in the vicus, a solitary figure that those with no wish to know the gods' wills studiously avoided. But Cassia *needed* to know what the gods wanted of her. And Antiope's answer had led her here, to this most unwilling of sacrifices.

Presently, she felt Antiope push her upright. Cassia faced her and saw one of the woman's fingers dripping with the hare's blood. With it, Antiope drew lines across her brow and down her nose before inscribing some symbol upon her lips. Cassia closed her eyes, absorbing herself in the sharp odour of iron and mumbling around Antiope's handiwork, 'make me your mouthpiece.'

Antiope nodded and stood. Cassia's eyes fluttered open, focussing on the grey clouds overhead. She lifted her red palms to them once more. The nebulous babe of her distant past, she banished from her mind. The gods must know her intentions were pure.

'I am yours,' she whispered. 'Show me your will. Please, Nemesis, exact vengeance for the lives I didn't mean to take.'

The pair strode down the Via Praetoria, eyes focussed upon the fort's southern gates. The cemetery at her back, Cassia wished only for the comforting confines of the vicus. Antiope, one step behind at her shoulder, imbued her movement with purpose.

She strode past a contubernium of legionaries frolicking in the snow, pelting one another with handfuls of ice and powder. A group of carousing auxiliaries stumbled around the corner of one of the stable blocks, cheering and brandishing their wineskins high. As they tripped onto the path before her, Cassia checked her stride to sidestep the drunken Thracians.

'Io, Saturnalia!' They cheered, leering at the women. One, his eyes widening at the sight of Cassia's telltale garb, staggered away from his mates and stretched his arms out to her.

Cassia paused only long enough to smash her fist against the soldier's throat. He crumpled and fell to the ground amidst the jeers of his comrades. Cassia stalked on. At a raised palm from Antiope, the cavalrymen fell silent.

Cassia stormed past the half-insensible gate guards and made her steady way down the path to the settlement at the Sabrina's ford. Passing the bright lights and music emanating from Charis's brothel and the ragged fir garland encasing the bull on The Aurochs' painted sign, she turned down an alley marked by a silversmith's and didn't stop until she reached a plain door obscured in shadow.

Antiope stepped past her and unlocked the door. The women flowed into her humble abode, lit only by a couple of oil lamps perched on cobwebbed wall brackets. Dried bundles of herbs and stoppered jars cluttered the shelves lining the hovel's walls, competing for space with bundled straw, grinning deity statuettes, and wax figures. A collection of wind chimes shaped as phalluses tinkled above the door, warding their occupants against the evil eye. A small, dark figure darted across the floor and leapt into the window, emitting a high-pitched hiss.

'Poor Gale,' Antiope absently fondled the polecat's ears before turning to her desk. 'Have we disturbed your rest?'

The creature hunched its back and shrieked, glaring at the women.

'I can't stay long.' Cassia unwound her palla and patted her piled knot of curls. 'Charis will expect a full shift out of everyone tonight, given the holidays.'

Antiope shifted through a stack of papyri unrolled across her table and lifted a finger. She pulled out a star chart and took a seat, poring over its contents.

Cassia folded her arms and tapped her foot. 'Well? I did as the gods demanded. What next?'

'Patience, child. Their realm does not conform to a Roman clock.' In the half light, Antiope's handsome, patrician nose looked misshapen and bulbous, distorting the woman's beauty into a hideous shape. Cassia frowned and sucked in a nervous breath until Antiope lifted her head, revealing the image to be merely a trick of the light.

'One moon from Proserpina's return.'

Cassia furrowed her brow. 'One…you mean the spring?'

Antiope nodded. 'We cannot move the gods of vengeance to follow our own whims.'

'And what until then?' She thrust an arm expansively towards the outdoor world. 'How do I bring justice to Cook and my brother?'

Antiope shrugged, smirking.

'Give me one of your potions.' Cassia dropped herself into the chair across from Antiope. 'The one you learned from Locusta. I will take it to the Silure chieftain myself and taint his food, the sooner to serve Nemesis.'

Antiope tilted her head, her dark eyes dancing wickedly in the dim flames. 'It shan't do you any good. Nothing will happen until a full cycle has witnessed the earth's rebirth. And not a moment sooner.'

Cassia looked away, biting her lip. She noisily swallowed the lump in her throat and blinked back frustrated tears.

'Consider this an auspicious gift. It is time enough to carefully plan and prepare your attack.'

Cassia clawed absently at her face, flaking away some of the dried blood from the bridge of her nose. 'So be it. But I'll have my revenge.'

Gale hissed in response to the laughter that erupted from her mistress. Cassia frowned. This was no laughing matter. She stood and hurried out the door. Antiope's voice pursued her through the snow.

'All in good time, child!' Antiope cackled against her tinkling chimes. 'All in good time!'

III

'I say, that little imp of yours, Regulus, is quite the character!'

Decimus looked up at the kitchen doorway to see the imperial procurator's leering face. Catus Decianus's hands fumbled with his belt, evidently on his return journey from the legate's private latrine. He sagged against the sturdy frame, eyeing the assembled nobles in the kitchen with a self-satisfied smirk. The tufts of grey fuzz on either side of his bald dome stuck out in disarray, his pale green eyes lolling about the assembled party. His brow furrowed at the sight of Decimus seated on the floor beside Regulus, his daughters, and Tribune Cincinnatus; they gathered beneath the table Regulus's wife shared with the governor. 'What's this, Legate? Not enough chairs to go around?'

'In case you haven't noticed, Decianus, we're at the arse end of the empire.' Regulus glowered at the procurator. 'Space and building materials come at a premium in Londinium.'

The man threw a desultory glance at the limewashed walls. 'It appears the barbarians here have never fathomed constructing with anything other than timber and mud.'

Decimus carefully set his bowl aside, scowling. He hadn't been in the company of Catus Decianus long since arriving in Londinium, and he already couldn't wait to quit himself of the man's presence. The mere sight of him was enough to send a shudder up Decimus's spine. He ground his teeth. 'One more word about the barbarians on this island and you'll be answering to me. Saturnalia be damned.'

Decianus laughed, lifting the hand bearing his equestrian ring to his mouth to cover a belch. 'Stand down, man. Your little Brittunculus is looking quite charming this evening.' He held up his cup, sloshing some drops of wine to the floor. 'The influence of empire, eh?'

Decimus felt the legate's hand on his shoulder and closed his eyes, angrily resisting the urge to shrug him off and confront the procurator. Thankfully, he was saved from committing such impropriety when Aemilia sat up to ask her mother a question.

'Mama, his ring.' She tugged insistently at the lady's tunic. 'Why isn't he in here with us?'

'Because, little one, I'm a subordinate.' Decianus pointed to the governor. 'Every other day of the year, I do exactly what that man says.'

'That's not strictly true.' Tribune Cincinnatus raised his head. 'When the governor's away on campaign, the procurator governs in absentia.' He considered the drunken man carefully. 'During the summer, *you* answer to no one.'

''Cept the emperor.' Decianus raised a toast. 'Long live Nero!'

'Enough, man!' Governor Paulinus stood from his seat. 'I only agreed to letting you dine with the slaves to prevent you making a donkey's arse of yourself. Which is precisely what you're doing now!'

'Ah…ah…' The procurator grinned, tripping over his feet before catching himself in the door frame. ''Tis the season!'

'Which ends tomorrow!' Paulinus pounded his fist on the rickety table, making everyone jump. 'Have you considered why Governor Paulinus of Britannia had to host the citizens' Saturnalia feast at the beginning of the week and not the final day of the festival?!' He gestured towards Regulus on the floor. 'At least the legate's got walls and a roof to host within, which is more than either of us can say!' He narrowed his eyes. 'And I'll be making sure the architect working on our quarters knows to leave your residence for last.'

Decimus bit back a smile as he watched the procurator's eyes grow wide. Having spent a considerable amount of time in the governor's offices, he was only too aware of their half-constructed state. Outside of the rooms needed to conduct the province's business, the building was far from complete. The governor and his staff, when in town, were forced to barrack themselves within the garrison fortress. It was a far cry from the governor's palatial residence in Colonia Camulodunum.

'It's a good thing, then, that I'm only in this pigsty for as long as I need to be.' The procurator lifted his hooked beak imperiously. 'The moment we've finished collecting the annual tribute, I shall make my return to the capital.'

'On the morrow.' Paulinus pointed a stern finger at the tax collector. 'In the meantime, you'll treat the legate's home and his guests with the respect they're due!'

Decianus seemed to sober, eyeing the governor. Decimus furrowed his brow. He'd seen the same defiant expression in Luciana's eyes only too often, and he knew exactly what it meant.

Catus Decianus stretched his arm out and slowly emptied the contents of his cup onto the floorboards, never breaking his locked gaze with Paulinus. 'To…fucking…Saturnalia.'

Decimus craned his head at the governor. The man had gone quite red in the face, but he held his tongue. Decimus sat uneasily in the silence that ensued. He slowly registered that everyone else, like him, was hesitant to draw so much as a breath to break the tension.

At long last, with a hiccup and a lurch, Decianus removed himself from the room with as much dignity as his sorry state could muster.

'The swine,' Paulinus breathed, collapsing back into his chair. 'I'll be only too glad to see the back of him!'

'Good luck!' Cincinnatus snorted. 'Why do you think the emperor assigned him to Britannia?'

Decimus turned to the tribune and smiled in approbation. 'Not so welcome in Rome, then?'

Cincinnatus sighed. 'The man's a parasite.' He flicked a piece of dirt from his clean linen tunic and ran an absent hand through his oiled chestnut curls. Decimus could easily see, from the tribune's smooth, pale complexion and classically handsome features, why he'd been a favourite of Emperor Nero.

A sharp rap on the door startled the legate to his feet. 'That must be your ghost, Cincinnatus. Janus! Janus, answer…' He trailed off, feeling the eyes of everyone in the room. He cleared his throat and straightened. 'I, uh, forgot. I'm Janus today. Go join everyone else in the triclinium.' He straightened his cockeyed freedman's cap and stormed down the hall. 'Io, Saturnalia!' His voice trailed down the corridor.

Decimus groaningly rose to his feet and followed the rest of the party down the hall. 'You hired the ghost?' He asked Cincinnatus.

The tribune grinned. 'My freedman, Lucius. The man's got an ear for gossip like no other, so I suggested he regale us with some of the most frightening stories from Rome.'

Decimus's severe brows lifted in surprise. 'More frightening than the threat of pulling us out to abandon the province?'

'Quite.' Cincinnatus turned to him. 'You know, now that I'm on the ground, I'm beginning to see things Nero's way. This swamp would be no great loss to the empire. And the locals seem to be more trouble than they're worth.' His eyes widened at Decimus's dark look. 'Your woman excepted, of course.'

Decimus grunted and stalked over to Luciana's dining couch. She lifted her head at his approach and propped herself up on her elbows, smiling. Decimus felt a lurch in his chest as he seated himself on the floor before her. The sight of her sparkling green cats' eyes and powerful, lithe form quickened his pulse, filling him with longing.

'Io, Saturnalia.' She reached out to straighten the conical tip of his hat and giggled. More golden tendrils had escaped her imperfect updo, twining their sensual way over her bared shoulders.

He regarded her as sternly as he could, though he knew she could read the clear desire in his eyes. 'You're so fucking beautiful.'

'What an impertinent thing to say.' She playfully slapped his shoulder before reaching down to toss one of the last remaining olives into her mouth.

He trapped her wrist and pressed his lips to it. 'Forgive me, my lady. It must be a trick of the occasion.'

A golden projectile suddenly whizzed past Decimus's ear. They turned their heads in time to see Gaius dancing a jig on top of the dining couch. He swung his wand and cheered gleefully before lobbing another must cake across the room.

Luciana withdrew her hand from Decimus's grasp and trailed her finger along his neck. 'Well,' she breathed, 'I suppose it *is* a time to be naughty…'

He shuddered, swiftly turning away. He saw a rather squat figure with a sheet draped over its head appear in the doorway, waving its arms and moaning.

Everyone laughed, quickly taking their seats on the floor. The legate's daughters moved along the walls to dim the lamps.

'Ghost stories! Wonderful!' Hilaria clapped her hands. 'Dominus, you have outdone yourself this year!'

'Don't thank me, thank the tribune.' Regulus nodded towards Cincinnatus. 'He's brought us a ghost all the way from Rome.'

'My pleasure.' The young man lifted his cup. 'Io, Saturnalia!'

Luciana frowned. 'What is this?' She hissed, gesturing at the figure. 'This…clownery…this is a part of it, too?'

'Now, Luci, that's no way to speak about the dead!' Decimus smiled at her. 'You, of all people, know better.'

'Humph.' She inclined her dainty nose. 'And yet you mocked my Samhain traditions.'

'Oh, Saturn!' The figure intoned in a high-pitched, wavering voice. 'I beg your release! Doomed, doomed to walk the night among the lemures!'

Aemilia and Afrania took their seats before the ghost, giggling. Regulus gestured good naturedly. 'As the owner of this domicile, I ask you make your presence known, spirit. Who visits their mischief upon us this evening?'

'In life, my name was Julia,' the soft voice moaned. 'Julia…Agrippina!'

The party collectively gasped. In the ensuing silence, Gaius whimpered softly.

Decimus was the first to recover his voice. 'The mother of the emperor?

But…I thought you'd taken poison?'

'Silence, mortal! Listen! Listen to my tale of woe.'

Luciana sighed, resting her chin in her hand. 'Your shade certainly has a flair for the dramatic,' she whispered in Decimus's ear.

'I, Julia Agrippina, daughter of Nero Claudius Drusus Germanicus, granddaughter of Marcus Vipsanius Agrippa and great-granddaughter of the Divine Augustus, sister of Gaius Caesar Augustus Germanicus, wife of Tiberius Claudius Caesar Augustus Ger-,'

'We know who you are, spirit. Spare us the recitation of your inbred relatives,' Cincinnatus said, studying his nails. Decimus and the others couldn't contain their giggles. The door porter whooped a cheery 'Io, Saturnalia!' at the tribune's impertinence.

The ghost lowered its arms. 'Look here, who's telling this story? I've a mind to turn around and haunt somewhere else, where my audience might actually pay me!'

Cincinnatus shrugged, grinning. 'Who said you weren't getting paid?'

The party laughed harder. Decimus looked over his shoulder at Luciana, who attempted to hide her smile behind her hand.

'Silence!' The sheeted figure rattled its chains, wailing at the top of its voice until the room quietened. 'My tale demands to be heard. It's so incredible my son, Nero Claudius Caesar Drusus Germanicus, dare not repeat it. Yet the truth must be told. My agony…my immortal agony demands it!'

Gaius yelped, burying his face in the folds of his mother's gown. Luciana sighed and sat up, reluctantly committing her attention to the theatrics.

'*I* was the one who solicited Locusta for the poison that tainted my husband's meal. Yes, *I* committed the Divine Claudius to his grave so that my son would wear the purple. My precious son, emperor of Rome. And how does he repay me?' The ghost paused, then violently rattled its chains. 'By taking up with an *infamia!* And after everything I did for him!'

Decimus mouthed 'Claudia Acte?' in Cincinnatus's direction. The tribune confirmed with a brief nod.

'I threatened to elevate his brother to the throne if he refused to obey his mother,' the ghost continued. 'But I raised my boy too well. He thwarted me by murdering Britannicus the same way I murdered his father.

'But that wasn't enough, no. No, *then* he had the gall to remove me from the palace! The emperor's mother! My face upon the coinage, and yet I was refused residence on the Palatine! Refused protection as a member of the imperial family, forcing me to live like a…a common *senator!*'

The audience roared, turning towards Regulus and Paulinus. The pair smiled indulgently, nodding for the spirit to continue.

'Oh, the horror, the horror that was to follow!' The ghost swept its arms wide, revealing a flash of dark tunic beneath the sheet. 'I gave Nero that throne, and I foolishly believed I could take it away just as quickly! Ah, me! Just because I tried to punish my naughty, naughty boy, he conspired to kill me. I was too clever to go the way of my husband and his son, so my boy tried outsmarting me. He rigged the boat I meant to sail on. He hired a shoddy craftsman, however. Typical.' The ghost tsked, provoking another round of laughter. 'The ceiling fell in but failed to strike me, leaving the traitorous crew no choice but to sink the boat themselves. My son all-too-soon forgets my extended exile in Pontia, where I had little else to do but swim. I had the strength to make it back to shore.'

'What rubbish!' Catus Decianus roared from the back of the room.

'Rubbish, you say?' The ghost seethed. 'I am doomed to an eternity of restlessness, telling my tale of woe, and you call it rubbish?! May Pluto in Hades call me back this moment if I speak a lie!'

'You claim to survive this silly murder attempt, and yet you are dead.' Paulinus glared at the procurator as he addressed the ghost. 'Your tale makes little sense.'

'I haven't finished yet.' The ghost clanked its chains together for emphasis. 'I declare, you lot are more in love with the sounds of your own voices than you are with seeking the truth!'

'It's got a point there.' Luciana nudged Decimus's shoulder, grinning. He grunted good-naturedly.

'I returned home and went to bed.' The ghost resumed in a low, creepy tone. 'All was quiet. You could hear a mouse pitter across the floor.' The storyteller paused for emphasis, surveying its audience. 'In fact, it was almost as quiet as it is right now.' The sheet-draped head nodded. 'Yes, and just as dim, too.'

Regulus's girls swallowed their anxious cries. The party's lord of misrule had gone very silent and still in his mother's arms. Decimus felt the small hairs on his arms prick up as a shudder coursed down his spine. The tribune's man was good; he had to give him that.

'I could hear my heart throbbing,' the ghost whispered. 'Sleep evaded me. I called for my attendant,' the spirit swung towards Hilaria, 'but she didn't respond. I called for my porter,' the ghost lurched towards Janus, making him draw back. 'And he didn't respond. I called for the cook!' The spirit lifted an arm towards the legate's cowering chef. 'And she…didn't… respond. My servants had deserted me. I was left in my villa. Alone.'

The ghost suddenly struck the wall with a loud thump, making everyone scream. 'I heard a noise in the hall! I called out, "Who's there?" But everything fell still. I tried again: "Whoever you are, I demand in the emperor's name that you answer me!" Not a sound.

'I turned over in my bed, reaching for the dagger I kept beneath my pillow. Clutching it before me, I rose from my bed and crept to the door. I was determined to meet whatever dared disturb my domicile. I went out into the corridor.'

'And what did you see?' Afrania gasped.

The ghost regarded the group silently for a long moment. 'Nothing. Only darkness.' It lifted its foot and stomped. The girls shrieked. 'I heard a single footstep from the atrium!' It stomped its foot again. 'And then another. And another! And another!'

The figure leant over the audience. Decimus found himself shrinking back, though he barked a weak laugh at the effective performance. He glanced at Luciana out of the corner of his eye and swallowed another chuckle at the sight of her nonplussed expression.

'Slowly, slowly, the footsteps drew near.' The ghost stepped harder, heightening the volume. 'Just when I could take it no longer, a flint struck a torch in the darkness, and I came face to face with my assassins.'

Aemilia squeaked, lifting a hand to her mouth. Her mother tsked. 'How dreadful!'

'Dreadful indeed! For these horrible, leering eyes and twisted, gawping mouths regarded me from beneath the plumed helmets of the Praetorian guard!'

Regulus harrumphed uneasily, trading flinty looks with Decimus and Paulinus.

'I saw the long arm of my son at once. The men bore cudgels and lifted their arms to batter me. I knew it was over, and I could run from Death no longer.'

'Nero had his mother beaten like a common deserter?' Decianus snorted.

'No more interruptions!' The ghost screeched before lowering its voice. 'I stayed their hands with a sharp word. I told them I knew who had sent them. And then I handed one of the guards my dagger. I told him, "If your master must commit matricide, so be it. But you'll end my life here."' The ghost clanked its chains, motioning towards its loins. '"In the very place where I gave life to the murdering bastard."'

Regulus's wife cried out sharply. The legate folded his arms. 'Watch your language, spirit. There are ladies present.'

'My apologies.' The ghost bowed slightly. 'The guard did as I wished and ran me through the womb with my own blade. I collapsed on the ground and slipped away to Hades, cursing my treacherous son with my dying breath.' The ghost waved its arms. 'No grave, no cover, no honours for my memory! The emperor refuses me burial. My ashes shift listlessly on the sands of Misenum, forcing my spirit to wander the earth. I grow weak, and yet my feet compel me to continue my journey, seeking the peace forever denied my shade. Thus ends my tragedy. Farewell, farewell!'

The ghost whirled around and smacked into the doorframe, eliciting a sharp 'Ow!' from beneath the sheet. Stumbling, it felt its way around the door and disappeared into the corridor.

Gaius sent up a mighty wail, erupting into tears against his mother's side.

Hilaria groaned, hefting him on her shoulder as she stood. 'All right, Lord of Misrule. I think it truly is time for bed, now.' She nodded to her master and mistress before removing her squalling son from the triclinium.

Decimus sat up and clapped. 'Well done!' He touched Cincinnatus's arm. 'Is any of that true, though? Seems a bit fantastic, even for the emperor's mother.'

'Every word of it.' Cincinnatus smirked. 'Do you dare to question the dead?' He stood up and stretched. 'I think I'll see our spirit friend out, lest she run into anything else.' He nodded to the legate as he strode past.

'Liar,' Decianus snarled, lurching from his couch. 'The emperor would never be so stupid.'

'We're a long way from Rome, Procurator.' Paulinus glared. 'And I hardly think we'd have been notified of the truth if he had, indeed, committed matricide.'

'And you call *us* barbaric.' Luciana caught the officers' disapproving looks and lifted her cup in a playful toast. 'Io, Saturnalia.'

The room fell silent for a long moment.

'To bed, girls!' The legate's wife broke the tension. 'It is late.' She began gathering discarded dishes from the dining tables, grumbling under her breath about 'this farce being over for another year.'

Tor roused himself from beneath one of the couches and followed the legate's wife. His tail wagged hopefully as he gazed at the scraps of food she carried away.

Afrania and Aemilia reluctantly wandered into the corridor, heads bent close in whisper.

'Well, Centurion, you seemed rather entertained.' The legate turned to Decimus. 'What did you make of the tale?'

Decimus considered for a moment as he slowly unfolded himself from the floor. 'I'm inclined to believe it, given the troubling news Cincinnatus gave us about Seneca.' He absently stretched his hand out to Luciana, helping her to her feet. 'If Nero's decided to cast aside his former advisors, that would certainly include his own mother. It makes far more sense than Agrippina trying to do away with him, now that Britannicus is gone.'

'There's no love lost between the emperor and I.' Paulinus brooded, a faraway look in his steely eyes. 'Yet it stretches credulity, believing that toga-lifter would have the balls to do it.'

'I think it's a statement.' Decimus ignored the pleasant sensation of Luciana twining herself about his arm. 'Mummy's boy is all grown up and can do whatever he damn well pleases.'

'Like abandon Britannia?'

He felt Luciana studying his expression. His own gaze stretched through the wooden floorboards to the previous sixteen years he'd spent in the province. A sharp pain tore through his chest. He blinked. 'Mithras forbid,' he breathed.

'He'll certainly be wearing my guts about his neck if we don't take what he's owed from this forsaken land.' Paulinus clapped a hand on the legate's shoulder. 'I thank you for your hospitality, Regulus, and must quit you for the fort. There are taxes to be collected tomorrow.'

The governor collared a swaying Decianus and led him towards the door.

Decimus glanced around at the legate's small retinue of slaves. All of them, excepting Hilaria and her son, were natives procured at a local auction. 'Sir…' He glanced at Luciana uneasily before turning back to him. 'If we are recalled, what happens to this? To them?' He avoided Luciana's gaze, his words catching around the growing lump in his throat.

'I shudder to think, Centurion.' Regulus sighed. 'So, I won't until circumstances necessitate it. Meet me in the principia at the first hour tomorrow.'

Decimus nodded. As he pulled Luciana into the sconce-lit peristyle, his pace quickened. 'Get your cloak,' he barked.

Luciana frowned. 'Why? Where must we go so late?'

'Anywhere.' He snatched the Phrygian cap from his head and crushed it in his fist. 'I need some air. Now.'

Sighing, Luciana paused near the door to free her wolfskin from the pile of outerwear in the porter. Heavy grunting and a sudden clatter from within the porter's cubby made her pause, drawing back in alarm.

There, in the dim light of the atrium, Decimus and Luciana could just make out the tribune's bare backside as the man piled deeply into the ghost's broad bum. The stout apparition's member stood erect as he squawked with pleasure, clanking his chains in front of him. Cincinnatus, concentrated on the task at hand, steadied his rhythm to match his partner's groans.

Covering her mouth to contain her laughter, Luciana handed Decimus his scarlet cloak and the pair slipped silently out the door.

IV

Tullius shuddered, wrapping his cloak tighter about him as he tramped the frozen streets of Viroconium's vicus. It had taken an age to find Nicomedes after the prefect's Saturnalia banquet; the teen had finally shown up in his quarters long after dark, smiling and stinking faintly of garum. Were it not for Nicomedes, he wouldn't have felt the need to hunt for last-minute provisions for a modest Saturnalia meal. But it was a season where master served slave, and the boy deserved a treat.

Already, Nicomedes had dragged him away from the food stalls and into the store of a clothing merchant. While Tullius had noticed that Nicomedes had begun to outgrow his meagre garments, he hadn't intentionally set out to buy his slave an entire new wardrobe. Before he'd known what had happened, he held three new tunics and pairs of braccae in his arms, while Nicomedes immediately donned the fourth, a fine green tunic with red braid.

The Greek teen carefully smoothed the hem of his tunic over his new leggings and pinned his dark woollen cloak to his shoulder with a Celtic brooch Luciana had gifted him before she left. When he tugged on his socks and moved to refasten his caligae, he paused to finger the holes worn through the soles of his shoes. 'Sir, might I have these replaced as well?'

Tullius sighed. They moved on to the leatherworkers' stall and he forked over another denarius for a brand-new pair of sandals.

Tullius and Nicomedes emerged onto the slushy thoroughfare of the vicus, blinking in the dimming afternoon light. A girl toting a bucket sidestepped them, continuing her trudge towards The Aurochs at the end of the road. Nicomedes followed her movement before quickly averting his eyes. A bright blush crept up his cheeks.

Tullius, noticing his slave's reaction, heaved a small sigh. *So, this is what the shopping is for.* Perhaps he'd need to pull out the Ovid for the lad's lessons sooner than he'd thought.

'Thank you, Optio.' Nicomedes gestured to his attire before running a hand through his dishevelled dark locks. 'I know it's Saturnalia and all, but...I have to ask...' He pointed across the way at Porcius's tonstrina.

'Might I…get a haircut?' His dark complexion reddened once more. 'A nice one?'

'Why not? My purse seems to lighten, no matter what.' Nodding, Tullius hefted his food and clothing purchases under his arm and guided the boy to the shop's entrance. To his surprise, the normally crowded space was deserted, with Porcius nowhere to be found.

'*Salve?*' He called tentatively.

Steps clattered on the floor overhead and soon Porcius's hulking frame made its way down a rickety ladder at the back of the shop. He turned around and appraised the pair. A smile brightened his dark eyes and lined tan visage, his grin tugging his curly whiskers up around his prominent, classical nose. 'Optio Servius! Io, Saturnalia!'

'I-I'm sorry to disturb you,' Tullius stuttered. 'If you aren't open today, we can just…'

'Not at all, not at all!' He turned to his table and began pulling out shears, razors, and combs. 'Are you wanting your customary trim and shave?'

'Actually, I was hoping you'd help my slave boy here.' He nodded to Nicomedes, who took a tentative step forward.

Porcius glanced over his meaty shoulder at the boy. 'Kalosórisma, sympatriótis!'

Nicomedes's face lit up and he excitedly responded in Greek to Porcius as he clambered onto the man's stool. The pair fell into an easy conversation as Porcius picked up his shears and went to work. He good-naturedly answered Nicomedes's rapid-fire questions about his childhood in Halicarnassus, describing his family's farm.

Tullius set his purchases down and eased himself into a seat just inside the door. He folded his arms and watched the tonsor gradually tame Nicomedes's dark mop into neat, short curls. The man had been attached to the Fourteenth Gemina, dispensing his services to the men at every fort they'd occupied since landing in Britannia. Porcius didn't seem like a hairdresser; he looked more like one of the hulking brutes found in front of a barbarian horde with his tall frame, wide shoulders, thick torso, and muscular arms. He'd confided to Tullius long ago that a weakness in his knees had been the reason he'd failed recruitment training, though that hadn't dissuaded him from joining the legions in a noncombatant role.

The man's broad, dark hands lifted a grooming pick and stretched out Nicomedes's fingers to pare away the dirt under his nails. Tullius shook his head. He had to admit, the man had found his calling, for he was a defter hand with sharp implements than the legionary physicians. He'd never once drawn blood when shaving Tullius, and he'd rarely heard complaints of that sort from any of the men in his century. Perhaps that trust he'd developed among them was the reason they felt so at ease trading confidences with Porcius…Though, as Tullius listened to Porcius's effortless conversation with Nicomedes, that might just be because the man was a born communicator.

He blinked as Porcius unwrapped his sheet from around Nicomedes and handed the boy a mirror. The lad numbly stared at his reflection before reaching up to riffle the neat coils clinging tightly to his crown. Tullius sat up. Porcius hadn't only worked fast, but he'd turned his street urchin into a little princeling.

Nicomedes turned to Porcius, a delighted grin slowly breaking across his face. He handed back the mirror and grasped his arm in thanks before darting over to Tullius and enveloping him in a hug. 'Thank you, sir!'

Winded by the ferocity of the boy's embrace, Tullius patted Nicomedes's bony back.

Nicomedes quickly stepped away as Tullius groaned to a stand. He fumbled at the pouch by his belt before extending a denarius towards Porcius.

He held up a hand. 'Please, Optio. That's far too much. And it's Saturnalia. Allow me.'

'I insist.' Tullius nodded, waving the coin at him. 'The boy's my property and we're imposing on you during the holidays.'

'You weren't imposing. I prefer this place when it is lively.' Porcius grinned at Nicomedes. 'And your slave is certainly that!'

Tullius shook his head. 'You might be the first to welcome his inquisition!'

Porcius regarded him for a moment, lips pursed in thought. 'Tell you what. I'll take your denarius…' He grabbed the coin from Tullius's outstretched palm. 'But only if you let me throw in your trim and a shave.'

He stifled a laugh. 'We couldn't possibly-,'

'But you aren't imposing!' Porcius held up his sheet and gestured to his stool. 'Besides, it won't take me long!'

Tullius shrugged, giving in with a small smile. 'If you insist.'

Nicomedes watched and waited until Porcius had set to work, trapping Tullius in the chair. He grabbed his new cloak and pinned it to his shoulder.

Tullius turned his head and frowned. 'Where are you going?'

'Sir, would it be okay if I waited for you at The Aurochs?'

Tullius wrinkled his nose. 'Whatever for? That place is a dump!'

'It's just next door…and it wouldn't be as strange as me waiting around in the street.' Nicomedes leant close and lowered his voice to a conspiratorial whisper: 'The shopkeepers look at me like I'm trying to steal something.'

Tullius sighed and rooted around under the drape. 'Here.' He handed the boy a few copper asses. 'Get a pitcher of wine – heavily watered, the swill they serve is vinegar – and park yourself on a bench. I expect to find you there.'

Nicomedes's face lit up. 'Yes, sir! Thank you, sir! You will, sir!' He turned and darted out of the tonstrina.

Tullius shook his head and winced when the barber's shears clipped a lobe.

'Stop moving your head, Optio! I nearly took your ear off!'

'Sorry, Porcius.' Tullius sighed, closing his eyes. 'Whatever's gotten into that lad, I'll never know.'

'Isn't it obvious?' Porcius grinned. 'Your lad's been mooning over Metellus's daughter for the past month.'

'What?'

'Ever since the snows came. He's been quite the entertainment for the men here, watching him fall over himself in the street every time she passes.' Porcius shook his head. 'I believe that – what do you call Eros? Cupid! Cupid has struck Nicomedes with his lead arrow.'

'I feared as much,' Tullius groaned. 'I've dreaded the prospect of having to explain the facts of life to him for some time.'

'Well, you know.' Porcius shrugged. 'It's inevitable, isn't it? We all come to that realisation sooner or later.'

'I didn't.' Tullius shuddered, despite Porcius's delicate work. 'I never have.'

'Is that so?'

'Take the last time I travelled to Rome. It didn't matter the time of day or what I was doing, Antonia wouldn't shut up about "husbandly duties." I tried to leave the villa as much as possible because, whenever I was home, she'd corner me. It doesn't matter how many times she forces the matter, I…still…hate it.'

His eyes widened, surprised by his candour. He met Porcius's gentle dark gaze as the man clipped his straight fringe into a uniform line.

'Hmm. Forgive me if this sounds impertinent, but has it ever occurred to you…that you just might be doing it with…the wrong person?' He leant Tullius back and prepared the sharpest of his iron blades.

'Many a time!' Tullius chuckled 'I wish it were. But my friend's pulled me into Charis's den enough times to know it isn't Antonia. The act itself just…repulses me.' He stilled as Porcius carefully set to work. 'I've thanked Fortuna for giving her Jacobus. Perhaps, if I can suffer enough to father two more brats, Antonia will leave me alone.'

'That's a shame.' Porcius peered close, concentrating. 'Handsome man such as yourself.'

'Come off it.' Tullius pulled a small smile. 'I'm almost entirely grey; I'd be no great loss.'

'I know too well.' Porcius gestured to his own head of receding ringlets; only a few brown locks stood out in a dark grey sea. 'Time catches up with us all, in the end. It is, after all, the most valuable thing a man can spend.'

Tullius's eyes lit up. 'You've read Theophrastus.'

Porcius paused, sitting up. 'I didn't take you for a philosopher, Optio!'

'How else do you think I spend my spare time?' He grinned as Porcius completed his stroke, scraping the fuzz from his jaw. 'I prefer the Greeks to our own. Horace has some worthwhile ideas, but he comes across as too much of a country bumpkin for my tastes.'

The pair fell into a Socratic dialogue, considering each other's argument before offering a thoughtful riposte. They'd only worked partway through their discussion when Tullius felt Porcius's fingers, soaked in a heady unguent, comb their way through his short locks and caress his shorn cheeks. The tonsor righted the stool, still holding Tullius's face in his strong grasp.

'There.' Porcius playfully patted him and stood. 'As smooth as the day you were born.'

'I thank you.' Tullius removed the sheet and stood. He felt his heart drop a little at the prospect of pausing their dialogue. 'I…really enjoyed the chat.'

'It's a welcome change from the conversation I normally have to make.' He held up a hand in parting, reluctantly stepping towards the ladder. 'I hope to continue again soon, Optio.'

Tullius watched Porcius turn his back, his muscles rippling beneath his pale tunic. He tried to force his feet to move, but they remained rooted to the spot. Before he could stop himself, he uttered, 'Wait.'

Porcius paused and looked over his shoulder.

'We won't…I mean to say…at least *I* wouldn't…' He gulped and gestured towards the door. 'How about you join me for a cup of that swill Nicomedes bought? That way, we can at least finish getting to the bottom of the nature of time.'

He held his breath while the tonsor silently assessed him. Then his face collapsed into a relieved grin when Porcius nodded. 'Thank you, Optio. I'd like that.'

Nicomedes perched on a stool beside Metella, the proprietor's buxom, raven-haired daughter. She rattled a pair of knucklebones and tossed them onto the counter before moving her piece, absorbed in their game of Tabula. Nicomedes watched her move, his eyes dewy with admiration. He only looked away long enough to toss the *Tali* knucklebones Metellus kept for dice and consider his options, which was when Metella chose to smile at him. She bent her head close to suggest his next move, reaching across him to point at his counters. Behind the teens, a glowering Metellus watched them carefully as he swiped a rag over the bar.

'Well, they seem to be getting along.' Porcius turned to Tullius, settling into his seat across from the optio at one of the caupona's few tables.

'Hmm.' Tullius took a sip of The Aurochs' cheap, acidic wine, and winced. The tavern's stock hardly compared to Bakari's far superior product across the street. 'Don't think Metellus is too pleased, though.'

'Only because he is a slave.' Porcius shrugged. 'And he won't always be one. You said you were teaching the boy, so he'll not only be a freedman one day, but an educated freedman. There's far worse prospects for a legionary's daughter.'

'Especially when her options are few this far from Rome.' Tullius sighed. 'Which is where I suppose I'll be heading once my enlistment's up.'

Porcius cocked his head. 'Would that really be so terrible?'

'No more than the visits are, I suppose.' Tullius considered. 'I was looking forward to the prospect of returning with Decimus, my centurion, but…'

'But?'

Tullius frowned down at the tin cup in front of him. 'I don't know anymore. The man's changed, ever since his little British slave sunk her claws into him.'

'Forgive me, friend, but you sound bitter.'

Tullius shrugged. 'I've worked beside Decimus for more than twenty years. I know the man, or at least, I thought I did.' He shook his head. 'He never cared a jot about women before. Just wanted to pack up and get back to Rome. Then this barbarian witch cuts his slave's throat and all of a sudden, he's lost his head.' He downed another swig of the wine, relishing its sharp burn. 'It defies explanation.'

'Is this the same man who used to drag you to the wolf den?'

Tullius nodded. 'But not for whoring, though he still did plenty of that. There's a woman there, he grew up with her…'

Porcius stayed his arm when he moved to take another drink. 'It sounds as though your friend has always cared for women.'

Tullius closed his eyes, wrestling with an image of the courageous young Decimus he'd first met on the Rhenus and the jaded older copy who'd endured the trials of the invasion beside him. 'You don't know…'

'I've known this legion a long time, as well.'

He met Porcius's glittering gaze and froze, seeing his own anguish mirrored within the tonsor's eyes.

'"Nothing forces us to know what we do not want to know, except pain."'

Tullius dropped his cup, holding his head in his hands. 'I always found Aeschylus's treatment of Agamemnon the hardest to stomach.'

'Because his words strike at the very heart of the tragedy of man.' Porcius regarded the distance and stifled a laugh, absently stroking his beard. 'You know, I once saw Seneca attempt a recitation of Agamemnon many, many years ago.'

'Oh, dear.' Tullius grimaced in sympathy. 'Did the old windbag bloviate through the whole thing?'

Porcius clutched his sides and roared. 'You know he did!'

Tullius chuckled, his companion's laughter growing infectious. The thought of Decimus, no doubt curled around his concubine far away in Londinium, faded from his mind.

'I've…never been so *unmoved* by a performance.' Porcius wiped tears from his eyes. 'You got it in one!'

'He never uses less than a hundred words where one would suffice.' Tullius smiled. 'I don't think I could bear hearing him massacre Agamemnon.'

'Neither could I. From that day forward, I forswore readings, recitations, and the buffoonery you Romans pass off as theatre. Shame, as I rarely get the chance to share my love of literature with the grunting apes that fill my chair.'

Tullius laughed and shook his head. 'Then why'd you end up cutting soldiers' hair on the arse end of the empire?'

Porcius scoffed. 'Lack of culture aside, you lot aren't that bad. Besides, someone's got to keep you looking presentable.'

'A philosopher *and* a cynic?' He smirked. 'I'm not sure what to make of you, Porcius.'

The man regarded him evenly. The laugh lines crinkling his eyes uncreased as his expression grew serious. A worried furrow etched itself across his high, brown forehead. 'I'm wondering, Optio, what you might make of this.'

He leant close and hovered, uncertain. His beard twitched, the veins standing out prominently from his thick neck. The air surrounding them grew charged and Tullius's world shrank to the table and the man before him. Porcius must have found whatever answer he sought in Tullius's eyes because he closed the distance between them and planted a soft kiss on his lips.

He felt the man's curling whiskers tickle his chin, tasted his hot breath, inhaled his spicy pomade, and felt the clouds part from his befuddled mind. Before Porcius could withdraw, Tullius kissed him back, pressing his face close. He kissed him again and again and again, craving more, never wanting to let go.

Porcius, mindful of the children and the caupona owner across the room, extracted himself long enough to nod towards the door. Tullius stood as if entranced and followed.

Tullius blinked, letting his eyes slowly adjust to the gloom. Moonlight shone through the iron grate covering a window at his back, throwing the pale ticked mattress into stark relief. The sight of muscular shoulders, broad torso, and bare bottom cast its shadow upon the bed. It instantly quickened Tullius's blood. He regarded Porcius's bare backside, colouring at the sight of the man's sizable bum. He sank on his back and regarded the thatched ceiling. The implications of what he'd done, what it might mean, and the destruction it could cause hit him with a sweat-inducing sobriety. A stony faced-Antonia, her hands on the shoulders of his son, regarded him coldly from the depths of his memory. 'It wasn't a dream…' He whispered bleakly to whatever gods might be listening.

'Socrates believed dreams are messages from the gods.' Porcius rolled over towards him, smiling. 'So, what does that make this?'

Tullius turned and couldn't help but smile at the man's wry grin and tousled appearance. 'I don't know.' He reached out and ran his hand down Porcius's arm. 'I wish it were a dream. One I never had to wake from.'

Porcius cradled Tullius's face in his broad palm and kissed him once more. 'You enjoyed it, then?'

Tullius lowered his eyes towards Porcius's semi-erect cock. He sighed, feeling himself grow hard again as he danced his fingers along Porcius's shaft.

'I'll take that as a yes.' Porcius enveloped Tullius in his arms and drew him close, tenderly rubbing his back. 'Io, Saturnalia, Optio.'

Tullius's eyes flew open. Had midnight passed already? 'Nicomedes!' He tried to sit up, but the headiness of his lust thrust him back down on the bed.

Porcius chuckled. 'He's all right. Metellus is good at heart. He wouldn't have chucked your slave out at Saturnalia, even if his daughter was flirting with the lad too much for his liking.'

Tullius grunted. 'I suppose you're right.' He smiled at Porcius. 'And I suppose, after tonight, that you'd better call me by my name.'

'If that's what you want…Tullius.'

He relaxed against the blankets, a thrilled shudder coursing down his spine. 'Say it again.'

'Tullius.' Porcius began trailing kisses down the optio's torso, tickling him with his beard. 'Tullius…Tullius…'

When his lips enveloped Tullius's member, he arched his back and moaned. Why, *why* had sex with Antonia never felt like this?

Porcius tolerated Tullius's quick flight of ecstasy. He lovingly wiped his cock with a corner of the blanket before resting his receding curls on Tullius's stomach. 'You know, I'm starting to think you do like sex, after all…of a sort.'

Tullius hummed as he slowly came down from his high, relishing the warm feeling of Porcius's head on his lap. His eyes sought the shadows cast on the ceiling, seeing far more than what they held. 'And that's exactly what worries me.'

V

The fresh air did little to improve Decimus's brooding humour. He stalked down the dim street, forcing Luciana to hasten to keep pace. She skirted around a timber drain dividing the roughly cobbled path and followed the centurion's hulking shadow towards the quay. He turned to avoid the singing and laughter emanating from one of the nearby warehouses and made his way to the bridge spanning the Tamesis. Luciana, catching her breath, halted alongside him.

She gazed at him curiously. Decimus's flinty blue-green eyes took in the collection of homes and businesses built up on the islands dotting the river's far side. She touched his arm and felt him stiffen. She lowered her eyes to the bridge and watched the dark waves lapping beneath them.

'Strange place to build a town,' he murmured, shaking his head. 'It's nothing but a swamp.'

'The waters here are sacred. Their boundary between the living and the dead is thin.' Luciana crossed her arms, shuddering within the folds of her wolfskin cloak. 'It is too powerful for any one tribe to claim. But of course, you Romans have the hubris to believe you can.'

Decimus ruefully shook his head. 'It was just a ford and an earthen fort when I visited last.'

She cocked her head at him. 'I didn't know you'd visited Londinium before.'

His expression hardened. 'During the invasion.'

She heard finality in his tone and let the matter drop. She picked up one of his broad palms in both her own, twining her fingers through his. 'Has the air cleared your head?'

He didn't answer, eyes still locked upon the far side of the bridge. His grasp tightened as he squeezed her hands.

She felt the cool breeze whipping up from the quay and rested her head on his shoulder. A few pins fell free of her tresses, dropping into the inky waters below.

'I'm sure you'd celebrate…if we were to withdraw from Britannia and leave you be,' he finally said.

She clung tighter to his side and sighed. 'I wouldn't be *unhappy*, if that's what you mean. Though I wouldn't have any freedom to enjoy.' She glanced up at him. 'I'm your property, remember? I go where you bid me.'

He wound his free arm about her, drawing her into his chest. 'You know I want nothing more than to go back to Rome.' A lump rose in his throat. 'But I can't go yet. The legions can't go yet. Not after everything… everything that's been done.'

She gazed up at him. 'You realise that everything that's been done is precisely why we want you to leave?'

He lowered his head, brushing his whiskers against her brow. 'Do you?'

'Oh, Decimus.' She closed her eyes. 'I don't know *what* I want anymore.'

She tore herself away and shuffled along the pier, tightly clasping her cloak to her. The thought of her mother and the Cornovii women huddled in their prison cell sprang to her mind and she shuddered. *I have failed them. I've already turned traitor…and for what?*

The wheel of Taranis burned against her skin. She squeezed her eyes shut. *This is Gaius Nerfinius all over again. You've learned nothing, Luciana. Nothing. Do you think he loves you? Do you really love him so much that you would throw your freedom away? He is a Roman, after all…*

The wind whipped about her, freeing the rest of her locks. They tumbled across her shoulders in a golden cascade, ends pulled like a flag by the gust.

'Luciana.'

She turned to see Decimus still rooted to his spot, gazing after her. The moon peeked from behind the heavy clouds darkening the sky, illuminating all the emotion in his eyes that his stern face belied. Her pulse quickened, renewing the bond that drew her irresistibly to him. She tucked a fluttering strand behind her ear and smiled. *I suppose many have turned traitor for worse.*

She took a step towards him, though he stayed her with a hand. 'Let me watch you a moment longer.'

Luciana straightened, tossing her head. She gazed at the water, letting the wind buffet her about. Decimus slowly walked to her. She glowed under the admiration shining from his eyes.

He tentatively reached out and brushed her cheek. 'How can you be real?'

She warmed at his touch and stepped into his embrace. She took his grizzled cheeks in her hands and kissed him. Her thumb brushed the angry scar curving out of his beard, ignoring the way he winced and shifted away from her touch. Luciana recaptured his lips, savouring his hot breath and the aroma of spiced stew that clung to him. Decimus responded warmly, cradling her slim form as it melded into his.

When they finally broke off to catch their breath, Luciana met his eyes. 'It matters not what policy your emperor decides. For as long as I am yours, I go wherever you go.'

He studied her a long moment, a wan smile pulling at the corners of his mouth. Confusion darkened her brow. She tilted her head, trying to parse out his thoughts. His gaze alit on a bundle tucked within the folds of her cloak and he plucked it out to examine it.

'Excuse me!' She grabbed at the kerchief, but he held it out of reach.

Smirking, Decimus unwrapped the last of the mustacei from one of his army neckerchiefs and turned it over in his palm. 'Look at that. You're full of sweet surprises.'

'I was saving that for later.' Luciana lunged for the roll.

Decimus hunched over his prize and darted back the way they came. 'Io, Saturnalia!'

Luciana followed him with determined steps, pausing only to gather a handful of sludge from the reeds lining the road.

Decimus ducked to avoid the snowball that careened over his head. He laughed and darted around the side of nearby warehouses, running as fast as his boots would carry him over the slick, muddy path. Luciana bounded around the corner after him. She laughed and chased him to the legate's modest town home, her cheeks flushed with excitement.

Decimus skidded to a halt before colliding with a group of carousing merchants. 'Io, Saturnalia!' They brandished their wineskins and cheered as he made his way around them. One man hooted, eyes widening, when Decimus's pursuer raced into sight.

Luciana checked her pace only long enough to glare at the trader. He clutched at the phallus pendant hanging from his neck and averted his gaze. She scurried on, eyes locked in pursuit of the centurion's billowing scarlet cloak.

Decimus glanced over his shoulder and squeaked. He flung open the gate to the legate's side door and hurtled around it. Luciana caught the heavy wooden door before it fell back on its hinges and slipped inside, pausing to lock it behind her. When she turned around, she just caught sight of Decimus entering the unlocked garden door. Shaking her head, she pursued him into the house, down the narrow peristyle, and up the stairs to the chamber she shared with him.

Decimus unlocked the door to his guestroom and darted inside. Before he could slam the door, Luciana's shoulder pushed back against it. One small foot crossed the threshold, barring the door's path. Smirking triumphantly, she slithered inside and threw off her cloak.

'Right, then!' She closed the door for him and held out her hand. 'Give it here.'

Decimus ruefully glanced at the treat secreted away in the folds of his cloak before meeting her gaze. 'Must I?'

'You must.' Luciana stepped closer and lifted her fingers to tickle his whiskered chin. She laughed at the delighted smile that grew across his face. 'Tis the season, after all!'

'Fine.' Decimus threw back his cloak and drew the last of the mustacei from behind his back.

Luciana wrinkled her nose, pulling back in surprise when he suddenly pressed the sweet must roll against her lips. His warm, deep chuckle serenaded her ears. She took a few nibbles, relaxing. Decimus stooped to meet her height and clapped his jaws about the opposite end. They gazed into each other's eyes, lost in the delirium of the moment. Then, in a matter of moments, the roll had been devoured between them. Their lips pressed urgently together.

Luciana kissed him, savouring the sweet taste of honeyed mulsum upon his lips. His full, luxuriant beard caressed her chin, and she moaned appreciatively. She wound her arms over his shoulders and buried her fingers in his close-cropped ringlets, holding him close.

Decimus shut his eyes and gently placed his hands on her small shoulders. 'You know,' he breathed between kisses, 'I can't remember ever enjoying a Saturnalia as much as this one.'

'Oh?'

He hummed affirmatively. 'Even with…the ice and snow…the work… this stinking swamp of a settlement…far from home…You more than make up for it.'

She ran a hand down his chest, coming to rest above the strong thrumming of his heart. She felt her own pulse sync with his and she pressed herself to him with new urgency. 'The pleasure is all mine, Centurion.'

He grunted in sudden remembrance and pulled away, breaking their hungry kiss. He grinned and held up a finger to quiet her protest. 'Wait. I have a gift for you, Luci.'

'A gift?'

'It is the custom to bestow gifts on your servants and loved ones during Saturnalia.' Decimus strode over to his chest and rummaged about in the clutter. He located a small wooden box and snatched it up in his palm.

'But…but I didn't know. I have nothing for you,' she murmured.

'It doesn't matter.' The soft smile upon his lips and the twinkle in his eyes when he presented her the box melted her resistance. He pressed it into her hands. 'For you, my love.'

Breathlessly, she slowly opened the casket. Inside lay a silver ram's head pendant on a chain. She gazed at it for a moment before lifting her head. 'Cernunnos?'

'Capricorn.' He smiled and pulled the pendant free of its container. 'It's the legion's mascot. Augustus, who reconstituted the Fourteenth Gemina, was conceived beneath Capricorn. Though I suppose it does bear resemblance to your horned patron god.'

'Yes.' She smiled and took the delicate chain in her fingers. 'Perhaps we Romans and Celts are not so different, after all.'

'Perhaps.' He gathered her hair up in his hand when she moved to fasten the pendant around her neck.

Luciana suddenly paused as her fingers brushed against the leather thong. She idly stroked the rough strap as she considered for a moment. Then, decisively, she lifted the thong from around her neck and thrust it at Decimus. 'Take this. My Saturnalia gift to you.'

He frowned a little at the lumpy bronze trinket in his palm. 'I've always wondered about this. What is it?'

'The wheel of Taranis. The fortunes of the world turn upon it.' Luciana fumbled with the Capricorn necklace as she spoke. 'My mother wore it for many years before passing it to me. It's supposed to bless the wearer with his favour.'

'Then I'll wear it with pleasure.' Decimus slipped the thong over his head and tucked the wheel beneath his red tunic. 'Who's Taranis, by the way?'

'He's one of the most powerful of our gods; a large, bearded man who rules the skies and summons the thunder.'

'Ah, I know the bloke.' Decimus nodded sagely. 'In Rome, he goes by the name of Jupiter.'

Luciana beamed. 'We really aren't so different, after all!'

They smiled at each other in silence. Then, squaring her shoulders, Luciana threw her arms about the centurion. She pressed her mouth to his, tightly clasping his rock-steady frame. One of her feet lifted from the floor and hitched itself over his hip. When she pushed against him, she could feel his hardening erection beneath his tunic. A laugh rumbled in the back of her throat.

Decimus's hands travelled down her sides and crossed over her spine. He felt the contours of her bottom and then squeezed it roughly.

'No.' Luciana broke away and smiled teasingly, her voice husky with emotion. 'We do this my way.'

'Today, I live to serve.' He craned his head down to place a tender kiss on her neck. 'Io, Saturnalia.'

'Good.' She flicked her tongue across her lips and gripped the hem of his tunic. In as smooth a motion she could muster for her diminutive height, she pulled the garment over the centurion's head. At the sight of his broad, bare shoulders and scarred chest, a thrill raced down Luciana's spine. The wheel of Taranis dully gazed back at her from against his pecs, and she lifted her eyes to his. He gazed back at her expectantly, his sea-coloured eyes sparkling in the dim room. With the gifted pendant, he looked even more a Gaul than he normally did.

Luciana took a deep breath, gathering her self-control. She placed a palm on his sternum and pushed him. Decimus backed steadily until he fell onto the room's cot. Luciana smiled down at his sprawled form for an instant. Then, in a flash, she picked up a set of kerchiefs from the heaped paraphernalia of his trunk and began binding each of his limbs to a bedpost.

'Mithras god,' he groaned, following her with his eyes as she ably knotted her ties. His muscles began to quiver in anticipation and his erection hardened.

'Well, what did you expect?' She smiled and ran her finger down his long, aquiline nose. 'You're a naughty boy, stealing off with your mistress's food.'

'It was worth it,' he croaked. His eyelids fluttered in response to her teasing caresses.

'So, you're not even sorry?' Luciana moved away from the bed.

Decimus sighed and weakly shook his head.

'We can't have that now, can we?' She turned around and slowly strode back into Decimus's sight. This time, he could see her holding his vine staff.

His eyes widened. 'Luci…you don't know how to use that.'

'Don't I?' She batted her eyes innocently before swatting the end against her palm.

'I mean it. You're not a centurion. You don't have the training.'

'Oh, if that's your only objection…' She stooped and picked his crested helmet up from the floor. She wrapped the felt helmet liner around her forehead before slipping the heavy apparatus on. The brim toppled over her eyes. One hand pushed it back and held it in place as she reappeared in his view. 'Better?'

He swallowed the low whine rumbling in his throat and writhed against his firm bonds.

Luciana slowly brought the staff down to his chest, the tip resting against his shoulder. She gently bounced it in place a few times, then laughed when she saw him flinch in anticipation. 'Oh, Decimus!'

'Fuck…' He gasped hoarsely.

The tip of the staff began to trail down his chest. It brushed his pierced nipples, skirted around his stiff erection, and came to rest across the top of his thighs. Once again, Luciana tapped the staff against his skin. After a few moments, it slowly shifted down, and down, and down.

Decimus tipped his head back against the pillow and sighed. The soft, tiny blows had a relaxing effect on him. The sound of her earrings jangling against his helmet's cheek guards provided a soothing, melodious soundtrack to her ministrations. Warmth stirred within him as a flush stole over his skin. 'By Juno, you're good,' he grunted.

Luciana ceased tapping his ankles and smirked. Moving around to the end of the bed, she took up a position beside one of the posts and prodded the bottom of his calloused foot with the staff.

'Luci!' He laughed and squirmed, desperately trying to jerk his foot away. The knots held him fast. 'Please!'

'Does that tickle?' She smirked, raising an eyebrow at him. 'I thought your feet had hardened from a lifetime of marching.'

'So had…my heart,' he rasped between giggles. 'You…put paid…to that!'

She let the staff fall for a moment, gazing at him with wide eyes. He strained against his bonds, his thick, bristled neck pulsing with laughter. His toes curled repeatedly, shaking and shirking from their torment. In his present position, he was as helpless to her wiles as he had always been. Tears brimmed in the corners of her eyes. She fervently blinked them away. 'Stop that. You'll make your mistress cry!' With a squeal, she whirled about and renewed her prodding on the opposite foot.

'Luci!' Decimus bellowed, shaking his head. He squeezed his eyes shut and tears of mirth streamed down his lined face. 'Luci! Mithras god, please stop! Stop! I can't take it!'

In response, she increased the tempo. When he'd been reduced to a sobbing mess, she finally dropped the vine staff to the floor.

'You've unmanned me,' he whimpered, still trembling from her touch.

Luciana carefully lifted the helmet from her head and set it aside. She pushed off the liner, shook out her hair, and settled her gaze on the centurion's cock. 'I rather think this fellow disagrees.'

She pounced onto the foot of the cot and crawled forward so that she sat poised between Decimus's legs. Eyeing him, she lifted her hands and danced her fingers across his testicles. They waved and circled about his penis, tantalizingly just out of reach.

Decimus seethed. 'Typhon take you, woman!'

She lifted one sleeve of her tunic and slid her arm free. As she repeated the gesture with the other sleeve, she tucked her head and smiled coyly. Her green eyes mocked him. The top of her purple tunic flopped down about her waist, exposing her small, spherical breasts.

Decimus's breathing grew laboured. His tongue darted out to wet his dry, chapped lips. He gazed at Luciana's form in astonishment; no matter how many times he'd seen it, the perfection of her naked body always stole the breath right out of his lungs.

With great care, she slowly leant forward, arching her back to avoid contact with his cock. When she'd brought her torso mere inches from his face, she lifted her hands to her breasts and began teasing the nipples erect.

'Oh!' He yelped, raising his head towards her as far as it would stretch.

Luciana winked and sat back, further beyond his reach. He could look, but not touch, and it tortured him. Suddenly, she clenched a hand about his cock, making him squeak. She arched a brow. 'Is this what you wanted?'

'You vile barbarian witch!' He let out a strangled moan. 'You accursed Celt! You cunning, sadistic, bloody-minded…*cunnus*!'

He arched his back from the bed, howling his last word, as Luciana's grip tightened about his penis. When his voice petered into a whimper, she slowly began dragging her hand up and down his shaft. Decimus groaned approvingly. His strained muscles went limp.

Luciana leant forward and placed her other hand on his chest. Her fingers nimbly fiddled with the wheel of Taranis. She smiled. 'Would you expect anything less from a royal savage?'

'Your wickedness is worthy of a queen,' he whispered.

Luciana paused a moment to rest against his chest. Her fingers flicked his nipple rings back and forth playfully. She stretched forward and pecked his lips. 'Aren't you a lucky plebeian, then?'

'The luckiest.' A satisfied smile stretched across his face.

She softened, fighting the urge to immediately shower him with kisses. She closed her eyes and forced a stony expression, slowly leaning away from him. 'Come, Decimus. Show me your warrior's heart. You must be a foe worthy of your queen.'

He growled, a fresh thrill pulsing through his veins. He hadn't felt the fire she incited so easily within his breast since his impetuous youth. 'If you want me to come, you must make me,' he murmured through clenched teeth.

'Fine.' She drew away from his cock and clambered down the bed. As soon as her feet hit the floor, her tunic pooled about her ankles. She kicked it aside.

'Luci…where are you going? What…are you…doing?' He rasped, straining his head. His short, greying ringlets lay plastered to his skull with sweat.

Suddenly, she threw a leg across his chest and eased herself down on top of his face. 'Why should I be doing all the work?' She purred.

Decimus let out a low groan of approval. He breathed deeply of her heady scent. The wispy blonde hairs tickled his face. He parted his lips and stroked her entrance with his strong, girthy tongue.

'Oh, yes!' She tossed her head and grabbed his cock. His wet, assertive touch, his coarse whiskers brushing against her genitals, his adoring lips that pursed every few seconds to kiss her sex brought stars before her eyes. She enthusiastically pumped his shaft, wriggling her toes wildly. 'Yes! Decimus!'

He shuddered violently in response to her ministrations. His panted grunts increased with the tempo of her tugs. His tongue probed further and finally brushed against her clit. He clenched his bound hands into fists and fought against the climax rising within him. His tongue circled her a few times, feeling her engorge in response to his touch. Then, finally, he took her clit between his teeth.

Luciana threw her head back and yowled. Her body convulsed and she nearly collapsed on top of him. Weakly, she clung to his shaft and attempted to stroke him further.

A satisfied smile pulled at the corners of Decimus's parted lips. He sucked on her clit, batting it about in his mouth with his tongue. He released it only to pop it between his teeth again, savouring the feel of her warm, shuddering walls against his face.

'Decimus!' Luciana screamed. She tightened and released, the flood carrying her over the abyss. Her head fell forward. She rested against his abdomen, lost in the elated waves of her own pleasure.

Pride flushed his face. He gently kissed her still trembling flesh, murmuring her name over and over.

When the world stopped spinning and dropped her back onto the bed, Luciana lifted her head and gazed at the centurion's still-erect cock. She pressed her feet against the sides of the bed and lifted herself from Decimus's face. 'Right,' she murmured, her limp grasp tightening around his shaft. 'We still have to do something about this…'

He watched, his grin widening, as she sat up and then slowly impaled herself on him. Her warm, wet walls stretched to fit him as easily as though they were a comfortable sock. He gazed yearningly at her pert, round bottom and writhing spine. His fingers extended from the posts, desperate to rake themselves through her sleek golden hair. 'Luci!' The strangled cry escaped his lips.

She moaned, eyelids fluttering softly, as she took him deep inside her. The tip of his penis brushed against her still throbbing clit, setting her nerves off anew. Slowly, she began to rock, expertly rotating her hips and grinding against his chest.

'Mithras god!' He whined. Steadily, the friction increased, and his muscles tightened. His breaths came shorter, harder. The feeling of her lithe, perfect form writhing against him, her warm heat enveloping and tenderly caressing his cock, her short, sharp cries, dimmed his vision. Finally, when her pace became frantic, he could hold back no longer. With a guttural roar, he came inside her and fell limp.

Luciana fell forward and panted in relief. She nestled her head against the woollen comforter and sighed, relishing the feel of his thick seed pulsing inside her. When she'd regained her breath, she crawled off his flaccid penis and turned about towards his head. She laid her head across his chest and rested her palm against his scarred, muscled torso. She listened to the frantic drumming of his excited heart and smiled. 'My worthy, worthy servant.'

They lay together in contented silence, their bodies adhered to one another with sweat. Decimus, upon regaining his senses, lifted his head to gaze down at the top of Luciana's crown. The way she nestled against his body, the way she held him, the way she controlled him so completely felt so perfect it beggared belief. He blinked several times just to assure himself of her existence.

Luciana breathed out a long sigh and sat up. She untied one of his hands from the bedpost. 'Io, Saturnalia,' she whispered softly.

He flexed his newly freed wrist and followed her with his eyes as she moved across to the other hand. His fingers reached out and gently brushed against her shoulder. 'You're incredible.'

Luciana pulled the bonds loose and paused. She smiled at him in contemplation for a moment, then ducked her head to place another swift kiss upon his whiskered lips. 'You flatter me. I'm sure your friend Cassia has long accustomed you to nights like this.'

'Never like this.' He trapped one of her pale delicate hands between his palms and pulled it towards his mouth. He kissed it reverently. 'You're a queen.'

A blush stole across her cheeks. She shyly withdrew her hand. 'Well…' She rose from the bed and slunk away, her emerald earrings flashing in the dim light.

Decimus slowly pushed himself upright with a groan. He stared down at his feet and then stretched his arms to one of the bedposts. His fingers fumbled with the knots binding his ankle, but they made little progress. He grunted in frustration at the strength of her ties. 'Was your father a sailor, by any chance?'

'You know he wasn't.'

Decimus raised his head. His face suddenly became ashen. He watched in stupefied silence as Luciana, clad in her light purple tunic once more, held a chaplet of gilded oak leaves above her head. She laughingly settled it atop her crown and brushed a few strands of hair away from her face. 'I am a chieftain's daughter, and your triumphant mistress!'

'Where did you get that?'

Her eyes widened at his harsh, accusatory tone. 'I…I found it in the bottom of your trunk.'

'Take it off!' He tried to rise from the bed but remained bound in place by his ankles. His fingers set to the knots with renewed purpose. 'Take it off right now!'

Luciana backed away from the bed. Anger had flushed Decimus's face; his severe brows knotted together thunderously. His scar glowed white across his cheek. The muscles in his jaw flexed as she lifted her shaking hands. She pulled the chaplet off and held it by her finger and thumb. Fear welled inside her. 'What's come over you? I only just-,'

'Get out!' He roared, pointing to the door. 'Put that fucking thing down and get out of my sight!'

Luciana gasped and spun around. She threw the crown to the floor and flew out the door, nearly tripping over Tor huddled against it. Tears blurred her vision as she raced down the stairs, hardly knowing where she was going. Behind her, the angry bellows of her beloved echoed in her ears.

Her feet led her into the garden and around the back to a modest shed serving as a makeshift stable. She clambered over the rickety wooden partition and found the centurion's horse standing quietly at the back of the structure. She threw her arms about the bay's broad neck. He hardly paid her notice, accepting her fierce hug without a quibble.

'Oh, Aquila!' She sobbed, burying her red eyes in his coarse black mane. Horses, she understood; horses, she could manage. Beastly men with their beastly tempers were another matter entirely.

The stallion stood quietly, occasionally lifting his nose to nuzzle Luciana's hair, as she soaked his silky hide with her tears.

VI

Luciana blinked and lifted her head, squinting against the weak rays of sunlight streaking through the slats. Her lids, still heavy with sleep, protested the incursion. A snort sounded above her head, and she turned to see Aquila munching a tick of hay.

She sat up and looked down, wrinkling her nose. Her tunic, stained with Aquila's manure, clung haphazardly to her body. Gooseflesh pimpled her pale, exposed arms. Hay peeked from her hair, with a few straws protruding from between the golden fringe of her earrings. She sniffled, her bright red nose numbed and crusted with her frozen snot. She watched her breath dispel into a cloud of smoke in the crisp air, hugging her arms to her chest.

The memory of the night before jarred her awake. 'Oh, fuck,' she whispered. She still wasn't sure what she'd done, but the centurion's response…

Luciana looked at Aquila. She sat in silence for a long while, studying the stallion's rippling muscles beneath his shiny bay coat. He was broad and well-proportioned, with a deep chest, sound, sturdy legs, and an intelligent, handsome head. In almost every regard, he was a perfect match for his master.

The horse lazily twitched his ears and snorted, burying his muzzle contentedly in his straw bedding. Luciana palmed away fresh tears and sighed. 'If only he had your temperament!'

Aquila lifted his head. His liquid brown eyes regarded her placidly.

She looked past the horse, into the far reaches of her mind. A shudder coursed through her at the thought of Decimus. She knew that fire and fury pulsed within his cold, disciplined frame, but the aggression in his voice, the curtness with which he'd treated her…it was almost as if she were nothing to him. Fresh tears brimmed in her eyes at the thought; he had told her he'd loved her, and she had believed it. A contemptuous, strangled laugh rose to the back of her throat. He sure had a funny way of showing it.

At least Gaius Nerfinius rejected me by leaving the country. She hadn't thought Decimus could be as callous as her old tutor, but his brusque dismissal stung just as harshly as when her teenage self had learned why Nerfinius had vanished. But this time, she couldn't leave him behind. No matter what he now thought of her, she remained his *property*. 'Bastard,' Luciana spat under her breath. She brushed her face against her folded arms and frowned up at Aquila. 'They're all bastards!'

The stallion continued to nibble his straw bedding, unperturbed.

She sniffed. 'I think I'll live with you from now on, Aquila. After all, we're both just the master's things.'

The bolt slid back on one of the garden doors and the sound of male voices filled the yard. Luciana rose onto her knees, peering over the top railing of the shed. The scarlet helmet crests of Decimus and the legate stood at right angles to one another as the men conversed, wrapped in their dark scarlet cloaks. Decimus stamped his feet in the cold, breathing into his hands. Regulus gestured and the pair exited onto the street, still deep in conversation.

She waited for their voices to fade and slipped out of the makeshift stable. Aquila snorted gently at her back, and she absently patted his soft muzzle. Still squinting in the cold light of day, her frozen feet stumbled across the yard and entered the town home through the kitchen door.

'I know I was pleased, but I'm fit to murder that tribune now.' Hilaria's broad backside quivered indignantly as she leant against the sideboard, facing the busy cook.

'Oh, dear. The little one still upset?' Cook murmured, chopping a turnip.

Luciana crept past them, trying not to draw attention to herself. Cook turned in Luciana's direction, but Hilaria leant closer, blocking her view.

'Six times Gaius woke up screaming in the night. Six! Said he saw the guards coming to murder him next. I ask you…'

Luciana slipped free of the kitchen and quietly stole up the wooden staircase. Tor's tawny bulk suddenly appeared at the top, whining and wagging his tail in greeting. Luciana patted his head and entered the room she'd quit so hastily a few hours ago.

The chamber hadn't been tidied, which didn't surprise Luciana in the least. The kerchiefs she'd used to bind Decimus lay where they'd been discarded at the base of each bedpost. The blanket covering the straw tick rested askew, slipping partway onto the floorboards. Decimus's dirty tunic lay wadded up against his trunk. The source of their argument perched atop the garments spilling from within.

She walked over and picked the crown up. Her fingers traced the ribbing of the gilded oak leaves. What about this gaudy chaplet could have induced the rage she'd seen last night?

She dropped it back on his trunk with a sigh. 'Who cares, anyway?'

Tor dogged her steps, bumping his wet nose against her leg.

She turned to him as she pulled a clean gown out from the mess. 'What's the matter, boy? Did the master forget to feed you?'

The dog's large eyes regarded her steadily as his tail thumped the floor.

'Poor thing.' Luciana unhooked her earrings and tossed them down beside Decimus's beard oil. She grabbed his bone comb and ran it cursorily through her hair. 'He's neglected all of his *things*, recently, hasn't he?'

Tor barked.

She had just pulled a pair of woollen socks over her blue toes when a shout in the street arrested her attention. Frowning, Luciana quickly padded over to the window.

'Stop, thief!' A familiar red head pushed through the crowded market stalls lining the muddy cobbles, desperately pursuing a cloaked figure hastening towards the quay.

Luciana gasped and stepped into her leather boots before racing down the stairs. Tor bounded at her side, baying. She grabbed her wolfskin cloak from the alcove and pushed her way past the doorman as she darted into the sunlight, following the route she and Decimus had taken the evening before.

If I hurry, I just might intercept him. She leapt over a pair of children playing in the drain and skidded in the slush accumulated at the corner of one of the warehouses. Tor darted ahead of her, ears pricked.

'Get him, boy!' Luciana cried, making directly for the man racing across the bridge.

Tor took the initiative and lengthened into an arrow. He leapt up at the hooded man, who staggered in surprise. The purse he'd been holding slipped from his grasp and disappeared into the Tamesis below.

A scream of dismay sounded from the direction of the Walbrook estuary. Luciana turned to see a face from her past race towards them.

'Leave it,' Luciana murmured to Tor, who, growling, reluctantly relinquished his hold on the thief's hood. The gaunt man, eyes wide with fear, picked himself up and raced on towards a collection of huts south of the river.

'I'm sorry, Boudicca.' Luciana patted the dog's head and straightened, panting. 'I tried to stop him.'

'Luigsech of the Cornovii?' Boudicca stopped short, shock widening her bright eyes. 'What in the name of Andraste are you doing here?'

She smiled ruefully. 'I could ask you the same. We're a long way from the lands of the Iceni.'

Boudicca's face darkened. 'We were bringing the tribe's yearly tribute to the Roman scum.' She gestured to the water. 'It belongs to the gods now.'

Luciana frowned, regarding the woman. Boudicca, her childhood foe in the Beltane chariot contests, had always been a proud, fearsome woman. She'd refused to admit that her tribe's horses could ever be bested, even when Luciana and her plucky mare, Belena, had done exactly that. She'd also been held up by Luciana's parents as a shining example of everything that Luciana ought to be. Boudicca, they'd pointed out, had married for the sake of strengthening cross-tribal alliances. She'd borne children and risen to tribal leadership alongside her husband. She'd used her knowledge of the Romans to avert further retribution after a failed Iceni insurrection had stripped the tribe of their weapons. She had it all, and she still had time to breed and race ever-swifter ponies. If only Luciana, who'd resisted such a fate, could have done the same.

Looking at Boudicca now, Luciana felt vindicated in her choices. Though of roughly the same age as Luciana, the Iceni queen looked far older. Her noble features had creased with worry, her skin frighteningly pale and clammy. Her form looked a bit hunched bundled in its furs and woollen finery, despite the gold glinting from her thin hands and the beautifully struck fibula in the shape of a hare that held her cloak in place. Her long, bright red tresses, neatly coiled at the nape of her neck, showed streaks of silver amid their gold. The once fierce warrior she'd raced in her youth seemed a shadow of her former self.

Boudicca heaved a broken sigh, choking down her sobs. 'You did what you could, I suppose.' She spun on her heel. 'Come. I need to make sure my husband's all right.'

Luciana and Tor fell into step with Boudicca. The trio fought the bustling crowds eyeing up trinkets and fresh-caught oysters hawked by merchants on the quay, heading west. Boudicca sharply veered when they reached the Walbrook's marshy banks, clattering up cobbled Roman paths.

'I hope the gods enjoy their bounty, for it means our demise,' Boudicca said bitterly.

Luciana matched her strides, frowning thoughtfully. 'Surely, you can explain to the procurator and ask for an extension?'

Boudicca laughed. 'Hardly! We're already trying to pay off last year's back taxes. The Romans won't give us yet another extension.'

Luciana cocked her head. 'Have things been so bad?'

Boudicca lifted her set chin, glaring straight ahead. 'Do you have any idea how being unable to hunt has crippled us? With the droughts, we can hardly grow enough grain to feed ourselves, let alone set any aside to pay the Romans.' She lowered her voice as they passed a group of uniformed legionaries in the street. 'Too many have starved to death, and more still won't survive the winter.' She glanced at Luciana's drawn brows. 'I'm sure the Cornovii have been well-fed with the forests you have to hand.'

Luciana grimly shook her head. 'The Cornovii are no more.'

'What?' Boudicca checked her step, bumping into a dark-complexioned sailor toting a heavy sack. 'But old Suliac brought us word of a Cornovii troupe staying among the acolytes on Mona.'

'That would be my brother and the warriors.' Luciana ducked underneath a line of washing strung across the path. 'The Romans killed the old men and the boys, including my father. The women and children live for now, locked in the prison of the Viroconium fort.'

'How did you ever escape?'

'I didn't.'

When Boudicca stopped and turned to her, Luciana sighed. 'I'm enslaved to a Roman officer.'

Sadness glittered in Boudicca's pale green eyes. Her hand clasped Luciana's. 'It seems we have both fallen victim to their tyranny.'

'My lady!' A man with dark mustachios and a gaunt, wild-eyed look, gestured frantically from further up the street.

Boudicca dropped Luciana's hand and raced towards him. 'How is he?'

Luciana whistled a wandering Tor to her side and followed Boudicca's billowing yellow and black cape. She stopped just behind the queen's shoulder and gasped. There, stretched out upon the ground and supported by his warriors, lay the mighty Prasutagus, chieftain of the Iceni.

'Husband!' Boudicca knelt, gently palpating the bruise at the back of Prasutagus's head. The Iceni men closed ranks around her, nearly blocking the scene from Luciana's view. She stepped forward and muscled in beside the wild-eyed man. She regarded the pair in shock, dumbfounded by the profound change time had wrought.

Luciana remembered Prasutagus as a tall, hulking figure, taller even than his formidable wife. There had been a power about his stern glare and deep voice, one that could intimidate his listener even when he spoke words of peace. As amenable as he was to Roman rule, Prasutagus hadn't been a man you'd choose to cross. And yet, the figure before her was a frail, shrivelled old man. He was small, bent, having lost all semblance of bulk or muscle. The skeletal fingers that clutched at his fur cloak repulsed her as much as they fascinated her. The flesh had fallen from his face, leaving his eyes and cheeks sunken into his withered, wrinkled skin. His raven hair had greyed and receded from his brow, hanging in lank, thin strands down his stringy neck. A rheumy film had cascaded over his eyes; they gazed sightlessly beyond his wife's shoulder, staring through Luciana into the sky.

His thin, dry mouth opened to reveal a largely toothless maw. 'The…

money…?'

Boudicca shook her head, taking one of his claws between her hands. She bent her head over it, holding his knuckles against her cheek. 'We are doomed, my love.'

His pale visage whitened further.

'There has to be something we can do.' Luciana knelt beside the couple, glancing between them. 'When are you supposed to meet with the procurator?'

'Luigsech…' Prasutagus slowly turned towards her. 'How fares… Gruffydd?'

'My father resides in the Otherworld.' Luciana patted his shoulder. She turned to Boudicca expectantly.

The queen shrugged. 'One of our men has been queuing amongst the other tribes since the first hour. There is no telling when the procurator might get to us, but he certainly will.'

Prasutagus tried to shake his head, but Boudicca stilled him. 'She knows about the debt.'

Luciana regarded him sadly. 'I'm just sorry I couldn't catch your thief in time.'

'The swamp rat,' Boudicca spat a gob of phlegm onto the road. 'Scurrying back across the river. Who steals from a tribal chieftain?! Of the Iceni, no less? Roman scum!'

Prasutagus winced as his wife's fingers brushed against the growing lump on his crown.

She lifted her head to the warriors ringing them. 'You have failed to protect your lord.'

'My queen, we never saw the man coming! He had his back to us one moment and running off with the purse the next!'

The other men nodded their agreement with the speaker.

'Don't blame them.' The chieftain lifted a trembling hand. 'I am the one who failed.'

Boudicca snorted. 'Don't be ridiculous. It's this Roman settlement.' She clambered to her feet and gestured for the warriors to take up the litter carrying her prostrate husband. 'There never should have been people living along the confluence of the sacred waters, let alone conducting business!'

'I doubt the procurator will see it that way.' The chieftain's sallow face gazed blankly up at the glowering sky.

'My lord!'

Luciana, rising to stand beside Boudicca, saw another man in checked trousers and a heavy cloak waving frantically from outside the governor's office.

Boudicca motioned to the warriors. 'Come, then. Let's get this over with.'

The women allowed Prasutagus's retinue to begin carefully making its way down the cobbled street before falling in behind. Luciana sneaked a quick glance at Boudicca's grim expression before continuing in uneasy silence.

'He's dying.' Boudicca finally broke the tension, her tone blunt and defeated.

Luciana sighed, letting her words tumble out. 'How? A man like Prasutagus…?'

'It started a couple of winters ago. He became weak, then he dropped weight. Soon, he could hardly eat at all. We sent for every healer around, tried everything they told us. I have prayed and made promises to every god I could name. And yet he only grows worse.' Boudicca lifted her head with a resigned air. 'I have watched him waste away every day. Nothing I have done,' she choked down a sob, 'nothing I have done can stop it.' She shot Luciana a sad smile. 'I doubt even your mother, with every resource to hand, could save him.'

'I am…very sorry.' Luciana averted her gaze, her features crumpling.

'I have made my peace with it.' Boudicca blinked away the tears gathering in the corners of her eyes. 'It's the girls I worry about. They're still too young to marry, and without their father…'

Luciana thought back to the last time she'd seen Boudicca's family, at a large inter-tribal Beltane gathering four winters ago. She remembered the woman's daughters, Emer and Rioghnach, tumbling about outside the horse pens. The eldest hadn't yet been old enough to partake of the festival's courtship and handfasting rites, though Boudicca had told her she suspected Emer would be initiated into womanhood soon.

Their conversation abruptly ceased as they mounted the short wooden steps to the large, heavy doors of the governor's office. A pair of legionaries flanked the doors on either side, barring the way for Prasutagus and his retinue.

'Make way for the chieftain of the Iceni!' Boudicca bellowed to the guards in heavily accented Latin.

'State your business with the governor, *Brittunculi*,' one of the soldiers sneered.

Luciana saw Boudicca's fists clench tightly at her sides. 'We have no business with the governor. We have come to see the procurator about our annual tribute.'

The other guard rapped on the door box and murmured something to the porter who shoved the window aside. When he received his answer, he nodded to his colleague and stepped back. 'But leave the mutt here.' His eyes fell on Tor, who flattened his ears and growled.

'I shall tell Centurion Decimus Maximus, primus pilus of the Fourteenth Gemina, that you disapprove of his personal hound.' Luciana turned to Tor and uttered a sharp command.

Tor reluctantly sat outside the door, eyeing the suddenly uneasy guards.

Boudicca inclined her nose as she passed the legionaries before letting her anger burst anew over her features. 'How dare they.'

Luciana noticed a peristyle to her right and studiously averted her gaze when she caught sight of Decimus's retreating figure following the governor along the corridor. His tall, broad frame followed the forms of several other high-ranking military officers before disappearing into a room. Luciana felt her own quiet rage fomenting in the pit of her stomach.

The legionary leading them down the hall stopped beside a doorframe and brought a fist to his chest in salute. 'Catus Decianus, imperial procurator of Britannia!'

'What's this?' The man lifted his bald dome from a series of unfurled scrolls on his desk. A pair of bronze scales perched precariously on the edge, within reach of a much smaller table allocated to a secretary. Luciana's nostrils flared as the procurator's weaselly eyes narrowed. 'Why in Jupiter's name have these barbarians brought me a corpse?'

Boudicca shouldered Luciana and the warriors aside, stepping up to the desk. 'My husband, the noble Prasutagus of the Iceni and loyal client of Rome, has been ill for some time. Yet he still made the effort to visit you himself regarding the matter of our taxes.'

Decianus cocked his head to meet the prostrate chieftain's gaze. 'And this woman of yours would be...?'

'Queen Boudicca of the Iceni!' She thundered. 'And I demand you address me when I speak to you!'

The procurator lumbered to his feet. He brushed at the broad purple stripe lining his rather handsome linen tunic, regarding Boudicca with the self-satisfied smirk Luciana had grown to detest the night before. 'Or what, *woman?*'

Boudicca gritted her teeth and lifted a fist. Luciana caught it, holding her back before the sentries at the door could protest.

'Boudicca, don't...' Prasutagus wheezed from his litter.

Decianus crossed his arms. 'Oh, dear. Let me make something perfectly clear to you. I don't have to address you or call you anything. You're a queen of...what? A collection of mud huts? I am the emperor's trusted deputy to this province. You may have heard of him? Emperor Nero? The most powerful ruler in the known world?' He chuckled as Boudicca's eyes widened with rage. 'And, as his representative, my person is also sacrosanct. I'm not sure how you're used to conducting business, but we Romans have far more civilised methods than resorting to violence.'

The queen's complexion reddened to match the hue of her auburn knot. She reluctantly allowed Luciana to wrestle her arm down to her side. 'That, procurator, is highly debatable.'

Decianus inclined his head. The grin spreading across his face sent a shudder down Luciana's spine. 'Tell me, Chief Prasutagus, have you come with the year's taxes plus interest on the previous year's debt?'

Boudicca opened her mouth but was silenced by a stern look from her husband. Luciana glanced between them, biting her lip.

Decianus shrugged. 'Well? Or do you let your women do all the talking for you now?'

Prasutagus lowered his filmy gaze. 'We do not have it.'

'Oh, dear. Oh, dear.' The procurator chuckled and shook his head. 'What are we ever going to do with you Iceni?'

Boudicca stepped towards him. 'We've come about an extension…'

'Please!' Decianus grimaced and held up a hand. He turned to the thin, mousy secretary seated behind his cubby. 'Volsius, do you believe it would be wise for Rome to extend their line of credit with a tribe that has twice defaulted?'

The secretary lowered his head. He measured denarii on his scale and scratched numbers on a tablet. 'Doesn't seem like sound business sense to me,' he mumbled.

Decianus turned back to Boudicca with a shrug of feigned helplessness. 'There you have it.'

'You said yourself that you are the emperor's man in Britannia.' Boudicca wrung her hands. 'Surely, your emperor would like to be considered a…gracious and…magnanimous ruler.'

Decianus ignored her, riffling around some files shelved and tagged in a cubby. 'Now, if I recall correctly, the terms of your loan last year specify that if you failed to make the necessary repayments…Ah!' He pulled a roll of papyrus from the vault, unfurling it. 'Then, as the imperial procurator, I have the authority to seize all lands belonging to the Iceni in the name of Rome, effective immediately.'

'We…we didn't agree to that!' Boudicca attempted to bat the document away. Decianus lifted it from her reach and pointed to an untidily inked line.

'Read it here, my dear. It's plain to see.'

Boudicca scowled defiantly. Luciana, reading the document over her shoulder, saw the poorly drawn 'X' indicating Prasutagus's signature and sighed inwardly. She knew Boudicca and Prasutagus had learned what Latin they commanded by ear; likely, neither of them could read the Latin characters on the page.

Boudicca whirled to meet her gaze, eyes beseeching. 'Tell them they can't do that, Luigsech. That wasn't part of the agreement!'

She glanced at the document. Her friend's pleading look choked her, filling her eyes with tears. 'I'm sorry,' she whispered.

'Decianus.' Prasutagus lifted a skeletal hand, beckoning the procurator to his litter. Decianus rolled up the papyrus and complied, slapping the document against his hand.

'I am a very ill man. I have…I hope…served Rome well as its client?'

Decianus reluctantly nodded. 'Yes, and?'

'You have a copy of my will, I believe? From…from the time of my cousin's revolt? When you recognised me as…client-king of the Iceni?'

Decianus turned to his secretary, who nodded. He sighed. 'Your point, Prasutagus?'

'If I made a gesture…of good faith, would that…potentially…extend the debt?'

'It would depend on the gesture, sir. I must say, for someone deep in default on your previous loan, you don't have a lot to bargain with.'

'I still have my life.' Prasutagus rested his trembling arm against the procurator's. 'For now.'

'Volsius! Find the chieftain's will.' Decianus turned and stalked towards the shelves of records situated at the secretary's back.

Boudicca ran to her husband's side. 'What are you doing?'

'What I must.'

Luciana drew back, folding herself against the wall. Decianus waved to one of the legionaries stationed by his door and the pair met not far from where she stood.

'Get me a noble to witness the changes.'

'Sir?'

'A senator or an equestrian. The governor's surrounded by them. He can spare one for a few moments!'

'Yes, sir.' The soldier withdrew into the hall.

'There we are!' Decianus grabbed the will out of his secretary's hands and unfurled it across his desk. 'Now, what would you like to do with this, Prasutagus?'

He weakly cleared his throat and gestured for Boudicca and his warriors to prop him into a sitting position. 'I, Prasutagus, chieftain of the Iceni-,'

'Not yet, man! Roman legal matters require a witness.' He elbowed his secretary and sniggered. 'Barbarians, eh?'

Luciana bristled as the men laughed. One glance at Boudicca told her she was feeling a similar ire.

When the guard reappeared, he had Decimus in tow. Luciana, eyes widening, glared at her master as she flattened herself against the wall.

'You sent for me, Procurator?' Decimus stood rigidly at attention, his crested helmet tucked beneath his arm.

'I'll need your signature and the seal of your ring in a moment's time.' Decianus sobered and gestured to the chieftain. '*Now* you may proceed, Prasutagus.'

'I, Prasutagus, chieftain of the Iceni, do declare…'

Decimus glimpsed Luciana out of the corner of his eye and turned towards her questioningly. Luciana, nostrils flared, avoided his gaze. The rage the procurator had stoked roiled wildly within her.

She felt his eyes burn holes into her neck. Luciana folded her arms, refusing to respond.

'…bequeath half my kingdom, including my residence, my personal effects, and the lands encompassing our tribal centre and the sacred bogs, to my daughters, Emer and Rioghnach.'

The secretary, furiously scribbling with a reed pen across the document, leant towards Decianus. 'How do you spell-,'

Decianus swatted him away and motioned for the chieftain to continue.

Prasutagus drew a long breath. 'The remaining half of my kingdom, including the harbours and the lands bordering the kingdoms of the Trinovantes and Catuvellauni, I leave to Emperor Nero of Rome.'

Boudicca drew back, scowling at her husband. 'You can't do this!'

'Please.' Prasutagus held up a hand. He gazed steadfastly at the procurator. 'Would such a gesture be considered sufficient to cancel our debt?'

'Hmm.' Decianus pretended to mull over the proposition, reading the words as Volsius transcribed them onto the document. He ignored the growing unease of the Britons in the room.

He's enjoying this, Luciana seethed, studying Decianus. *The worm!*

'It is a most generous gift. Willingly given, of course.' Decianus finally lifted his gaze. 'I think the emperor would be most pleased. You may… consider the debt cancelled.' His eyes flickered cruelly.

Prasutagus bent his head in grateful acknowledgement.

'I can't believe you.' Boudicca glared at her husband. 'How could you do this to your daughters? To your people? To *us?*'

He regarded her sadly. 'What other choice do I have?'

Boudicca swiftly looked away. Luciana caught sight of the tears the Iceni queen fought to stifle.

'Centurion.' Decianus motioned Decimus over to the clerk's desk. 'Your signature, please.'

Luciana glared at Decimus's back as he strode over and scribbled on the indicated line. He pressed the gold equestrian ring on his left hand into a fresh dollop of wax Volsius had deposited next to the line, leaving his intaglio imprinted on the document.

Decianus arched a brow at the prone chieftain. 'Are you capable of making your mark anew, my most noble friend?'

Prasutagus grunted and gestured to be given the reed pen.

Decimus retreated from the desk, standing beside Luciana along the wall. Staring blankly ahead, he growled under his breath, 'What in Jupiter's name are you doing here?'

Luciana couldn't help but study the stern lines of her centurion's bearded jaw from the corner of her eye. 'None of your concern,' she snapped. 'Just as your trinkets are no business of mine.'

His nostrils flared. 'That was no *trinket!*'

'How am I supposed to know? You never tell me anything!' Luciana coolly nodded to the Iceni couple as their retinue prepared to depart. 'Queen Boudicca is an old rival of mine.'

'For *him?!*' Decimus's thin lips drew down in disgust as he took in the emaciated chieftain.

'*Racing* rivals. We used to pit our tribes' best chariot horses against each other every Beltane.' Luciana smirked. 'Boudicca still wants to crow that the Iceni breed the best ponies in Britannia, even though Belena never allowed one of her nags to draw past her.'

He inclined his head. Luciana noted the softening of his eyes.

She folded her arms and sighed as Decianus curtly dismissed the centurion. She fell into step beside him as they followed the Iceni litter down the peristyle. 'There. I can keep nothing from you.'

He merely grunted, though one of his vambraces brushed against her wrist. Luciana quickly withdrew her arm from reach.

She waited, searching his stony expression for some clue that his apology would shortly be forthcoming.

The modest cubby substituting an atrium loomed before them. Luciana made to follow her fellow Britons into the street. Before continuing along the corridor, Decimus paused and faced her, pulling Luciana up short.

'I expect you to be ready when I dine with the legate and his family at the eleventh hour.'

'Of course.' She held out an arm and bowed mockingly. 'Will that be all, *master?*'

For the first time, his eyes clouded with doubt. 'I don't...I don't mean...'

'What?'

He closed his eyes. Pain creased the folds of his skin. 'I don't mean to treat you like that.'

'Like what?' Luciana folded her arms. She arched a brow at the sight of his discomfort. 'Go on. Tell me.'

'Luci…' He gulped. 'I really can't…'

'*Tell me.*'

He reluctantly met her gaze. 'You don't deserve what happened last night. I…was upset…and I unfairly took it out on you. That was wrong. And I apologize.'

She softened. She didn't see cruelty reflected in Decimus's emotive eyes; she saw nothing but pain. She tentatively placed a hand on his breast. 'Was that so terrible?'

He coloured and looked away.

Luciana blinked back frustrated tears, resting her head against his chest. 'Why do you do this to me? One moment you're the most miserable man alive. And the next…' She felt him wind his arms about her and she sobbed.

'I'm sorry,' he whispered in her ear.

'You know…' She sniffed and lifted her head to meet his gaze. 'You don't have to use misery as a weapon. If there's something upsetting you, you need only tell me.'

He immediately stiffened, releasing her. 'No.' A guarded look fell over his eyes. 'I can't.'

She frowned. 'But-,'

'Maximus!'

Decimus whirled to face the governor and his attendant officers, who were emptying from one of the chambers into the peristyle.

'On me!'

'Sir!' He obediently straightened and hastened to catch up with the men.

Luciana sadly watched his retreating back.

VII

'Tullius!'

Decimus clasped his optio's arm and tried to pull him close for a greeting kiss on the cheek. To his surprise, Tullius shrugged him off and pulled away.

'Centurion.' Tullius rifled through the tablets under his arm, the black-and-white plume on his helmet quivering in the frigid breeze.

Decimus frowned. 'What's the matter with you, man? Didn't enjoy the holidays?'

The optio didn't answer, handing him one of the missives. 'Here you are, sir. Eighty-nine effectives, ten recovering from illness according to the hospital, and fifty still detailed to the Twentieth Valeria at Glevum.'

Decimus snatched the tablet, not looking at it. He studied his friend's drawn, thin-lipped expression. 'Your boy isn't ill, is he?'

Tullius visibly whitened. 'No, sir.'

'Come off it!' He slapped Tullius across the back. 'Did you hear from Antonia at all?'

'Not recently, but they are well. Why wouldn't they be well, sir?' Tullius ducked his head and strode across the snow-strewn intervallum. 'The men are practicing close combat with Prefect Corvus. I thought you'd like to check with the quartermaster about the supply requisition you put in for next summer's campaign.'

Decimus stopped behind Tullius, studying the man's set shoulders. Had he been blind these past several months, or was something clearly bothering his optio more than it should?

'I have a better idea.' Decimus folded his arms. 'Since you seem to have the supply matter in hand, why don't you go down and sort details with the quartermaster? I've got a pile of correspondences to attend to.'

Tullius froze. He slowly turned around. 'I don't think that would be wise, sir. There's a matter of choosing the proper materials, the need to make substitutions…decisions to be made. Decisions that will bear significantly on the summer's campaign.'

Decimus sighed. 'Is that what this is about? Your preternatural lack of initiative?'

'You know I've never wanted promotion to the centurionate.' Tullius sighed. 'I can't take on that sort of responsibility.'

'You should thank the gods you've never had to.' Decimus walked past Tullius, snatching a tablet from his hands. 'I shudder to think what might happen if you find yourself leaderless. Delegate the role to someone else?' He raised his eyebrows. 'I know Antonia is the real paterfamilias of your household.'

Tullius winced. 'Can you *please* stop talking about my wife, sir?'

'All right.' Decimus furrowed his brows. He knew there was no love lost between Tullius and the patrician girl his father had forced him to marry, but it seemed to bother him more than it usually did. Almost as if it pained him, in some way.

Tullius silently fell into step beside Decimus, who studied him thoughtfully. Decimus thought he knew Tullius better than he knew himself. They'd hardly left each other's sides since their first meeting more than a lifetime ago, when they'd been forced by their contubernium to share a bunk as the two new recruits to their century. They'd been blooded together, which forged the strong, brotherly bond that had kept each other alive in the years since. They'd always felt perfectly at ease in each other's company. There was no man Decimus trusted more. But now…?

Decimus narrowed his eyes. Tullius frowned, squaring his shoulders and staring straight ahead. It wasn't like Tullius to be so cold. Decimus laid a hand on the optio's arm. 'Are you sure, Tullius, that all is well? You may speak freely.'

Tullius gruffly shrugged Decimus's arm off. 'Perfectly, sure, sir. Though now is hardly the time. I want you to look first at the last shipment of replacement loricae Corvus signed off on…'

Decimus sighed as Tullius prattled on, back on the topic of his supply records. He made a mental note to take the man to Bakari's as soon as possible. Perhaps some fine Falernian would loosen his friend's silent tongue.

'How was Londinium?' Nicomedes dumped Nero's grain into his feed trough. He quickly stepped out of the way as the grey stallion muscled past him. He went to the stall door and glanced at the partition dividing Nero's stall from Aquila's. 'Did the legate host a grand Saturnalia?'

Luciana shrugged, picking up a brush to run across her charge's silky bay hide. 'Fine enough, I suppose.'

'I would have expected a better response than that!' His impish face appeared over the partition. 'Tell me, did the centurion forget to give you a present?'

She scowled in his direction before immediately doing a double take. 'What happened to you?'

The boy blushed and self-consciously tugged at his new cloak, backing away from the partition. 'Um…present from the optio,' he mumbled, gazing at the floor.

'Well, I think you look very nice.' Luciana flicked the dust from Aquila's flanks, then turned to pick up a comb. 'At least one of our masters has the good sense to treat his slaves properly.'

Nicomedes's face reappeared. 'So, something *did* happen between you and the centurion!'

'Never you mind.' She tousled his neat, short curls.

'Come on!' He ducked out from under her touch. 'Tell me!'

'No, you tell me.' Luciana smirked. 'You can't fool me, Nicomedes. Who is she?'

The Greek immediately fell quiet. A long silence ensued between the pair, with only the sound of Nero crunching his grain and Aquila snorting softly to punctuate their work.

'You must have it bad,' Luciana teased, catching sight of the teen pitching soiled bedding out of Nero's stall. 'I don't believe I've ever witnessed you so quiet.'

'Not as bad as you do, clearly.'

'Oh, no.' Luciana waggled a finger. 'If you can stay quiet about your love troubles, then so can I.'

Nicomedes groaned. 'What else is there to talk about?'

'Your Saturnalia, for one. Tell me, how did my plan turn out?'

The boy's face lit up. He grabbed a rag that hung over the stall door. 'I did what you asked and passed your denarii on to as many of the village children as possible. They were in and out of the kitchens all day while the prefect's slaves were preparing the feast, and I picked out the scraps that were worth saving from the legion's trash.' He rubbed the rag across Nero's powerful hindquarters. 'I don't know what your people said when I brought the food, but they sounded appreciative. I'm not sure if they liked the garum, though.' He wrinkled his nose.

Luciana grimaced in agreement. 'I don't see how the centurion can eat the stuff.' She smiled. 'Did all seem well?'

'As well as they can be.' He sought her gaze. 'They're very weak, Luciana.'

She sighed. 'I feared as much. Though the cell's the safest place for them until the weather changes.'

'Do you still plan to get them out?'

'Umm.' She bit her lip and studied the underside of one of Aquila's hooves, nodding.

'How? Won't it be harder now? And what about your loyalties? How are you going to do that when you and the centurion-,'

'Ah, there's the Nicomedes I know and love!' Luciana pointed her strigil at him. 'I knew he had to be lurking somewhere within that lovelorn puppy!'

His bronze complexion reddened. He quickly shut up.

Luciana chuckled. She could get used to having this newfound advantage over Nicomedes's bottomless questioning.

'But really…where *do* your loyalties lie?'

Luciana closed her eyes. She saw Boudicca and Prasutagus, impotent with rage. She saw the slimy, triumphant smirk of Catus Decianus. She saw the huddled forms of her tribespeople in the cell, hands outstretched for the food she brought them. Her mother's words suddenly leapt into her mind:

When the head and the heart are in conflict…

She reached for her collar to touch the Wheel of Taranis. Instead, her fingers found the delicate charm of the legion's odd ram-mermaid mascot. She felt the unfamiliar ridges of the pendant, seeing Decimus's pale eyes light up with love. Decimus, caressing her body with his sure touch. Decimus, primus pilus of the Fourteenth Gemina, standing steadfastly by her side.

She shuddered, dropping the silver Capricorn. She blinked in the morning beams and forced a tight smile across her face. 'Never you mind.'

'But-!'

'I'll only say if you promise to reveal the secrets of your heart.'

Nicomedes scowled and turned away.

Her triumphant expression faded as the pair resumed their work. If she were completely honest with herself, she hardly knew where her allegiance lay anymore. She desperately hoped she wouldn't have to choose, but the tensions she'd noticed in the past year had only grown stronger. If things continued, there was bound to be a reckoning soon.

Which side of the battlefield would she be on?

PART TWO
EARRACH

VIII

Cassia moaned, running her hands along the oiled torso of the tattooed warrior grunting beneath her. She bounced up and down on his cock and flung her head about, desperate to bring the man to a climax.

An extended grunt died into a whimper and the Silure slackened against her bed.

'Finally,' Cassia muttered, crawling off him. She sat up at the edge of her mattress and regarded the Brittunculus. The man was so dirty it was hard to tell just what on his skin was ink and what was mud. Beneath the grime, his grim mouth was largely hidden beneath a long, flowing moustache. His square jaw jutted forward proudly, set in what seemed to be a permanent scowl. A bright, twisted scar marred the shape of his bulbous nose, which was missing a chunk near the bridge. His bright blue eyes regarded her ceiling vacantly, framed by long, matted blond braids that surrounded his head like a nest.

Cassia's eyes fell on the warrior's armband. Gilded and carved to resemble a scaly serpent with onyx eyes, it would have fetched a pretty penny from the jeweller. She was surprised she'd missed it when raiding their hunting camp last winter.

She rose from the bed and sauntered over to her cosmetic table. Her fingers tapped the offering bowl that sat before a statuette of Nemesis on the corner. She contemplated the shrivelled fruit husks within, sprinkled with dark, dried drops of her blood that she'd offered to the goddess. Her fingers fell upon the ceremonial dagger resting next to the bowl, curling around its grooved hilt.

A cool, steel blade suddenly pressed against her throat. 'Drop it.'

Cassia stiffened, releasing the dagger. She tried to see the Silure warrior out of the corner of her eye but only saw the grubby fist poised to slice her open. His other arm snaked over her shoulder and pulled her back against his slick chest. Cassia closed her eyes and winced.

'Where are they?'

'I don't…I don't know what you're talking about.'

She gasped as the blade pricked her skin. The warrior tightened his grip.

'You know.'

'I...I'm sure I do not.' Her swallow scraped painfully against his iron edge.

'You took a load of very valuable items from our camp. Things that weren't yours to take.' The man's fetid breath curled her nostrils as he leant close to her ear. 'The chieftain wants them back.'

'Then your chieftain should have paid me, as previously agreed.' She scowled. 'Roman law prohibits you reneging on a transaction.'

'Fuck you Romans and your Roman law.' He tightened his grasp. She felt hot, searing droplets bead along her neck. 'The law of my people says to take what's ours or take your life. You decide.'

Her eyes widened. Weakly, she pointed to a curtained shelf in the corner of the room. 'There...'

The warrior loosened his hold just enough to march the pair over to the cubby. Cassia tentatively lifted her hands. 'I'm just going to get it...there's a cask...'

She drew back the curtain to reveal a shrouded Antiope. Her polecat hissed from its perch on her shoulder and flew at the warrior's head. He released his lock on Cassia and fell to the floor.

'Get the knife!' The old witch straddled the fallen warrior, pinning his straining arms to the ground. The man writhed as Gale bit down on his nose. Cassia carefully prised his whitened fingers free of the blade and took it up herself.

'Enough!' Antiope commanded and Gale released his nose. It slunk into the darkened shadows of Cassia's bedchamber, spitting contemptuously.

Cassia crouched beside Antiope, holding the weapon where the warrior could see it. His eyes widened and he stiffened beneath Antiope's firm hold.

'So Morcant sent you?' Cassia blew a stray blonde curl out of her eyes. 'I should have known. Why pose as a customer?'

The Silure bared his teeth. 'You looked like a good fuck.'

Cassia bit her lip hard, bringing a droplet of blood to its split surface. She grabbed the man's testicles with her free hand and twisted. He winced, inhaling deeply. A soft yelp escaped his lips.

'You can tell your lying, murderous snake of a chieftain that the jewels have gone.' She hawked up a mouthful of phlegm and spat on the man's face. 'And they didn't make up for even a quarter of the promised payment.'

He groaned as she continued to twist his manhood.

'A friend of mine is dead because of him, as well as my brother!' She squeezed, crushing the Silure's testicles in her grasp. Antiope muffled his shrill scream by placing her full, comely mouth over his.

When his cries had died to a weak whimper, Cassia released him and watched the witch clamber off. She leant in close, scowling at the twin rivers of tears streaking down the Silure's face. She held the knife up for a moment longer, before lowering it to her side. 'No. I'm not going to kill you.'

She stood and kicked the still whimpering native in his ribcage. 'Go back to Morcant. Tell him the daughter of Nemesis sends her regards, and he will endure far worse than castration before she's exacted her payment.'

Cassia lifted her head to see Antiope sitting on the edge of her bed, stroking a writhing Gale in her lap. The older woman's eyes glittered. She nodded at Cassia approvingly.

Nicomedes strolled down the path snaking from the fort to the river Sabrina. The collected buildings comprising the vicus surrounded its ford. He glanced over his shoulder at the fort's southern gate, making sure he hadn't been followed. Facing forward, he smiled and hastened his steps.

Beneath his dark cloak, he clutched a crude clay figure in his fist. No bigger than his palm, the shape vaguely resembled a person. He'd managed to sneak it into the kiln in the brickyard when the optio's century had taken their turn at construction duty a few weeks ago. Though he wasn't much of an artist, he prayed that Metella might appreciate the effort.

He passed the cruder, native-type dwellings and farmhouses that gave way gradually onto tenements and shopfronts. He passed along Porcius's stoop and waved to the tonsor inside. The burly man gave him a jaunty salute with one of his razors before returning to his customer.

Nicomedes straightened his shoulders and slowed as he approached The Aurochs. It wouldn't do to seem too eager. His eyes fell from the large, white bullock on the sign to the graffito advertisements scratched onto the caupona's walls. His welcome piece of news, 'Livius has gone! Thanks be to Jupiter!' remained where he'd etched it into the paint just a week ago. A small smile tugged at his lips; he certainly wouldn't miss Tribune Titianus's bullying boy. The smile faded as he turned to the door. He swallowed the lurch of anxiety rising in his throat and ducked through the entranceway to the dim tavern.

It took a moment for the boy's eyes to adjust. As they did, the peeling red paint along the walls, the bubbling cauldrons of stew sunk into the dingy counter, and the shapes of the customers standing along its length slowly came into focus. He passed tired legionaries, sad-eyed merchants, and jaded retirees, nodding between their heads at Metellus serving them behind the counter. The man glared at him in return.

Nicomedes glanced at the men clumped about The Aurochs' two tables, frowning when he failed to spy Metella serving or sitting at either.

Nicomedes went to the wooden staircase leading to Metellus's living chamber and rented room. He glanced over his shoulder at the proprietor, making sure the man's attention was clearly focussed on his customers. He took a breath and darted up the stairs, huddling to make himself as small as possible.

He paused at the top upon hearing muffled voices inside the rented room. The door stood ajar, soft lamplight shining through the gap. He tried to peer through the slit, glimpsing just Metella's back before accidentally pushing the door wide.

The girl whirled about from her seat on the floor, gasping. A series of thin metal bangles rattled around her wrist. Her companion, a squat, unshaven man with glittering dark eyes, frowned at the intrusion. 'Oi! What's this?'

Nicomedes blushed, righting himself. 'I…I was looking for you,' he mumbled in Metella's direction.

'Well, I'm busy, all right?' She stuck out her wrist. 'I'm trying on Lucius's wares for him. Aren't they pretty?'

'Picked those up in Bithynia. The bloke who sold them to me said they came from even further east.' Lucius stood and moved over to a trunk propped open against a wall. 'Can I interest you in anything, young man?'

'He's a slave. You'd have to ask his master.' Metella waved a hand dismissively before admiring the way the bangles sparkled in the soft light.

'Are you, then?' A guarded look fell over the man's scrunched-up features. 'Who do you serve, boy?'

'Tullius Servius. Optio to the primus pilus of the legion.' Nicomedes lifted a hand to run it through his curls before pausing, remembering the little figure he still held. He considered it for a moment before glancing at Metella. The girl was still rapturously studying the bangles adorning her arm. Closing his fist around the sculpture, he thrust his hand deep inside the folds of his cloak.

'One of the higher-ups in the rank and file, eh?' Lucius considered for a second. 'Might he be interested in some plush carpeting for his quarters? I brought some samples all the way from Parthia…' He reached down and shifted some heavy bags aside in his trunk. The sacks clinked with a heavy metallic sound.

'No, thank you, sir. I don't think he'd be interested.' Nicomedes eyed the wrapped wares. 'You brought quite a lot of bracelets.'

'They're popular, aren't they?' Lucius gestured in Metella's direction. 'And they travel quite well.'

Metella blushed, drawing her arm against her chest. 'I doubt Pater will want to spend any of his cash on these.'

'Then he doesn't have to spend any.' Lucius sauntered to the bed and leant over her. 'The company of his charming daughter is payment enough.'

She lifted her head, dark eyes sparkling. 'And you'll still drive me in your cart, right? You promised you would.'

Nicomedes's heart lurched when he saw the lascivious leer stretched across the man's stubbly chin.

He stepped between the girl and the merchant, drawing the man's ire. Nicomedes crossed his arms. 'I'd be careful, sir. Metellus is quite protective of his daughter.'

'Be quiet, Nicomedes!' Metella slapped him across the back. 'Lucius is our guest. He's a man of means. Pater told me to see that he's settled in.'

Nicomedes reluctantly stepped aside, gazing sadly at Metella. Her wide brown eyes saw past him, trained only upon the ugly little man with his trunk of exotic jewels. He bit the inside of his cheek to keep his mouth from falling into a disconsolate frown.

'Now, if you haven't any business to conduct on your master's behalf, little slave, I think you should be going.' Lucius grabbed Nicomedes's arm, shoving him back towards the door.

Though considerably younger than the shabby merchant, Nicomedes's adolescent height was sufficient for him to look the man in the eye. He didn't like the cruel, glassy light that reflected in his gaze. 'You hurt her and you'll regret it,' he snarled softly in Greek with as much menace as he could muster.

'Stay out of my way, you rat!' He growled in perfectly fluent Greek. Nicomedes's eyes widened.

With a final push, the dark-haired merchant shoved Nicomedes onto the narrow landing. Without another word, he slammed the door in the boy's face.

Nicomedes hung his head and slowly made his way down the creaking stairs. Ignoring The Aurochs' sullen customers, he slunk out the rear entrance to a dirty yard that abutted Charis's brothel. A light flurry of snow dusted the frozen mud, encasing the area in a delicate white haze. Nicomedes glanced at his misshapen pottery figure before angrily hurling it into the snow. With dejected steps, he slowly walked towards the fort.

He didn't stop until he reached Nero's stall and slipped inside. The stallion lifted his head and snorted, alert to the unusual presence of Nicomedes in his stall after his second feed.

'Easy, boy.' He extended his palm for Nero to sniff, studiously avoiding his gaze. 'It's only me.'

The stud breathed in the boy's familiar scent and lost interest, attacking his manger once more.

He absently ran his hands along Nero's broad spine, working up towards his withers. He paused to scratch there, knowing it was one of Nero's favourite itchy spots. Still chewing, Nero extended his neck and shuddered, whickering appreciatively.

'I'm glad you'll still talk to me,' he murmured softly to the horse.

'You say something, lad?'

He looked up at the question posed in Greek and winced. The sight of Decurion Tiberius Claudius Tirintius would normally be a welcome one, but he presently would have preferred a bit of solitude.

'Look here, what's that for? You look like you've choked on a nettle!' Tirintius tied the lead for his black charger, Rhesus, to a ring in the aisle and cautiously entered Nero's stall. 'What's happened?'

'Nothing.' Nicomedes buried his face in Nero's mane, willing the friendly Thracian to go away.

'Don't tell me Metellus's girl shafted you already!'

He whirled around to face Tirintius, frowning.

'We all know you've been pining for her, lad. It's hard not to see as much when you're looking out at The Aurochs from Porcius's chair.' Tirintius ran a hand through his black ringlets, which looked as though they hadn't seen a barber's touch in weeks.

'Oh.' A bright blush crept up Nicomedes's dark cheeks. He stared at the floor, absently kicking around wisps of straw at his feet.

'Let me guess.' Tirintius took a couple of bow-legged strides towards him. 'You've got a rival?'

'The new merchant in town. Lucius.' Nicomedes raised his head. 'He also speaks Greek. And he's been all over the empire.' His face crumpled. 'And I'm just a slave.'

'Hey, hey,' Tirintius patted the boy's back as a sob racked his thin frame. 'You're not *just* a slave, lad. You've got all sorts of skills.'

'Like what?'

The Thracian thought for a moment, tapping his bearded chin. 'You can read.'

Nicomedes scowled. 'So can he!'

'Well…' Tirintius turned towards Nero. The grey stallion still had his head tucked into his hay, though his swivelling ears indicated he was listening intently to the humans. 'You can pick a fine horse. And ride him well, too.'

'How does *that* help? Lucius has a mule cart.' Nicomedes frowned. 'I saw it in the vicus. Metella said he was going to drive her around.'

'There you are!' Tirintius's face lit up. 'Show up at her door in a chariot and take her for a ride. That's better than a mule cart any day of the week. The lads in the ala just put one together using the parts we got in our shipment from Londinium.'

'But I can't drive a chariot. And the optio's horse can't pull one.' Nicomedes leant against the stall partition and sighed.

'You can learn, can't you? And so can he.' Tirintius jerked a thumb in Nero's direction and stooped to meet the boy's sullen gaze. 'I'll teach you. Been years since I last picked up the traces, but I reckon you never lose it.'

Nicomedes sniffled, regarding the decurion guardedly. While the leader of the Thracian auxiliary cavalry always provided solid companionship, he'd never previously offered so much as a riding lesson.

'Come on!' Tirintius punched his arm. 'You have to fight for love! What do you say?'

A cautious smile slowly crept its way across Nicomedes's face.

IX

'**R**ight.' Tribune Cincinnatus slapped a missive shut and bound the boards tight. 'I'm calling it a night before we lose any more daylight.' He stood from his seat on one of the benches lining the officers' meeting room and sauntered over to Decimus and Tullius, who were still studying the new notations made in the local map by Regulus's scouting parties.

The pair looked up at his approach, faces wooden. He paused, glancing from one to the other. 'You've both been here long enough. Tell me, what passes for fun in this backwards bog?'

Decimus lowered his head back to the map. Tullius shifted the helmet tucked under his arm and shrugged. 'Getting a drink at Bakari's. He gets the best shipments around. Some of the men hold dice games and throw *Tali*, though they're careful to keep any betting pools hidden from our eyes. I prefer *latrunculi*, myself.'

Cincinnatus chuckled. His dark eyes took on a mischievous glint. He moved his tongue against his cheek, considering his words. 'What about the more…physical pursuits?'

'Go to Charis's for that.' Tullius, losing interest, bent his head over Decimus's shoulder to study the map.

'You're talking about the wolf den?' Cincinnatus shook his head. 'It's just…my man's taken up lodgings in the vicus and, according to what he can see from what's scrawled out front…your lupanar only serves those desiring female company.'

'Is there any other sort worth two coppers?' Decimus snorted, slapping his palms against the unfurled map. 'This is the army on the arse-end of nowhere, not the Caelian hill. Hermaphrodites are a bit harder to come by in these parts.'

'As you so astutely pointed out, Centurion, this is the army. Isn't an army teeming with…men?' Cincinnatus shrugged.

Decimus's face darkened. Tullius caught his friend's look and stiffened, focussing on the map's notations. He felt his cheeks burn under Decimus's disapproving look. He felt bile rise into his throat, ashamed of what he feared he might be.

'Don't you have your *man* to help you with that?' Decimus's words dripped with disgust.

The tribune inclined his head. 'Lucius is busy at the moment, working on my behalf.' He held up the sealed letters. 'For one thing, he's got these to deliver for me immediately.'

Decimus grunted. 'Please yourself.'

'I don't like your tone, Centurion.'

Decimus turned to meet the tribune's gaze. He narrowed his eyes as he met the haughty disdain of Cincinnatus's scowl.

'You may have crawled your way to the top of this place, but you're not at the pinnacle. Nor will you ever be.' Cincinnatus flicked a dismissive hand. 'And I refuse to be judged by a classless brute like yourself.'

Decimus chuckled. He grinned at Tullius, who ducked his head and studied the table. 'Yes, sir. I apologise, sir, if my tone displeased you.' He straightened and made to move past the tribune, then paused and clapped a hand on the man's ornately tooled cuirass. 'Just remember, *sir*, that this classless brute stands between you and the blue-skinned Britons baying for your blood.'

Cincinnatus's eyes widened and his nostrils flared. Decimus ignored his gaze, clapping his crested helmet on his head as he exited into the principium complex.

'I say!' The tribune turned to Tullius. 'Are they all as bad as that?'

'Couldn't say,' Tullius mumbled, gathering his cloak up with trembling hands. He quailed under the tribune's gaze and immediately stiffened when Cincinnatus placed a hand on his arm.

'Come on. You can tell me…where are you getting it?' The tribune breathed heavily in Tullius's ear.

He knows. Tullius twisted away from Cincinnatus. *He sees what you are.* He gathered up the campaign maps, shaking his head. 'I-I-I'm sure I don't know what you m-mean.'

Nodding towards Cincinnatus with averted gaze, he hurriedly shambled down the aisle in Decimus's wake. He felt Cincinnatus's gaze burn into his back, accusing him.

It was only the once! Tullius emerged into the evening air, drawing a heaving gulp. *That doesn't make me one of them! I can't be!*

Shaking his head, he stalked off to his quarters. He waved at any soldier who saluted him in passing, not looking up from his feet. Nicomedes jumped up at his arrival, but he marched past the boy into his bedroom and slammed the door. He dropped his maps on the floor and rested his forehead against the wall. The disgust dripping from Decimus's words and the slimy insinuations of the tribune played on a loop in his mind. He closed his eyes and gently banged his head against the wall. *Go away! Stop!*

He turned to his washbasin and threw handfuls of water over his head. Once he was drenched, he gripped the sides of the basin and panted, staring into its bottom.

The flickering lamplight from a nearby tripod illuminated his dim reflection in the water. He gazed in despair at himself. He was a soldier, an officer, a father. Grey-haired, lined face, squared jaw tightly clenched. He didn't look like a catamite. But no matter how hard he tried to frown, his eyes seemed to betray him.

He punched his reflection and heaved over the side of the basin, vomiting onto the floor.

Nicomedes knocked on the door. 'Sir, are you all right?'

'Leave me,' Tullius moaned, gripping the sides of his head. He crashed facedown onto his bed, humming. He squeezed his eyes shut, heightening the pitch of his note in a vain attempt to shut out the accusatory looks and words haunting his mind. *Stop! I can't be, I mustn't be! Stop this! Stop!*

Cassia ducked out of a side door and conscientiously straightened her tunic. She looked both ways along the busy market-day street and tucked a wayward blonde strand behind her ear. Her bright paints had faded on her face, barely disguising dark circles and bloodshot eyes. She glanced at the door one last time and shook her head, remembering the arduous evening she'd endured for the sake of a few denarii. *And Nemesis.* Then, clutching her dark palla at her throat, she strode off into the crowd.

The sun strained to break behind a low veil of clouds on a surprisingly dry mid-spring day. Children darted among the teeming bustle as civilians, slaves, merchants, and soldiers alike crowded the streets. One waggon, bearing amphorae full of garum, trundled its way up the road; another, containing wool, had paused so a woman could inspect its wares. The mules hitched to its shafts swished their tails lazily, heads drooping low. A pair of children chasing each other scurried between the idle beasts' legs. A squat man she didn't recognise clanked cheap bangles together, decrying his wares from the back of a splendid-looking cart.

Cassia glanced at the looming Roman fort beyond the vicus streets. Her heart lurched into her throat as the thought of Decimus leapt to her mind. She'd hardly seen him since midwinter. There'd been several nights, particularly after the hunt that left him injured, when she'd hoped he might arrive at her door to pass an evening in her company. He hadn't. Only reports from customers within his cohort kept her informed of his wellness and whereabouts.

The fort's large gates suddenly creaked open and a rider issued forth, heading for the woods beyond the moor. A tall, dark man mounted on a bay…

Was it? Cassia caught her breath and pushed through the throng before emerging onto the via praetoria. She stood to the side of the path and smiled. It *was* Decimus!

He looked a picture astride Aquila. His stern face frowned impassively at the vicus, his sea-coloured eyes roving the landscape. His close-cropped ringlets stirred gently in the breeze. Cassia could almost swear his trim, handsome beard looked even greyer than it had the year before. He was clad in his dull red tunic and calf-length boots, offset by his metalled belt and a baldric slung across his broad torso. He looked well, his muscles shapely and his bearing erect. Cassia closed her eyes, imagining the vision before her rendered in richly painted stone and placed atop a pedestal overlooking the streets of Rome.

She sighed and blinked her eyes open upon his mortal, moving form. Decimus's lack of helmet and greaves clearly indicated he was off duty for the rest of the day. Cassia raised a hand to call his name.

Decimus looked behind him and the sound died in Cassia's throat. Emerging through the gap, trotting on his tail, came his native wench straddling a leggy buckskin gelding. Her long, flowing hair with its collection of sparse plaits shimmered behind her like a golden train in the late afternoon light. Her bright green tunic rode up above her knees, giving way to a delicate pair of sandals that wound their straps about her ankles. She edged her horse up beside Aquila, her sensual lips parted in laughter. She smiled at Decimus teasingly, eyes sparkling, before prodding her horse into a swift canter down the road.

Decimus shouted and followed, trailing in her wake as the pair made for the woodlands encircling the settlement. Cassia watched them go, her face crumpled in bitter disappointment.

'Luciana!'

She glanced behind her and saw Decimus charging fast on her tail. He gazed ahead with determination, his hunched form swiftly urging Aquila forward. She shrieked and buried her nose in her own horse's mane. Clapping her knees tightly against the cavalry mount's sides, she pressed him harder still.

The pair flew across the overcast moor and disappeared into the gloomy trees. Decimus felt low hanging branches brush past his hair, and he flattened himself against Aquila's neck. He turned his head to keep one eye cocked forward, following Luciana's progress through the whipping black strands of Aquila's mane.

The two horses thundered down the narrow forest track, probing deeper into the woods. The trembling aspens and majestic elms shaded the path with newly grown leaves. A couple of wrens startled from their perch as the horses galloped past, fluttering their wings as they rose into the sky.

Luciana veered her mount to the right, vanishing from Decimus's view. The centurion cursed and sat up, bringing Aquila down to a canter so he wouldn't miss the turn. He seamlessly pivoted onto the smaller track, only to see no trace of his slave or her horse. He frowned down the shady lane. 'Luci!'

Her mocking laughter echoed back to him. Decimus growled and nudged Aquila forward. 'Luci, come back here! This isn't funny!'

Aquila slowed to a trot. Decimus sat back in his saddle, surveying the terrain ahead. The foliage grew denser along this part of the path, the trees closer together. An eerie sense of foreboding took hold in the centurion's heart. His brows knitted together with worry. "Luci!"

He rounded a bend in the trail and suddenly came on her buckskin, now riderless. The gelding stood at the edge of a dense grove of oak trees, his reins trailing upon the ground. Decimus eased Aquila to a halt and slid from his back.

Cautiously, he made his way around the horses and stopped at the edge of the clearing. He'd seen such places before, and they never failed to strike fear in the pit of his stomach. Through the opening of the grove, he could just see a large stag's skull nailed to one of the oak trunks. He gulped; it was a druid's circle.

'Halt, Roman.'

Decimus whipped around to see Luciana standing just inside the grove, one hand stretched out in warning. The dim light from the open circle bathed her in an almost ethereal glow. The folds of her tunic and the ends of her hair stirred gently in the breeze. A smile played upon her lips. 'You must remove your belt and sword.'

He frowned. 'What?'

'Iron is forbidden within the sacred circle.' She spread her arms wide. 'Products of war exploit nature and its order, and this angers our gods.' She spun round and lifted her head towards the skull. 'Especially Cernunnos.'

'It sounds more like a ploy to disarm me,' Decimus grumbled. One hand adjusted the strap of his baldric and rested on the hilt of his gladius.

Luciana shrugged and strolled to the other end of the clearing. 'Don't put them down, then. But pursue me no further. I will not invite the wrath of Cernunnos upon your head.'

He watched her saunter out of sight, his blood beginning to boil. The slim shape of her body in the grove, the way her tunic accentuated her glowing green eyes, the poise and confidence in her step stirred his loins and tightened his chest. He gritted his teeth as a strangled growl escaped his throat. He slung off his baldric and unbuckled his belt, letting his baltea and sheathed gladius drop. Decimus lowered his head and charged after her into the clearing.

As soon as he entered the grove, time seemed suspended. Luciana glanced over her shoulder and shrieked. She broke into a run, giggling. Decimus followed, quickly closing the space between them. Her unfurled tresses licked at his face, bobbing in the breeze behind her. Decimus bunched his fists and quickened his pace, pumping his muscular legs even harder. In a matter of heartbeats, he threw his arms about her shoulders and lifted her from the ground.

'Decimus!' She kicked out, squealing with delight. The trees blurred before her as he swiftly whirled her about, then her feet landed in the grass. She found herself gazing up into his eyes, marvelling at the way they winked in the light. His dark ringlets, freshly cut in their customary military crop, had become dishevelled in his pursuit through the woods. The scar on his cheek glowed white in the dim light. Luciana ran her fingers along his broad shoulder and cupped his grizzled chin in her other palm. She lifted onto her toes and leant forward, seeking his mouth.

Decimus curled his head, drawing towards Luciana. He stopped cold at the sight of a large grey shape over her shoulder. He stiffened and glared past her.

Luciana furrowed her brow. 'What's…' She followed his gaze to the large stone altar looming behind her. It sat in the centre of the clearing. A small wooden bowl perched on one corner beside the charred remains of a chicken. Evidence of old fires were marked by a large, blackened circle in the middle of the altar. Brown rivulets of dried blood stained the edges of the stone. A small pile of gold and silver coins, statues, and bracelets lay heaped at its base.

Luciana turned to Decimus, an amused smile on her face. 'Does it frighten you?'

He glowered. 'How many of my men met their end on that altar?'

'If I had to hazard a guess? None.' Luciana stepped towards the stone, pulling on his wrist. 'Come here, I'll show you.'

As they neared the altar, the stench of rotting intestines curled their nostrils. Around the side, they came upon the mangled remains of a goat. At their approach, a few crows fluttered into the trees, cawing angrily about their interrupted meal.

Luciana stopped and gestured. 'Tell me, don't good Roman citizens sacrifice animals on the altars of their gods?'

Decimus pressed his lips together in a grim line, shaking his head. 'Not so often as you might think. The haruspex charges a bloody fortune for an augury these days.'

'So do the druids.' She laughed dismissively and indicated the wooden bowl. 'The only human blood you will find is there, and it is all British. Token flesh offerings made by those who accidentally violate the sanctity of the grove with their weapons. Usually hunting parties.' Her expression hardened. 'Obviously, no Romans have violated the grove. Your soldiers would have stripped the altar clean of its offerings and never looked back.'

Decimus sucked in a breath. 'Trust me, none of my men have ventured close enough to try. The druids are monsters.'

She studied his face quizzically. 'Do you really believe that?'

He turned to Luci. Her penetrating gaze and brazen expression belied her noble heritage; he could not gaze upon her and fail to forget she was a Cornovii princess. *And the granddaughter of a druid priestess.*

Decimus cleared his throat. 'I…I'm not sure what I truly believe anymore.'

'Well,' she grabbed his hand and led him upwind of the rotting carcass. 'Your suspicions wouldn't be entirely unfounded. There are some that do perform occasional human sacrifices. But only upon those chosen by the gods, and only in times of direst need. An unwilling sacrifice would only anger our deities and bring shame instead of honour upon the victim's family.' She stopped and drew his arm about her waist. 'According to my mother, the last human sacrifice here took place in the first days of your invasion.'

His expression hardened. 'Then why have we found Roman corpses on the altars of your gods?'

She flinched. Decimus placed his hand on her wrist and softened his gaze, feeling himself drawn once more into the spell cast by her bewitching green eyes.

'Why do you think?' She drew a long breath. 'The druids know the fear they strike in the hearts of your soldiers. The very same soldiers who have stolen property, destroyed homes, and violated the natural order of our lands ever since they got here. They have carved apart our tribes and clapped us in chains, leaving thousands of widows and orphans in their wake. Those brave enough to stand against Rome must leverage every advantage they have. So, if they stage a killing to make it look like a sacrifice?' She shrugged defiantly. 'It is only natural to do what you must when your home is under attack.'

'And is that what you think of me?' Decimus loosened his grip about her.

'I have no doubt of the cruelty you have inflicted upon my people,' she tentatively reached up and brushed her fingers against his scar, 'or of the cruelty they have returned in kind. There are forces greater than you or me at work upon these lands, Decimus. I do not know if your people or mine will triumph in the end. We can only do what we must and leave the rest in the hands of our respective gods.' She nodded over his shoulder at the horned skull before pulling the wheel of Taranis out from under his tunic. She held the amulet against his breast. 'I do know this: you have a warrior's heart, Decimus. One that, despite everything, does your Celtic ancestors proud.'

'I'm not sure about that,' he murmured, letting his hands slide down her body as he knelt upon the ground. He closed his eyes and pressed his whiskered lips to her skirt. 'There is only one Celtic goddess I choose to worship.'

Her lips curled into a satisfied smile. 'Then please, don't let me interrupt you.'

Luciana closed her eyes and sank softly into the grass, spreading her arms wide. She gathered her skirt up over her hips and opened her legs invitingly. Decimus cupped one knee in his calloused palm and hitched it over his shoulder. Then, lifting her other leg into the air, he held it close and pressed his mouth against her thigh.

Luciana gazed up at the grey sky and shuddered.

Decimus caressed her soft, yielding flesh with his tongue, trailing a path along her pale skin. He lingered over each freckle he encountered and traced their shapes lovingly. He pressed his sharp Roman nose against her, inhaling her intoxicating scent. 'You're beautiful,' he mumbled through his kisses.

'Oh!' She arched her neck as she savoured the feel of his whiskers tickling her sensitive skin. His lingering kisses set her nerves afire, kindling a warmth within her core that quickly spread throughout her body. Luciana sighed and smiled blissfully.

Decimus reached the top of her thigh and paused. He nuzzled the wild golden tufts at her core and drew a long, heady breath. He placed a couple of soft, gentle kisses on her walls before resting his tongue against her entrance.

She trembled. 'Oh, yes,' she murmured, entwining her fingers in the grass. 'Yes, *carissime*!'

He buried his face in her, caressing her with his mouth. Luciana felt her body lurch, her breath temporarily snatched away by his adoring touch. She moaned weakly and reached down, her fingers just brushing the top of his head. Low, keening whines escaped the back of her throat.

Decimus felt her heat, her fire, flush his face. He breathed deeply of her, quietly enjoying her sacred grove. He lovingly kissed and stroked her walls with his tongue, her approving moans ringing melodiously in his ears.

Luciana lifted her head and gazed down at the gruff centurion. His powerful, scarred physique crouched reverently before her, his stony face buried tightly against her flesh. His surprisingly deft, gentle touch sparked deep feelings of affection within her guarded heart. She lay back against the grass and stared up at the tall, forbidding oaks surrounding them. A haze seemed to settle over the grove and her heart raced along to the beat of an ancient chant echoing through her mind.

Decimus effortlessly slid two fingers into her. Luciana cried out, writhing her head to and fro. He eased them back and forth, mapping and stretching her tight walls. Her body pulsed in perfect rhythm with his movements. His fingertips brushed up against her and paused, feeling her suddenly tense beneath his touch. He remained there, lightly rubbing his fingers against the spot. Her moans intensified and her body heaved. Decimus smiled, feeling himself harden in response.

He pulled back his head and let his lips travel north, above her entrance. Soon, his probing tongue brushed up against her engorged, glistening clitoris. He traced a path around it. She sobbed in anticipation. 'Oh, Luci,' he whispered, placing a kiss directly on it. His beard bristled against her, and she cried out again. He maintained his gentle ministrations against the inside of her walls and took her clit between his teeth.

'Decimus!' Another immense shudder wracked her lithe frame. She tilted her gaping mouth to the sky and threw her arms wide as he teased her with his mouth. His fingers quickened inside her and she felt herself go limp. Suddenly, it seemed as though she were disconnected from her body. She could look down at herself and Decimus in the grove. She felt as though she were Danu gazing on a worshipping acolyte. A warm aura of devotion cloaked her. She smiled regally. Her lips began to move, silently repeating old prayers she'd heard as a child in her native tongue.

When the mists lifted, she found herself in her earthly form upon the ground. Decimus's bronzed, brawny arm stretched across her torso. His nose lay buried in the tresses collected at the crook of her neck. When she turned to face him, his eyelids fluttered drowsily. A damp spot in the grass where he'd finished himself off sat just beyond their entwined forms.

She caressed the back of his neck. She smiled at him, slowly shaking her head. 'Oh, my brave heart. You are a man of many talents.'

'No talents. Just love.' He grinned and bussed her cheek.

'Why, Leucus Decimus Maximus.' She linked her arms around his stout neck as he lifted onto his elbows and braced himself over her. Her eyes danced teasingly. 'Could there possibly be a romantic hidden in there under your soldier's clothing?'

He chuckled softly and lowered his head to hers. 'With all due respect, my dear, you can fuck right off.'

She tightened her hold as his lips met hers. Her body curled beneath his sturdy frame as she captured his mouth, savouring the taste of his lips and his invigorating musky odour.

He held her close. The power and vitality encased within her small body stirred something deep within him. Her courage, her confidence, her earthy and regal poise were so unlike the soft, shrinking modesty of the other women he'd known. He felt her curl her ankles around his torso and he deepened his kisses with wild abandon. He felt like an oarless bireme crashing against her rocky beaches - helpless to stop yet thrilled and awed in equal measures.

He broke off to nibble her slim, graceful neck, sinking into the grass beside her. Luciana sighed and stared at the gloomy sky. 'It is such a perfect day,' she murmured absently.

Decimus followed her gaze, wrinkling his nose. 'You really like it here.'

'Of course I do. It is home.'

'I have spent most of my life far from home.' A wistful note crept into his voice as he remembered the warm, sunny days of his childhood: the scent of ripening olive trees, the sounds of merchants calling to one another, the gentle Mediterranean breeze whipping through his hair… He blinked fervently and turned to her. 'If you had the choice, would you ever consider leaving it?'

She didn't answer, humming to herself as she wriggled her toes.

'Luciana.'

She opened one eye and turned to him. 'Yes?'

'You had a name before your father Romanised it, didn't you? A British name?'

She slowly nodded. 'I did indeed.'

Decimus ran his finger along her arm. 'What was it?'

'Luigsech.'

He recoiled, his brows furrowed.

'What? It is a very noble name!' She sat up and tossed her head defiantly. 'Lugh Long-Spear, the protector of our warriors in battle, bestowed the same name on his own daughter!'

'Easy, love.' He wrapped his arms about her and squeezed her to his breast. He kissed her stony face as one hand travelled down to stroke her thigh. 'It is a fine name for a Briton. Especially a woman of your mettle. But I prefer Luciana all the same.'

'Well...' She melted into his embrace, falling back onto their bed of flattened grass. 'If you keep touching me like that, you can call me whatever you like.'

X

Tullius stepped back from his vantage spot between the oaks, trying not to make a sound despite his disorientation. The world spun around him, making him sick.

He tripped over a thick root and stumbled down the dark, wooded path. Aquila rumbled a low wicker from where he stood tied beside the buckskin gelding. Tullius ignored the horses and looked down, studiously avoiding Decimus's weapons lying at the edge of the grove.

Bile rose in his throat. He closed his eyes and shook his head, furiously trying to forget what he'd just seen.

But no matter how hard he tried, nothing could erase the image of his friend, his blood brother, defiling himself in the most wretched, debased way. Decimus, a *cunus lingere!* Nothing demeaned a man of *virtus* more than soiling his noble mouth, the source of his words, by servicing a woman. And Decimus had placed himself beneath a *barbarian* woman, no less!

Tullius pushed on along the trail. He didn't stop until he came within sight of Nero, stationed far downwind from the other two horses. Sufficiently free of the toxic grove, he collapsed to his knees and rocked, clutching his head.

He didn't know how long he crouched there, as each time he remembered what he saw, he fought his tears again. Tullius gazed at the ground, swallowing his tortured cries.

How could he? How could *he?!* There was no undoing what had been done. The man Tullius had come to regard as the closest embodiment of perfect Roman manhood had forever fallen in the vilest possible way.

'That *witch,*' he breathed, furiously wiping his eyes. It was her fault, he knew. Decimus would never have become a *cunus lingere* if she hadn't taken him under her spell.

He stood, squaring his shoulders and drawing deep breaths. He rearranged his features into a stern frown and marched over to Nero, who stretched his nose out curiously in his master's direction.

Tullius absently shoved Nero's head aside and grabbed hold of the saddle's double pommels. With a groan, he hauled himself up and threw his right leg over the stallion's back. Reluctantly, he gathered up his reins and prodded Nero into a walk, back to the site of Decimus's horrific emasculation.

To his dismay, he hadn't gone far when Nero whinnied a greeting. A moment later, the offending pair appeared mounted on their horses. The adoring look Decimus gave a triumphant, smug Luciana, her back straight and sure in the saddle, made the bile rise anew within Tullius's throat. He looked down, willing the light-headedness to pass, and forced a word between his gritted teeth:

'Sir!'

Decimus looked up as he and Luciana rode out of the trees. Darkness had started to fall. He squinted in the dying light at Tullius. He reined Aquila to a halt and waited expectantly.

With a slow, deliberate step, Nero brought Tullius closer. He drew rein and swallowed his bile. He didn't trust himself to speak for a long moment, willing his nausea to pass.

Blowing a small, impatient sigh over his shoulder at Luciana, Decimus straightened and cleared his throat. 'Yes, Optio. What is it?'

'Sir.' Tullius stiffly clapped a fist to his chest. 'Legate Regulus requests your presence in his quarters.'

'Very well.' Decimus's face twisted. Tullius watched his wretched lips struggle for words. *Has she cursed your speech, you dog?!*

Decimus, oblivious to his attention, sat deeper in his saddle and nudged Aquila towards the fort. 'You may tell the legate that I will be by directly.'

'Begging your pardon, sir.' Tullius's dark eyes flashed as he clenched his jaw. 'The legate specified you come as directly as possible.'

Decimus traded a puzzled look with Luciana. She seemed to enchant him, for his handsome features fell into a blank expression. He nodded up the path. 'Remember, today's password at the gate is *Miles Gloriosus*. I will see you later in my barracks.'

Without a backwards glance, he spurred Aquila into a canter. Tullius scowled at Luciana before wheeling Nero about to follow. He felt her eyes watching their retreating backs in the twilight. Tullius ignored her burning gaze and looked steadily between Nero's ears, trying to quell the rising nausea within him.

'What's gotten into you, Tullius?' Decimus turned to him. 'You look like you've spent the afternoon sucking on vinegar at The Aurochs!'

'Just following orders, sir. As an officer of the legion *should*.' Tullius avoided Decimus's gaze, focussing on the path before them.

Decimus frowned. 'Naturally. I would expect no less.'

The men lapsed into silence. Tullius growled the watchword to the guards when they approached the fort and the pair trotted inside without checking stride.

'You'll find the legate in his office at the Praetorium.' Tullius halted and grabbed hold of Aquila's bridle. He nodded down the straight cobbles to the limewashed brick domus sitting directly to their left. 'I'll take the horses.'

He gazed blankly ahead, ignoring Decimus's curious look as the centurion slowly dismounted and sauntered towards the building. Tullius's guts wrenched again. He narrowed his eyes. *You mincing fool.*

XI

'About time you showed up! This is a most unfortunate turn of events!'

Decimus stood at attention before the legate's desk, staring blankly ahead. Legate Regulus angrily strode around to him, hands linked behind his back. 'What sort of a fool takes off into the forest when he's in charge of preparing an entire legion for campaign?!'

Decimus pressed his lips together. He gazed directly at the wall, waiting for his superior's tirade to end.

'And what's the meaning of your appearance?' Regulus slowly stormed behind Decimus, eyeing him contemptuously. Without his armour or helmet, the centurion's rumpled tunic and casually adorned baldric made him look downright slovenly. 'How *dare* you present yourself at headquarters without your proper kit?! Do you think this is some spring holiday camp we're running here? Do you?!'

'I'm sorry, sir,' Decimus replied through gritted teeth. 'In my haste to obey your summons, I didn't have time to make myself presentable.'

'And whose fault was that?!' Regulus looked up, pausing inches from Decimus's chin. 'Maximus, you are *not* some newly promoted ranker, much less a useless tribune! You are the senior officer in charge of this legion! I expect nothing less than professionalism from you!'

'Yes, sir.'

'If you weren't my primus pilus, I'd have you posted to latrine duties for a year!' Regulus grabbed a sealed tablet from his desk and stomped over to the door. He drew back the iron bolt and stuck his head out. 'Catullus!'

'Here, sir.' His aide emerged from the shadows just outside his office.

Regulus thrust the tablet at him. 'Run this over to the imperial courier. Ensure that it makes its way back to Rome with all due haste.'

'Yes, sir!' Catullus turned and anxiously hurried away down the open-air peristyle.

The legate relocked the door and turned to Decimus. 'At ease, Centurion. I have a lot of confidential information to impart and not much time to do so.'

Decimus relaxed and let his gaze follow the legate. His expression silently implored Regulus to continue.

The legate collapsed into his chair and propped his elbows on his desk. He leant towards Decimus, his voice low and measured. 'The western tribes may be preparing to start their offensive sooner than we originally thought. As you're aware, the governor has spies planted within the native populace. He learned of whisperings of a war council from his Ordovician contact, but the spy warned him that the Silures' plans were still unknown amongst the neighbouring tribes.'

Decimus's brow furrowed. He gripped the edge of the desk. 'Doesn't Governor Paulinus have a spy within the Silure tribe?'

'Yes.' Regulus nodded. 'Or, rather, he did. He'd begun to worry that his Silure spy had turned traitor when several months passed with no communication between them. Then, just a few days ago, he turned up on the alley step of the governor's Londinium palace. In a bag. In pieces.'

Decimus winced. 'Morcant got wise to him, then?'

'Which is likely why he's been reluctant to share his plans for this impending council with the other tribes.' Regulus closed his eyes, shaking his white head. 'We need a replacement plant within the Silures, and quickly. The chieftain will be on his guard now he's discovered Paulinus's man, which means the translators on our staff are out. They'd be sure to stand out, given their mere passing familiarity with the British tongue. What Rome needs is a genuine Briton, one who wouldn't be suspected.'

'One of the locals in the vicus?' Decimus mulled over the prospect. 'I'm sure we could find someone willing to risk his neck if the governor makes it worth his while.'

Regulus waved a dismissive hand. 'That won't do. Our contact must be completely trustworthy. Risking such delicate information with some idiot loose-lipped civilian would jeopardise our entire campaign plan.' He met Decimus's eyes. 'That's when I remembered that barbarian whore of yours.'

Decimus stiffened. 'Luciana?'

The legate nodded. 'She obeys and answers to you, doesn't she? No one would suspect her if she rode into their camp, asking questions about the war council. In fact, her story would be all the more credible after what happened to her tribe last summer. No one could question her motive for revenge.'

'Sir…' Decimus clenched his fists, struggling to find the right words. 'You can't…you can't expect me to order my slave to spy on her own people?' He gestured helplessly. 'Who's to say she wouldn't take this opportunity to run away and take her revenge? Or to feed us lies about the tribe's intentions? She has no love or loyalty to Rome, sir. What you're asking is preposterous!'

'Mmm.' Regulus nodded. 'But she is loyal to *you*, is she not?'

Decimus paused and considered. After all they'd been through together, he hoped she did, but he did not know how far her loyalty extended. Especially when it came to comparing her love for him to her love for Britannia. 'If she is loyal to me, sir, it is only because she chooses to be.'

'That's going to have to be enough.' Regulus stood. 'And that's why you're going to accompany her.'

'Me?' Decimus paled. 'But sir-!'

'You're there to keep an eye on her, make sure she doesn't double cross us. We can't trust her to do right by Rome, but I think we can rely on her doing right by you. Especially if you're placed in such perilously close contact with the enemy.' He smiled humourlessly.

'Sir, I protest!' Decimus planted his feet wide, his expression stony. 'I don't know one word of the barbarians' tongue! I would stand out worse than one of your translators!'

'Nonsense!' Regulus stood and came around his desk. 'You're not there to speak to the locals. That's your wench's job. You can remain at her side as her mute bodyguard, or lover, or what have you.' He touched the centurion's shoulder. 'Besides, you've got enough facial hair to blend in with that lot.'

'But what about the legion? Sir, I'm needed here to oversee the men's training!'

'I'm sure your officious optio can handle some mere exercises until you return. I only need you in there long enough to learn where the Silures stand, infiltrate their war council, and divine their plans for the summer. Besides,' the legate's expression darkened. 'It seems that you're satisfied enough with the legion's progress to take a lazy rendezvous in the wilderness.'

Decimus gulped. 'Sir, I appreciate the faith you have in myself and Optio Servius. But I respectfully concede that I have no business in the world of political espionage. I am a soldier, and my place is here with my men.'

'You misunderstand me, Maximus. This isn't a plea. It's an order.'

Decimus's heart sank. His gaze fell to the floor and his knees swayed. A tight, sick feeling welled up within the pit of his stomach. The mere thought of cosying up to the wretched Silures, even for a short duration, made his blood run cold. And one wrong move would land his head amongst Morcant's grisly collection. But he had no choice. Reluctantly, he stiffened his spine and drew his fist up in salute. 'Yes, sir.'

Regulus sighed, knuckling his desk. 'If I had anyone else able to infiltrate their lot, I wouldn't order this. But it *has* to be your woman, and therefore you *have* to go. I'd hate to see you killed, but this intelligence is crucial to our campaign. More critical than any one of our lives.'

Decimus swallowed his nausea. 'Understood, sir.'

'Right.' Regulus backed away, nodding sternly. 'I expect you and that girl of yours at the south gate before the first hour tomorrow morning. There, you'll be provisioned and receive your final instructions.'

'Yes, sir.' Decimus nodded stiffly.

'And watch your back, Centurion. Don't take any unnecessary risks. I can ill afford to replace you right before the summer's campaign.' Regulus returned to his desk and lowered his head over his paperwork. 'As far as the official record is concerned, this conversation never took place. Dismissed.'

Luciana grabbed Tor by his new leather collar and crouched beside the bars of the fort's dank cell. 'Mother?'

'Luigsech.' Gwenfrewi weakly extended a hand up to the grate. Her fingers just brushed against her daughter's before falling back at her side. 'I thought you'd forgotten us.'

'Never.' Luciana bit back tears, shaking her head. 'You're still here, aren't you?'

'Is that a good thing?' The dull, glassy look of her mother's once vibrant eyes tugged at Luciana's heart.

'Better than the slave market in Londinium.'

Gwenfrewi shrugged. 'You're a slave. You're at least getting fed.'

Luciana reached under her cloak and handed a wrapped parcel through the bars. 'It's not much, but it was all I could smuggle in without their noticing.' She huddled closer to Tor's panting body, frowning at the back of the legionary standing guard a few feet away.

Gwenfrewi didn't unwrap the parcel, passing it absently to a dirty child that eagerly snatched it away. She nodded at Tor. 'Is he yours?'

'The centurion's.' Luciana blushed. Her fingers vigorously rubbed the hound's tawny coat. 'But he's of good British stock. A Regni man bred him.'

'The centurion seems to be collecting quite the local menagerie.'

Luciana looked away. She frowned at the floorboards surrounding her, struggling to quell the furious shame roiling inside her. 'Mother...'

'We're not leaving this place, are we?'

'Don't say that!' She snapped, making the guard look at her. She frowned at him, switching to Latin: 'It's impolite to stare!'

The legionary turned away and Luciana lowered her gaze to the pitiful women and children gathered below. 'I have sworn, before our gods, to free you. And I will.' Her fingers twined about the metal bars. She leant closer. 'But I will not endanger you further. The opportunity must present itself.'

Gwenfrewi sighed. 'If the opportunity doesn't come soon, we will perish here.' She lifted her reproachful gaze to her daughter. 'It's already too late for some.'

'I know.' Luciana tucked a blonde strand behind her ear and stood. 'We are all living on borrowed time.'

'May Taranis grant you the time you need.' Gwenfrewi reached towards her own bared neck.

Luciana likewise touched her throat and froze when she felt the silver Capricorn beneath her tunic. She coloured and clucked to Tor, turning away from her mother's curious gaze. 'Yes…yes, may he bless the wearer indeed.'

When Luciana re-entered Decimus's living quarters, Tor hastened his trot and barked a greeting. She followed him down the narrow corridor to their shared bedroom. She found Decimus just as he turned from his armour rack. Tor leapt up and placed his paws on the centurion's stomach, wagging his tail happily.

'Down, boy.' Decimus gently brushed the hound away, motioning to a pile of blankets by the fire. Ducking his tail between his legs, Tor whined and reluctantly padded off to his bed.

'There you are, *carissime*!' Luciana smiled pertly as she held her hands to the hearth. She shook off her last shudder at the cool spring evening and hurried over to him. When she saw his handsome face, she remembered the deeds it had so expertly rendered earlier. Luciana felt the flush of desire burn her cheeks. Rising onto her toes, she planted a kiss on his grizzled cheek.

'Get off me, woman!' Decimus curtly flung his arm up and pushed her away. He stormed down the hall and sank into his desk chair. Muttering to himself, he fumbled about the clutter surrounding his correspondence and opened a blank tablet. Moving a clay oil lamp closer to his hand, he picked up his stylus and began scratching away in the wax.

'I'm sorry!' Luciana folded her arms and stormed after him indignantly. 'What happened to the man I was with this afternoon?'

He didn't answer her, head bent low over his furious scribbling.

'I am sick of this! I really am!' Luciana paced the floor behind him. *How many more times must I endure this? I'm not some thing to be thrown about every time he's in a mood!*

She frowned and looked at the usually barren dining table lining the side of the room. Decimus had tossed his vitis on it sometime earlier, where it lay forgotten. She picked up his vine staff and studied it a moment, turning its twisting, rough shaft about in her hands. Then, with a cruel smile, she lifted one leg and cracked it apart over her knee. She smiled triumphantly at his turned back, holding the pieces high over her head before letting them noisily clatter onto the floor.

Decimus continued writing, unfazed.

'Humph.' Luciana lifted her nose in the air and flounced into the bedroom. She flung her cloak aside and disrobed, stripping down to the sheer undertunic she'd purchased the summer before. She flopped onto his bed and drew a warm pelt about her. Tor lifted his head from the corner of the room. She studied the fire and absently twiddled her legs in the air.

I'm beginning to tire of these mercurial moods of his… She sighed, gazing at the ceiling. Who even knew what could be troubling him this time?

Her gaze slowly travelled down the whitewashed brick to his trunk, situated along the wall beside their bed. She narrowed her eyes, knowing the stupid chaplet of oak leaves sat buried at its bottom. 'What power do you hold?' She asked the trunk. 'Why do you change him so?'

She lay back against the pillows, fingering her Capricorn pendant. She sighed and waited for his fury to find her once more.

A short while later, Decimus clapped the tablet closed and poured a spot of wax over the hinge. He pressed his ring into the seal and waited a moment for it to harden. Then he threw back his chair and quickly crossed the corridor to the door. Throwing it open, he bellowed into the night: 'Tullius!'

Something stirred in the twilight. His eyes fell upon the small dark face of Nicomedes. 'Please, sir. The optio is asleep. Must I wake him at this hour?'

Decimus blew a short sigh through his nose and shook his head. 'Here.' He thrust the sealed tablet at the boy. 'Make sure he sees this immediately upon waking. Tell him I expect my instructions followed to the letter.'

'Yes, sir.' Nicomedes took the tablet and shrank from the door. He tucked it under his arm and gazed up at the centurion inquisitively. 'Sir, what's-?'

Decimus nodded and slammed the door shut before the boy could utter another word. He shuffled into his office, rubbing the back of his neck. He stopped short, seeing the remains of his vine staff littered on the floor. His visage whitened.

'Oi! What's the meaning of this?!' He picked up the pieces and stormed into the bedroom, holding them up at Luciana.

She shrugged, fanning herself across the bed. 'You'd just tossed it aside, so I figured it didn't matter anything to you.'

'Have you *any* idea how many years...?!' He squeezed the severed pieces, seething. The vitis, gifted to him during his initiation into the centurionate a lifetime ago, had hardly left his side. His hands had worn grooves into the gnarled wooden head, melding it perfectly to his grasp. And in a single evening, she'd destroyed it. He closed his eyes and took a long, deep breath. When he spoke, his voice was low and cold. 'I suppose I won't need to use it to keep the men in line for a while. Perhaps never again.'

'How was I supposed to know you valued it? You treat all your possessions so callously. Even the living ones.' She lifted her head and gazed at him coolly.

Decimus dropped the broken staff and sat down on the bed beside her. 'Luci...there is no easy way for me to say this.' He stared down at his boots.

Luciana sat up, curling her legs beneath her. 'What is it?'

'I suppose you would enjoy spending time among your own people again?'

She stiffened. 'What do you mean?'

'I mean...living...' Decimus scrunched his face. '...with Britons again.'

'You're freeing my people!' Luciana swiftly rose, her face brightening. She threw her arms around him and kissed him. 'Oh, *carissime!* You're letting the Cornovii go!'

'No, I...I said that wrong.' Decimus gently pushed her away. He looked into her crestfallen eyes. 'Luciana, I can't do that.' He turned away. His cheeks burned as he felt her gaze turn frosty. 'I'm trying...to make our assignment sound a bit better. You won't like it, but you have no choice in this matter. Nor do I. We are being sent to live among the Silures for a while.'

'What?' She frowned, wrinkling her nose. 'You? Live among the Silures? But they'd kill you!'

'They might,' he said. 'If we fail to convince them we're on their side.'

'Their side?' Realisation slowly dawned across her face. 'We're being sent to *spy* on the Silures?'

He nodded. 'We leave Viroconium in just a few hours.' He gestured to Tor, who regarded them intently. 'I've arranged for Centurion Fortunatus to care for the dog while we're away.'

Luciana sat back and stroked the furs covering the bed. 'You know I have no great love for the Silures. They are responsible for the decimation and enslavement of my people. But to serve Rome…?' She shuddered and met Decimus's gaze. The revulsion evident in her expression made him turn away in shame.

'I know. I told the legate as much. But what you think, or what I think, doesn't matter. We either do this, or we die.' He balled one hand into a fist and punched it lightly against his knee.

'There's another option.' She curled up next to him and stroked his arm. 'We use this opportunity to run away. Far away from everyone who knows us. And take my people with us. We'll escape into Caldonia and resurrect the Cornovii tribe. We could be happy?' She cupped his bristled chin in her hands and tilted it towards her.

His gaze softened and he sadly shook his head. 'You know that's impossible.'

She sighed and looked down at his lap. 'I know.'

'I am sorry, Luci. Please believe me when I say I don't want to do this any more than you do.' He clasped her hands tightly in his own.

She thought for a moment. 'You need me, don't you? *You're* under orders to do this mission, but *I* am not. I am not in the Roman legion. Your legate has no control over me. And without me, you're as good as dead.' A hopeful light sparkled in her eyes.

Decimus frowned. 'Yes, but you are my slave, and you will do as I tell you.'

'Or what?' She cocked a brow in challenge.

'Or I will have to sell you away with the rest of your people.'

'Bollocks!' She laughed in his face. 'You couldn't bring yourself to get rid of me and you know it!'

He winced and hardened his gaze. 'Luci, please…'

'I will agree to do your dirty work. On one condition.' She sat back, smiling triumphantly. 'You free what's left of my people in return.'

Decimus shook his head. 'Luci, you cannot demand that of me. I do not control the fate of your people!'

'Really? Who will be responsible for handing them over to a slave trader?' She batted her eyes.

He sighed. 'The garrison.'

'And who is in charge of the garrison?'

'Legate Regulus.'

'And after him?'

'Tribune Cincinnatus.'

'And after him?'

'Prefect Corvus.'

'Come now!' She huffed. 'Do you really expect me to believe any of those striped skirts have ever so much as *looked* at the prisoners? Whose task will it be to ensure my people are sold away?'

He gazed at her for a long moment before he looked away and sighed. 'Knowing Corvus as I do, I suppose it shall fall to me, in the end.'

'Exactly.' She lifted a finger and absently traced it across his back. 'And who's to say the escort you send to Londinium doesn't, say, fall victim to an ambush? Forcing your men to fight for their own skins until they're forced to abandon their prisoners?'

'This is ridiculous!' He shrugged away from her touch. 'What you're asking me to do is treasonous! You hold no power over me, woman! You are in no place to bargain!'

'Don't I?' Her smirk maddened him.

'Enough!' He stood and shoved her against the pillows. 'Tomorrow, we become British nomads! We enter the Silure camp, learn their plans for war, and report everything back to the legate! And that's the end of it! Understood?!'

'Y-yes,' she breathed. A sliver of fear stabbed through her heart. The angry man who threw things had returned. She blinked as the shiver passed. A bland expression settled over her features.

With a grunt, he strode over to his side of the bed. He untied his boots and pulled his tunic over his head before throwing himself down beside her. 'Let me get what rest I can.'

She turned away from him, stiffening her shoulders. 'Suit yourself.'

Despite his words, he frowned up at the barracks ceiling, his fingers tapping nervously against his hardened stomach. The prospect of leaving the fort for a bed amongst the enemy filled him with disgust and dread. He blinked, trying to reconcile the task in his mind. *You must do this. You must do this and live so that you may return to Rome at summer's end…*

The thought that everything he'd done, everything he'd worked for, might end with this dangerous, silly game of the legate's irked him to no end. *Why does he single me out for this? I thought I was too senior for this shit…*

Luciana gazed out at the darkened room, finding sleep just as elusive. Her thoughts, however, turned to an ever-brightening future.

She slid out from beneath the skins and walked over to Decimus's household shrine. His lararium was tucked into a cubby above the mantle. Her own additions, a pair of stag antlers and a few crudely sculpted heads, he'd reluctantly crowded into the cubby behind his revered statuettes. Luciana reached in and grabbed one, turning it over in her palm. Its ridges identified itself to her in the dark: Danu, the earth mother in triplicate. Shaking her head, she replaced the fused trio and reached instead for the bigger, bulkier carved visage.

She felt the heft of Taranis's bulk and the curve of his wide, gaping eyes beneath her fingers. Smiling, she carefully set him beside the offering dish and picked up the bronze hilt of her dagger, resting in its new place beside the plate. The weapon glinted in the moonlight.

She pricked her finger on the tip of the blade and held it over the bowl. She watched dark blood droplets collect at the cut's mouth and drip slowly onto the dish. She glanced over her shoulder at Decimus, who still frowned at the ceiling. Her prayers would have to be silent.

She faced the shrine and closed her eyes. *Taranis, great and powerful, thank you for providing this opportunity. Grant me the wisdom to use it properly, that my people may go free. If you permit this, I vow to give you the whitest and youngest lamb I can find in gratitude.*

She waited for the pinprick to clot and opened her eyes. She withdrew her hand and padded back to the bed, slipping beneath the coverings.

Decimus still frowned at the roof, not seeing her. Instead of leaving him be, Luciana turned and curled against his side, a smile tugging at the corners of her lips. It didn't seem to recall him from wherever his mind had travelled, but she didn't care. The excitement of the adventure awaiting them brought a giggle to her throat and she kissed his scarred shoulder. Despite her master's rebuff, her mind already mulled over the possibilities she might find once amongst her own kind.

XII

Cassia coughed, scrunching her nose up at the cloud of incense surrounding her. She fidgeted on the floor of Antiope's hovel, eyes closed. Her legs had long since gone numb from holding her folded position. She didn't really hear the rattling sistrum or Antiope's foreign chants; they had gone on for so long that they'd faded into white noise. The sounds swirled about her head as Antiope paced in a small circle around her.

Suddenly, the ringing sistrum grew louder. Cassia bit her lip and flinched as she felt Antiope hover before her. She slowly opened her eyes to see Antiope, still chanting, dip her finger into a bowl of oil. Her gnarled finger deftly anointed Cassia's forehead. Cassia made to rise but stopped when Antiope held her hand above Cassia's head. The seer's cant grew louder, her sistrum more insistent. Cassia shuddered, feeling a powerful warmth that seemed to emanate from the woman's fingers.

Finally, Antiope fell silent. She moved away, the sistrum limp at her side. Her piercing dark eyes regarded Cassia for a long moment. She turned away. 'It is done.'

Cassia slowly unfurled her limbs and clambered to her feet. She waved in front of her face in a futile attempt to see through the incense. 'The enchantment holds?'

Antiope sat at her table and nodded. 'You will go unrecognised by those that know you. Including the man you seek.'

Cassia smiled. She picked up a dark veil and draped it over her head. The thin silk fell over her hair, swept into a tight knot and braided with small charms from Antiope's chest, and completely over her face. The fabric just touched the neck of her dark linen tunica. Two amulets hung around her neck: one a phallus to guard Cassia from the evil eye, the other beaded with the bones of three human fingertips. Cassia touched them and turned to Antiope. 'A full moon has passed since the first spring thaw.'

'You are ready.' Antiope motioned to the door.

Cassia picked up her bag and stuffed her statuette of Nemesis into it. 'And I need to find…?'

'The short man selling woollen braccae. He will take you where you need to go.' Antiope lowered her head over one of her charts. Gale hopped onto the table from the floor and slunk across the drawing.

Cassia stepped into the alley. The tinkling chimes over Antiope's door faded as she rounded the corner and came upon the remnants of the market day bustle. The crowds had gone, leaving only a few merchants packing their wares and driving out of the vicus. Oyster shells, frayed ribbons, and clay sherds littered the ground. Cassia stepped over them with a stately grace, peering through the dark film of her veil for any shadowy obstacles.

She saw the portly wool dealer Antiope had mentioned. He was folding the last of his brightly coloured trousers in the back of his waggon. She stalked over to him, swaying slightly in the sharp breeze.

She cleared her throat. 'You are heading for Silure lands.'

The merchant jumped and whirled to face her, banging his knee against the cart. He regarded her warily. 'How…how do you know that?'

'You will take me there.' Cassia marched up to the driver's seat and clambered on.

'Now, wait just a moment!' The little man huffed, scurrying after her. 'Who said you could…'

He stopped short when Cassia glared at him. She regarded him for a long moment, holding his frightened gaze. 'You will take me there,' she repeated.

The man slowly nodded.

Cassia smirked as he stumbled away to finish securing his load. She felt Antiope's enchantment working. It wouldn't be long, now, before she could finally take her revenge.

'Ah, Centurion. Punctual this morning, I see.'

Decimus glared at Legate Regulus as he tramped into the stable block, jaw tightly shut. Clad in his sandals and a dull grey tunic, his short ringlets dishevelled, he keenly felt the absence of the spit-and-polish normally demanded of him. His eyes, bloodshot from his sleepless night, betrayed his resentment as he snapped to attention before the legate. 'Centurion Decimus Maximus reporting for duty, sir!' He called, drawing a salute.

Regulus winced. 'No need for parade ground volume at this hour.' He glanced over Decimus's shoulder and smiled. Luciana skulked behind him, the cowl of her wolfskin cloak pulled over her head. 'Ah, yes, good. I see your little piece of cunny has accepted her mission?'

Her jaw dropped in shock. Decimus glanced at her uneasily and shook his head. He turned to the legate. 'Sir, I ask that you might remember Luciana is perfectly fluent in Latin.'

'Of course, she is! How else would she be able to translate for you?' Regulus glanced at his aide, Catullus, and Centurion Fortunatus, ranged alongside him. He slapped Decimus's shoulder, barking a short laugh.

Fortunatus's squat, muscular form suddenly lowered to the floor as he caught sight of the tawny wolfhound at Luciana's side. 'There's the lad! Come here, boy!'

At Luciana's prompting, Tor padded over to him and tentatively licked his chin. 'Who's a good boy? Who's a good boy?' Fortunatus murmured enthusiastically, rubbing his hands along the dog's hide. Tor wagged his tail and planted himself in front of the centurion.

Decimus arched a brow at the second spear. 'I know you said you liked dogs, but I didn't realise how much!'

'Love 'em.' Fortunatus's tubby fingers tickled Tor's chin. The hound lifted his head and closed his eyes, clearly enjoying the attention. 'I've got four pups myself back in Rome. Brother writes to keep me informed of how they're getting along.' He lifted his head. 'You won't have to worry about this one. I'll care for him as if he's my own.'

Decimus nodded. 'Thanks, all the same.'

He turned to Regulus, who appraised him with a critical eye. 'Right, off with your clothes.'

Decimus frowned. 'Sir?'

Regulus gestured to Catullus. The aide offered Decimus a folded bundle of brown and red tartan. He took the garment from Catullus and shook it out. He frowned. 'Sir, these are just trousers!'

'Can't be helped, Maximus.' Regulus shrugged.

Decimus glared long and hard at him before slowly stalking into a nearby stall.

Regulus nodded to Catullus. The aide slipped between the horses to Luciana, who stood stroking Aquila's nose. He gestured to the mount standing saddled beside him. 'Horses good, yes?'

She glared at him silently before turning back to the placid bay stallion.

Catullus moved along the animal's hide and patted the saddlebags extending either side of the seat's high cantle. 'Food here.' He mimed an eating motion. 'And blankets.' He pointed at the long saddle cloths that extended farther along the horse's flank than was customary. 'Leave these be.' He lifted the rear fold to expose the brand of the imperial cavalry on the horse's hide. 'No let the Silures see.' He sternly shook his head.

She sighed and brushed past him to adjust the cinch and breast collar. 'Yes, Catullus. I understand the need for discretion. Now, if you would allow me to fix the poor job you made of tacking these animals up?'

The aide clapped his mouth shut in embarrassment and stepped away.

Decimus slowly strolled into the aisle, clad in his tartan braccae. Luciana paused and smiled appreciatively at the sight of his bare torso. He ruefully held his waddled tunic before handing it to Catullus.

'What's that?' Regulus frowned, pointing to the wheel of Taranis still hanging from its leather thong about his neck.

'This?' Decimus fingered the trinket. 'Just some piece of local jewellery.'

The legate's face creased into a smile. 'Good! You look more like one of those heathen bastards already!'

Catullus dropped the tunic. He picked up an oval shield and long scabbard from the floor.

Regulus nodded to them as Decimus took the items. 'Some of the kit we captured from the Cornovii last summer. Hopefully, you won't have much need for them. But you can't be too careful.'

Decimus slipped the strap of the baldric over his head. The long blade touched the ground, the bronze-wrapped hilt standing ready to be drawn at his side. He tested his grip on the oval shield and gulped. He wasn't used to wielding such a small, ungainly piece of work. He studied the thin wooden sheet, decorated with its swirling design. A small boss protruded from the middle of a vertical wooden ridge that bisected its length. The shield's leather backing felt none too sturdy. The Roman scutum was larger and of far better construction. He lowered it to his side. 'Is that all, sir?'

'Yes.' Regulus glanced over his shoulder at Luciana and lowered his voice. 'You know what's expected of you. Find out the Silures' intentions and report back here as quickly as you can. Don't take any unnecessary risks. Their chieftain is bound to be suspicious. Make your return by the south gate; I will tell the duty centurion the watchword that will let you pass. When they ask you to halt and state from whence you came, answer: "where roses are red – and where the rose wine is mellow." The watch will be instructed to conduct you directly to me.'

Decimus nodded. 'I understand, sir.'

Catullus handed Decimus a dingy brown cloak and fell to his hands and knees by Aquila's side. Decimus ignored him. With a small hop, he effortlessly vaulted onto Aquila's back. The pair stepped out of the stable. He glanced over his shoulder to see Luciana right behind, mounted on the other provided horse. He nodded. 'We're ready.'

Fortunatus straightened and clapped his fist to his chest, smiling bravely at Decimus. Tor sat at his feet, gazing up at his temporary master. Regulus and Catullus followed the mounted pair as far as the south gate.

'The gods go with you, Centurion.' Regulus tapped Catullus on the shoulder. The aide barked an order to the men manning the gates. The legionaries lifted the locking bar and groaningly pushed the doors wide enough to allow a horse through. The two shrouded figures filed through the gate in tandem and disappeared into the predawn gloom.

'Easy, lad. Easy does it…Outside rein, outside! Don't drop your other hand, take up that slack!'

Tirintius sternly repositioned Nicomedes's quaking arm. The teen stood braced in a stationary chariot in the middle of the stable row, steering imaginary horses. His traces ran from his fingers to twin hitching posts. Nicomedes groaned, fumbling with the pairs of reins as they slipped from his grasp.

'You dropped your whip again!' Tirintius stooped by a wheel and picked it up.

'I don't know how I'm supposed to hold it when I've got all…this!' The teen clenched his fists around his four tangled reins.

'One day, you might be able to hold them with one hand.' Tirintius snatched the traces from Nicomedes and deftly wended them through the fingers of his left hand. 'Like this. Then you've got your other hand free to hold the whip, or wave, or cuddle your sweetheart.' He straightened them out and handed the newly separated reins to Nicomedes. 'But for now, we'll stick to one pair in each hand. Keep your whip tucked in your palm, like so.' He opened the lad's fingers and embedded the whip handle in his right fist.

Nicomedes looked at its dastardly braided tail trailing over the cobbles. 'Is it really necessary?'

'For driving, yes. Wait until we hitch this up. Trying to communicate with your horse is a lot harder when you don't have your legs or seat to help you out.' He lifted Nicomedes's arms higher. 'Now show me how you'd ask for a turn to the right.'

Nicomedes fumbled with the traces, sawing back on one pair before accidentally letting the other slip through his grasp. He collapsed his arms to his sides with a strained gasp. 'Please, Tirintius, can't we be done? I can't hold my arms up any longer!'

'Hmm.' Tirintius eyed the boy's thin forearms. 'You're going to need to build your strength before I put you behind some horses. I've got some weighted flays you can use, and I'll show you how to practice with them.

Put some muscle on those twigs.' He playfully knuckled Nicomedes's shoulder. 'Give you something to show off to your girl, besides.'

Nicomedes reddened and stepped down from the chariot.

'What girl?'

The pair turned to see Optio Servius walking towards them, an opened tablet clutched firmly in his hand. He paused before the pair, his gaze flinty beneath the visor of his crested helmet. 'My Greek may be a little rusty, but I definitely heard you mention the word "girl." You're talking about Metella?'

'Umm.' Nicomedes squirmed as he helped Tirintius untie the traces from their hitching posts. 'The decurion's teaching me how to drive a chariot, sir. That way, I'll be ready to become a driver at the Circus Maximus once we return to Rome.'

A small smile tugged at the corner of the optio's mouth. 'And in the meantime, impress Metella?'

Nicomedes scowled and ducked his head.

Tullius sighed, turning back to the missive in his hand. His eyes scanned the tablet, the lines on his face creasing into a scowl.

'Bad news, Optio?' Tirintius nodded to the letter.

'Not sure.' Tullius tucked it under his arm. 'Don't forget you've got a living horse to tend once you've finished untacking this pair.' He held up the empty bridle attached to the reins Nicomedes struggled to unknot. 'I passed Nero's stall on the way here and he rushed the door. Nearly bit my hand off. He needs a good workout, and I've got business in the vicus. You know that horse goes mad when he spends too much time in his stall.'

'Yes, sir. I'll get on it right away, sir.' Nicomedes stifled a groan and hefted the bridle up. He turned to Tirintius, who'd gathered a rag and a vial of oil.

'Cheer up, son.' Tirintius grinned, holding out the tools. 'Nothing will get those biceps growing like hacking an angry horse after scrubbing down these reins!'

Blowing a long sigh, Nicomedes grabbed the items and plonked onto a trunk. He sat there for a long moment, gazing blankly down the road from the stable aisle. The limewashed praetorium, off in the distance, glittered in the late afternoon sun. Nicomedes's muscles protested lifting the bridle, let alone cleaning it. With exaggerated slowness, he hefted the harness across his knee.

Movement farther down the via praetoria pulled his attention. He sat up as Lucius, the new merchant, appeared with the tribune. He waddled beside the officer, toting an amphora of wine. The tribune stopped with Lucius beside his mule cart and placed a hand on his arm. Though

Nicomedes was too far away to overhear their conversation, it looked serious.

Finally, Lucius nodded and watched the tribune enter the praetorium. He whistled and tossed the amphora around before loading it onto his wagon bed.

Nicomedes frowned. He knew from toting the optio's supply that sealed wine amphorae were considerably heavy. If Lucius handled one as easily as that, he had to have arms of iron. No wonder Metella had taken to him!

He glanced down at his own trembling arms and winced. He'd need to work hard to catch up to Lucius.

'*…You are to serve as primus pilus in my absence. Coordinate the ordering of supplies for heavy campaigning this summer with the depot. Deliver updates on amassed quantities to Legate Regulus as soon as they're compiled. Work with Corvus to ensure that the following training regiment is carried out according to the schedule outlined below…*'

Tullius's eyes jumped down the etched words as he flipped to the next tablet, looking for any more clues within the lines he was beginning to learn by heart.

'*…I do not know when or if I may see you again. Please ask no questions, for no one can answer them. Know only this: it has been an honour and a pleasure to serve alongside you, my blood brother.*'

He lowered the tablet to his lap, gazing blankly at the unadorned wall of Porcius's spartan apartment. 'I don't know what to make of it,' he murmured.

'Make of what?' Porcius sat up behind him, wrapping his burly arms about Tullius's shoulders. He looked down at the missive. 'That from your centurion?'

'Mmm.' Tullius's hands trembled. *Primus pilus in my absence…* 'It's my worst nightmare come true.'

Porcius sat up, reading over his shoulder. 'He's given you control of the whole legion.'

'Exactly.' Tullius gasped. Immediately, he felt overwhelmed by the gargantuan task Decimus had left him. He needed to write to the quartermaster. He needed to meet with the other cohort centurions. He needed to delegate the watch and the scouting parties. He needed to hold periodic reviews. He needed to attend the high command officer meetings.

He needed to communicate any pertinent information to the rest of the legion. He needed to lead from the *front*.

'What's the matter?'

Tullius leant away from the hand Porcius ran up and down his spine. 'I can't…I don't…' His breathing quickened. Panic seized hold of his tongue and froze his mind.

'Isn't promotion what all Roman officers crave? Even an acting promotion?'

'Not this one,' Tullius choked.

Porcius took hold of Tullius's arm and turned him round. He tried to capture Tullius's gaze. 'You know, I have always wondered why you never made the centurionate. You've seemed to me like an officious, competent sort. Your centurion has nothing but praise for you anytime he's in my chair.'

'I…' Tullius's mind raced through his past. He saw himself as a cowering legionary at the front of a shield wall, at a loss for what to do until his centurion screamed instructions down the line. He saw himself in forage parties, frozen with uncertainty when encountering hostile natives. He saw himself meekly following his father's shouted instructions, hastening to complete a task as quickly and ably as possible. '…I never wanted it,' he whispered.

'Hey.' Porcius tilted Tullius's chin up, forcing him to meet his eyes. 'It's okay to be unambitious. It's not for a lack of ability. You're incredibly capable…'

'It's not that!' Tullius roared, leaping to his feet. 'I can't! It's too much! I can't figure out the best course of action quickly enough to do anything.' He slowly sat down, burying his face in his hands. 'It's always been, "use your head, Servius!", "figure it out, boy!", "do I have to tell you to wipe your arse before you'll do it?"'

Porcius scooted next to him and pried one of his hands away. He linked his fingers through Tullius's. 'This is your chance to prove all those voices wrong.' He nodded at the tablet.

Tullius lifted it, scanning the words again. 'Decimus knows. He knows I've never wanted this. Why did he leave this responsibility to me?'

'Hard to say.' Porcius frowned. 'It reads as rather officious. Sounds quite cold and impartial, aside from that last bit.' He kissed his lover's cheek. 'Whatever you may think of him, he certainly thinks the world of you.'

'We joined the legion within days of each other.' Tullius squeezed Porcius's hand. He pictured himself and Decimus on the day they'd met: two scared legionaries scrapping on a muddy, forested path in Germania. 'We needed each other, though I think I needed him more.' Tullius shook his head.

'And I think you're selling yourself short.' Porcius playfully ruffled the optio's hair.

Tullius ducked out from under his touch, lifting the tablet.

'It's a beautiful thing, the brotherhood of the legion.' Porcius nodded. 'I knew there had to be more to you than Plautus's boastful buffoons.'

Tullius smiled ruefully. 'There's not much to boast about once you've seen the reality of war.' He looked away. 'Though I won't deny, the centurion is a force of beauty out there.'

'Sounds like you might admire him still.'

Tullius frowned. The sickening sight of Decimus playing woman to his little British whore leapt to the front of his mind. He swallowed the bile rising in his throat. 'I did, once.' He gazed at the letter. 'And this is how it ends.'

'You don't know that.' Porcius gently pried the tablet out of Tullius's hands and set it aside. 'It sounds more like governing business to me. And besides, you don't seem to object to *my* filthy mouth.' He turned Tullius's smooth chin towards him and tenderly kissed his lips.

A thrill raced up Tullius's spine. He closed his eyes, ignoring the feeling of self-loathing in his gut. He inhaled Porcius's scent. It was a heady mixture of sandalwood, wildflowers, red wine, and musky sweat. The man's impeccable beard tickled his face and his firm shoulder pressed invitingly against him.

Tullius embraced him and kissed him back. The pair fumbled at each other's broad sides, twining together at the edge of Porcius's bed. Tullius's appreciative moans were matched by Porcius's deep, rumbling chuckles.

They broke off at Porcius's insistence. He moved away, lifting a finger. Tullius reluctantly let him go.

'I have some more pleasant reading I thought you'd enjoy.' Porcius stood and deposited the tablet on a side table. 'We can leave your centurion to the gods. His fate is in their hands, now.' He knelt over a chest and riffled through a pile of scrolls. 'I discovered my copy of this and immediately thought of you...'

Tullius stood and wandered over to the window. As his euphoria faded, his shaking breaths fought a fresh wave of nausea twisting his guts. *You're a pathetic excuse for a man. One kiss is all it takes to turn you into a disgusting catamite...* He frowned and shook his head.

He peered through the window's iron grating. Below, the cobbled street in front of Porcius's shop lay quiet. A couple of figures crowding a merchant's wagon drew his eye.

Tribune Cincinnatus, out of uniform but resplendent in a cloak trimmed with purple fur, had paused to speak to a rather ugly looking tradesman with sunken features and a scraggly beard. The merchant, clad in a nondescript tunic, furtively grabbed rolls of papyri from the tribune's hands. He placed them inside an amphora on the back of his cart.

Tullius frowned. *What is Cincinnatus doing?*

He felt a strong hand on his shoulder and turned from the window. He smiled softly at the eager light in Porcius's eyes. The voices in his head grew quieter, drowned out by a wave of affection surging through his veins.

'Here.' Porcius led him to the bed and passed him a scroll.

Tullius settled against the pillows and unfurled it to read the title. '*Phaedrus.* Is this one of Plato's dialogues?' He chuckled. 'I haven't read this since my student days!'

'Shall I read Socrates or Phaedrus?' Porcius settled beside him, tucking his curly head beneath Tullius's chin.

'Oh, I'll read Phaedrus. You're much wiser than I.' Tullius grinned.

'You just want to listen more than read!' Porcius playfully batted his arm.

'Blame yourself for having such a pleasing voice.' He placed a kiss on Porcius's head. 'Come. Let me hear you declaim.'

Porcius cleared his throat, turning to face the parchment. '"*Phaedrus, my friend! Where have you been? And where are you going?*"'

Tullius relaxed into their snuggled position and smiled. '"*I was with Lysias, the son of Cephalus…*"'

XIII

Cassia stood in the centre of Morcant's cavernous hall, swaying slightly on her feet. Lamps ensconced around the circular room enhanced a thin stream of natural light beaming from a hole in the hall's conical roof. Thick furred carpets covered the tile floor. To one side, an odd old man sat and drew painted streaks along the wall. He muttered to himself, intermittently slashing new, curling marks amongst the old. Tribesmen with woad tattoos and silver collars about their necks flanked the hall and throne. Their polished spears and sheathed swords induced a shudder of fear down her spine.

Before her, seated on a sturdy oaken chair with silver and gem-encrusted ornaments, sat Morcant, chieftain of the Silures. His long, matted black hair and flowing mustachios made him look slovenly. His dress, however, was richly appointed: his silken shirt sported an intricately woven gold braid along its trim, and his brightly coloured braccae gave way to fine, well-oiled leather boots. Braided tassels and charms dangled from the laces binding them to his feet. He was cloaked in a mantle of deep, Tyrian purple, trimmed with bear fur. One hand, missing the tips of three fingers he'd lost in a Roman skirmish, lay curled in his lap. The other, sporting glittering iron rings, tapped the arm of his chair. A tattooed rectangle of dark woad on his brow proclaimed his chieftainship. He leant forward, scowling at her.

Cassia raised her chin. She swallowed her fright and met Morcant's gaze. He couldn't clearly make out her features through the veil, thought Antiope's enchantment would ensure her anonymity even if he did. She touched the bone necklace at her throat and smirked as Morcant shifted uncomfortably.

'You say…your visions brought you here,' he said in his coarse Latin.

'I do.' Cassia straightened. 'All oracles speak true, and they agree that you are poised to become quite powerful in this land.'

A smile slowly spread across his face. 'So, even your inferior Roman gods are in agreement.' He turned and said something in his native tongue to the old man seated by the wall.

'But you cannot attain this power alone. You require help in this quest.

Help that your gods alone cannot provide.' Cassia folded her hands in front of her.

He frowned. 'This power you say I will have…what shall I do with it?'

Cassia closed her eyes. She'd spoken with Morcant often enough in the past. She knew exactly what he wanted to hear. 'They have shown me Roman homes in flames. Roman temples crumbling to the ground. Romans leaving Britannia to a united, reclaimed people.'

'And what of the druids?'

'What of them?' She cocked her head, brows furrowing. She hadn't expected this.

'What takes the place of these…crumbling Roman temples and buildings?' He gestured to the wizened man. 'Are my people's religious leaders restored? Are the groves reconsecrated? Are the druids allowed to freely traverse the land and guide the tribes in peace and war as they once did?'

'Yes, yes, all of that.' Cassia waved a dismissive hand. 'Because you will be high king of all Britannia. You will be able to do whatever you want.'

'Restored…to what we were before the Romans came…' Morcant studied her for a long, silent moment. Finally, he said, 'and what makes *you*, Roman seer, come to aid me in this thwarting of your own people?'

'I cannot disobey the will of the gods.' Cassia fondled the bones at her neck. 'They compel me here, to you, to aid you in this. The great Sybils were told by the gods everything that shall happen, for millennia hence. It is beyond us mortals to know their whims. But they direct Rome elsewhere, away from Britannia. And you are the one chosen to make this happen.'

Cassia bit her lip as Morcant turned to converse with the old man. She felt her heart race and her hands go clammy. The words they spoke sounded harsh and unfriendly; were they rejecting her, or was that just the way their barbarian tongue sounded? They traded long remarks before Morcant nodded and turned to her. Cassia held her breath.

'You may advise me, seer. But only when I ask you for your gods' guidance. Taraghlan,' he gestured to the old man, 'is my senior and most trusted advisor. You are secondary to him. Be warned: if the word of your gods conflict with the word of mine, I shall always follow mine.'

'Of course, Lord Morcant.' Cassia breathed a long, silent sigh as she dipped her head.

He growled something in his native tongue. A female slave in shabby native dress scurried into the room. He nodded to her. 'You'll be shown to your quarters. Once you are settled, you are to be ready to attend upon me at any time.'

'Yes, Lord Morcant.' Cassia bowed and followed the slave through a screened walkway. She trailed the slave's slouching figure up a creaking flight of stairs. She could hardly hide her triumphant smirk; now, she was perfectly poised to bring Morcant harm.

Nemesis, you smile upon me!

'I think we've travelled far enough to the south.' Luciana reined her horse abreast of Aquila. The day had brightened into a grey morn, allowing her to see the centurion's stern features. 'It is safe for us to circle back.'

He nodded and turned Aquila westward on the barren moor.

'No.' She prodded her horse in the opposite direction. 'We go east.'

He halted and frowned. 'But if the fort's at our backs, the Silure territory's that way.' He pointed to a distant treeline.

She sat up in the saddle and met his gaze. 'Decimus, you must trust me now. Your life depends on it.'

A long silence fell between them. Finally, he sighed and turned Aquila about. 'Very well.'

Luciana lifted her nose and led the way to the left.

They rode in silence for several more hours. Decimus pulled a strip of dried mutton from one of his saddlebags. He chewed it absently as he followed Luciana's rump. Slowly, the landscape shifted from flat moors to hilly terrain. Something about their environs seemed eerily familiar.

Then, as they crested one of the hills, he saw it: Viricio. The charred, flattened ruins of the fort atop its lofty hill loomed in the distance, grey and forbidding in its dismal squalor.

He frowned. 'Luci, where…?'

'Trust me,' she answered glibly, turning away from the hillfort.

The hills flattened into a vale. Before long, they came across an occasional round hut. The fenced pastures surrounding the structures stood weedy and barren; no smoke drifted above their conical thatched roofs.

'Where is everyone?' Decimus craned his head about.

Luciana didn't answer.

The abandoned structures became denser, spotting the landscape regularly, before thinning out once more. Soon, a larger building loomed ahead. A rickety shed and a vast, untended field surrounded its perimeter. Decimus's eyes widened; they were travelling directly for its entrance.

'Luci!' He called.

She ignored him. Instead, she stopped before the door and dismounted. She looped her reins around one of the fence posts and gestured for him to follow. 'Come inside.'

He halted and glared at her. 'Do you know these people?'

She rasped a hollow chuckle. 'I would think so. This was my home.'

Before he could respond, she turned and flounced through the door. She halted just inside as the comforting, familiar odour of home flooded her nostrils. Though the roundhouse had sat unoccupied for several months, she could still taste the lingering aroma of the hearth fire, of her mother's tinctures, of her father's musty togas. Tears sprang to her eyes. She quickly wiped them away, looking around. The entry hall looked just as it had on the day they left it, with their most valuable possessions heaped on the family's altar to Cernunnos in an alcove. Their Samian ware lay scattered on the large oak table that filled their dinner hall. Luciana stepped around it, running her hand along the elegantly carved chair at the head of the table. 'Oh, father,' she murmured in her native tongue. She paused in the doorway to the bedroom she had shared with her brother and saw two piles of pelts still stacked neatly on the floor. She stooped beside her old chest and traced her fingers along its flowing, ridged design. Opening the latch unleashed a stale odour in her face. Quickly, she rummaged past scrolls and fabrics to find the small vials of cosmetics she'd kept in the bottom. Her fingers closed around the bottles and she pulled them up, a smile curling across her face.

'Nice place.'

She paused. Had Decimus just *complimented* her barbarian hut?

Decimus gazed about the dining hall, waiting for her to reappear. He trailed his hand along the pottery cluttering the table and stopped to admire the Roman frescoes stretching around the room. Just behind the head of the table, Apollo stood against a brilliant ray of sunshine, his silver bow drawn towards the monstrous Python of Delphi. Decimus studied the confident, elegant lines and nodded appreciatively. The figures were well-proportioned. The sinuous, sinister form of the Python and Apollo's curling golden locks were surprisingly lifelike. He traced his finger along the meadow they inhabited, almost surprised to find it had the texture of brick instead of grass. 'The artwork's nicely done,' he murmured.

'You think so?' She called, stepping into her mother's room. Bundles of dry herbs covered a spacious table; jars and bags sat haphazardly along the many shelves. She took a deep breath, feeling the presence of her mother in the room where she had worked her old magicks. A soft prayer to the gods bubbled forth from her lips. Blinking, she pulled down some materials and mixed them in an empty mortar.

'I do.' Decimus sat in one of the chairs against a wall. He drew back a little at the sight of Jupiter the bull charging directly beside him. 'I didn't think you could find such a skilled artist this far from Rome.'

'My brother did them.'

'Your brother?' Decimus frowned. 'You never mentioned a brother.'

'That's because you never asked.' She laughed softly, scooping a generous helping of ashes from the extinguished hearth into a large pail. She set the bucket on the floor and hiked her dress up, squatting over it to relieve herself. 'Timoteo was rather enamoured with Roman arts. Painting, sculpture, poetry, music, all that nonsense!'

'So's Emperor Nero. I reckon the two would have a lot to talk about together.' He smiled a little, then paused. 'He isn't…?'

'Dead? I don't believe so.' Luciana gathered her wares and moved through the screened chambers. 'Father made him leave with the rest of the Gaesatae before the tribe retreated to The Viricos.'

She stopped short, dropping her supplies beside a rear entrance. She paused, staring at the door for a long moment.

'Luciana?'

'Just a moment. Wait here.' She slowly stepped outside.

The rolling pastures that greeted her eyes hadn't changed. The hills faded away into thick forests, where her tribe's cattle had once lounged in the shade. She strolled down the slope from the back of the house, trailing her fingers over stray heather shoots bursting forth from the renewed soil.

She stopped before a crudely constructed hut and pried open the door. There, in the gloom, she could just make out the disused harness and farming equipment her family had been forced to abandon. The heady smell of leather filled her nostrils as she reached for a shape draped over a peg just inside the door. Her fingers found the familiar, grooved strap. A small cry escaped her lips when her hand revealed Belena's bridle. She rubbed along the ribbed surface of the mare's chunky browband and scraped at a bit of dried grass pulp staining the iron bit. Tears burned anew, blurring her vision. Choking on a sob, she moved deeper into the shed to run her hand along the twin pommels of her saddle.

'Belena…'

Sighing, she stepped outside. Her hands still clasped the bridle reverently. She paused in front of the open pastureland, remembering the many times she'd waited with headstall in hand for her spirited little mare to come galloping over the rise. She whistled her old call out of habit.

A strong breeze gusted from the east, fanning her hair behind her. She closed her eyes against it, indulging her fond memory of bygone days. If she ignored the Roman centurion currently sitting inside her family's deserted home, she could almost imagine the events of last summer had never happened…

She sighed and dragged her feet towards the house. She stopped, however, when she thought she heard the distant sound of rollicking hoofbeats.

It can't be! Can it?

She turned around, almost afraid of what she might see. At first, she thought she must have imagined it. Then, over the crest of a hill popped a familiar, pudgy brown form barrelling in her direction.

Luciana gasped and raced to meet her. 'Belena!'

The mare whinnied a greeting and put her head down. Her stumpy black legs became a blur as she bounded over the grass.

'Belena, you're still here!' Luciana cried. She stopped and held her hands to her mouth. Her fingers brushed against tears flowing freely down her cheeks.

The little brown pony hopped and bucked as she drew up, throwing in a half rear and a squeal for good measure. She pranced to a halt and lowered her jug-shaped head to Luciana's pockets, seeking her customary turnip.

'I have nothing for you, girl. I didn't expect to ever see you again!' Luciana threw her arms around Belena's neck, hugging her fiercely. The mare nipped playfully at Luciana's braids, leaning into her mistress's affections.

'Oh, girl. Oh, my beautiful girl…' When she could finally tear herself away, Luciana immediately combed through Belena's unruly black mane and felt her thick, fuzzy back. She ran her fingers along the mare's stout legs and feathered fetlocks, assessing every inch of her beloved friend.

'You're perfect,' she breathed at last, smiling as Belena bared her teeth. 'I'm so glad you're well, even if a little hungry.'

Belena stomped an impatient hoof, pinning her ears.

'Still as bratty as ever.' Luciana batted her muzzle away and kissed the mare's cheek. 'I love you.'

'Luci!'

She looked at the house to see Decimus emerge from the doorway. He gestured to the mare. 'What have you been doing? And where the fuck did that horse come from?'

'Run to the saddlebags and grab a handful of that uncooked barley porridge. Then come down here!' Luciana laughed. 'Belena will be most happy to meet you if you come bearing snacks!'

'So, this is your Belena.' Decimus stretched his flat palm to the mare's mealy muzzle, watching her scuffle up another lump of barley. 'She's a bit smaller than I expected.'

'You say that about all our horses!' Luciana nudged his arm, smirking.

He shook his head, running his gaze over her wide barrel and stout legs. 'It's just…you said she's never been bested in a race.'

'And she hasn't.' Luciana stroked the mare's forelock. 'A bigger horse isn't necessarily a faster horse, as Boudicca of the Iceni learnt the hard way.'

He chuckled. 'I guess I'll have to believe you. She sure doesn't look like much, though.'

'She's the best horse my father ever bred!' Luciana hugged Belena's shaggy neck. 'And I'm not saying goodbye to her again.'

Decimus closed his eyes. 'You can't take her with us.'

'Why ever not?' Luciana stepped behind Belena, letting the mare's bulk divide them. 'I've still got her tack. We can use that gelding your legate gave me as a pack animal.'

Decimus crossed his arms. 'And what about when we get back to the fort? You're my slave, Luciana. You can't requisition a stall for a native pony.'

'Belena's never needed a stall!' She stretched her hands across the mare's back. 'And I don't expect her to have one now.'

'She can't walk free around a legionary fort. She isn't a pet, Luci.'

'No. She's my friend.' Luciana lovingly stroked Belena's thick brown hide.

Decimus turned away and sighed. The too-familiar adoration in Luciana's eyes panged him. The pride that radiated from her touch mirrored the way Decimus handled Aquila. He couldn't bring himself to insist the mare stay behind. 'I'll…I'll see one of the farmers in the vicus about grazing her with his stock.'

Luciana ducked around the pony and grabbed him, kissing his cheek. 'Thank you.'

'Come on, then.' He nodded to the roundhouse. 'Get her tacked up and let's be off. We've tarried here long enough.'

'Not yet! We aren't ready!' Luciana shoved the bridle into his hand and darted up the rise. 'I wasn't expecting Belena. There's more to sort out at the house.'

He frowned, watching her frantic steps.

She paused by the door and smiled. 'Can you tack her up and lead her around to the front with the others? I should have everything set by the time you finish.'

Decimus sighed. 'If it gets us out of here faster…'

She blew him another kiss and disappeared into the roundhouse.

A short while later, Decimus led Belena around to the front of the building. He looped her reins around a fence post not far from where Aquila and the cavalry mount stood. The mare pinned her ears and pawed the ground when Decimus approached the doorway.

'Don't get mad at me! This was her idea, not mine!' Decimus shook his head and ducked inside. He stood a moment to let his eyes adjust to the gloomy interior before moving between the screens, rounding one that shielded the family's impressive dining bench from view. His eyes ran over the tasteful murals lining the wattle-and-daub walls.

'My brother did them…'

He frowned momentarily. He cursed himself for failing to learn much about her family before. What would a brother of Luci's be like? Older, younger? Strong, no doubt, and wilful, if his sister was anything to go by. He must have been formidable to be sent from the hillfort before it fell. Where might he be now?

'Sorry.' Luciana hastened into view, toting a bucket and several assorted items. 'I think everything's in order.'

His eyes lit up at the sight of her. She'd painted her lips a bright, rich colour and her toenails were a brilliant shade of blue. She'd shed her cloak, revealing a beautiful cerulean gown; gold trim adorned the bodice, which hugged her body before giving way to a long, diaphanous skirt. The sleeves travelled up her arms before stopping short of her shoulders, leaving the top corner of her woad tattoo exposed. He growled appreciatively at her appearance. Then, as she set her containers on the dining room table, he wrinkled his nose. 'What is that? It smells like a fucking fullery!'

'It can't be helped, *carissime.*' She turned to him, hands on hips. 'Now, it's time to finish your disguise.'

He tittered, gesturing to his checked trousers. 'The legate's already seen to that.'

Luciana shook her head. 'I'm not taking you to the Silures looking the way you do now. They'd see you for what you are in a heartbeat. And the last thing I want is you parted from your precious head.' She tickled his bristly beard and tugged at his baldric. 'Come on. Put your sword down. It's time you started looking like a proper Briton.'

He shrugged his weapon off and knelt on the floor at her gentle prompting. Behind him, Luciana rolled up her sleeves and drew a deep breath before dunking her arms in the acrid bucket. She swirled the mixture about before gathering up handfuls. 'Close your eyes. This wash is going to burn.'

He obliged, keeping a stony face as she heaped the mixture on top of his head. As her hands returned to the pail for more, his scalp slowly started to tingle. The feeling crept over him, rapidly touching off nerve after nerve. His lips drew back in a grimace. By the time Luciana dropped the next coating on, his entire head felt like it was on fire. 'Mithras god, Luci!' He whined. 'What are you doing to me?'

'I told you it was going to be unpleasant.' Luciana buried her fingers in his hair, working the solution through. His short, soft ringlets grew thicker and coarser as she stiffened them into spikes. She caressed the contours of his skull and smiled. 'Seems a shame to let you keep your head, though. It would make such a beautiful ornament.'

'Don't get any ideas,' he growled.

A teasing laugh rumbled in her throat. 'You might just have to sleep with one eye open, *carissime*.' She stepped back and examined her handiwork before turning to the other bowl on the table. 'Right. Now for the fun part.'

Decimus felt her crouch before him. He cautiously opened his eyes. 'And that would be…?'

She dabbed a small brush in her mixture of dark blue woad and waggled it with a flourish. 'I get to draw all over you.'

He watched as she made bold strokes along his forearm, deftly creating intricate swirls, stripes, and waves on his skin. She bit her lip in concentration as she moved along his shoulder and began to create a large design over one of his pectorals. He studied her face, his expression soft. How beautiful she was! Her brush left a cool tickle against his skin. He looked down to study her handiwork. 'This isn't going to end up like your mark, is it?'

'What's that supposed to mean?' She drew back in dismay. 'I thought you said you loved my woad!'

'And I do.' Decimus nodded. 'That doesn't mean I want the same permanently etched all over my body.'

'Oh, is that all?' She laughed and tossed her hair behind her shoulder before resuming her work. 'Don't worry. The markings are only permanent if you use needles to draw them into the skin. Otherwise, they will begin to fade after a few days.' She nodded to the bowl. 'Which is why I'm going to take the rest of this with me. I may need to touch you up before we leave the Silure camp.'

She moved around and drew across his back. Decimus lowered his head and gazed at her intricate handiwork. 'Does all of this mean something?'

'Of course it does,' she murmured. 'All our symbols hold sacred meaning.'

'So, what does this mean?' He pointed to a triad of swirls she'd painted across the upper corner of his chest.

'The triskelion?' She glanced over his shoulder. 'It represents the movement of life, comprised of the past, present and future. There is a triple nature at work in the world, which provides the balance of our existence.'

He nodded. 'And these three leaves in a circle?' He indicated one of his arms.

'The triquetra?' She drew a long, curving line along his broad spine. 'It embodies unity of spirit.'

'Unity of spirit with what?'

'With earth.' She smiled softly. 'Danu, the Great Mother, gave our spirits our earthly forms and the lands we call home. The circle is to ensure that the unity of spirit is not broken. It calls upon the Morrigan, who controls our wars and our fates, to ensure our success.'

He snorted. 'In Rome, we are taught to believe that the Parcae are three ugly old hags who cut and spin the threads of our existence.'

Luciana smiled. 'The Morrigan is pretty frightening in appearance, as well.' She made some sharp strokes and sat back to study her handiwork. 'The signs I have drawn on your back are evocative of the bull, which is very sacred to the Druids. It not only symbolises success, but strength and virility as well.' She danced her fingers along his shoulder. 'And we both know how apt those descriptors are.'

Decimus shuddered and playfully snapped at her, a low growl rumbling in his throat. If truth be told, he already felt different; earthier, fiercer. It was as if the woad markings had unleashed something primal within him that had long since been suppressed by the trappings of Roman civilisation. Perhaps Luciana had been right all along about the strength of the Gallic blood that coursed through his veins.

Luciana moved around to face him. She lifted her brush and ran it down the bridge of his nose. 'That represents protection,' she murmured, indicating another of the symbols with her free hand, 'and that represents life. Beside it is the symbol of truth, which we hope to uncover, and along your other arm are the marks of luck, honour, and love.'

'And what are you putting on my face?' He murmured softly.

'The Awen.' She smiled as she finished the diminishing point of the line streaking up his nose. 'These strokes up your cheeks represent the male and the female. The line in the middle,' she broadened the mark at the end of his nose, 'symbolises the harmony between the two.' She finished by dabbing three blue circles, one above each brow and one higher in the centre of his forehead.

'The balance between us.'

He slowly leant close. She shrank away, setting her tools aside. 'I chose it so the woad would distract from the very Roman shape of your nose.'

Decimus snorted. 'I'd imagine after all your doodling, I hardly look very Roman at all!'

'No.' She sat back and studied the full effect of her handiwork. She nodded, as though satisfied, and held up a blue and green checked garment that wildly contrasted with his braccae.

Decimus frowned. 'What is that?'

'It belonged to my brother.' Luciana tore a strip from the cloth and stretched it diagonally across Decimus's bare torso. She fastened it at his waist and positioned the cloth so it masked both the centurion's pierced nipples. 'Best not draw attention there. Doesn't look very Belgae.'

He grunted and shrugged. 'If you say so.'

She finished adjusting the material and sat back. A smile tugged at her lips. 'Oh, dear.'

He frowned. 'What?'

Luciana leant forward, linking her arms around his neck. Her eyes slowly flickered over his countenance. 'At least now I know I don't love you because you're a Roman.'

Even with his patrician profile and trim, shapely beard, he looked utterly transformed. His hair, bleached a dirty white colour and stiffened with lime, stood up and away from his face in a series of short spikes. The bright woad on his features only accentuated the captivating colours of his sharp, intelligent gaze. His severe, bushy brows drew together towards the corners of his almond shaped eyes, lending his expression a savage air. Luciana shuddered, tilting her chin up with desire.

'Luci,' He rumbled, grasping a fistful of her hair.

'Leucus,' she whispered.

Their lips crushed together with a desperate urgency. Luciana closed her eyes and moaned, capturing his mouth. Decimus wrapped his broad, tattooed arms about her slim form, resting his fingers against the waist of her delicate dress. He savoured her sweet, hot breath, feeling familiar flames of passion spark within his breast. She cupped his face, stroking his beard as she deepened the kiss. Decimus moaned and sat straighter, tilting back so she could probe him deeper. He reached up and roughly caressed her breasts.

'Oh, *carissime!*' She breathed. Her pulse began to race at the thrill of his brutal touch. Her core quivered. She pressed even tighter against him.

He grabbed the top of her dress and yanked it down. With a sharp tear, the bodice split in two and the top of the ruined garment fell about her waist.

'Decimus!' She pulled back, stunned. 'You animal!'

His broad chest heaved. A numb astonishment mingled with awe in his stormy gaze. He'd surprised himself at the barbaric way he'd just torn into her.

Then she flung herself at him again, kissing him with a renewed fervour. Decimus gathered her into his arms and flung her on top of the table. The pail containing the putrid remnants of the limewash crashed to the floor, spilling its contents. His bare hands made quick work of her skirt, leaving it in tatters about her naked form. Luciana pushed down his trousers and eagerly fumbled for his erect cock. He let out a high-pitched yelp before pushing her back, slamming her down against the table.

Decimus loomed over her, panting. His knees locked overtop hers and his hands firmly clamped her arms, pinning her to the table. His throbbing member quivered, hovering over her soft, glistening core. The wheel of Taranis dangled from his neck, suspended just above her heaving breasts. She gazed back at him, her hair framing her face in disordered array. Her eyes glittered with desire. She writhed against his hold.

'Take me,' she whispered. 'Take me, you savage brute.'

With a primal roar, he swiftly and ferociously obliged.

XIV

'Straighten, straighten!' Tirintius grabbed Nicomedes's outside trace.

'I don't know how!' Nicomedes hollered, a note of panic in his voice.

'Correct your bend! You're still telling them to turn!' Tirintius hauled back, letting the long reins slip between his fingers. 'Release your inside hand.'

Nicomedes relaxed his grip, all but dropping the ends.

'Not that much!'

'I'm sorry! It's just too fast!' The lad turned tearful eyes up from beneath his leather helmet. 'I can't remember everything!'

Tirintius sighed and clucked once. The pair of ponies in the traces, one grey and one seal brown, obligingly slowed from a walk to a halt. They turned their heads, eyeing the contraption they towed. They had nearly doubled back on themselves after Nicomedes failed to stop commanding them to turn.

Tirintius stepped out of the chariot and straightened the ponies in their traces. 'You're going to break the yoke if you're not careful!'

Nicomedes sat on the back of the chariot and wrenched his helmet off. 'This is never going to work! It's too hard!'

'Steady on, lad.' Tirintius squatted before him. 'You just need to remember to do everything you did at a standstill. There's nothing to it!'

'Nothing to it?' Nicomedes scowled. 'What do you mean? I'm so far back from the horses I can hardly smell them, let alone touch them! How are they going to listen to me?'

Tirintius shook his head, waggling a finger at Nicomedes. 'Charioteering isn't for the faint-hearted, young man. It requires both courage and skill. You've got the skill.'

Nicomedes made a face.

Tirintius shrugged. 'Okay, you've got the foundation to build skill. Now you just need the courage. Come on, I thought you wanted to be a charioteer in the Circus Maximus someday!'

'I thought I did, too.' Nicomedes looked down at his hands. He picked at the fresh blisters forming on his fingers. 'I just don't know if…'

His voice trailed off as he lifted his head, squinting over Tirintius's shoulder. There, beyond the edge of the treeline, he could just see Metella's short, broad form. She sat beside Lucius at the front of his waggon, arm linked through his. His portly mule plodded along, ears swinging, as the cart creaked over the cobbled path.

Tirintius stood and watched alongside Nicomedes, who couldn't take his eyes from the girl. Feeling his gaze, she turned in their direction and tugged on Lucius's arm to stop. As he did so, she waved. 'Nicomedes!'

He tentatively raised a hand in response, a smile pulling at the corners of his mouth.

'What are you up to out here?' She rearranged the folds of what looked to be a new, silken palla and preened.

'Nothing much, I…'

'Come on, lad!' Tirintius nodded his encouragement. 'Might as well!'

'Just…' Nicomedes coloured, rubbing the back of his neck.

'Is that a chariot?' Metella's eyes grew round. 'Have you got a chariot?'

'It's not mine,' he squawked. 'I'm just…driving…it.'

'Oh, my Jove! Lucius says you have to be well fit to become a charioteer!' She beamed at Nicomedes, ignoring the merchant's insistent tugs at her elbow.

Nicomedes looked away.

'What are you in such a hurry for?' Tirintius frowned at Lucius.

'I need to be away by nightfall. I've got an important shipment to deliver to Londinium.' The merchant nodded at the amphorae in his wagon bed.

'We won't keep you, then.' Tirintius turned to Nicomedes. 'Right, lad?'

He nodded, finally meeting Metella's gaze. The admiring look in her eyes made him freeze. Hope bubbled up within him.

'Would you take me for a drive sometime?' Metella's face suddenly jerked away as Lucius's mule lurched into action. She wrenched around to face Nicomedes and cheered at his enthusiastic nod.

Tirintius shook his head as he watched the cart disappear up the forested track. 'Strange. Thought the man needed to take the Londinium road. He's heading north.'

Nicomedes frowned. 'Why would he do that?'

'Not to drop the girl at home, that's for sure. He's going the opposite way.' Tirintius narrowed his eyes. 'There's something odd about that one. Not sure what your gal sees in him.'

Nicomedes brightened at the mention of Metella. 'Did you hear her, though? Did you? She wants me…' His voice trailed off as visions of Metella's arm tucked in his filled his thoughts.

Tirintius grinned. 'What did I tell you?'

Nicomedes startled from his reverie and refastened his leather helmet. 'Come on! Let's do this!'

The decurion laughed and clambered into the chariot after Nicomedes. He grabbed the curving sides and held on when the boy enthusiastically clucked to his ponies, launching them into a rough trot.

'Whoa, whoa!' Nicomedes lost his grip on one of the traces and the grey pony broke into a canter. The brown pony increased the speed of his trot, reluctant to go any faster.

Nicomedes bumped around inside the chariot, nearly shoving Tirintius out the back. 'Help me!' He squeaked.

'Zeus preserve me,' the decurion grumbled, reaching over to fix the boy's grip on the reins. 'Knees bent! Brace...brace! Take up the slack there. Not too much! You want to be smooth...I said smooth!'

Cassia tugged her skirts out from under Taraghlan's foot, rearranging them about her. She scowled at the druid. His grubby grey robes, matted white beard, and unwashed skin repulsed her. She felt unclean sitting in the spot she'd been forced to occupy beside him.

Taraghlan only twitched his foot and curled into a tighter huddle on the floor. He lay in a rather disturbed slumber after drinking some concoction he'd devised. Cassia had watched Taraghlan cut up various herbs and mushrooms, straining them into some liquid until the drink had turned an ugly, dark colour. She was surprised he'd drank such a thing so readily and had so quickly fallen asleep.

She frowned at the man's bald dome resting against the tile floor. What remained of his hair trailed in long, scraggly waves from the back of his head. He lacked the remote grace of the cave-dwelling oracles, the untouchable beauty of the Vestal Virgins, or the stately bearing of the pontiffs with their beautiful hoods and richly coloured togas. Even the enormous women posing as Venus outside her temples held more charm than Taraghlan. She found it hard to believe a man like him was capable of arbitrating, leading, and curating all the knowledge of these primitive people. Were all druids so ugly? She wondered.

'Get up.'

She startled, lifting her head to see Morcant hovering above her. He scowled. 'I need to know what your gods say.'

Cassia stood with as much dignity as she could, carefully arranging the folds of her dark tunic. 'This is the first time you've called on my services. I was beginning to think you'd forgotten.'

'I told you. I will only consult you when I wish to. And now, I wish to.'

'And the far more important gods of your people?' She gestured to the sleeping Taraghlan.

Morcant waved a hand. 'They speak to him now. But it may be days before they release him back into our realm.' He pointed at her. 'My Roman contact, however, hasn't communicated with me for some time. I am beginning to worry I've displeased your gods. You must speak to them and demand I receive word. It is critical I do so.'

Cassia inclined her head. 'You cannot order the gods to do as you please. I may ask on your behalf, but they are not compelled to answer.'

'They'd better answer.' Morcant glowered.

Cassia brushed past him. 'Fetch me stones. Small ones.' She spread her arm around the great hall. 'I need some from the north, south, east, and west of your dwelling.'

Morcant sighed and nodded to one of the guards. The man lowered his spear and exited the hall.

Cassia sat at the head of a long dining bench pushed against the gradually sloping wall.

'What do you think you're doing?! You cannot sit there!'

'Can't I?' Cassia rounded on him. 'You wish me to intercede with my gods on your behalf, yet you refuse to show them any respect! Is it any wonder they're angry with you?'

He pounded his fists on the table and leant close. 'If they are going to make me as powerful as you claim, they ought to be bending their will to mine.'

'That is yet to be decided. My visions will only come to pass if you receive my help.' Cassia scowled.

'Is there a woman in any of your visions?'

Cassia's eyes widened. 'Pardon?'

'You heard me.' Morcant's gaze intensified. 'Does a *woman* enter into or play a part in any of your visions of the future?'

She shrank back. He seemed to care very deeply about this, though she could hardly fathom why. *Nemesis, please give me the words he desires.* 'There is no woman…beside you…in this future.' She bit her lip. 'Does this disappoint you?'

To her relief, a smirk slowly spread across Morcant's face. 'I knew it.' He glanced over his shoulder at Taraghlan. 'The druid tells me that a *woman* will lead my people to freedom from Rome's tyranny. But if you disagree, he must be mistaken.'

Cassia frowned. 'So, my gods only take precedence over your gods when they agree with what you want? I don't think…'

He narrowed his eyes. 'What?'

She hesitated for a moment, then continued. 'You cannot pick which prophecies to believe and which to discard. It is not the way of the gods. They may say different things, but the ones you serve the most are the ones you must believe. You choose which gods you make obeisance to, sacrifice to them, serve them humbly, and accept any favours they deign to give you.'

'Roman gods and the gods of our people do not exist on equal planes.' He shrugged. 'Your Roman gods are so much smaller, control so little. Yet they are many. If they change a matter here, a matter there, what is it to our more powerful gods? They have too much to see to. They do not bother with human fates the way your puny Roman deities do.'

Cassia saw the guard re-enter and beckoned him to place his gathered pebbles before her. She straightened in her seat and coolly regarded Morcant. 'Just remember that my gods require sacrifice. They will not do anything for you unless you do something for them.'

Morcant harrumphed impatiently. Cassia slowly gathered the pebbles in her palm. She shook them, intoning a few nonsense words. Watching Morcant, she cast the stones upon the table.

He drummed the fingers of his intact hand against the wood. 'Well?'

Cassia bent her head, pretending to study the pattern of the rocks. This was it. Now, she would destroy him, piece by piece. She sat back, smiling. 'The gods will bring word from your Roman contact *if* you give them a sacrifice.'

Morcant sighed. 'And just what do they want me to sacrifice?'

Cassia's gaze hardened. 'Your right hand.'

He froze. The intact fingers of his left hand curled as he drew his arm away. 'My…right hand?'

'If you wish to receive this most crucial word you ask for.' Cassia nodded. 'Nothing less will do.'

Morcant studied her for a long moment. Finally, he turned to regard the sleeping druid. 'I suppose I would call Taraghlan my right hand.'

Cassia frowned. 'I don't think…'

Morcant barked at his guards. They hauled Taraghlan up and dragged him across the hall. They stopped before a brazier, which one of the guards lit. Morcant followed, commanding in his native tongue all the while.

Cassia watched in rapt horror as one of the guards stretched Taraghlan's right arm out and pinned his weight against the druid. The other warrior dealt a hacking blow to his wrist. Cassia gasped and shrank away, wincing. Taraghlan awoke from his stupor with a deep, agonised howl.

The sound echoed off the cavernous walls, forcing Cassia to cover her ears.

The guard had to deal two more cuts before the hand came free. The man holding Taraghlan immediately thrust the druid's bleeding stump into the brazier. Taraghlan's screams mingled with the acrid stench of burning flesh. Cassia studied the floor, feeling her gorge rise.

Morcant walked over and chucked the severed hand onto the table before her. 'Give this to your gods. And tell them I expect they uphold their end of the bargain.'

Cassia glanced at the wizened, ropey limb, dripping bright red droplets onto the oaken surface, before fainting and tumbling to the floor.

'Optio Servius!'

Tullius, shifting through the mountain of tablets stacked in front of him, glanced over his shoulder at the entrance to his cramped office in the principia. 'Enter!'

A centurion strode into the room and halted smartly before his desk. 'Mucius, first century, fifth cohort. I left a request with the primus pilus concerning the recall of a detachment of my men last week. They've tarried long enough at the auxiliary fort, and I need them to supplement my century for routine details. Our numbers are down after a stomach sickness tore through my men.'

'Let me see…' Tullius threw down his stylus and shuffled through the towers of tablets. 'I haven't yet come across anything about recalling a detachment…'

'The primus pilus *assured* me he'd attend to the matter with no delay! He should have received a reply from the fort by now.'

'I can't…' Tullius opened more tablets, scanning their lines before tossing them aside. 'Um…'

'Respectfully, Optio, I need-,'

'Optio!'

Tullius threw up a hand at the entrance. 'In a moment!'

'Sorry, Optio, I cannot wait.' One of the junior tribunes on Regulus's staff marched into the office. 'I need your most recent strength reports for a letter that needs to be sent with the imperial courier *tonight.*'

'He told you to *wait*, sir,' the centurion growled. 'I was here first!'

'And I outrank you!' The tribune scowled, drawing himself up.

Tullius scrambled through the pile on his desk. 'I know I saw that current strength report just a moment ago…'

'Hang on! Where's the reply regarding my men?'

'Optio Servius!' Corvus, the camp prefect, pushed past the two men and leant over Tullius's desk. 'I sent a lad round requesting the duty rotation an hour ago! Not one of the decurions has a fucking clue whose turn it is to send patrolling parties. Nobody's been out all day!'

'I told your man, sir, that I'd sent for last week's rotation from the decurion princeps. But my messenger hasn't returned with that schedule.' Tullius ran a hand through his hair. *Damn that Nicomedes!*

A legionary tentatively knocked on the door and crept up to the desk. He set down a new stack of tablets beside Tullius's elbow. 'Correspondence from the quartermaster's office, sir. I've been told to wait and deliver your reply to the message on top immediately.'

'Fuck the quartermaster!' The tribune yelled. 'The governor needs a current strength report *now!*'

'Not before I get a duty rostrum for the auxilia!'

'What about my detachment, sir?!'

Tullius dropped the tablet he'd just opened and clapped his hands to his ears. He stared at the mess scattered across his desk, completely at a loss. *Make it stop! Someone, tell me what to do first! I can't do this! I can't!*

'What the fuck is going on here?!' A commanding voice bellowed.

The room fell silent. Everyone turned to see Centurion Fortunatus standing in the doorway. He clasped his arms behind his back, seeming taller than his diminutive stature.

'How are any of you going to get what you need when you're talking over each other?!' He marched through the crowd, scowling at the men crowding Tullius's desk. He came around behind Tullius and placed a hand on his arm. 'Can't you see you're running Optio Servius here ragged?!'

Tullius closed his eyes, breathing a long sigh of relief. At last, someone to take charge of the situation!

'Go into the hall, all of you!' Fortunatus pointed. When the men tried to protest, he cut them off. '*Now!* And do *not* re-enter until you're summoned!' He eyed Corvus and the tribune. 'Respectfully, sirs!'

The men reluctantly shuffled into the colonnade, grumbling.

Fortunatus straightened one of the towers of tablets and began sorting through them. 'Optio, look for anything pertaining to that infantry detachment. I'll find the latest strength report.'

Tullius gratefully took up his singular task. His hands gradually stopped trembling as he worked. 'Thank you, Centurion,' he murmured.

'That's what we do. We help a brother in need.' Fortunatus frowned, sorting the tablets into new, smaller piles.

Tullius opened one and paused. 'Here's a mention of the fifth cohort detachment.' He read Decimus's lines and frowned. 'Seems the primus pilus started the recall letter but never got around to finishing it.' He slowly placed it on the table.

'Give it here. I'll finish it and send it off tonight.' Fortunatus took the tablet and set it aside.

Tullius sat back, happy to let Fortunatus assume the initiative.

Luciana nudged Belena along the banks of a small brook. The mare lazily nodded along, her fierce energy spent by the long ride. Decimus rode Aquila beside her. His repeated winces and scowls told her he was just as tired.

'How much longer, Luci?' Decimus rubbed his trousered bottom. 'We've been at it since dawn. I lost all feeling in my legs ages ago!'

'That's funny. I don't seem to recall any trouble in your legs when we rested at midday.' Luciana smirked.

Decimus's eyes lit up. He lowered his voice to a sensual growl: 'I said I'd lost all feeling, not all power.'

She giggled. 'Don't worry. The Silure tribal seat isn't far from the brook.'

They rode a few more paces before Luciana heard a splash. She drew Belena up and silently motioned for Decimus to halt. They listened to the sounds of someone – or something – wading in the water.

'Wait here,' Luciana whispered. She slid from Belena's back and crept through the trees shading the bend.

She caught sight of bright red hair through the branches. She stopped and watched a woman standing in the shallows, her skirt tucked above her knees. Her back to Luci, the woman pounded a damp cloth against a large stone on the bank, beating it dry.

Luciana eased back through the trees, careful not to snap a twig. She hastened over to Decimus.

'Well?' His brow furrowed anxiously.

'It's a Briton. She might be a Silure. I can't be sure.'

'She? Just the one?'

Luciana nodded. 'She's alone.' She turned to Decimus. 'This might be our chance to escape an interrogation with Morcant's guards, if she is a Silure. Follow me, and for the love of both our gods, *don't say a word.*'

They nudged their horses along the rutted track. Mounted on a small native pony and a slightly larger Roman horse, leading the gelding behind them, they made quite a sight as they emerged into the dappled afternoon sun. The trees fell away, exposing the grassy banks of the brook.

Luciana nodded to Decimus, who halted at the water's edge. She leant forward, murmuring encouragement to Belena. The mare scrambled into the water, throwing a great splash up with her hooves. Luciana laughed and clung to Belena's thick mane as the brook soaked her hem. The water was shallow, never reaching higher than the mare's belly. Luciana sat up and smiled brightly as she steered Belena towards the woman.

'Greetings!' She drew rein as soon as she came within earshot. 'Are you of the Silures?'

The woman had drawn back to nervously watch her approach. She slowly began to gather her laundry from the rocks, never taking her eyes off Luciana. 'Who wants to know?'

'Forgive me.' Luciana slid from the mare's back and waded towards her. 'I am Luigsech, of the Cornovii.' She pointed over her shoulder at Decimus on the opposite bank. 'And my companion is Leucus. Belgae. We've come in search of the Silure settlement. Are you a Silure?'

The woman frowned. 'Might be.' She studied Decimus, who scowled at her from atop his mount. 'I don't want to cause any trouble, mind.'

Luci turned and glared at him. *Don't spoil this. You must trust me.* She maintained her gaze, willing her thoughts into his mind. *Relinquish control. I must take charge, now.*

After a long pause, he turned his face away. Luciana inclined her head. She stooped to gather the rest of the woman's garments and handed them over, a gentle smile on her face. 'Please don't feel alarmed. We are friends, seeking vengeance against Rome.'

'I wouldn't know about any of that.' The woman looked at her feet and shook her head. 'Matters of war aren't for my head, apparently. Morcant and his ring don't take to-,'

'Morcant?' Luciana laid a hand on her arm. 'So, you *are* a Silure, then?'

The Briton reluctantly nodded. 'I don't *know* the chieftain, so much as I know *of* him. As much as I need to know of him, in any case.' She narrowed her eyes at Luciana. 'How do you know Morcant?'

Her cheeks momentarily flushed. She struggled to find words, demurely lowering her gaze. 'We…have a history of sorts.'

'Right.' The woman hitched her basket under her arm and turned away from the brook. 'Best be getting on, then. I'll leave you to your… vengeance.'

'Wait!' Luciana leapt after her, pulling at her sleeve. The native whirled around from the force of the tug.

Luciana released her grip, smiling. 'We heard rumours of a war council among the western tribes. It hasn't happened yet, has it? We wanted to come, to learn the will of the ancestors in our resistance against Rome. And to fight alongside our countrymen if we can.' Her eyes widened. 'Please tell me we're not too late.'

'I don't know anything about any war councils.' The woman drew away. She glanced from Luciana to Decimus and back again. 'When it comes to consulting ancestors, though, I doubt if you'd receive permission to speak with The Old One. Only the sidhe are permitted to look upon her. But…'

'But?' Luciana's eyes lit up encouragingly.

The woman hesitated. She turned away from Decimus's piercing eyes. She leant close, lowering her voice. 'There is a druid who's taken residence with Morcant. He…he came with the last waning of the moon.'

Luciana drew in a breath. 'Might we speak with him?'

The woman thought for a long moment. Time seemed suspended. *Please, please…* Luci made her eyes go round. *Please say you'll take us to Morcant.*

The woman, at long last, nodded resolutely. 'Follow me.'

Luciana swallowed her delighted squeal and raced back to Belena. She mounted and waved to Decimus, falling into step behind the Silure woman. She leant low over Belena's back. 'What is your name, by the way?'

'Saibh.' The woman hefted her basket and shot Luciana an uneasy smile.

XV

'Well, well, Luigsech. We meet again.' Morcant drummed his cauterised, stumpy fingers against the arm of his varnished throne. 'Or should I say…Luciana?'

She cast a furtive glance at the sentries stationed around the chieftain's vast dining hall. 'How *dare* you call me by that name?'

The Silure chieftain chuckled. 'I don't recall you scorning your Latin title when you were mooning over that tutor of ours, Gaius Nerfinius.'

Her nostrils flared. A suppressed moan of rage rumbled in her throat as she leant forward and pursed her lips, hawking up a gob of phlegm that landed at Morcant's feet.

The chieftain promptly sat up and smacked her across the face.

'You *monster!*' She shrieked, recoiling. She backed a safe distance away and panted, her fists balled tightly at her sides. 'I am *not* your subject, and I am *not* your wife! I have no grounds to respect you!'

Morcant stood from his throne. 'Is *this* not enough?!' He pointed to the woad rectangle tattooed across his forehead. 'Nobody challenged my claim to the chiefdom! The elders elected me unanimously! Ocelus *chose* me to rule the strongest and bravest tribe in Britannia!'

Luciana crossed her arms. 'Ocelus would *never* approve of an unworthy traitor to his own kind and country!'

'Traitor?!' He thrust his finger against her chest. '*Your* tribe were the traitors! Your people scorned your heritage, your strength, your land, and your gods by rolling over and accepting the ways of your Roman conquerors! You more than deserved your fate!'

'*Don't* touch me again unless you want to lose the rest of that hand,' she snarled.

A small cough behind Morcant caught her attention. Her eyes alit on an aged man in white robes who sat within a chalk circle to one side of Morcant's throne. Beady grey eyes glared back at her from his wrinkled face. A long, white moustache obscured his mouth, and his iron-grey hair had been shaved in the druid's tonsure, bald on top with the rest trailing in long, scraggly locks from the back of his head. He was missing one hand, his bandaged arm tucked tightly to his side. He hunched over a pair of bronze divination spoons in his only hand, tracing the pattern of ashes scattered across their surface and making calculations under his breath.

Luciana turned towards him. 'I suppose *he* told you Ocelus approved of your plan to destroy my people?'

Morcant bristled. 'Nobody tells the chieftain of the Silures what to do!' He cast an absent glance at the druid. 'Taraghlan merely acts in an advisory role to my decisions. Mine.'

'I'll take that as a yes, then.' Luciana shifted her weight and crossed her arms. 'It doesn't matter. I eventually escaped my Roman captors. But I didn't choose to come here on your account. My father's offer of marriage died with him.'

Morcant sneered, parting his lips to reveal dirty, tannin-stained teeth. 'I'd never have taken you for a wife if he'd begged me. Insolent woman!'

Her countenance darkened. 'You dishonour our Mother Goddess by spurning women in this way! Where are your female warriors? The ladies of your tribal elders? The druidesses to advise your foolish head?!' She gestured to the hall's entrance. 'The woman who guided me here said you don't even permit them to sit at the nobles' councils and make decisions pertaining to war!' Her fists clenched. 'This is *not* what Danu and our ancestors intended! If I didn't know any better, I'd take you for a woman-hating Roman or a toga-lifting Greek!'

'Silence!' He snapped, his voice ringing around the vast room. 'I have no patience for your wicked words! Women have no place in the affairs of tribal leadership!'

'Never have I heard a weaker man speak!' She sneered. 'Mark me, Morcant: you have no chance of *ever* uniting the western tribes, much less of defeating Rome! You will fall before them as pitifully as my father did!'

'Interesting.' He stroked his bare chin, lips curling into a smirk beneath his flowing black mustachios. 'Taraghlan tells me a much different story.' He turned to the druid. 'Isn't that so?'

Taraghlan sat up, turning his steely gaze on Luciana. 'The time is upon us. The wrath of Andraste waxes bright in the heavens. Enemies shall become allies, and Rome shall be put to fire and sword. None shall be spared.'

Morcant smirked at Luciana. 'It sounds to me as though the gods have predestined my success.'

'Except for one thing.' She arched a brow. 'It is the wrath of Andraste the prophecy calls upon, not Ocelus or Lugh Long-Spear. I hardly think a goddess of vengeance will work through a boor who spurns female warriors.'

He huffed. 'The gods care little about our petty affairs. It is beyond us to know who they choose for greatness.'

'And you think you're such a one?' She laughed and turned to leave. 'Very well. I had come to offer the services of myself and my companion as warriors for your cause, but if you have no need for a woman at your war council…'

'Wait.' He halted her. 'I suppose I *could* have a use for that big Gaesatae brute you rode in with.'

'Leucus?' She faced Morcant, hands on her hips. 'I doubt he would be much use to you without me. The man is a deaf-mute.'

Morcant frowned. 'Is he?'

'I came upon him shortly after I escaped the Romans. He took me into his home. He clothed me and fed me.' She allowed a slight blush to creep up her neck. 'After a time, we grew…closer, and we forged our own way of communicating with one another. I learned that he was Belgae, who retreated north to the hills and forests after the Romans defeated his tribe. He cannot hear, and he cannot speak, but he has a warrior's heart.' Her eyes glimmered. 'I've seen him hunt. I've seen him take down a patrol of legionaries who ventured too close to our home. He is the ablest fighter I have ever seen, and he shares my hatred of Rome.' Luciana shook her head. 'But I doubt you could move him without me on hand to communicate for you. He is as devoted to me as he is to Britannia.'

The chieftain grinned. 'Of course, the only man who could ever love you is deaf and dumb to your shrill, impudent voice.'

Luciana abruptly turned on her heel and marched to the entrance.

'Halt!'

She hesitated and slowly turned.

Morcant's eyes narrowed. 'Very well. Your idiot lover may have a place among the warriors I take to the council convening at the next full moon.'

'And I…?'

'Will accompany him.' He held up his mangled hand, his expression stern. 'In an interpretive role *only.*'

She was silent for a long moment, then nodded. 'We shall stay.'

She spun around and marched to the doorway. A movement out of the corner of her eye drew her gaze and she stopped short. The veiled woman rearranging her dark skirts, studying the ground, looked exactly like Cassia. Luciana watched her for a long moment, and when the woman's bright blue eyes flicked her way, her jaw dropped in recognition. It *was* her!

Cassia froze. She sat very still, holding Luciana's gaze. When Luci's mouth finally began to move, she subtly shook her head.

Luciana stifled her voice and swiftly turned away. She marched out of the reception hall, fists clenched. She needed to warn Decimus, and quickly, before Cassia gave them away.

Cassia nodded to the slave hovering in her shadow. The woman silently followed Luciana out.

Morcant frowned as he watched Luciana leave. 'I do not trust her,' he murmured to the druid.

Taraghlan stood beside him. 'The warrior or the priestess?'

Morcant snorted. 'Is there any woman truly trustworthy?' He frowned. 'The warrior.'

'It would be wise to watch that one. Remember, the gods proclaim that a female warrior will guide our people to victory.'

Morcant bristled. 'The gods are wrong. It is *my* destiny. And I don't intend to let any female warrior stand in my way.'

Decimus sat just outside the chieftain's hut, arms clasped around his knees. The two sentries flanking the entrance had disarmed him and barred his path after admitting Luciana. Their message had been plain enough to Decimus, who resigned himself to wait until Luciana resurfaced. The sentries cast sideward glances at him every so often, though their watchfulness escaped Decimus's attention. He scowled blankly ahead with his back against the daub and wattle wall, trying to quell any outward show of anxiety.

The sentries' oval shields, painted with their distinctive, swirling designs, stood propped on either side of the doorway. Above the entrance, a series of bleached human skulls grinned lifelessly back at Decimus from their deeply embedded perch. He tried to ignore the decorations and his growing sense of dread. In the distance, a cow lowed and the murmur of women conversing in alien tones hummed through the British settlement. Outside the entrance to the nearest hut Decimus could see, a couple of naked children sat on either side of a lined drawing they'd carved in the dirt. They each took turns moving stones in intricate patterns across the crudely chequered image, engaged in some sort of native game.

He felt uncomfortable surrounded by so many Silures; he'd only previously viewed them this closely over the edge of his scutum. When the sentries murmured to one another in their native tongue, a small part of him couldn't help but fret that they spoke about him. What were they saying? What were they thinking? Could they see right through his disguise? Could they sense he was not one of them? Decimus gulped and set his jaw.

By Mithras, he vowed, he would *not* give away any outward tell!

Not far from the chieftain's hut, a couple of warriors slung a stag carcass down beside a large, open cookfire. They straightened and laughed, conversing in loud tones. One, a squarely built man with a wide scar bisecting his chest, had so many woad tattoos crowded on his body that his skin was hardly visible. The other, a bit tanner and wirier than his companion, brandished a bejewelled metal band high around one arm. A couple of silver chains dangled from his neck and his clutch of spears clung tightly to his torso with a leather strap. His dark blue eyes glimmered as he roared a response to his companion. Both men's hair had been spiked with lime in a similar fashion to Decimus's own.

The square warrior caught sight of the centurion over the wiry man's shoulder. He pointed across the way and shouted an inquiry. Decimus flicked his stormy gaze in the man's direction as disinterestedly as possible. He carefully refocused his stare beyond the two warriors.

The square warrior called out another question, barking a contemptuous laugh. His companion turned to Decimus and joined in. The caustic note to their voices made Decimus's pulse quicken, but he refused to look at the warriors again.

More British invective flowed his way, a growing belligerent tone to the questions. From the periphery of his vision, Decimus saw both men walk towards him. His body tensed for action and his right hand reached towards his hip, grasping for the hilt of his gladius. His fingers closed impotently about empty air.

Sandalled feet crunched to a halt before him. Toes delivered a sharp prod to his ribs and a hand gruffly pushed at his shoulder. The two warriors leant over, their faces fixed in angry scowls. Decimus recoiled, his heart thudding in his throat. Tentatively, he shook his head a fraction. To his dismay, the warriors grew angrier. The men's words came hard and fast, peppering him as incessantly as their rough jabs.

One of the warriors delivered a particularly heavy blow to the side of his head and Decimus reeled. Stars flashed before his eyes, and when the world refocused, he saw only red. With a roar, he leapt to his feet and struck out at the warriors.

The Silures shouted and redoubled their efforts, balling their hands into fists and battering him between them. The centurion fought back, blocking as many of the punches as he could while simultaneously striking out whenever the moment appeared. But one man's defences weren't enough to effectively fight two attackers.

Decimus caught one of the wiry man's blows aimed at his groin and feinted up to jab the man's stomach. Just as the wiry Silure stumbled backwards, the square warrior landed a cutting hit to Decimus's kidney. He howled, doubling over in pain. Above his head, the warrior's mocking laughter rang in his ears.

Decimus drew in shallow, quaking breaths, staring at the men's feet. Gritting his teeth, he slowly drew himself up and slid one foot forward to hook behind the square warrior's heel.

The wiry man, having recovered his breath, rushed up with his fist trailing behind him, swinging it in a wide arc. Decimus scowled at him, following the line of the punch before jerking his foot forward. The square warrior wobbled, waving his arms to recover his balance. Decimus ducked his head inside the arc of the wiry man's punch at the last moment, allowing the square warrior to absorb the blow instead. With an angry howl, the square warrior wheeled away, holding his head.

The wiry man paused, frowning at his companion. Decimus took the opportunity to pounce on him and strike the man unconscious. Wordlessly, the wiry warrior crumpled at his feet.

Decimus glared down at him, wincing and breathing hard. He tenderly reached to feel along his side when he heard the square warrior's angry voice. Suppressing a groan, Decimus lifted his head.

To his surprise, he saw Luciana race from the chieftain's hut, rushing to place herself between Decimus and the warrior. The Silure barked something at her and tried to shove her away, but Luciana angrily responded and pushed back. She planted her feet in front of Decimus and belligerently lifted her chin, her words coming harsh and fast.

The warrior drew up against her, hollering back, but it was hard for him to get a word in edgewise. Though he had no idea what they were saying, Decimus could clearly hear Luciana's voice winning the war of words. He gazed down at the top of her head, his expression softening with pride.

From the corner of his eye, a motion attracted Decimus's attention. He gazed in the direction of the chieftain's hut. There, Morcant of the Silures, the man who'd thrust his sword in Decimus's thigh last winter, hulked menacingly. His sharp, venomous glare sent an involuntary chill down Decimus's spine. The man's right hand remained tucked against his thigh, hiding his deformity. His long, scraggly black hair framed his lean, hungry features. Decimus gulped and met the chieftain's gaze, staring blankly back. The scar on his leg began to throb as memories of that cold morning on the moor flashed through his mind.

He stirred from his reverie when Luciana took his hand and began chattering at him imploringly. He frowned at her as she spoke in her native tongue, befuddled as to what she might be saying. He saw her gaze flick to their linked hands. He slowly became aware that her thumb was insistently tracing patterns against his skin. His brows drew together in concentration as he felt the Latin letters her finger wrote across his palm: *nod*. He paused for a moment, then tersely complied.

Luciana glanced over her shoulder and snapped something at the square warrior, gesturing to Decimus with her free hand. The warrior shrugged and growled a few words. Luciana sneered and replied dismissively.

When the warrior spoke again, Decimus lifted his head away from the conversation. He still felt the chieftain's glare burning into his neck. Did he look familiar? Might Morcant be trying to place Decimus's face? The centurion tensed as a cold feeling of anxiety gripped his stomach. He knew that if *he'd* been the one who'd lost his fingers, he wouldn't forget the perpetrator in a hurry.

Luciana wrapped her arms around his neck and pulled his gaze back to her. She crowded close against him, her breath warm and sweet on his face. She kissed his lips, mumbling senseless words against them. He was so stunned by her sudden, affectionate proximity that several moments passed before he realised she was writing with her finger against his chest: *again*.

Decimus eased away from her and nodded vehemently. Luciana turned and grinned at the warrior. He turned away, dragging his unconscious companion by the arm. Luciana took Decimus's hand and pressed against him in the opposite direction. He didn't need much prompting to escape Morcant's gaze.

'Luigsech!'

The chieftain's voice drew Decimus's heart into his throat. He stopped marginally before Luciana pressed him to a halt. His back remained turned as Luciana cautiously faced the chieftain.

Morcant growled at the pair in his garbled tongue. Decimus poised himself to flee, every muscle within his body taut. The voice sounded so inherently threatening that he couldn't tell if the words were spoken in anger or not.

Luciana merely offered him a curt nod, then tugged at Decimus's arm. It took every ounce of power within him not to hustle after her hurried steps, maintaining a steady, even pace in her wake. She averted her face, taking care not to look at him, until they came to their horses.

He watched her unsling the pack horse's saddlebags and followed suit, loosening the girth of Aquila's saddle. The bay stallion breathed a relieved sigh in response. Decimus patted his silky hide. He breathed in the horse's earthy odour and ran his fingers along the leather martingale. Finding himself with a familiar companion in this alien world touched something deep within Decimus; it temporarily soothed his fraught nerves.

A woman's lilting voice sounded nearby. Decimus tensed again, keeping his head down. He glanced the woman who'd led them to the Silure capital standing in the doorway of her home, wiping her hands clean against her skirt. She spoke to Luciana, her eyes darting in his direction every so often. Decimus fiddled with a buckle on Aquila's bridle. A brief exchange between the women ensued before Luci turned to him, nodding in the hut's direction. '*Come,*' she silently mouthed.

Luciana wiped clean the last of the bronze dishes and handed it back to their host with a smile. 'Thank you kindly for the meal. I can't tell you the last time I've eaten so well.'

Saibh shrugged as she placed the bowl on a shelf. 'Just a bit of stewed beef, is all. I've plenty to share, and seeing as you've got no place to go…'

Luciana gently touched the woman's shoulder. 'I still appreciate it all the same. Leucus would echo my sentiment if he could speak.' She nodded to Decimus, seated on a pile of furs against the wall.

Saibh glanced at him and lowered her voice. 'There's something about him that unsettles me, it does.'

Luciana laughed. 'Don't worry, he cannot hear us.' She followed Saibh out a rear door to her garden and pasture. 'Leucus is harmless. You have nothing to fear from him.'

'I know.' Saibh scooped some dried barley into a bucket sitting by the door. 'But his very *look* unsettles me. Something unnatural about that one. The sidhe must have left him for a changeling.'

'He is a warrior.' Luciana climbed onto the top rail of the pasture fence and watched Saibh empty the bucket into her pigs' trough. 'His strength defies even the gods' curses.'

'I do not doubt it.' Saibh turned from the trough to scatter the remaining barley around her chicken pen. The birds clucked and scattered at her approach. 'Word is he left Eaden and Fearghas with dirtied noses.'

Luciana nodded.

A shrill whinny from the pasture greeted her and she laughed as Belena bounded up to the fence. She hopped down, smiling, as the mare halted and whiffled her muzzle over the top of Luciana's head.

'You two are quite the bonded pair, then.' Saibh slipped through the pasture fence and shooed a few of the chickens blocking her path.

'She expects I've brought her a treat.' Luciana pulled a chunk of bread from her pocket and giggled as the mare inhaled it. 'To be fair to her, she's rarely wrong.'

Her eyes languidly followed the Silure's progress to where Aquila and the gelding stood just inside the pasture. She gasped as she watched Saibh reach for the long saddle blanket on Aquila's back. 'Wait! Don't do that!'

'It's fine.' Saibh tugged at the folds. 'There's plenty room for them three in the pasture with my mare. No need to let them…' Her voice trailed off as she lifted the blanket and caught sight of the imperial brand on Aquila's flank.

Luciana winced. She slowly strode over to the Silure woman. 'Saibh, I know what you must think…'

The woman turned to her, eyes wide. 'You stole them from the Romans.'

Luciana halted, her body swaying slightly in the evening breeze. Silently, she nodded.

'I wondered how you might have come by such fine animals, considering how different they look from your girl.' Saibh admiringly patted the stallion's shoulder. Aquila, oblivious to the humans, lowered his head to graze. 'I hate to think what the Romans might do to me if they discover them.'

'You are under no obligation to let us stay here.' Luciana hastened forward. 'If you'd rather we left, please say the word and we will go.'

Saibh shook her head as she pulled the blanket from the back of the other horse. 'No. Please, stay. Your home is a hard two days' ride away, and you haven't any friends among our tribe. It would be more dangerous if you stayed outside our village.' She faced Luciana, a defiant spark to her gentle gaze. 'Let the Romans do what they will. I shan't quake in fear of their tyranny any longer.'

Luciana relaxed, grinning. 'Perhaps the old druid is right; the wrath of Andraste *shall* take hold in the hearts of our people!'

Saibh snorted. 'Little hope of *that* in a tribe whose chieftain won't give women their rightful place on the battlefield.'

Luciana cocked her head. 'Are there many who share your frustrations, Saibh?'

'More than a few, I reckon.' Saibh folded the Roman saddle blankets and tucked an auburn wave behind her ear. 'The elders, for one, feel that Morcant has shown nothing but disrespect for The Old One since he took power. The warriors and noblewomen resent losing their positions and their voices among his council. As for me,' she shrugged and met Luciana's gaze. 'I just resent being told I have no say in the affairs of my own people.'

Luciana gazed at her thoughtfully. 'You're a warrior, aren't you?'

'How did you know?'

'The markings on your shield.' Luciana nodded towards Saibh's house.

'The one hanging on your wall. You come from a family of warriors.'

Saibh nodded. She watched the horses for a silent moment, brows furrowed. 'And I don't intend for my generation to be the last,' she breathed.

'What do you mean?'

Saibh turned to her. 'As I'm keeping your secret, you are bound to keep mine.'

Luciana nodded.

'I'm training the younger women in swordcraft,' she sighed. 'Every few days, the older warriors and I take them out to the forest, claiming to gather wood. Instead, we practice battle tactics. We're keeping our skills sharp and training up the youngsters.' She regarded Luciana evenly. 'We'll be ready, when the time comes, to serve a chieftain that knows our worth.'

'I might have to see one of these training sessions for myself.' Luciana smiled. 'It seems you Silure women have found a way to reclaim your voices.'

Saibh shook her head. 'Hardly. It's an impotent protest, one confined to the shadows. We shan't have any say in our tribe's future until Morcant is gone. But I won't let my sword go rusty just because he says so. It isn't the natural order of things. It isn't how our ancestors or our neighbours say we should live.' She wrinkled her nose. 'It reeks of Roman and Greek civilisation.'

'Quite!' Luciana laughed and fell into step with Saibh as they headed for the house. 'I'm glad to know we are of one mind!'

***

'Well?'

The slave woman glanced around the screen shielding Cassia's quarters from the rest of the chambers on the hall's second floor. She dropped to the ground by Cassia's skirts and bowed her head. 'The woman is lodging with Saibh, the one with the pasture and pigsty on the edge of the settlement. She is with a man, and they have three horses.'

Cassia stilled. 'A man?'

The slave nodded.

'What did the man look like?'

The woman scrunched her face in thought. 'He was…tall. He wore native clothing, including a sash across his torso like so.' She motioned a diagonal pattern from her shoulder to her opposite hip. 'He had the spiked hair of the Gaesatae and…a wheel pendant around his neck.'

'How old did he look?' Cassia sat forward. 'Did he have a beard? Was it grey?'

The slave studied the wall, brows furrowed. 'Yes…he had a beard. He looked older than the woman I followed.'

Decimus. It had to be. Cassia clutched her phallus charm. 'And nobody saw you?'

The slave shook her head.

'Nemesis preserve me.' Cassia sat back on her pallet, studying the conical ceiling. What were they doing here?! She was so close, and they were about to spoil everything! She had seen the look Luciana had given her in the hall. She had recognised her. Had Antiope's spell lost its power so quickly? Would Morcant now see her true identity?

If he doesn't, Luciana could tell him. I have to get rid of them. I need to stop them before they stop me. Cassia lifted her head. She met the light brown eyes of the slave. 'At first light, you will seek the woman out. Tell her to take her man to the woods west of the settlement at the eleventh hour. I wish to speak to them both.'

The woman fidgeted. 'And…if she refuses?'

'Threaten her. Tell her that an assassin will come for her man. That her eyes will fall out. That Morcant will eject her. I don't care what you say, just make sure she complies!'

The slave hung her head. 'Yes, Domina.'

Cassia quickly sat up. She narrowed her eyes at the woman. Her black hair hung in loose, untidy tresses and her native dress, free of any fibulae or adornments, was frayed at the hem and sleeves. The heavy iron collar at her throat and a woad character running down the side of her face marked her, like the other servants in Morcant's hall, as a slave. Her dark complexion didn't stand out from the Silure people, who seemed darker than other Britons. But there was something about her that didn't look British, even if Cassia couldn't quite put her finger on it.

'Of course…' Shame flushed Cassia's cheeks behind her veil. 'You're a Roman, aren't you?'

The woman mutely nodded.

She should have realised it the moment she heard the woman's fluent Latin, untainted by the throaty accent of natives attempting to speak it. She glanced at the statuette of Nemesis, standing among a makeshift altar of candles and offering bowl at the foot of her pallet. Had revenge so blinded her that she'd failed to notice?

She placed a hand on the woman's shoulder. 'How…?'

'The Silures raided a few settlements outside the vicus at Glevum. They waited for the legion to leave on campaign before they attacked. Two summers ago, now. They killed any men they found, raided our farms, and took the women captive.' The slave quickly swiped at her reddening eyes. 'I was one of the ones taken.'

'I'm so sorry.' Cassia squeezed the woman's worryingly thin arm. Having been born a slave herself, she knew the frustrating limits of such servitude. But working as a slave in a wealthy senator's villa was worlds apart from being in thrall to a stinking barbarian chieftain.

Cassia studied the top of the woman's head. 'What is your name?'

'I have no name.' The slave stood, shrugging her off. 'I am no person.' She marched to the screen and paused, looking at Cassia over her shoulder. 'I live only to serve. And I will do as you wish.'

Luciana opened one eye in the darkness and slowly let it adjust. She cautiously lifted her head from Decimus's chest and gazed across the room. The fire Saibh had lit in her central hearth had long since died, dousing the room in gloomy shadows. The walls, adorned simply with a brightly coloured woven blanket and a couple of bull skulls, communicated the middling status Saibh held within her tribe. An oval shield stood against one of the gently curving walls, one corner glinting dully in the darkened room. It had been shoved behind a tightly bunched group of woven baskets containing Saibh's food stores. Her meagre dishes and cookware stood piled on a low wooden shelf built into the wall, with her tiny wooden table and single stool tucked directly underneath. The round posts used to form the building's frame visibly ringed the perimeter of the single room. Their beams stretched above the daub and wattle walls and gradually sloped inwards, supported by meticulous latticework that fortified the conical thatched roof. Saibh lived a far cruder existence than the life Luciana had led as a chieftain's daughter.

The woman in question lay on the other side of the room, bundled in blankets and stretched across a narrow wooden bedframe. Her face was turned to the wall, hidden from Luciana's sight. She watched her closely for signs of alertness. Saibh's frame steadily rose and fell in the shadows for a long while. A small groan sounded in her throat as her legs shifted on the frame. Then the moment passed. Her steady breathing resumed.

Luciana lowered her head and slithered along Decimus's body. She clasped his arm and whispered his name in the darkness.

'I'm awake.' He glared up at the funnel-shaped ceiling. 'I've been awake.'

'My love, relax.' She kissed his collarbone, stroking one finger along his arm. 'You're doing marvellously.'

'Am I?' He swallowed, his gaze still trained on the latticework; to his mind, it resembled the domes of birdcages he'd seen in crowded market stalls housing exotic birds from Africa and the far east. 'I have no fucking clue what I'm even doing here.'

'You seem to be holding up.' A smile pulled at her lips as she tapped his skin. 'Those Silure warriors you met seemed to be sufficiently cowed.'

Decimus winced, his bruised body still throbbing from the earlier encounter. 'I think it might have been the other way around.'

'Come, now. Morcant seemed impressed.'

He alertly met her gaze. 'What did he say about me?'

'That you were a handy and capable fighter.' She frowned. 'Why do you care so much?'

'He knows who I am. He remembers that skirmish on the moor.' He turned his head away and gazed across the room. 'I know it.'

'You don't know a thing.' She gently took his whiskered chin between her hands and tilted it towards her. She smiled at the bright streaks of woad lining his face. 'Do you think he'd have allowed you a place on his war council if he recognised you?'

His eyebrows flew up. 'You know when the war council will convene?'

'Hush!' She glanced furtively at Saibh before nestling her head tightly against his. 'The western tribes are convening at the next full moon,' she whispered into his ear. 'Morcant will allow you to accompany his contingent, and I am to go as your interpreter.'

'How soon will that be?' He breathed.

She considered for a moment. 'In another week, I should think.'

'That long?' Decimus gulped. He felt the anxious knot in his stomach twist with a sickening lurch. 'I don't know if I'll make it that long.'

'Of course you will, my brave heart.' She kissed his cheek, idly fingering the wheel of Taranis about his neck. 'Your courage shall not fail you.'

He grunted. 'It's not that. It's this playacting bollocks in a nest of headhunting vipers that worries me.'

'What playacting? You *are* half-Celt, after all.' She smiled sweetly in response to his scowl. 'Just keep your wits about you and your eyes open. Morcant's up to something more, and I don't like it.'

'What do you mean?'

She laid a finger across his lips and glanced at Saibh. 'Keep your voice *down!*' She lowered her head and nuzzled his cheek. 'I'm not sure yet,' she breathed. 'I don't know why Cassia's here, and it worries me. We need to get rid of her before she blows our cover.'

'Hmm.' Decimus drummed his fingers absently. 'I still can't believe you saw her in Morcant's hall. You must have been mistaken.'

'I *wasn't*. It was her. Trust me.' Luciana pursed her lips. 'And it's not just her presence that bodes ill. It might have been something the druid said, or the way Morcant's been treating women since he assumed leadership. But there's more to this than their plans for war.'

'I take it your reunion wasn't on the best of terms?'

'Clever lad.' She kissed his lips. 'Don't worry. I can take Morcant's abuse.'

He stiffened, drawing his burly arms around her spine. 'You shouldn't have to.'

'No?' She cocked a brow. 'I've received plenty of the same at your hands, if I recall.'

'But that is very different,' he murmured, nibbling at her ear.

She giggled. 'How so?'

'Because you give as good as you get.' He trailed his hands along her back and squeezed her bottom. A low growl rumbled in his throat. 'And I love it.'

She squeaked and saw Saibh groggily lift her head in the darkness. 'Oh, Leucus!' She cried, capturing his mouth with hers. She kissed him hungrily, digging her nails into his broad shoulder. Her other hand reached into his pants and eagerly clasped his penis.

Their hostess lay down. She turned her back on the lovers as they began to roughly fumble one another across the floor.

XVI

'Get up! Tullius!'

Tullius's eyes flew open as he sat up in bed. He stared at the trunk clothed in shadow at the end of the bed. He drew in deep gasps. A rivulet of sweat ran down the side of his nose.

Gradually, his head stopped spinning. He heaved an enormous sob. *It was just a dream. It wasn't real. Just a dream…*

'Tullius.' A broad, comforting hand ran along his spine.

He slowly turned. Porcius sat up against the pillows, frowning. He slowly stroked his back, eyes glittering in the darkness.

'You were screaming.'

Tullius nodded. He ran a hand through his hair and swiped at his damp brow. 'The son of Night disturbed my slumber.' He smiled. 'Thanks for chasing him away.'

'Not a pleasant dream, then?'

'Mmm.' Tullius eased himself down next to Porcius. The tonsor lifted his fingers and began to idly fondle Tullius's damp locks.

'A copper for your thoughts.'

Tullius met Porcius's gentle eyes. He could hardly make out the taut lines wrinkling his brow. The noble angle of his impressive nose swathed half his face in shadow. His strong, bearded jaw trembled slightly. A small, inviting smile pulled at the corners of his lips.

'I…' Tullius closed his eyes. 'I don't deserve your kindness.'

'You needn't shoulder your burdens in solitude.'

'Hmm.' Tullius nestled his head against Porcius's solid, formidable chest. He deeply inhaled Porcius's musky scent and felt himself relax as completely as if he were beneath a drape in the tonsor's chair.

The pair rested in silence for a long moment. The distant laughter of male companionship and the clinking of wine pitchers trickled through the open bars of Porcius's window.

Porcius's reassuring touch enveloped Tullius. He felt a warm, contented glow rise through his stomach, envelop his shoulders, and smooth over the worried lines pinching his face. He sighed. 'My father was a medicus.'

Porcius stilled. 'I don't think you've ever mentioned the gens Tulii.'

'There isn't much to say for them.' Tullius buried his nose in the crook of Porcius's neck. 'I hated him.'

'Well…' Porcius kissed Tullius's crown. 'I suppose we all have that spectre to contend with.'

'He *forced* Antonia on me.' Tullius scowled. 'He thrust that child bride into my hands and then immediately enrolled me in the legions.'

Porcius ran a hand along Tullius's arm. His fingers paused to carefully trace every scar he encountered. 'Do you think he knew?' He finally breathed.

'He couldn't!' Tullius wrenched himself up, arms propped over Porcius's naked bulk. He squinted in the shadows, meeting Porcius's eyes. '*I* haven't…I didn't…until we…'

'Tullius…' Porcius's face fell. 'It isn't wrong. Who we are, what we're doing…it isn't wrong.'

'Tell that to my wife and child.' Tullius clambered off him and sat up on the edge of the bed. He buried his face in his hands.

He heard the blankets rustle behind him. He felt Porcius's gaze boring into the back of his head. His fingertips pressed harder against his brow as a wave of nausea gripped him.

'Aristotle wrote that there are three kinds of friendship, two incidental and one perfect.'

'Spare me your philosophy,' Tullius groaned.

'Friendships that only provide service or pleasure are easily dissolved.' Porcius paused. 'You once told me that giving your wife a son was a loathsome husbandly duty.'

'And I *owe* them that duty!' Tullius sat up, clutching his stomach. He stared at the ceiling, willing the bile to stop rising in his throat. 'It's… selfish…'

He promptly leant over and studied the floorboards. The revulsion swirling within him threatened to empty his stomach. He clutched at the bedsheets, breathing heavily. He trembled violently as he fought the urge to vomit. When the danger finally passed, he collapsed against the mattress.

'"Those who wish well to their friends for their sake are most truly friends; for they do this by reason of their own nature and not incidentally."' Porcius's fingers lightly rested on his shoulder. 'I only wish you *well*, Tullius.'

Tullius choked and stood from the bed. He grabbed his clothes, hating the way his cheeks burned, hating the warmth stirring in his belly, hating the way his loins reacted to Porcius saying his name.

'You don't have to go.'

Tullius pulled his tunic over his head and grabbed his sandals. He gazed at the floor, shaking his head. 'I can't do this, I can't…'

'If you'd only wait until morning. You're not well…' Porcius reached for his wrist, just brushing it.

'I'm not a fucking catamite!' Tullius backed away from his touch. 'None of this…makes me…a catamite!'

Porcius regarded him silently, features masked by the darkness.

A fresh wave of nausea gripped Tullius. His head swam, haunted by the demons in his dreams. Doubled over, he darted down the ladder and out the back door of Porcius's shop.

Luciana sat up and gazed about Saibh's darkened home. The inky sky through the window announced the coming dawn. She stifled a moan and crawled out from beneath the blankets. She'd grown too accustomed to waking with the buccina calling the first hour.

She stole across the room and slipped silently out Saibh's back door. A cool breeze kissed her skin as she leant against the wall. The dewy grass tickled her ankles. She inhaled deeply, relishing the dawn. As her eyes slowly adjusted to the dark, she listened for voices or movements. Nothing. Not even a whiff of a reignited hearth. The Silures were yet to wake.

Luciana pushed away from the wall and stepped around Saibh's sty. A few of the hogs grunted, but the chickens made no peep. With a quick glance back at the house, Luciana slipped between the boards fencing Saibh's pasture. She could just make out the shadowy forms of horses standing in a cluster, snorting and swishing their tails. She whistled softly.

One of the horses broke away and slowly ambled over. Luciana felt Belena's hot, sweet breath as the mare shoved her muzzle against her chest. 'Good morning, girl,' she cooed, burying her fingers in Belena's thick, wiry mane.

'Domina…'

Luciana spun around alertly. She frowned at the sight of an unfamiliar woman cowering just outside the fence. An iron slave collar hung about her throat. 'Who are you?'

'Domina, please. I come from my mistress, the priestess, bearing a message.'

'The priestess…' Luciana stilled. *Cassia*. She knew it.

'She says-,'

'Wait.' Luciana held up a finger. She pushed Belena's head aside and ducked through the fence. 'Stay here. I'll be back.'

She darted into Saibh's house and padded silently across the dirt floor. She glanced once at Saibh. The woman's form steadily rose and fell, her back to the hearth. Luciana bit her lip and knelt beside Decimus. To her relief, he was awake. His blue-grey eyes glittered in the pre-dawn gloom. The grim lines pinching his mouth belied his anxiety. Had he even slept at all?

'Come.' She whispered, taking his wrist. She helped him slowly clamber to his feet, pausing every few heartbeats to check Saibh hadn't stirred. Then, as quickly as she could, she ushered him out the rear door.

He didn't speak until they'd rounded the pig shed. 'What in the name of Mithras-,'

'Shh!' Luciana scowled at him. She drew him to a halt before the slave woman and gestured to her. 'She comes from Cassia. Who has a message for us.'

Decimus's eyes widened.

Luciana faced the woman. 'Well?'

'My mistress wants to speak to you.' The slave glanced uneasily between Luciana and Decimus. 'She says you are to meet her at the clearing with the rock, on the western edge of the settlement, at the eleventh hour tonight.'

Luciana scowled at Decimus. 'I told you it was her. Do you still doubt it?'

Decimus's nostrils flared. 'But why? What could *she* be doing here?'

Luciana shushed him. She turned to the slave. 'Tell your mistress we'll be there, at the eleventh hour.'

The woman nodded and stepped back.

Luciana straightened. 'And also…'

'Yes, Domina?'

Luciana narrowed her eyes, meeting the woman's timid gaze. 'Tell her I know.'

She frowned. 'Is…is that all?'

Luciana nodded. 'She will understand.'

The slave turned and slunk away between the houses.

'What do we do until then?' Decimus breathed. His guarded gaze followed the woman's progress until she disappeared.

'We carry on, doing what we came here to do.' Luciana bit her lip. She crossed her arms and hugged herself. 'She won't give us away until we've spoken to her first.' She glanced up at Decimus. 'Won't she?'

He shook his head. His tense shoulders and taut jaw betrayed his own doubts.

She wished he didn't look as uneasy as she felt.

Cassia scowled, carefully stirring a mixture before her. She sat on the dirt atop a small but rather steep rocky hill behind the chieftain's hut, Morcant and Taraghlan nearby. She added tinctures she'd taken from Antiope to a silver bowl brimming with a golden, hoppy liquid the natives were fond of. Every now and then, she glanced at the men.

Taraghlan hunched over a speckled hen. He had instructed Morcant to hold the bird down while he shakily split it open with his remaining hand. He bent close to study its entrails, heedless of the ripe, gaseous odour emanating from the chicken. Morcant paced behind him, fists clenched at his sides.

Cassia noticed her slave cresting the rise and she beckoned her to her side. She continued preparing her mixture with studied disinterest as the slave knelt on the grass beside her. 'Well?'

'She will come.'

Cassia arched a brow. 'And…?'

'She will bring the man.' The woman turned to face Cassia. 'She told me to tell you she knows.'

Cassia's spoon clattered against the side of her silver cup. She nodded, swallowing the knot of anxiety rising within her. 'Very good,' she breathed.

The slave bowed her head. Cassia stared at her veiled reflection in the amber drink. *She knows.* She already knew Luciana had recognised her, but she felt the message held more than that. Had she figured out that Cassia had sicced the legion's lecherous former tribune, Titianus, on her last winter? Cassia had watched from her window as the tribune had nearly raped Luciana. If it hadn't been for the intervention of that girl from the caupona, he would have succeeded. She hadn't wanted to do it, even if she did resent Decimus's obvious affection for Luciana. But her brother, Cato, had been killed by Luciana's hand. It was the least she'd deserved in retribution. Wasn't it?

An angry bark from Morcant startled Cassia back to the present. She turned to see him hovering over the druid's shoulder. He pointed at the chicken guts and then at the sky, waiting for Taraghlan's response.

Taraghlan spoke in a solemn, measured tone. He shook his head, gazing at the bird. Whatever he'd said had evidently displeased the chieftain, for Morcant shoved him aside and stormed over to Cassia.

'Taraghlan says Andraste's prophecy is unchanged.' He pointed at her cup. 'I heard from my Roman contact soon after I made your sacrifice. Tell me, what do your Roman gods want now?'

'In exchange for altering a greater god's prophecy?' Cassia gently swirled the liquid. 'You ask for quite a lot.'

'Just tell me what to do!' He snapped.

Cassia smiled and lifted the cup. 'Drink this, and they will tell you all.'

Morcant snatched it up and gulped the mixture down. Taraghlan made an alarmed sound, rising from his seat. Cassia smirked. It was too late now.

The chieftain gripped his head and sank to the earth. He stayed upright, rocking back and forth. Cassia waited, chin lifted. She heard Antiope's voice counting steadily in her head. *Now his vision will swim…now he loses control of his limbs…* She watched Morcant's arms fall limply to his sides. *And now…he is entranced.*

'Morcant of the Silures, do you hear me?' She intoned.

He answered in his native tongue, though his head dipped in assent.

Cassia turned to her slave. 'Keep Taraghlan busy.' She watched the Roman woman scurry off and swipe the druid's sacrificial knife. She turned back to Morcant. 'You, Morcant of the Silures, must journey to realise your ambition.'

'Tell me…' he muttered, '…where to go.'

'Rise.' Cassia stood, motioning with her hand. Morcant followed her as obediently as a dog. Out of the corner of her eye, she spied Taraghlan's turned back as he chased her slave. *Perfect.* 'Now turn to the east.' She twirled a finger.

Morcant turned in place until he faced the steepest edge of the bluff.

'Now, walk forward. Do not stop until I tell you to.'

Her heart began to race as he took one halting step, then another. He shuffled closer to the edge of the hill.

Cassia followed, looking over his shoulder. In just a few steps, the ground would fall away. Large, pointed rocks studded the hill's side and the ground below. He wouldn't fall far, but it was deadly enough. With Nemesis's blessing, he wouldn't survive the drop. 'Keep going,' she murmured. 'Don't stop now…'

Morcant hovered just over the edge. A few pebbles dislodged from underfoot and clattered down the steep escarpment. Cassia grinned. A giggle slipped loose at the thought of Morcant's demise. *This was it!*

Taraghlan hollered behind her. His lone hand reached out, grabbing Morcant just as he lurched forward. Morcant's legs crumpled under him and battered the side of the hill, sending a shower of small stones down the treacherous side.

Cassia's shoulders slumped. She stepped aside as Taraghlan hauled Morcant back from the ledge.

The slave, thinking quickly, tossed Taraghlan's knife over the steep ledge. He stood and advanced on her, shouting and angrily waving his arm. She shrank behind Cassia, clutching her shoulder.

Cassia hardly heard his garbled invective. She stared at the ground, stupefied. It hadn't worked…*why* hadn't it worked?

Taraghlan whirled about and stomped. He couldn't drag Morcant down the hill with one hand, and the warriors guarding the chieftain's hut stood all the way at the bottom. Unarmed and alone, he posed little immediate threat.

The slave tugged her towards the hill's descent. She squeaked in alarm when Taraghlan turned and planted himself in their way. He narrowed his eyes, fingers splayed in Cassia's direction. He chanted some threatening cant in his own tongue before hobbling down the rise.

Cassia sank to her knees. She didn't know what sort of magicks the druid had cast her way, but there was no mistaking her place in Morcant's retinue had been lost. She wouldn't be welcome in the chieftain's hall anymore. If they believed Taraghlan as much as they seemed to, Morcant and his warriors wouldn't hesitate to kill her should they see her again.

Her stomach churned. She felt an anxious knot in her chest slowly travel up her throat, where it remained trapped. Tears streaked down her cheeks. All this preparation, all this planning, gone. And Morcant still lived.

She lifted her head to the sky. 'Nemesis, why have you forsaken me? Please, show me out of this! I am your loyal servant!'

The Roman slave hovered next to her and shook her shoulder as Cassia crumpled to the ground. 'Domina…Domina, we must leave this place.'

Cassia groaned. She held her breath for several long moments, fervently praying for a sign.

'Domina…'

When she opened them again, she found herself gazing directly into the blank, beady eyes of a brown toad.

She stared at the creature for a long moment, mouth agape. Finally, she managed to croak, 'Messenger of Nemesis…tell me what the goddess desires.'

The toad blinked, nestled within tall grasses. It sat near the edge of a puddle that filled a tiny gulley on the hilltop's uneven surface.

Cassia took measured, silent breaths to keep from disturbing the creature. Still rapt, she slowly shook her head. 'I…I don't understand. I know that, but what is it supposed to mean?'

The toad hopped to one side, angling its body away from her.

'But it's all gone wrong! I can't continue in my guise. What am I supposed to do?' She sat up, beseeching the disinterested toad.

It wriggled over a corner of the puddle and leapt into the reeds sloping down the hill's western slope.

Cassia stood and fixed her veil, nodding. 'I won't claim to understand your wisdom, great goddess, but I trust in you. And I shall follow.' She turned to the slave. 'Come. Let's leave before Morcant realises we've gone.'

The pair strode down the knoll, following the direction indicated by the toad.

Luciana strode across the settlement, frowning. Her mind raced, fretting over Cassia's summons. Why send a slave with the message? And what could she be *doing* here? She absently chewed a nail, tasting the bitter dirt caked underneath. She'd spent the morning and most of the afternoon helping Saibh tend her animals and weed her pastures. She'd soon found herself growing impatient and slipped away when Saibh disappeared into the forest. She'd invited Luciana to help her train the Silure women, but Luciana had declined. She needed to learn what Morcant was up to, and the slave woman's message made her uneasy. Was Cassia about to ruin everything?

'Enough with this mystery! Are you with us or not?'

Luciana raised her head in the direction of the voice. Morcant lurched outside the entrance to the chieftain's hut, his druid advisor in tow. They met a mounted contingent of Britons who'd just ridden into the settlement. The man who'd spoken slowly dismounted. He was cloaked in a rich blue garment and bejewelled vambraces. A group of bare-chested warriors closely flanked him.

Morcant shook his head, looking around furtively. 'We must discuss this matter civilly and privately.' He gestured to the entrance of his hall.

The visitor curtly nodded and fell into step behind Morcant and Taraghlan. A lithe, hulking man tossed his reins to another warrior and hastened to the visitor's side.

Luciana slowly glanced around to make sure the other Silures milling about paid her no mind. She crouched behind a stone not far from the chieftain's doorway.

Morcant stopped just outside and whirled to face the man in blue. 'Leave your bodyguard outside.'

The visitor drew himself up haughtily. 'Osgar goes where I go. If you won't permit his presence in our party, I shall leave this moment.'

'You wouldn't dare,' Morcant sneered.

The middle-aged noble glared back, his expression stony. Neither moved for a long, breathless moment.

Finally, with an angry growl, Morcant threw up an arm and shrugged. 'Have it your way, then, Muireach!'

As the party trooped inside, Luciana turned away, slumping against the boulder. *'Muireach,'* she mouthed. She knew the name well enough, but she wondered what the chieftain of the Ordovices needed to discuss so urgently with Morcant.

She peered around the edge of the stone. One of the sentries posted at the entrance of Morcant's hut had stalked off to the Ordovice warriors, pointing at their mounts and proffering directions for food and shelter. The other sentry remained on watch beside the door. The blond man stood with erect bearing, the long shaft of his wooden spear ground firmly at his side.

Luciana glanced around as she slipped away from the stone. Once she'd travelled far enough from the hut to appear inconspicuous, she straightened to a stand and marched confidently around in an arc towards the entrance. Her eyes stared directly at the door, her steps sure as she made to move past the lone sentry.

'Halt.' The warrior, surprisingly soft spoken for his frame, laid a meaty palm on her shoulder. He jerked her back to stand before him. 'What do you think you're doing?'

'I need to speak with the chieftain. Immediately.' Luciana ducked her head and tried to skirt around him. In one step, her face collided against his bare, hulking chest. The pungent aroma of fresh sweat and a foul, acrid body odour curled her nostrils.

'Morcant's busy. He's left instructions not to be disturbed. You may speak with him later.' The soft-voiced warrior frowned down at her, refusing to budge.

Luciana opened her mouth to retort, then thought better of it. Her fiery words died in her throat as a sensual smile spread across her face. 'Very well. I'd rather see you than Morcant, anyway.' She wound her arms about his neck.

The warrior's eyes widened. 'I'm not looking for trouble. What about that Belgae brute you rode in with?'

'What about him?' She tilted her head and cocked a brow, letting her fingers dance down his cheek before trailing over his tattooed stomach. 'What he doesn't know won't hurt him.'

Beads of perspiration broke across the warrior's forehead. He groaned, taking Luciana by the arm. Her fingers grabbed his penis through his braccae. She watched his face carefully. Then, with a sharp twist, she wrenched him around by his manhood. Her smile hardened in satisfaction as the warrior whined, eyes widening.

The sentry stumbled aside, both hands clasping his throbbing crotch. He sobbed, heedless of Luciana, who'd coldly turned and marched inside Morcant's hut.

'…make the first strike.'

'But why? By standing together, all the tribes possess an equal share in the fortunes of war. Surely the pursuit of glory cannot goad you to make such a demand.'

Luciana crept up to a small anteroom sectioned off from the vast banquet chamber. She crouched just outside, cautiously peering around the doorframe.

Morcant's limber form sat on one side of a small, sturdy oaken bench, his back to Luciana. Taraghlan perched just beside his right shoulder. Muireach, chieftain of the Ordovice tribe, sat cattycorner to the Silures across a central hearth. Luciana studied his broad, craggy face, his soft brown hair curling about his shoulders, his grey, drooping moustache. His brown complexion whispered of his Sidhe ancestry, which had, alongside his intelligence, bolstered him to a position of reverence among his people. His bare-chested bodyguard hovered directly behind his seat.

'The rest of you don't stand a chance without my warriors. All I ask for is the vanguard. That my men attack the Romans first.' Morcant idly stroked the stumps of his shortened fingers. 'I have my reasons.'

'So, the Silures strike first and then fall back to our lines?' Muireach frowned. 'Then your warriors will cooperate with the rest of our host?'

'If we must,' Morcant growled.

'And just when is this first attack to be?'

'When the Romans are least prepared for it.' A dark chuckle rumbled in Morcant's throat. 'When they emerge from their fortress to wage war, their line of march shall take them directly through a narrow, forested vale lodged deep in your mountain passes. My warriors shall lay in wait until the entire snake, from the vanguard to the baggage train, is inside the trap. They'll be annihilated.'

Muireach pursed his lips. 'How can you be sure the Romans will take that path?'

'I have my ways.'

'Wouldn't such an attack only call reinforcements to our front?'

Morcant shrugged. 'All the better. More Romans for your men to kill, and a depletion of Rome's presence in the north will only aid Venutius in his bid to regain the Brigantian throne.'

'Hmm.' Muireach crossed his arms and sat back. Morcant lowered his hand to his lap so his fingers could drum silently against his trousers, unseen. Finally, after an interminable silence, the older chieftain sighed. 'I don't like it, Morcant. There's something unnatural about the whole business. But I can't fault your logic. The more we impede their line of march, the safer Mona will be.' His gaze darkened. 'And if that means letting you act alone in the first battle, then I shall reluctantly agree.'

Morcant's shoulders straightened. 'Very wise. I knew you'd see sense. The question is, what about the others?'

'I shall speak to them in advance of the council. Banna, I think, should be agreeable.'

Morcant snorted derisively. 'She would.'

'*You* would be wise to listen to her. The Demetae are a proud, spiritual people. They pay our gods more than just dues, they keep to themselves, and they are cunning in the ways of territorial defence. Their leader is likewise nothing short of formidable.'

'She is a woman.' Morcant shook his head. 'Women cannot be trusted. They are quick to change allegiances to whomever serves their own interests best. I'd sooner trust her to surrender our forts than lead our host to victory.' He turned his head and spat a wad of phlegm on the floor. 'She's no different from that bitch Cartimandua and every other British queen.'

Muireach's frown deepened. 'You do our noble queens a great dishonour. One dirty traitress does not outstrip the loyalty of the rest!'

'*I*, dishonour?' Morcant pressed his palms against his knees and leant forward. 'You'd better think long and hard before throwing such words at me, old dog, if you wish for the cooperation of my men!'

The sound of hurried footsteps behind her made Luciana's heart leap into her throat. She withdrew her head and pressed tightly against the wall, cloaking her form in the dining hall's long shadows.

A dark-haired man in mud-spattered trousers and leather jerkin bustled past her into the room.

'What is it?!' Morcant shouted irritably from the alcove.

The man must have bent close to Morcant's ear, for Luciana could hear nothing more than an indecipherable murmur. As the Silure relayed his message, feet scraped against the compacted floor. Suddenly, the hem of Taraghlan's white robe floated before her. Luciana recoiled, gazing up at the priest. It seemed the druid's gaze bore directly through her. Then, to her relief, he turned and stole away.

Though his gait seemed as stately and forbidding as ever, something about the priest's demeanour seemed strange. Glancing around to make sure she hadn't been spotted, she rose into a crouch and followed him. As she passed the alcove, three of the messenger's muttered words inflected high enough to reach her ears: *'Prasutagus…Iceni…dead.'*

Luciana closed her eyes as a dull pang tore through her heart. The news was hardly surprising, but the defeat of such a proud, sure warrior to his wasting disease saddened her. She spared a thought for Boudicca and her daughters. They must be terrified now they'd lost the man standing between their tribe and Rome.

She blinked, letting her eyes adjust to the shadows. She watched Taraghlan slip outside and hastened to keep him in sight. She approached the doorway and paused, risking a glance at the sentries. The absent man had returned. He stood with his back to the door, angrily trying to make sense of the other guard's sob-mangled words. Ducking her head, she darted past them and rounded a hut. In the distance, she saw Taraghlan making for the forested hillside beyond the river basin. She turned her steps and went the opposite direction, passing several homes on her way to the livestock pens.

Her hair fluttered behind her, dogging her purposeful steps. She turned her head about, inspecting the settlement. Everything and everyone suddenly seemed vaguely threatening, despite the slivers of pale spring sunshine illuminating the village. A placid cow chewing her cud gazed at Luciana, following her path. Unnerved, Luciana rounded the next house and slowly circled back to the hills.

She cut a path across a meadow and entered the woods just as the druid did several paces away. Gathering her skirt about her hips, she skipped through the brush, eyes locked on her target. Taraghlan's grey head disappeared and reappeared through the trunks and shady branches, guiding her along a twisting, trailless route through the forest's undergrowth.

Luciana swallowed her breaths, panting shallowly through her nose. Thorns and twigs caught at her hair, threatening to pull her back. She ploughed on, leaving the occasional gold strand trailing in her wake.

Suddenly, Taraghlan stopped. Luciana halted and crouched beneath a shady elm. She watched the druid round a sizable boulder just within a sacred oak circle.

A twig snapped on the forest floor behind her.

Choking back a gasp, she whirled in the direction of the noise. The gorse surrounding her rustled gently and a squirrel leapt out. It scrabbled up the trunk and disappeared into the branches above her head.

Luciana closed her eyes for just a moment to calm her nerves. She turned back to her quarry.

Taraghlan had vanished.

She raced into the grove, searching for some sign of the druid. He couldn't be far! Which way had he gone? Had he seen her? Was she in danger?

She spun in a tight circle, the trunks blurring before her eyes. She imagined she glimpsed a pair of eyes, a flash of woad – a mirage? A shade of her ancestors? – before dizziness overwhelmed her. She sank to her knees, gasping.

Luciana waited for the world to stop spinning. Then, cautiously blinking, she swept her gaze over the brush for any clue to his trail. She crawled over to the rock where she'd last seen the druid.

Nothing. Not even a footprint or trampled branch to guide her.

Luciana ran her hands over the boulder. It looked and felt to be just a stone like any other. When she tried to push or pull it, the stone refused to budge. She wound a tight circle around it, reaching along its crevices for any clue as to where Taraghlan had gone. She'd made three thorough sweeps around the rock before giving up. She straightened, scanning the tightly packed trunks gathered around her. The hills' utter silence stirred a tight feeling of unease in her breast.

Where had he gone?

XVII

Tullius pulled his helmet off and gulped. He stared at the open doorway of the tonstrina, watching Porcius carefully clip a customer's hair. The man studiously avoided his gaze, concentrating on his task.

He'd resolved to never come back. He hadn't wanted to come back. And yet something within him seemed to drag his steps to Porcius's shop. He felt his stomach clench. With determined steps, Tullius strode inside and sat on the bench facing Porcius.

'*Salve*, Optio.'

He turned and noticed the squat, plump man waving from the chair. He nodded. 'Centurion Fortunatus. I…thank you for…assuming the primus pilus's responsibilities.'

'Think nothing of it. Couldn't have the legion dissolving into chaos, now, could we?'

Tullius nodded, feeling his cheeks burn. *Yet another failure of character I'll have to live with.*

'Saw those reports from the quartermaster. The food stores are excessive for this time of year.'

Porcius leant closer, carefully trimming the edges of Fortunatus's beard. 'Hold still, please, sir.'

Tullius shrugged. 'Well, we're getting ready for the summer's campaign, aren't we?'

'Hmm. I suppose.' Fortunatus muttered. 'It just…it doesn't look like the normal campaign preparations. As if we were going to be undertaking a large-scale, coordinated action instead of just punitive policing.'

Tullius studied his hands, twisting his black-and-white crested helmet in his lap. 'You might be right, at that. I don't know what's on the legate's mind. Or the governor's, for that matter.'

'I just wondered if the primus pilus mentioned anything of the sort to you.'

Tullius frowned. 'No, he didn't. Why do you ask?'

'He's the most likely of us to be in the legate's confidence. And the governor's. Didn't he spend the Saturnalia holidays with the pair of them in Londinium?'

Porcius met Tullius's eyes. Tullius quickly turned away, colouring at the memory of his own Saturnalia. 'Yes. Er…I believe that's correct.'

'There you are, then.' Fortunatus stood as Porcius whisked the towel away from his shoulders. He whistled and Tor roused himself from a cozy corner at the back of the shop. The hound padded over to Fortunatus's side.

Tullius frowned. 'Hang on. Isn't that Decimus's dog?'

'It is. I was told to look after him until further notice.' Fortunatus crouched to stroke Tor. 'I also happen to know he rode out of here with his woman, carrying a barbarian sword.' He glanced over his shoulder at Porcius. 'You didn't hear that from me.'

Porcius held up his hands.

The centurion turned to Tullius, his voice hushed. 'That's as much as I've got. I was wondering…if you might know anything more?'

Tullius wrinkled his nose. 'I don't. Why would you think that?'

'Because the pair of you are closer than a pair of arse cheeks, man!' Fortunatus slapped his shoulder. 'He really must be knee deep in the governor's affairs if you're just as clueless as I am.'

A small smile pulled at the corners of Tullius's mouth. He nodded.

'Come on, I'll stand you a drink at Bakari's.' Fortunatus moseyed to the doorway. 'He's been keeping broth bones for Tor here. Stingy old Metellus needs his for his *paying* customers.'

Tor barked, wagging his tail.

'Sorry, I…' Tullius felt his mouth go dry as he glanced between Porcius and Fortunatus. The pudgy centurion crossed his arms expectantly while the tonsor cleaned and packed away his blades, his back to Tullius.

'I…can't. I-I came in for a haircut myself.' Tullius sat down on Porcius's stool.

'You're a bit late, mate. The shop's closed. I had his last appointment.' Fortunatus pointed at the hours painted just outside the doorframe.

'It's all right, Centurion. I can squeeze the optio in.' Porcius draped his sheet around Tullius. 'Though he really must be my last one. If you wouldn't mind hanging up my closed sign on your way out…?'

Fortunatus glanced between them. Tullius couldn't help but burn beneath the suspicious light that sparked in Fortunatus's eyes. 'Yes…Yes, no matter. Another time, then, Optio.'

Tullius lifted a hand as Porcius grabbed a pair of shears. 'Another time.'

Fortunatus whistled and Tor followed him outside. He closed the door to the shop behind him, affixing Porcius's 'closed' sign to its customary nail.

Porcius sighed as Tullius stood from the seat. 'You came back.'

'Believe me, I didn't want to.' Tullius tossed the sheet at him. He walked across the room, blowing out the oil lamps perched on their sconces lining the shop.

'There's no reason to be ashamed, you know. It's okay if they know…'

'Know what?' Tullius whirled around, fists clenched at his sides. 'Why should the men know? Our affairs are no business of theirs.'

Porcius sidled up and took his hand. He lifted it to his lips and kissed Tullius's callused fingers. 'There's plenty of us within the legion.'

Tullius withdrew his hand, narrowing his eyes. 'What do you mean by "us?"'

'You know!' Porcius crossed his arms. 'Why else would you be here?'

'You mean catamites, don't you?' Tullius froze, disgust marring his features. His stomach churned, threatening to empty itself.

Porcius winced. 'I wouldn't use so ugly a word. Rather, I'd say we were men who preferred the company of other men.' His face softened. 'A beautiful, trusting bond between men who are good and alike in virtue…' He reached out to touch Tullius's cheek.

Tullius shrank away. 'I never so much as kept the company of other men until I joined the legion!'

'The desires of one's heart are often kept secret even to oneself.' Porcius shrugged. 'It doesn't matter if you didn't…'

'No! Stop!' Tullius held up a hand. 'I *won't* debate this in a seminar with you.' He pointed to the ladder. 'Now, come on. Get up there and shed your garments.'

'Is that all I am to you?' Porcius's face fell. His brow darkened. 'Just a vehicle for *sex?*'

'Why else did you think I'd ever come back?' Tears burned in the corners of Tullius's eyes. He swallowed them down, desperately trying to quell the bile rising in his throat. He frowned defiantly at Porcius's growing anger. 'You needn't despise me for it! I assure you, I'm plenty capable of despising myself!'

'I thought I was more than that.' Porcius slowly shook his head. 'I didn't just enjoy your body. I enjoyed your presence, your company, your *mind*. It was never just sex for me.' He breathed a shaky sigh. A tear fell free of his eye and trickled down his nose. 'And you mean to tell me…that to you, I've just been a piece of meat?'

Tullius's face burned. 'I don't see what the problem is! I have a need, and you fill it! It's no different from what Charis's whores do for the men!'

'But I am *not* your whore!'

Porcius's fist suddenly collided with Tullius's eye. Tullius staggered backward. His head swam as his vision blackened, merging the images of family members and men that haunted his dreams.

'I *don't* despise you. I pity you.'

Tullius gripped his head and cracked his good eye open. The room slowly stopped spinning, bringing Porcius into focus. The way his lined face crumpled with pain struck at something deep within Tullius; it was the expression he'd seen on his own son's face in his nightmares. And it hurt more, far more than he'd thought it would. The dull throb of his eye paled in comparison to the shame wrenching his chest.

'I thought ours was a lasting friendship, Aristotle's perfect bond between men who like one another for nothing more than the other's sake.' Porcius's voice trembled. 'But if I'm just someone you used for pleasure, then you can consider our friendship dissolved.' He pointed to the door. 'You need to go.'

Tullius felt his swollen eye weep and he covered his face in his hands. 'I can't…' He breathed, suddenly light-headed. 'I can't…'

'I can't help you anymore, and I was a fool for thinking I ever could. You can accept yourself or die miserable. But darken my door no longer.'

Tullius haltingly stumbled to the shop's rear exit. 'I'm…sorry!' With trembling fingers, he slammed the door behind him.

Decimus sat on the grass outside Saibh's hut, a few strips of leather unfurled in his lap. In need of something to occupy his nerves, he'd grabbed them and begun weaving them together into a bridle strap. Saibh had even paused on her way past to say something about his work. Though he'd no clue what she said, he gathered from her tone that she'd approved.

He glanced over his shoulder at the horses in the pen behind him. The sight of Aquila provided a desperately needed comfort. If worst came to worst, Decimus resolved, he could always leap onto the horse's back and gallop far away from the enemy's clutches. When all else failed, Aquila wouldn't fail him.

He stared down at his work, expertly weaving the rein together. As he did so, his mind retreated to the days when Amyntas, a grizzled decurion, had taught him this task.

'Halt a minute, lad. See this?'

Decimus stared at a kink in the knotted leather.

'You crossed the wrong two. That'll create a weakness in the strap. Go back and do it over, Decimus. Only thing for it.'

Decimus grunted to himself. He unwound the strips to his error and carefully began again.

'…settled…battle?'

He paused a moment before resuming his work. The old Greek's voice had rung so clearly in his head, he could've sworn he'd actually heard his words uttered in this forsaken land.

'The Ordovices…agreed…location we desired.'

From the corner of his eye, Decimus spied a bearded merchant hunched over the seat of his cart. He conversed with a short, shaggy-haired Silure. Their words cut clearly through the jargon of British that flowed through the settlement, for they indeed spoke Greek.

He shifted in his seat and hunched forward, anxious to seem oblivious. Despite its remote location, it seemed even Britannia traded in the common tongue of the wider world. Though he'd worked hard to become fluent, Decimus's Greek had never been particularly strong. He listened closely to the pair, parsing out every word he could distinguish.

The short Silure, clad in a rather tattered pair of leggings, stood on tiptoe. 'Morcant requires assurance of his payment.'

The merchant frowned, glaring directly at Decimus seated close by. 'Keep your voice down!'

'For what? Nobody understands…' The Silure followed the merchant's gaze and pointed, grinning cruelly. 'That man is an idiot. Can't hear a thing.'

The merchant clasped his hands over his knees. 'My client is not yet satisfied with your terms. He's afraid that, if discovered, things would go quite badly for him. This reaches all the way back to the imperial court.'

'No payment until you hand it over. Morcant is firm. We cannot trust a Roman's word.'

Decimus frowned intently at his work, trying to study the merchant from the corner of his gaze. There was something vaguely familiar about the man's flat face, large nose, and gleaming dark eyes. Had he seen him somewhere before? In the fort? In the vicus? Both? He accidentally wound another kink in his leather and undid the work, huffing in frustration.

The merchant fumbled behind him and heaved a small amphora from the bed of his cart. 'Take this as a sign of our good faith. My client will produce the rest at the agreed upon meeting. But he will expect to be paid in full upon delivery.'

'I'll see that it's delivered.' The small man uncorked the vessel to glance inside. Satisfied, he tucked it under his arm and strode away. There was a waddle to his walk, almost as if his hips were too wide for his stunted legs. Seeing Decimus, he sidled up and babbled a series of taunting words in his native tongue.

Decimus kept his gaze averted, ignoring the small man.

The Silure laughed and scurried away, weaving a path among the roundhouses.

He turned to see the cart disappearing along a forest track. The merchantman was heading northeast, he noted. In the direction of Viroconium.

He sighed and set the bridle rein aside. The implications of what he'd just witnessed settled on his shoulders like lead weights. The future of every man in every legion in Britannia pressed at his conscience.

I'm a soldier, not a spy, he fumed, scowling absently at women making cheese across a field. His mind raced at a frantic pace. He wasn't a deep thinker like Tullius. If he had, his rash decisions wouldn't have led to…

The scar on his cheek burned bright. With an impotent groan, he tossed his leatherwork aside.

A sound startled him from his reverie. He turned to see two children seated not far from him. His rein had landed on top of their scratched-out playing board, scattering the stones they'd been using as tokens. The boys regarded him with baleful stares.

He stood and walked over to their board. He snatched the rein away and paused. He watched the children's fingers nimbly return the stones to their starting positions. He cocked his head, looking at the darker stones arranged along one side of the grid and the lighter stones lining the opposite side. The game seemed to resemble *latrunculi*, a favourite pastime of Tullius's.

One of the boys met his gaze and gestured for him to join them. With a small smile, Decimus knelt. He glanced between them. The child beside him, clad in a homespun tunic, vaguely resembled himself as a young lad. The boy's dark hair tumbled to his shoulders in unruly waves. He blew it out of his eyes as he moved one of his stones. His opponent, wearing a pair of brightly dyed trousers, regarded the move with steely brown eyes. His broad brow and stiff, sandy locks made Decimus think of his optio.

The boy rested his chin on his fist, considering his options, before finally moving one of his white stones. Decimus's companion pointed, whispering excitedly in his native tongue. Grinning, he leapt one of his stones over the other boy's and swiped the white stone from the board.

The sandy-haired boy frowned. The trio stared at the game board for a long moment.

Decimus couldn't be sure of the game's rules, but if it was anything like *latrunculi*, he saw an opportunity for the boy. Touching the lad's shoulder, he motioned for him to take one of his white stones. He pointed out the circular path it could take to capture both black stones on the board.

The sandy-haired boy smiled, triumphantly capturing the pair of counters.

'Artacos! Teilios!'

All three turned towards the cheese-making women. One stood regarding them, her cloths gathered in one arm.

The boys swept up their stones and scuffed out the board in the dirt. Waving to Decimus, the pair gambolled off to their waiting mother.

Decimus watched the trio pick their way through the fields to one of the roundhouses. The children joined hands as they trailed in their mother's wake. Even out here, far from civilization, Decimus marvelled, he could find a pair of *sanguinem fratres* playing the very same games.

His face suddenly fell. The Romans and the Britons played the very same games…that turned wily boys into ruthless soldiers.

Luciana forced her way through the trampled brush, leading Decimus by the hand. Every time he made a noise, she glared at him over her shoulder. Decimus raised an arm to shield his brow from the bracken as he followed Luciana's mad path. She hastened, tugging him insistently until they neared the edge of the grove.

When the boulder appeared, she halted at a break in the trees several paces upwind of the curious stone. She whirled to face him, flushing in panic as he began to form words.

'Wha-?'

Luciana silenced him with a kiss. He tried to pull away, but she held fast. One hand tightly clutched his jaw while the other traced across his breast: *we are watched.*

Decimus felt his pulse roar. Fear and anticipation bubbled inside him before erupting into the cool, grim determination that settled over him before every battle. He growled his understanding and relaxed into Luciana's embrace. He opened his mouth when she pressed her tongue against it and wrapped his arms about her waist. She hitched a leg over his hip and writhed against him, moaning. Her supple, graceful power thrilled his heart. He tightened his grasp. He tried to suppress his anxiety and lost himself in her. The higher his uneasiness mounted, the deeper he kissed.

When they came up for breath a third time, Luciana broke away. She squinted at the shadows. After a long moment, she sighed. 'It's all right, now. They've gone.'

He frowned about the forest. 'I still feel as though we're being watched.'

'I know what you mean.' She sat on the forest floor. 'I think it's just the area.' She nodded at the stone. 'I lost Taraghlan's trail right there this afternoon. One moment he was there, and the next he was gone.'

Decimus stumbled off to inspect the stone. He made several circuits around it, feeling about the crevices and thoroughly inspecting the ground. After a while, he ambled back over and plopped down beside Luciana. 'There doesn't seem anything strange about it to me.'

'Me neither.' She shrugged in dissatisfaction. 'It just seems strange I lost him so quickly.'

'And he wasn't gone long, either. I caught him hanging around Morcant when they brought a chicken up for his dinner.' Decimus paused a moment. 'Well, either dinner or an augury.'

'Morcant's planning to spring a trap on the Roman forces,' she murmured, lowering her voice. 'I overheard him discussing his plans with the chieftain of the Ordovices earlier today.' She mulled over the conversation. 'It was as if he knew exactly which route your legions plan to take in the spring campaign.'

'I might know the reason why.' Decimus arched a brow. 'I overheard something curious myself.'

'You? How?'

'Some short, little bowlegged fella was speaking Greek to a merchantman. I couldn't make much sense out of what they said, but I heard them discussing payment and a plan involving Morcant. The Silure was given an amphora to pass on to him.'

'Did you get a good look at this merchantman?' Luciana's eyes lit up.

He shook his head. 'Not really, no. But I'm sure I've seen him somewhere before.'

'Do you think Morcant has his own spy within the Roman fort?'

'That, or the vicus.' He nodded. 'It would explain why he's so sure he knows, or *will* know, our marching route.'

'But who would be working with Morcant? And why?' She frowned. 'The Silures cannot possibly offer a Roman more than what your emperor can.'

'That I don't know.' Decimus thought for a long moment, studying the ground. Finally, he tossed a pebble down and sighed in frustration. 'One thing's for sure, Luci. Something strange is afoot. And I don't like it one bit.'

XVIII

Cassia cautiously made her way through the dense woods. She hitched her skirts higher to clear the rough stones and broken branches lining the forest floor. Her slave woman silently dogged her steps.

After leaving the hill that morning, the pair had traversed the western edge of the settlement. They'd passed the pastures belonging to the woman sheltering Decimus and Luciana, which the slave had pointed out to Cassia. They'd entered the forest and found a clearing not far from the place she'd instructed them to meet her. Cassia settled her skirts about her in the shadow of a few shady elms not far from the clearing. The slave woman stretched out before her in the brush. She supposed this meeting with Luciana was what the goddess wanted.

Cassia must have dozed, for the next thing she knew, night had fallen. She could hardly see her hand when she held it up before her.

'Jupiter's cock!' She lurched to her feet, accidentally kicking the slave with her toe. The woman startled and roused beside her.

Cassia looked about, trying to regain a sense of direction in her blackened surroundings. 'We've missed the appointed time!'

She whipped her veil from her head, batting away the branch that suddenly brushed her face. She glanced a streak of moonlight through the leaves and lurched in its direction. She stumbled over a tree root and nearly lost her footing. The slave woman collided with her back. Cassia bit her lip, swallowing her cry. 'Nemesis, help me!' She hissed.

A pair of low voices hummed in the distance. Cassia stilled and listened. Finally, she moved in their direction, pausing every so often to check if the voices grew louder.

'…your emperor can.'

Cassia frowned, stopping short. But that sounded like…no. They couldn't still be here!

'…I don't like it one bit.'

Her heart soared. She'd know Decimus's voice anywhere. But what in Tartarus was he doing *here*, in the land of the Silures?

She caught sight of two figures not far from the boulder in the clearing.

She motioned for the slave to hunker down behind her. She stayed in the shadows of the grove, wanting to watch them for a moment.

The scars cutting their lines across Decimus's broad back gleamed white in the moonlight. Inky whorls of paint stretched between his shoulders and down his arms. The checked cloth crossing his chest cut a dark swath across his torso. Cassia's lip curled at the sight of his lime-stiffened hair and the leather thong about his neck. Native dress didn't suit him in the slightest.

As she watched, he rested a hand on Luciana's arm. Luciana had drawn her feet up in the grass, her gown hiding the shape of her body. Her long hair trailed on the ground behind her, looking rather wiry and unwashed. She turned to Decimus, and Cassia felt a pang as she saw Luciana's reassuring smile.

He leant close and kissed her on the lips. Instead of immediately pulling away, he leant closer, seeking her mouth again. A soft moan escaped Luciana's throat. She cupped the back of his head, holding him close.

How could he? Cassia couldn't wrench her eyes away, though the sight tightened her chest. Heat flushed her cheeks. Her fingers clawed at the dirt. It wasn't fair. She knew Decimus better, loved Decimus more than Luciana ever could! She'd loved him since they were both children, playing together in The Senator's peristylium. She'd followed his legion across Germania and into Britannia, because she loved him. She loved him so much, she'd even borne his…

Cassia squeezed her eyes shut. *No. I've given that up to Nemesis.* She clutched her sides, waiting for the pang gripping her heart to pass. *I can't think of it again.*

She refocussed on the pair across the clearing. They sat companionably now, Decimus's arm wrapped around Luciana. Cassia sighed. What was it about that barbarian bitch that made Decimus so tender, so affectionate? He'd never been that way with any woman, even when copulating. He'd sooner shrink away from Cassia than accept her kisses. And yet there he was, cuddling his little Brittunculus.

She punched the earth. It wasn't fair!

As she watched, Decimus lifted his head. 'I need time to think about all this. Can we leave?'

'We can't.' Luciana sighed and rested her chin against his shoulder. 'We're meeting Cassia here, remember?'

'I still don't understand it. How does she even *know* Morcant?' Decimus shook his head. 'No wonder that bastard's been looking at me strangely!'

'We don't know if she's said anything to him about us.' Luciana placed a hand on his arm.

'We must make sure. Where is she, then?'

'I don't know. It's well past the eleventh hour, but she hasn't showed up.'

'Mithras god.' Decimus grabbed the boulder and lurched to his feet. 'We have to leave, Luci. Now. We're as good as dead. Cassia can't keep a secret to save her life.'

Cassia arose indignantly. 'How little you know!'

She marched into the grove, glowering at Decimus. A small part of her rather thrilled at the sight of the pair's shocked expressions. Luciana slowly stood, mouth agape. Decimus's thunderous gaze had widened slightly. Was he afraid?

Cassia roughly shoved his shoulder. 'You have no *idea* how many secrets I hold. Many of them yours!' She closed her eyes, banishing the sudden thought of tiny fingers reaching for her. She gestured to Luciana. 'I didn't tell her everything about us, you know! Not even about the corona-,'

'Fine!' He barked, holding up a hand. 'You're right, that wasn't fair of me to say.' His gaze softened as he lowered his voice. 'And I'm sorry. I'm sorry that when we last parted, it wasn't on better terms.'

Cassia's eyes watered. 'Oh, Decimus.' She reached for him.

Luciana caught her arms and wrenched them back to her sides. 'So, you've finally shown up. Tell us what in Danu's name you're doing here. And more importantly, have you told Morcant about us?'

Cassia shrugged her off. 'I've told Morcant nothing! I'm here to punish him for what he did to Cook!'

Decimus turned to her, puzzled. 'Wait. Morcant knows Charis's cook?'

Cassia sniffed. 'He killed her.' She turned her vengeful gaze on Luciana. 'Just as surely as she killed Cato.'

'Cato?' Luciana frowned.

'My brother!' Cassia's voice rose, her fury mounting. 'You murdered him!'

Decimus's arms suddenly enveloped her. He pressed her face against his chest. 'And you will murder all three of us if you don't keep your voice down. Would Cato want that?'

She wrenched her head up and met her oldest friend's remote gaze. 'And if it were only my life in peril? Would you?'

He slowly shook his head.

Her breaths turned into sobs as tears blurred her vision. She leant into him, feeling her hatred crumble within her. She clung to his neck, burying her nose in the checked cloth at his shoulder to avoid a heavy stench of urine that overpowered his familiar musk. She felt one of his hands cradle her head. She dug her nails into his skin.

'I am sorry,' Luciana murmured.

Cassia peeked over his shoulder to see Luciana regarding her with a stricken expression. She scowled. 'Much good your words will do him in Hades!'

'Shh…shh…' Decimus planted a kiss on Cassia's brow. 'Be quiet, now…'

'I do not know whether my brother is alive or dead. My father went to the Otherworld on the same day as your brother.' Luciana's hands hovered uncertainly at her sides. 'I didn't know who he was or who he belonged to…'

'It doesn't matter, does it?' Cassia snarled. 'You got his master in the end, you filthy barbarian witch! You don't regret it at all!'

'Cassia!' Decimus hissed sternly, taking her face in his hands. She trembled at his fierce expression. 'We aren't the Fates! Wishing for things that didn't happen cannot change what did! Cato chose to disobey me and enter the fort! His death was no one's fault but his own!'

She sniffled, shrinking from his intense gaze.

'Looking to the past accomplishes nothing,' he intoned.

Cassia scowled. 'Says you!' She pressed a thumb to the livid scar marring his cheek. Decimus wrenched his head away, letting her go.

'Hang on!' Luciana grabbed Cassia's wrist. 'Is *that* why you arranged for Titianus to rape me? Because I killed your brother?'

'What?' Decimus barked.

Cassia snatched her hand away. She glanced at his bewildered face. 'I…I don't know what you're talking about.'

'Yes, you do.' Luciana leant close, blocking Decimus from Cassia's view. 'I know you do. You told Nicomedes that Decimus wanted to meet me there. He knows as well as I do.'

'Well, it's too bad your only witness is a slave. He'd have to be tortured to testify against me.' Cassia sneered.

'Cassia, is that true?' Decimus's voice rumbled.

'So what if it is?' She rounded on him. Her heart sank as his hazel eyes fixed her with a penetrating stare. His thin mouth had drooped in grim disappointment. She trembled, fresh tears stinging the corners of her eyes. 'I can't sink any lower in your estimation than I already have!'

He slowly shook his head. His expression didn't change.

She stumbled away, pointing at Luciana. 'You need to leave, both of you. So I can figure out how to solve this mess without you getting in the way!'

'And what mess is that?' Luciana folded her arms.

'Morcant and I have unfinished business.' Cassia refused to meet Luciana's gaze.

'And the last person Morcant had business with ended up dismembered,' Decimus said.

Cassia stiffened. She slowly turned. That tinge of fear had returned to Decimus's steely gaze. Did…did he still care?

'He's already suspicious of us. Your presence would consign us to just as worse a fate.' Luciana shook her head.

Cassia's face fell. 'Just why are you here, anyway? What's so important that you're risking your own necks?'

'And you aren't?' Decimus touched her elbow, drawing her back to him. 'I'm not allowed to tell you why. All I can say is we need to watch Morcant for a while, and then leave before he figures out who I really am.' He ran a hand along her knotted braids and brushed a small bell woven behind her ear, making it jingle. He smiled. 'You don't want me to end up as a bag of bones, now, do you?'

Cassia sighed. 'But he must *die.*'

'I agree.' Decimus squeezed her shoulder. 'But he can't die now.'

'Oh, Nemesis.' Cassia closed her eyes. 'What do you *want* from me?'

'What are we going to do?' Luciana said, regarding her coldly. 'Are you still staying in Morcant's hall?'

Cassia shook her head. 'I…can't. I…well, I can't go back there.'

'Domina?'

The trio turned to see the slave woman hovering uncertainly at the edge of the clearing. Luciana blew an exasperated sigh. 'Oh, great. *Another* one!'

'We need to send her to the nearest Roman fort, at Glevum, before Morcant realises she's gone.' Cassia looked up at Decimus. 'But please, don't send me with her. To be honest, I have no idea what to do next. But if whatever you're doing will ultimately harm Morcant, then I want to help you. If I can.'

'Who is this?' Luciana grabbed the slave by the arm and marched her over to Cassia and Decimus.

'I have no name anymore!' The woman sobbed.

'You'd best remember it, because we're setting you free.' Cassia fingered the iron slave collar encircling the woman's throat. 'Do you think we can get this off?'

Decimus lifted it and turned it about. His fingers stopped when they brushed against a seam. 'It was sealed while she was wearing it. Might be able to force a break here, where the pieces joined.' He turned to Luciana. 'We need to look for tools in Saibh's barn.'

Luciana crossed her arms. 'And what about Cassia?'

He frowned at Cassia, lips pursed. She smiled tentatively.

'We haven't gathered enough intelligence yet. Another set of eyes and ears could only help us?' He shrugged, turning to Luci.

'You can't be serious!' Luciana's mouth dropped. 'Nobody is supposed to know what we're doing here! And you said yourself she can't keep secrets!'

Decimus winced.

Cassia pushed past him, coolly meeting Luciana's gaze. 'If either of you knew what secrets I've held, you'd never doubt my discretion.'

'Speed is also of the essence, here.' Decimus gently touched Cassia's arm, regarding Luciana evenly. 'If we don't figure this out before the council, this will all have been for nothing.'

Luciana's shoulders sagged. She hated having to admit when Decimus was right. After a moment of considering the proposal, she narrowed her eyes. 'You're forgetting that she can't go back to Morcant. She'd be far safer in Glevum.'

'Hmm. You're right. She'd have to have another disguise.' Decimus considered, regarding the two women. 'You look enough alike. Could we tell Saibh she's your sister? Give her one of your frocks to wear?'

Luciana tapped her chin, mulling over his words. She narrowed her eyes at Cassia. 'Does Morcant know you by sight? Would he recognise your face?'

Cassia slowly nodded. Luciana sighed. 'Well, that's not going to work, then.'

Decimus pried Cassia's discarded veil out of the slave's clenched fist. He considered it for a moment. 'Is there a way we might explain covering her face up?'

Luciana snorted. 'Maybe if she were a leper.'

'That's it, then. We tell Saibh your sister, who suffers from leprosy, followed us here. It also means she and the others would have to keep their distance from her.'

'That's ridiculous!'

'It's going to have to work.' Decimus frowned. 'We can't leave yet. And three have a better chance of solving this than two.'

Cassia felt her heart lift as Luciana reluctantly acquiesced. The four tramped back through the woods to the Silure settlement. This wasn't what she had expected, but something told her this was the path forward. Perhaps Nemesis hadn't deserted her, after all.

'There.' Luciana finished tucking the end of her torn skirt hem behind Cassia's ear. She stood back and surveyed Cassia's disguise. She wore a dark green gown Luciana had grabbed from her pack, one with long sleeves and loose, billowing skirts. Luciana had fastened her dark checked mantle about Cassia's shoulders and pinned it in place with an enamelled fibula. Boudicca had gifted her the pin at Beltane a long time ago. Luciana smiled as the red, blue, and yellow plates lining the fibula's curve winked in the moonlight from the barn window. She'd long destroyed the Roman pieces given by her old Latin tutor and former lover. This one, however, so beautifully crafted by Iceni hands, had survived her jewel box's purge.

Luciana's eyes fell to Cassia's hands. While the long dress and mantle helped, Luciana still worried Cassia's creamy palms would betray the leprosy lie. She'd painted as many symbols on them as she could with her spare woad to mask their health. If people kept their distance, she hoped, they shouldn't notice.

She met Cassia's gaze. Cassia's bright blue eyes were the only part of her face still visible. Luciana had wound the torn fabric scrap about her head, masking her brow, hair, nose, ears, and chin. If leprosy had disfigured her, she wouldn't bear any more of her face than she'd need to. Luciana doubted Morcant would recognise Cassia from her eyes alone.

'I think you're ready, sister.' Luciana smirked. 'I think it's best if you slept in the pigsty to keep up the story.'

Cassia narrowed her eyes. 'How dare you.'

'You couldn't very well cosy up with anyone if you had leprosy, now, could you?' Luciana shrugged. 'Remember, you asked for this.'

Cassia clenched her fists. 'Nemesis preserve me.'

They both turned to Decimus, who'd been steadily banging and cursing behind them. He stood over the slave woman, gripping her collar while pounding and pulling it with a hammer. He'd stuffed a wadded saddle blanket between the woman's neck and the collar, granting her a thin layer of protection from his work. She still grimaced from her seat on the hay-strewn floor, head cocked at an extreme angle.

'Are you getting any closer?' Luciana strode over, Cassia in tow.

Decimus didn't answer, concentrating on the iron seam. His hammer rang true, gradually denting the collar. Sweat coursed down his cheeks, marring his faded woad. 'Come on, you son of Dis!' He growled.

The collar suddenly came apart, dropping to the floor. The woman cried out, toppling over beside it. Decimus sat back, panting. Luciana glanced furtively at the door, hoping they hadn't aroused Saibh. She thought the barn was far enough away from Saibh's roundhouse, but Decimus had been making a considerable amount of noise for most of the night.

'There. You're free.' Cassia knelt beside the woman and took her hand. The slave wept, curling into a ball.

'Thank you. Thank you, Domina…' she sobbed.

'Enough of that.' Cassia turned to Luciana. 'Is the horse ready?'

Luciana nodded. She'd tacked the Roman gelding and tied him by the pasture gate. If the woman made it to Glevum, the legion there could take the horse. She glanced outside. 'She'd better leave. She needs to be far away from here by dawn.'

Cassia helped the woman to her feet. 'Have you remembered your name?'

She nodded. 'F-Fabia.' She turned to Cassia and drew in a shuddering breath. 'But I would like to be called Fabia Cassia, with your permission.'

Cassia's eyes watered. She squeezed Fabia's hand. 'I would be honoured.'

The women crept outside, leaving Decimus to catch his breath in the barn. They moved silently through the grass until they arrived at the pasture gate. The pigs grumbling in their sty nearby muffled the sound of the latch swinging open. Luciana slipped inside to retrieve the gelding.

'Did you leave anyone behind in Glevum?' Cassia cocked her head at Fabia. 'Anyone you can return home to?'

Fabia looked down. 'I was seeing a legionary with Valeria. Gaius Aelius.' She wiped her nose. 'He was on campaign when I was taken. I…I don't even know if he still lives.'

'I hope he does.' Cassia patted her back. 'You'll go straight to the fort?'

Fabia nodded. 'I might as well. Nothing remains of the farm.' She sighed. 'And I can then learn Gaius's fate.'

Luciana reappeared, leading the gelding through the gate. She stroked the horse's muzzle and murmured soothingly. Cassia led Fabia around and cupped her hand. She took one of Fabia's feet and vaulted her into the saddle. Fabia looked around uneasily as she picked up the reins.

Luciana led them around the pasture and pointed. 'That's east. Head that way and don't stop until you reach the bank of the Sabrina. Once you do, follow the river's course north. That will take you directly to Glevum.'

Fabia nodded.

'May the gods go with you.' Luciana stepped back.

Fabia hesitated, then reached down to clasp Cassia's hand. 'Thank you, Domina. I will never forget what you have done for me.'

'I'm glad the Fates crossed our paths.' Cassia patted the gelding's rump. 'Go. You're not safe until you're under Roman protection.'

Fabia nodded tearfully. She prodded the gelding into a walk. Slowly, she rode along the edge of the settlement. Luciana and Cassia watched until the trees at the camp's eastern edge had swallowed her completely.

XIX

Luciana glanced over her shoulder. Saibh rushed past her, sword held overhead. She led the group of both seasoned and inexperienced female warriors who raised their voices in frenzied battle cries. Their target, a line of long twigs erected in the ground to represent a Roman shield wall, awaited their attack at the far end of the clearing.

She watched a few young girls dart past, awkwardly trying to hold their swords aloft, and joined the charging horde.

Her eyes locked on one of the posts and she hastened towards it. She thrust her shield forward, weapon held close to her body. Her sandalled feet skipped through the damp grass, carrying her to her target. The post loomed closer, and closer, and closer still…

At precisely the moment before she stepped within sword range, she raised her blade high and brought it down on the post with an ear-splitting shriek. The weapon shuddered against the ash rail, splitting the wood down the middle before it lodged several inches in. Frowning, she wrenched her sword out and punched the post over with the butt of her hilt. She followed the arc of the rail's fall, inserting her weapon one final time in the middle and giving it a satisfying wrench.

She pulled her blade free of the post, breathing hard from the exertion. Just as she did so, another sword awkwardly swung over her stooped back, narrowly missing her.

'Oi!' Luciana screeched, dodging the clumsy efforts of a young Silure girl. She straightened and glared at the child. 'Control your weapon!'

'Sorry!' The girl meekly drew back, lowering her head. 'It's so heavy!'

'Here.' Luciana stood behind the young woman. 'Work to strengthen yourself so.' She held the girl's arm up and flexed the wrist of her weapon hand. 'It's all in here. Once your wrist is strong, she'll always stay where you need her.'

The girl nodded, watching her blade glint in the late afternoon sun.

'Work with your target, alternating cuts and angles.' Luciana nodded to the post and stepped out of sword range as the girl clumsily set to work.

She looked up the row of battling women and saw Saibh detach herself from the pack. She made a few approving comments to some of the women as she strolled along the line to Luciana.

'They fight well,' Luciana called as Saibh came within earshot.

Saibh slung down her shield and nodded. 'The older warriors haven't let their skills grow dull. The younger girls would improve faster if they didn't have to train in secret, but…' She shrugged at the ground.

'I agree.' Luciana nodded. 'It's a pity Morcant would let such a valuable resource go to waste.'

'Morcant is weak!' Saibh spat. 'He's a fool to think women aren't fit for war. The older women who fought with Arthmael more than deserve their place alongside the male Gaesatae.' She tucked a wayward strand of hair behind her ear. 'It is hard, suppressing everything you know, everything you were raised to do. All because one man decided such things are dangerous in a woman's head.' Her eyes narrowed at Luciana. 'Remember, you are not to breathe a word of this training to anyone in the settlement. As far as the men are concerned, we're gathering nuts and kindling.'

'I understand.' Luciana glanced at the edge of the clearing, where a bundled Cassia looked on. 'As does my sister.'

'Strange, her turning up here.' Saibh studied Cassia's figure. 'What with her being a leper and all.'

'I told her to stay behind, but she wouldn't listen. She's the only family left to me, even if I must keep her at a distance.' She let her gaze roam over the horde of old and young women pouring their efforts into their swordsmanship. 'At least your women are free enough to train in secret. The remaining women of my tribe remain trapped inside that accursed Roman fort.' Her fists clenched at her sides.

'How did you ever manage to escape?' Saibh cocked her head.

Luciana reddened. 'I'd…I'd rather not say.' She looked at the ground, desperately banishing the thought of Decimus. 'It's certainly not a path any of the others could follow. I don't want to give up on them.' She lifted her head. 'Aside from my sister and I, they're all of the Cornovii that's left.'

'I know.' A shadow crossed Saibh's expression. 'We were not party to that decision. It was the first move Morcant made, after barring us from the warrior caste. Such a senseless waste.' She clicked her tongue. 'The Romans would have done enough to force you to our side. And we'd be stronger against Rome with the Cornovii than without them. But what would I know of such matters?' She shrugged. 'I am only a woman.'

'I wonder…' Luciana crept closer, lowering her voice. 'Might your group of female warriors…break what's left of my people free?'

Saibh frowned. 'How?'

'I can take up residence in Viroconium, after the war council. I know enough Latin to understand what the Romans' plans were for my people. They're to be sold to a slave trader and taken into Londinium, where they'll be auctioned off for the mines. I can keep an eye on the fort and leave some sort of sign on the road to your settlement when the trader takes my people away.'

'What sort of sign?'

Luciana drew in the dirt with the tip of her sword, brows knitted in concentration. Then, suddenly, her expression cleared. 'Like this!' She grabbed Saibh by the hand and led her to the edge of the clearing. She stopped just before the treeline and roughly sketched a shape resembling a stag's skull in the dirt. 'Cernunnos. I will draw him on one of the trees just beyond here.' She pointed through the foliage. 'We are not far from the moors that lead to Viroconium through Dobunni territory. I can find this place again. Every time you convene to train, come check for my signal. Once it's there, bring your women through Dobunni lands to line either side of the Londinium road. There, you'll be able to ambush the slave train and set my people free!' She lifted her chin.

Saibh thought for a moment, then nodded. 'I'll do it.' A small smile lifted the corners of her mouth. 'Perhaps the gods will see fit to forgive the Silures their misdeeds against the Cornovii for this.'

Luciana sighed and blinked back tears of relief. 'I would be pleased to take my place alongside you.' She clasped Saibh's arm, then drew her into a tight hug.

Luciana frowned at Cassia over Saibh's shoulder. A movement deep within the forest had drawn Cassia's attention. It was a figure, moving with purpose. Tall, black haired, cloak pulled up over his head. Pale hands, a flash of a golden torc…*Morcant?*

Cassia turned and met Luciana's gaze. Luci nodded. She watched Cassia slink away after the figure.

'Saibh, can I ask you one other question?' She frowned as she pulled away.

'You haven't another daring mission for me, do you?' Saibh arched a brow.

'It's just…there's this strange man I've seen skulking about your tribe.' Luciana wrinkled her nose. 'Short, shaggy hair, bit of a waddle to his walk. Odd looking fellow.'

'Diarmait?' Saibh nodded. 'He *is* a strange one. He disappeared from the tribe as a child and only returned a few years ago. Said he'd been pressed into merchant work after straying too far along the Sabrina one day. Had to serve his time before his masters would let him go, or something like that. I'm not sure any of us believed him. He keeps himself to himself, and the rest of us try to ignore him, but he's got Morcant's ear. I'm honestly surprised he trusts the little fella enough to keep him around, let alone talk to him. Especially after he discovered that Roman spy sleeping among us earlier this spring.' She shuddered.

'Hmm.' Luciana nodded, watching a distinctive, bandy-legged shadow dog the chieftain's footsteps. They disappeared, Cassia's trailing form only just visible between the trees. She gasped. 'Could you excuse me for a moment, Saibh? I think I need to heed nature's call.'

Without waiting for the woman's reply, she hitched her skirt and sprinted into the trees.

Cassia ducked low as she followed the men's path. The branches broken by the men kept her from losing them. Her heart soared as she darted along. *Nemesis, you have led me to this moment. I know I am doing your work.*

She slid and spun on her heel as the pair swerved to the left, heading back towards the hill country. Cassia stumbled over a branch but kept running, anxious not to lose them. They came to a halt underneath a particularly impressive oak. Cassia hid behind a thorn tree several paces away. She took long, measured breaths through her nose, regaining her composure. Then, cautiously, she peeked around the trunk to observe Morcant.

A hooded figure stepped out from behind the oak and approached the pair. The man's face was obscured by his cloak, though his bare knees and caligae betrayed him for a Roman. As he moved, something flashed in the gloom beneath the dark fabric. He stopped before Morcant and addressed him in a tongue she did not recognise.

The chieftain silently scowled at him. When the man's voice halted, the bandy-legged fellow answered him in the same tongue. Though he spoke, the Roman's gaze remained on Morcant. The pair eyed each other with mistrust as the little man prattled on.

When the Roman began to speak again, Cassia frowned. His voice sounded familiar. She had heard it before. She squinted, trying to make out any distinguishing feature.

He produced a scroll of parchment from his sleeve and he placed it in Morcant's outstretched hand. The dim light revealed enough of his face for Cassia to see. His expression was grim. His patrician nose protruded from his thin, bony face; his full mouth curled down in guarded displeasure.

The little man answered for the chieftain again, his words tumbling over one another. He reached out to lay his hand over the scroll and Morcant coldly swatted him away. The fellow made his apologies, bowing to the Roman. The cloaked figure nodded and replied curtly. Then he spun around and strutted back towards the north. As he wheeled, Cassia saw the momentary gleam of his armour beneath.

After giving the man enough time to put some distance between them, Morcant and his aide walked away. Their path curled into the hills that ringed the Silure settlement.

Cassia leant against the thorn trunk. She drew long breaths through her nose, reeling from what she'd just seen. She recognised the Roman. Of course she did. After all, she had facilitated his first meeting with Morcant.

Luciana plunged deeper into the woods. She skipped over the ground, darting between closely woven branches. She hunched over, keeping low as she struggled to follow Cassia's trail. A crow silently swooped down from the trees and glided just ahead of her, almost as if it were silently leading her along the path. Her progress was measured and slow, the trajectory eastward. She frowned to herself as she ducked a wayward aspen branch. She was fast approaching the moors dividing Silures from Dobunni and Cornovii.

The crow cawed once and settled into a branch high above her. Luciana slowed to a stop and straightened. She frowned, turning in a small circle. The trunks surrounding her seemed to stretch for miles in every direction. She could see no trampled brush, no broken branches. There was no sign of Morcant, Dairmait, or Cassia.

The crow cawed a couple of times and ruffled its feathers. Luciana studied the bird. Why would it lead her here, away from Morcant's trail?

'You seek the wisdom of the Ancient One.'

She gasped at the voice in her ear and spun around. There, standing immediately behind her, was a dark-haired, woad-painted man no taller than her. His naked body was lithe and lean. His large, round dark eyes gazed into hers searchingly. Luciana panted, placing a hand at her breast. She couldn't believe the figure had snuck so close without her notice. 'Where… where did you come from?' She stammered.

'Come.' He held out his hand. There was a strange lilt to his voice, though he spoke her native tongue fluently. It was…otherworldly. 'I will take you to her.'

Luciana cautiously stretched her fingers to his stout palm. With lightning quick reflexes, he snatched her wrist and yanked her close. A small cry escaped her lips, and suddenly the world went dark. She reached up with her free hand and clawed at the cloth he'd wrapped around her eyes.

'Do not struggle. Golden People are not permitted to look upon the Ancient One.'

Luciana stilled, suddenly aware of just what the stranger was. The sounds of the forest grew louder around her: the gentle spring wind ruffling the budding branches, the snap of a twig under a creature's foot, the lonely calls of a wren in search of a mate. When the man grabbed her wrist again, she silently followed him.

They stole across the forest floor. Luciana heard her own feet trip over stones, branches, and protruding roots as they travelled, but the man made nary a sound. After a while, the ground began to incline. They were trekking into the hills.

She panted to keep up with him. Every time she lagged a little too far behind, an abrupt jerk on her arm brought her colliding into his back. She drew in a long breath every time he did so, trying to gauge the man. He smelt of nothing, nothing but the wooded landscape enveloping them.

Gradually, his steps slowed as they travelled a sinuous, twisting path. Luciana lost all sense of direction. She only knew they were somewhere deep within forested hills, a place no Briton or Roman could ever hope to discover.

The man paused. 'Careful,' he muttered, placing Luciana's hand against what felt like a large stone. 'The path is narrow.' Tugging her more gently now, he drew her along a very narrow track. Luciana felt her way along the rock, turning sideways when she felt stone pressing against her other side. Slowly, they edged their way up the thin track before it widened into verdant grass, the stones falling away.

She lifted her head and sniffed. There was a small cookfire, somewhere. The unmistakable aroma of roasting hazelnuts greeted her nostrils. The man led her up a steeper incline, past the comforting flame.

He stopped before what felt to Luciana like an unscalable grass knoll. 'I stay here.' He held her wrist out. She felt it being passed to a smaller hand. 'Take her to the Ancient One.'

Silently, Luciana's new guide led her along the side of the knoll. Then, suddenly, she was pulled to the ground. 'You must duck to enter,' a small female voice intoned.

Luciana brushed her fingers along the grass. She hunched over, feeling for anything that might resemble an entrance. Then her fingers slid down and felt a small opening. At first, it didn't seem large enough to enter, but as her fingers probed, she felt the earth give way to air. She couldn't find the tunnel's ceiling. Bending double, she crawled into the earthen tunnel behind the guide.

After shuffling a few steps, her guide pulled her up. Luciana winced, expecting her head to collide against the tunnel roof.

'You may stand.'

Cautiously, she straightened to her full height. To her surprise, she didn't connect with the chamber's ceiling. She couldn't hear much but a crackling fire and the soft breaths of her female guide. Luciana stood quietly, unsure of what to do next.

'Just a few more steps,' the woman said, tugging her forward. Luciana followed deeper into the cavern and knelt when prompted.

'Keep your eyes down,' the voice warned as she untied the rag from Luciana's eyes. She obligingly kept her gaze trained on the floor, though she could see nothing but blackness. She remained still and silent as her eyes gradually adjusted to the dim light. A popping fire off to her right cast the shadows of several seated forms before her. Just at the edge of her vision, she saw the folded feet of an even more diminutive figure than the man who'd brought her here. A white shroud wound loosely about thin, knobbly legs. Yellowed, chipped toenails curled outwards from the tips of shrivelled brown feet.

'Oh, Ancient One.' Luciana reverently touched her forehead to the ground and raised her palms in supplication. 'Voice of Danu on high! Please take pity on my poor, wayward spirit!'

A pair of trembling, gnarled hands took one of her palms. Several heartbeats passed in silence as the fingers traced their way along her lines. When at last the old woman spoke, her voice rang authoritatively in a rich, strong tenor: 'You seek answers.'

'Yes,' Luciana gulped, quivering. She gazed at the dirt in awe. Was she dreaming?

'You ask the same as those that came before.' Did Luciana detect a note of weariness in the Ancient One's voice?

'I…I don't,' she stammered.

'Andraste's wrath springs from the flood and all she knows shall bathe in blood.' The oracle paused, tracing new lines farther along her palm. When she next spoke, her voice took on a decided interest. 'You seek more. Your heart is divided.'

Luciana sucked in a breath and nodded.

'When heart and home are torn in two, to one's home one must be true.'

She frowned a little. 'But Decimus…?'

'Head of stone and heart of ice, he must always go home twice.'

'You know him, then.' Luciana smiled. The gods of the centurion's ancestors had not forsaken him. 'Is he…? Will he leave…?' She couldn't bring herself to say the words. Tears gathered in the corners of her eyes. 'Shall he fulfil his wish?'

The oracle fell quiet. Luciana breathed shallowly, fearful that her question had in some way angered Danu. Then, out of the silence the Ancient One spoke:

When the world turns dark and the skies all burn, to the land he's trod he shall return.'

Luciana frowned. Was her home to be engulfed by flames again? Did that mean the gods had turned their backs on her race? Would Decimus leave her home in ashes, to parade triumphantly through the streets of Rome? Or would he likewise be consumed in the fire and only his ashes borne home?

The Ancient One released her hand and she reached out. 'Wait. What is to become of my people? What of the coming battles between us and Rome?'

'You seek no further guidance. You already know the answers.' The Ancient One spoke with finality. She fell silent, refusing to acknowledge Luciana's further entreaties.

'But I must know! Does Danu still favour her Golden People? What have the Cornovii done to bring decimation upon us? I don't have the answers, tell me!'

Without thinking, Luciana began to raise her eyes. Almost immediately, a cloth sack came down over her head. She got no more than a fleeting glimpse of a thin, ghost-white torso before the world became dark.

'The Ancient One has spoken. It is time for you to leave.'

Luciana struggled against her captor, but the small woman dragged her away from the feet of the Ancient One. The guide circled and veered to the left and right, pulling Luciana by both arms. Once she'd become sufficiently disoriented, Luciana reluctantly gave up and staggered to her feet. The guide led her out to the cookfires.

As soon as she emerged from the cave, Luciana felt a light patter of raindrops on her head. Cautiously, she followed the woman through the narrow, stony pass. As they descended the hillside, rain beat on her skin with increasing ferocity. The ground turned to shifting mud beneath her feet. Luciana haltingly slid behind her guide as they made their way down.

Once they'd travelled far enough, the woman lifted the sack from her head and pushed her through a gap in the trees.

'Keep walking straight. You will find the village of the Golden People.'

Luciana blinked through the steady sheets of rain and took a step. She glanced over her shoulder to thank her guide, but the woman had already disappeared.

Dazed, Luciana stumbled forward. She hadn't gone far when she caught sight of Cassia slowly walking towards the Silure village. She frowned when Cassia turned. A deep furrow ran between Cassia's clear blue eyes.

'Cassia, what's…?'

'I saw Morcant. With his Roman…'

Luciana grabbed her arm. 'His Roman what?'

Cassia cocked her head. Tears glimmered in her eyes. 'Oh, gods, what have I done?'

XX

'Hurry!' Luciana groaned in her native tongue. The rain pelted her cheeks as she led Decimus to Saibh's barn. Mud splashed about her skirt, but she hardly felt it. She only thought about what she needed to tell him.

Decimus hastened to keep up, glancing around. He pushed his sopping ringlets off his brow. His ferocious hairstyle had grown limp under the deluge. Hot rivulets of limewash stung his skin as they dripped down his face. He gritted his teeth and squinted through the rain, stumbling in Luciana's wake.

Luciana paused only long enough to throw the wooden door wide. She jerked on Decimus's arm and disappeared inside the barn's dry, dark recesses.

As soon as Decimus entered the barn, Luciana threw her arms round him and pressed her lips to his. The centurion pulled her close and kissed her back, relishing her warm breath.

Luciana kicked the rickety door closed and it swung noiselessly before settling into place. She gripped Decimus's grizzled cheeks and continued to kiss him, letting her eyes adjust to the darkness. She felt his broad hands wend about her sopping tresses and moaned appreciatively.

Reluctantly, Decimus pulled back. Concern fought with desire in his eyes. 'Now, what is-?'

'Shh!' She laid a finger on his lips. She stood on tiptoe and nuzzled his neck. 'It might not be safe.'

'Come now, Luci.' A small smile tugged at the corners of his mouth. 'I think this lot have learned by now that every time we sneak off together is to have sex.'

She arched a brow. A small thrill raced down her spine. *We've got all night. There's nothing we can do until the morrow. My news can wait just a few moments longer.* Her grin broadened. 'Well, then. We'd best not disappoint them.'

Her eyes fell on a chariot whip discarded behind Decimus. She picked it up and turned it over in her hands, feeling the ribbed leather bound about the stout chandle and the long, iron-weighted strips of leather that flayed from it. She slapped the flay against her palm and hummed in approval at the sensation.

As she turned to him, Decimus felt his blood run cold. His eyes widened as she continued to flick the studded flays against her hand. 'No… Luci…'

'What?' She asked in mock innocence. 'It's not so different from your staff.' She stepped closer and slowly trailed the whip down his bare chest.

He pushed the end of the flay away. 'That's *not* like my vine staff. That's meant for an actual horse!'

Smirking, she stuck the end of the whip under his chin. 'Don't provoke me, my love.' She stepped forward and Decimus obligingly backed a pace. With measured steps, she backed him behind a large pile of hay at the rear of the barn. She saw Saibh's double-pommelled saddle sat atop a rail, oiled and ready for its next use. Luciana's grin widened. She turned to Decimus, whose flinty expression conveyed nothing.

'We must be careful we're not overheard.' She picked up the oiling rag from beside the saddle and tied a knot in the middle. She stretched both ends taut and held it up to Decimus's mouth. 'Especially one Latin-tongued warrior.'

He grunted but parted his lips to take the gag.

'There we are,' she murmured, switching back to British as she knotted the rag behind his head. She let her hands rest a moment in his hair, more dark than ashen now that most of the limewash had sloughed away, before trailing down to fiddle with the wheel of Taranis about his neck.

Her gaze fell past him to the saddle. There, overtop the pommels, a stiff, newly woven bridle rein lay coiled. She picked it up and turned it over. There was something about the neat, tightly braided grooves that felt familiar in Luciana's hands.

She turned to Decimus and lifted the bridle rein. 'Your work?' She questioned lowly in Latin.

He nodded.

She bit her lip as she took first one of his wrists, then the other. She wound the strap around them, binding his arms together.

Decimus softly grunted behind the gag, face flushed. He admired the way her nimble fingers expertly worked the leather, the chariot whip tucked against her side. Her confidence and poise touched something deep within Decimus, something that melted his hardened innards. She was his match, his equal, in absolutely every regard.

She flexed his wrists against their new bonds and nodded. 'Good.' She cupped her hands around Decimus's face, capturing his gaze. She saw the storm roiling within his eyes and smirked. Then, without breaking their gaze, she shrugged free of her dress. It collapsed about her feet in a heavy, dark puddle. She shook her long, wet tresses about her head.

Decimus let out a long, low sigh. His muscular form quivered with desire.

'Come, my love,' she purred in her own tongue. She grabbed him by his bound wrists and led him to the saddle. With a few prods from the whip, he leant over the saddle's side, his bound arms stretched before him. He stared down into the sweet-smelling straw, his stomach pressed crosswise into the saddle's seat. Luciana strolled around him, savouring the sight of him helplessly prostrate before her. She stopped at his backside, regarding his bum propped in the air. Grabbing hold of his trousers and the loincloth beneath, she yanked them down, exposing his smooth, shapely buttocks.

She tore her gaze away and studied the whip in her hands. It was, indeed, quite a different entity from the centurion's vine staff. The stiff, ribbed leather shaft was far wider and harder. She gently flicked the flays between her fingers and bit her lip as the leather burned against her skin. She would have to proceed with far more caution than she normally would.

She turned to Decimus. Gulping in a ragged breath, she leant over him. She trailed the ends of the whip over his shoulders, allowing the leathers to crisscross his spine as she traversed downward.

Decimus moaned, shaking his head.

Luciana danced the flays up along his calves, alternating long strokes with lightning-quick touches. She gently tapped the whip back and forth between his thighs before reaching his bottom. Curling her tongue around her upper lip, she clapped the whip against Decimus's undercarriage.

Decimus lifted his head, a deep guttural sound rumbling in his throat. He trembled as the flays trailed along the cleft of his buttocks.

Luciana laughed softly, drawing small circles over his flesh. She nudged his cheeks apart and touched one studded tip against his cavity. She held it there for a moment, savouring his strangled squeaks before dropping it away.

A shaft of light streaming from the door caught her gaze. The wind must have blown the barn door open. Shaking her head, she dropped the whip and wiped the sweat from her brow. She approached Decimus again, her face flushed with exhilaration.

'Come, Leucus.' She grabbed his outstretched arms and lifted him to his feet. She turned him around and giggled as soon as she saw the rock-hard erection he sported. 'My work is already done for me.' She ran her fingers along the shaft, stroking him gently. 'It looks like someone rather enjoys this.'

Decimus coloured, looking away.

Luciana met his gaze and curled her finger under his bearded chin. 'Don't despair, my love.' She stood on tiptoe and placed a quick kiss on his forehead. 'We're just getting started.'

She grabbed his bonds and stretched his arms over his head. Stepping forward, she pushed him into the saddle. Luciana ran her hands over his shoulders and curled her neck, drawing in a deep whiff of his heady, intoxicating musk. 'It's okay.' She lifted a knee and pressed it against his hip, encouraging him to drape himself over the saddle. 'I've got you.'

Decimus fell back against the leather and stared up at the barn's thatched roof. He gulped and shifted his torso.

Luciana loomed over him. She looked down at Decimus's throbbing member, perched perfectly atop the centre of the double-pommelled saddle. Another wave of excitement passed over her. Placing both hands on his stomach for support, she vaulted up and impaled herself on him, facing his chest. Her eyes rolled into the back of her head as soft, sharp cries escaped her mouth. Her legs came to rest on either side of the saddle's perch, toes resting just off the floor.

Decimus let out a long, low groan at the sensation of her tightening around him. He flexed his outstretched arms and settled. He relished the feeling of her warm palms on his stomach, her limber thighs resting over his hips, her body embracing his own. No matter how many times they did it, the moment of connection always felt charged between them. He gulped and waited for his partner's next move.

Pressing a little harder on his abdomen, she rocked her hips back and forth. She panted, leaning so far forward her wet hair swept over her shoulder and tickled his chest. She shifted a little from side to side, trying to find just the perfect angle. Decimus pressed his feet against the sides of the post and tried to lift his hips towards hers, willing her to find it. Suddenly, Luciana let out a sharp cry. His cock rested against the spot he'd found in the grove. She froze for a moment, feeling all her nerves come alive at his touch. Decimus watched her, his face shining with admiration.

Pushing herself a few inches off him, Luciana moved up and down. She closed her eyes. 'Oh, Leucus!' She quickened, each new thrust sending a fresh shockwave of pleasure up her spine.

Decimus grunted, holding firm. His muscles remained tense, anxious to stay in position for her. Perspiration slid down his forehead, dripping from his prominent nose onto his bared lips. He felt himself growing even warmer just watching her commanding performance. He began counting in his head, trying to stave off his rising orgasm.

She moved faster still. The friction increased between them. One of her arms gave way slightly and she nearly fell off him. Decimus lifted a leg to catch her, letting out a panicked shout behind his gag. With a shrill cry, she stopped herself and rested, panting, against his sweaty chest.

Decimus took the deepest breaths he could manage before lifting his head, straining to look at her. Though his whole body screamed from the tension and intensity, he needed to know she was all right.

Luciana looked up at his strangled snorts. Rapidly collecting herself, she grabbed Decimus's arms. She brought them over his head, pulling them both into a sitting position. They faced each other upright on the saddle, still locked together in coitus.

Decimus studied her as she lowered her head. Her fingers, still trembling, swiftly unknotted the rein from his wrists. As soon as it fell away, she reached behind his head and untied his gag. Decimus felt along her back, his arms testing their newfound freedom. Her gaze met his and they stared deeply into one another's eyes. Her look told Decimus everything he needed to know: she was okay, but her energy was flagging. She was still on the edge. She needed him to help her over.

Luciana ripped the gag from between his teeth. She flung it away and immediately pressed her mouth to his. Decimus happily kissed her back, strengthening his embrace. Luciana savoured the feel of his whiskers brushing against her chin. She ran a hand through his limp ringlets, scrubbing them vigorously, before coming to rest against the back of his head. She stretched her fingers, locking her grip around him. Her other hand slid over his shoulder and came to rest at the base of his sturdy, stubbled neck. She suddenly rocked her weight forward, nearly shoving him over. Decimus resisted, pushing back in alarm. Luciana broke free from his lips and shook her head. 'Trust me, my love. Hold on.'

She pulled his head down, lodging his face between her breasts. With one more push, she sent him backwards over the saddle. His shoulders crashed onto the bed of hay, Luciana still tangled with him.

He let out an explosive grunt, absorbing the shock of the fall. Slowly, he relaxed against the cushion of straw.

'You're not hurt?' Luciana untucked his head from her bosom and cradled it in her arms.

'No more than you've already hurt me,' he panted. He turned to kiss her palm, tightening his arms around her. He smiled, cheeks glistening with perspiration.

'Good.' She lowered her head and locked lips with him. Without warning, she rolled onto her side, taking Decimus with her. He widened his eyes and held on. They rolled across the floor, hay prickling their naked bodies. They came to a stop at the far end of the barn with Decimus on top of Luciana.

She panted 'Come on, Decimus.' She linked her arms around his neck. 'Please!'

He sat up, locking his elbows behind her knees and pressing her hips against her torso. He felt her stretch as he reached deep inside her, her walls tightening around him. Gazing into her eyes, he thrust against her.

'Go!' She cried, quaking beneath him. 'Decimus! *Come on!*'

He tried to match her fervour, concentration clouding his gaze. Sweat poured off his brow and dripped onto her chest.

'Faster! Harder!' Luciana's hands wildly snatched about in the straw. Her fingers closed around the whip. She clapped her heels against his shoulders, striking his bottom repeatedly with the butt of the whip. 'Faster! *Faster!*'

He furiously increased his pace, his jagged breaths exploding into rough grunts under Luciana's blows. He gritted his teeth.

Luciana suddenly arched her back. Her walls tightly contracted before exploding with wave upon wave of pleasure. She tumbled over the abyss, losing herself to the warm, dizzying heights of ecstasy as her climax rippled through her body. She dropped her arms, collapsing limply against the straw.

As soon as he felt her relax around him, Decimus let himself go. He rocked against her a couple more times before releasing. He threw his head back and let out a long, low groan. It petered into a whine as his eyes rolled into the back of his head, his body convulsing. He collapsed on top of her, whimpering softly.

They lay in the hay together, breathless, slowly coming down from their highs. Decimus gradually became aware of Luciana beneath him and rolled off her. She weakly reached out, clasping for his hand, and he gave it to her.

The low thatched roof and wooden walls of the barn came back into focus. Luciana blinked, her face warm from the exertion. She turned to the man lying next to her. 'Oh, Decimus.' She ran her fingers through his hair.

He smiled, pressing his head against her fond, gentle strokes. He released her other hand and gathered her against his chest, enveloping her still shuddering body in his arms. His heart, still racing, surged with love for the woman he held close.

Her hand slid down to caress his cheek, her fingers ruffling his whiskers. She burrowed her head against his glistening chest and kissed the wheel of Taranis, the token she'd passed from her mother to him. 'You're incredible.'

Decimus coloured, grinning. He kissed the top of her head and held her close, brushing his thumbs against her.

A dark shadow shifted overhead, catching his attention. Decimus frowned, then his eyes widened. Something bright glinted briefly before plunging down towards Luciana's back.

He sat up and threw Luciana across the barn, absorbing the dagger's blade with his arm.

'Decimus!' Luciana shook her head, reorienting herself. As her vision, cleared, her gaze fell in alarm. Fearghas was locked in combat with Decimus. Dark blood dripped down Decimus's left arm, issuing around the knife hilt embedded deep in his flesh. She screamed and ran over, pouncing on the warrior's back. 'Leave him alone!' She screamed in British.

'Shut up, you traitorous spy!' Fearghas batted her away as if she were a fly. Luciana fell back in the straw with a thud. The warrior wrenched his blade out of Decimus's arm and wildly attempted to stab him again. Decimus warded him off with both arms, lips pulled back in a fierce grimace.

'Roman! Roman!' Fearghas cried, raising his voice. 'He's a Roman!'

Luciana gasped. She tried to shriek loudly enough to drown out his shouts. She balled her fists in the hay and suddenly felt something heavy and damp. She looked down and saw the knotted, discarded gag. Still screaming, she tackled Fearghas again, reaching around to stuff the rag in his mouth.

His shouts were abruptly cut short when the gag entered his mouth. He tried to spit it out, but Luciana worked too quickly, binding the cloth tightly behind his head. His arms, occupied in his tousle with Decimus, were helpless to break away to undo her knots. Luciana leapt away and rooted around for the chariot whip.

Decimus grunted, straining to dodge the warrior's frantic stabs. His fingers clasped Fearghas's wrist while his other arm kept the man's free hand at bay. He kicked up, trying to hit the man where it most hurt, but Fearghas remained solid. The frenzied look in his eyes alarmed Decimus; it was a look he'd seen on the battlefield. Fearghas wouldn't stop until one of them was dead.

Luciana stood behind Fearghas and arced the whip over her shoulder. She cracked it expertly, using as much force as she would driving a team of ponies. The studded flays cut deep into the warrior's back, creating fresh welts in his milky skin. Fearghas grunted in pain but didn't falter.

The world turned red before Luciana's eyes. She flayed him again, crisscrossing her lashes as she gradually laid his back bare. With each effort, the man seemed to weaken. But Luciana had gone so mad that she failed to notice Decimus overpowering him. He'd picked up the bridle rein from the floor and wrapped it around Fearghas's neck. He tightened the strap around his throat and pushed forward, turning him onto his back.

The iron tip of one of the flays struck Decimus across the forehead, cutting a bright crimson gash in his brow. Decimus howled and tightened his grip around Fearghas's throat.

Luciana immediately threw the whip aside. 'I'm sorry!' She stooped, concern gradually replacing the bright anger colouring her face.

He ignored her, grimacing as the blood coursed over his nose and dripped onto the warrior's face. Fearghas still thrashed about, waving his gory dagger in the air. Decimus squeezed the rein tighter against the Silure's throat, feeling his windpipe cave beneath him. Still gripping tightly, he picked the man's head off the floor and slammed it with as much force as he could muster against the ground, knocking Fearghas unconscious. He continued to squeeze, however, until he was certain the man had died.

'Decimus.'

He slowly released his hands from Fearghas's throat, watching the purple, atrophied lips for any signs of life. He turned to see Luciana crouched before him, arms clasped tightly about her naked shoulders.

'What do we do?' She whispered, eyes wide.

He searched for her sodden dress in the straw. He tore a long strip off the skirt when he found it and tossed it at her. 'Bind my arm.'

Luciana took the fabric and wound the cloth around the puckered, oozing cut. Her gaze flickered briefly to his blood-streaked face before concentrating on her work. 'I never meant for this to happen.'

He ripped out another bandage for his head, then tore up the rest of the dress with a cool methodism. 'When we get back to Saibh, ask her if she or any of her pals has Roman vinegar on hand. It will keep the wounds from becoming infected until I can get a surgeon to tend them.'

She nodded, then frowned as she noticed what he was doing. 'Why are you destroying my clothes?!'

'You will tell them,' He continued evenly, 'that this brute here tried to force himself on you without your consent. And I killed him to preserve your honour. If we're lucky, we won't be run out of here, or worse.'

Luciana picked up the second bandage and pushed his hair out of the way. 'How did he know? How did he get in here without our notice?'

'We were both…preoccupied. And you called me by my Latin name.'

She winced, remembering how she'd lost all control in the heights of her sexual ecstasy. 'I'm sorry. It won't happen again.'

'You're right about that.'

She paused, lowering her arms. 'What do you mean?'

'I mean, we very nearly gave ourselves away to the world for a bit of fun.' He glared at her. 'We cannot jeopardise ourselves and our mission. And it's clear we cannot trust ourselves when we get carried away. No more intimacy until we leave here. No kissing, no cuddling, nothing. For however long that may be, until we know what we came here to learn.'

Luciana's eyes widened. 'But Decimus…I know Morcant's Roman informant. Cassia saw him with Morcant in the woods.'

He regarded her for a long, silent moment. The rain drummed against the thatched roofing, roaring in the stillness. Finally, he sighed.

'Tell me.'

XXI

Morcant's roar reverberated through the village.

'No!' He furiously paced the hill behind his hall. 'I won't permit it!'

'You don't understand!' Luciana, tearstained, balled her fists at her sides. The tattered remains of her gown whipped about her. One sleeve of the garment had gone, leaving her breast exposed as the fabric sagged over her body. Decimus stood behind her, his gaze flinty.

'Fearghas is irreplaceable!' Morcant gazed over the rocky escarpment, clawing at his chieftain's torc. 'I needed him! *We* needed him!'

'What was he supposed to do?!' Luciana pointed at Decimus. 'Just let him take me? One man alone will not make the difference in our fight with Rome.' She scowled.

'Your brute has no right going around killing my best warriors, no matter the reason!' He snapped. 'And I will not let him accompany me to the war council. It is a privilege only for men of honour. Yours has none.'

'Men of honour.' Luciana spat at his feet. 'A man of honour doesn't fear and despise his female warriors. A man of honour doesn't try to bend the gods' words to his will.'

'I've been *chosen* by the gods!' Morcant stabbed his rectangle tattoo with a cauterised finger. 'And those closest to the gods make no mention of women in Andraste's prophecy! It *must* be about me!'

Luciana's eyes widened. 'You've…consulted the sidhe.'

He laughed bitterly, walking away. 'I've done more than that. You'll see. Everyone will see. *I* am the one the prophecy speaks of!'

'What about Taraghlan?' Luciana crossed her arms, glancing at the druid seated before a fire. 'I thought he was your most trusted advisor. Or is his word only to be trusted when it agrees with yours?'

Taraghlan scowled at the flames.

Luciana eyed Morcant's turned back. 'You're placing yourself above our gods. You cannot decide which of their dictates are true and which are not. Our religion does not conform to your-,'

'Silence!' Morcant rounded on her, fist raised threateningly.

Decimus moved to shield her, but Luciana shoved him away. She smirked at Morcant's enraged expression. 'Prove it. Prove I'm wrong. Show me how you'll convince all the western tribes to follow you at the war council.'

He narrowed his eyes, slowly lowering his hand. 'Fine. I will.'

Luciana nodded and turned to leave. She motioned for Decimus to follow her.

'But I *cannot* forgive what you've done to Fearghas. You and your man will remain outside the protection of my party, in a position of dishonour. You will not be permitted to ride with us or stand with us at the meeting. You will always stay at least thirty paces behind.'

Luciana shrugged. 'Of course.' She bowed her head. 'Thank you, my chieftain.'

She left him scowling as she prodded Decimus down the hill.

Cassia pulled her woollen blankets tighter and sighed as she stretched onto her back. The roughly thatched roof of the Silure woman's pig shed protected her from the rain, though the smell and the grunting company left more to be desired.

She frowned as she considered everything that had happened. The information she'd shared with Decimus and Luciana had pleased them. Decimus assured her it would bring vengeance down on Morcant. But, even if it did, the implications of what she'd seen still bothered her.

Tears burned at the corners of her eyes. She never should have accepted Morcant's initial proposal of payment for information. She should have stood her ground when he came demanding a Roman contact. She shouldn't have arranged for the incoming tribune to meet him. If she hadn't been so determined to find…

She frowned. *That's why you had to sacrifice him to Nemesis. Only by letting him go could you bring Morcant down.*

She pulled her statuette out of her breastband and ran her finger over the bronze goddess's dress. The figurine's mantle created many textured folds. She held a torch in one hand and the wheel of fortune in the other. Cassia studied the figurine's knowing smile. 'I know you punish hubris, Nemesis. I should have known you'd see to my own.'

She sighed and tucked the statue away. She rolled over in the straw, tugging her checked wrap over her shoulder. Decimus and his little whore had hardly spoken to her since she'd told them what she'd seen in the woods. They'd spent most of the afternoon away. When they'd reappeared at a distance, Luciana and Morcant had been screaming at each other. She'd later seen Morcant leave the settlement with an impressive retinue of warriors, Decimus and Luciana trailing behind.

That had been two days ago. Cassia had no idea where they'd gone, or if they'd even return. They'd taken their horses with them, suggesting they were travelling quite far. She worried they'd forgotten about her, leaving her here to while away her days standing near trees and watching barbarian women live their dull lives. She supposed she had to trust they wouldn't forget her. Decimus couldn't just abandon his oldest friend. Besides, they were her only chance of returning home now. She was helpless to do much but pray and wait.

She closed her fist around the statuette and pulled it out. She kissed the goddess's face and touched it to her brow. She closed her eyes, whispering, 'Nemesis. Your ways are mysterious to me, but I recognise your hand in this. Perhaps I can't do this alone. I need Decimus to help bring down such a powerful man. See that justice is done here.'

She opened her eyes. The murmuring seemed to continue after her lips closed. Cassia sat up, brushing the straw from her tightly wound scarf, as the humming grew in volume.

Through the rain, she saw a light emerge from her hostess's doorway. The redheaded woman strode slowly from her building, holding a torch aloft. She carried something in her other palm before her, and she moved with a stately grace. She wore an odd-shaped covering on her head, though it was hard for Cassia to make out in the dark. Woad lines had been drawn across her face, just visible in the light of her flickering flame. As she moved between the homes, similarly clad women emerged from their doorways to join her. The hum grew in volume to a low, otherworldly chant:

'Palug Fawr, Palug Cryf, Palug Fawr, Palug Cryf, Palug Fawr, Palug Cryf...'

As the voices began to fade, Cassia rose and followed at a distance. She watched the women step between the dark, forbidding trunks of the forest to the south, away from the path taken by Morcant and his followers. Their brandished lights illuminated their journey, making them easy to track. Slipping in the mud, Cassia skittered into the dense treeline, anxious to keep up with the chanting women.

She did not know how long she followed them. She occasionally glanced over her shoulder as she tripped along, stumbling over root and rock alike. The low, glimmering fires of the settlement had been blotted out by the forest, leaving her no choice but to continue forward.

She lifted a hand to her chest, feeling the figurine lodged back in her breastband. *Nemesis, please don't fail me now...*

She slowed to a halt as the voices grew louder. The party of women had stopped. Cassia cautiously approached, keeping to the shadows. Thankfully, the sound of the women's chanting obscured her rather clumsy stumbling in the dark.

She paused between a pair of ash trunks that afforded a perfect view of the women gathered nearby. They stood in a semicircle about the mouth of a small burrow, brandishing their torches high. In their collective glow, Cassia saw that the gathering wore woollen hats with small conical points on either side of their heads. The points of each cone on their headdresses were tufted with raven feathers. All the women at the cave's entrance had likewise painted woad lines across their faces. But only the first woman held an offering. She cried out something in her native tongue and placed whatever she held at the opening before stepping away.

Cassia placed a hand to her mouth. There, shadowed in the eerie glare of the torchlight, lay a man's disembodied sword arm and a shrivelled scrotum. The tattoo etched in the bicep revealed its former owner to be a native, not a Roman. But Cassia could not look away.

The women silenced, all watching the cave. Long moments passed. Cassia shivered against the growing damp and clutched at her mantle.

Suddenly, a pair of yellow eyes appeared from the cave. The group of Silure women collectively sank to their knees and raised their unencumbered hands. The eyes grew brighter as the face of a cat emerged from the shadows. It was unlike any cat Cassia had seen; it was larger than the desert cats worshipped by Bakari's ancestors, though laughably small compared to the African lions sent to entertain folks in the arena. Its light fur was studded with many spots. Its ears were large and tufted, like the headdresses worn by its acolytes. It lowered its head to sniff at the arm and the women reverently rejoined:

'*Palug Fawr, Palug Cryf!*'

The cat nibbled at the sorry-looking testicles before grabbing the arm. It dragged the limb back into the dark recesses of its lair.

The women cheered. A grey-haired woman, clad in a spotted cloak reminiscent of the cat, rose and chattered in excited tones. Whatever she said likewise enthused the women, who interjected their agreement as she spoke. She produced a silver chalice from Cassia knew not where and moved around the group, exhorting each woman to take a sip of the liquid within. Once they drank, each of the cat acolytes seemed to enter a trance. They swayed gently in place on the ground, yowling and murmuring by turns. Cassia couldn't understand a thing they said, but one word continually fell from every woman's lips: *Palug*.

She didn't know how long they rested there. Her legs began to grow stiff, and she let her back slide down one of the ash trunks. She ached to leave the hideous lair, but their lone flaming torch within the inky forest kept her rooted to the spot. The women, too insensate to notice her, lay in their collective circle about the cave.

The light rain made it difficult to tell, but the moon must have risen higher when the spotted woman stood and spoke. The acolytes clambered to their feet, relighting their damp torches from the spotted woman's steady flame.

Cassia lurched from her spot between the ash branches and followed, her muscles groaning in protest. She didn't want to think about the cat monster or the ritual she'd just witnessed; she only knew that she wanted to be as far away from it as possible.

The footsteps of the Silure horses beat a harsh, muffled rumble over the forest's dirt track. Their riders' faces were stony, focussed on the path. The Gaesatae held crackling torches out, casting their woad painted faces in a frightening light. At their centre rode Morcant, resplendent in his furs, bejewelled armbands, and heavy golden torc. His long, raven plaits streamed behind him as he moved, his mangled hand hidden within the folds of his cloak. Just behind him, Taraghlan stalked in his shadow. The hood of his whitish robe was drawn back, revealing his domed tonsure in the pale moonlight. He held his long staff at his side, just above his portly pony's hooves. Several paces behind the pack, just inside the lit aura of the torches, rode Decimus and Luciana.

The group had ridden almost continuously for two days, following the banks of the Sabrina. They had only diverged from the native track once, to avoid the Roman roads surrounding Glevum. The group kept irregular hours, often travelling through the night. As they neared Luciana's tribal lands, she began to worry they weren't going to the war council, after all. *Did Cassia let something slip? Has Morcant found out?*

Luciana squinted at Decimus in the predawn gloom. The profile of his prominent nose cast dark shadows over his face in the flickering torchlight. His hair, re-stiffened into pale spikes with a fresh application of lime, withstood the light, misting rain that fell about them. His forehead sported a fresh bandage wound tightly about his head, marred by a thin, jagged stain of dried blood. His pale eyes remained locked on the backs of the Silures in front of them, his expression grim.

She reached across Belena for his hand. He curtly swatted her away. True to his word, Decimus had refused to lay a single finger on her after they'd left Saibh's barn. It also seemed, to Luciana, at least, that he could hardly bear to look at her.

She sighed and gazed along the black, densely forested path. She supposed she could hardly blame Decimus for being angry with her. After all, they'd escaped discovery and certain death by the slimmest of margins. But they hadn't lost their place at the war council, and the position of dishonour made their task easier. Luciana would be able to translate for Decimus without anyone overhearing them. Things had worked out, hadn't they?

The full moon broke through dark rainclouds and treetops, bathing the narrow track in a soft, ethereal glow. Luciana frowned as they trekked to the north. The party had long since passed out of Silure lands. The wooded plains could belong to the Dobunni or the Ordovices; it was hard to tell. Though she had no clue where they were going, they were heading in the wrong direction. A feeling of unease rankled in her gut.

An owl whistled from the boughs of a fir high above them. Luciana glanced about the black trunks surrounding them and shuddered.

A short while later, Morcant's escort veered along a narrower tract to the left. They momentarily disappeared, leaving Decimus and Luciana alone.

'There's something familiar about this place,' she whispered.

Decimus said nothing, hastening to keep pace with the Silures.

They rounded a sharp turn and came upon a brighter congregation of torches ringing a druid's circle. The Silures had stopped and dismounted just outside the grove, where a hooded figure stood to greet them. Decimus and Luciana halted to maintain their distance. They watched Morcant's party drop their weapons in a pile outside the knot of trees.

'Iron is forbidden within the sacred circle…'

Decimus's eyes widened. He drew in a sharp breath.

Luciana turned to him.

'We *have* been here before,' he whispered. 'This is the place where we…'

Luciana glimpsed a white antlered skull through the trees and nodded. A cool shudder coursed down her spine. 'Say nothing,' she breathed, nudging Belena closer.

Decimus frowned at the hooded greeter as they drew near. He supposed it was another druid from its grey robes and amber studded staff. The cloak's cowl, however, consisted of a colourful array of feathers. Red, blue, white and grey quills covered the entire hood before giving way to a long, wooden beak that dipped low over the druid's head. Two bright amber stones atop the cowl winked in the flames, almost as if they were eyes.

Decimus dismounted and cautiously lifted his baldric over his head. He dropped his sword atop the pile beside the avian figure. Luciana said something to the druid, twirling to demonstrate her lack of iron. The headdress reminded Decimus of the Corvax initiates who served meals at his brotherhood gatherings, but this one seemed somehow more… ominous. He felt the glare of its inhuman eyes as he straightened. He didn't look away from the creature as Luciana took his hand and led him just inside the druid's circle.

They halted far behind Morcant's men. Taraghlan had pushed forward to stand beside the chieftain at their head. Decimus scanned the clearing. To their right, a fearsome group of men and women headed by a middle-aged warrior with a lined face stood. To their left, a collection of naked warriors led by a short woman with long, iron grey hair. A smaller contingent of Britons were just visible beyond the crackling flames of a large bonfire lit atop the stone altar. More druids clad in avian headdresses surrounded the altar. One older priest, his cowl drawn back to reveal his wizened, fearsome face stood apart from the rest. A pair of magnificent stag's antlers rose from the top of his head. The long white locks that flowed from his shaved tonsure gleamed in the dimming moonlight. He swept his gaze round the clearing, his eyes alighting on every face within the circle. Decimus shifted uneasily when the holy man's gaze connected with his. The druid narrowed his eyes a hair before finally looking past him. At a nod from his compatriot just outside the circle, he stepped onto the stone altar and called the council to order.

For a man of his apparent age, his voice rang clearly through the space. He spoke in a rich, deep baritone, his tone strident and commanding. Decimus listened to the druid prattle for a while before nudging Luciana.

She turned to him, surprised.

'Which tribes are here?' He whispered softly.

She gazed around the clearing. 'Ordovices…Silures, of course… Demetae…Deceangli…' She squinted across the way. 'And, I believe, a handful of Dobunni?'

Decimus nodded. He paused a beat. Then, 'what is he saying?'

'I don't know, do I?' She shot him an irritated look. 'Let me listen.'

Chastened, he looked away. The great, forbidding oak trunks seemed to close in about him. The atmosphere felt charged in a way it hadn't before. Though he scowled impassively at the spectacle, something deep within his hardened exterior cowed. None of the warriors' eyes were on him, yet he felt as if he were facing down a charging war host alone and unarmed.

He huffed and turned to the altar. If this was the world of his mother's ancestors, then he wanted no part of it.

As he took stock of the proceedings, he noted that the chieftain of another group had stepped forward to speak. The naked woman shouted something in response to what he said, which was quickly followed by Morcant's bluster. Decimus nudged Luciana. 'What's going on?'

'The druid is one of the Elders at Mona,' she replied. 'He speaks of the need to defend their stronghold from the Romans. He said the Romans threaten our gods and wish to eradicate them from our lands. That they will destroy our honour, our way of life, and everything we hold dear. It must not happen at any cost.' She sighed. 'Now the chieftains are sharing their experiences with the occupying armies. The Dobunni know too well what it means to incur the wrath of Rome. They are worried about what might happen if we should fail and Mona falls.' She glanced sidelong at Decimus. 'Morcant insists that we shan't fail.'

'Little does he know,' Decimus replied.

Luciana scowled. 'Do not be so sure. Every one of us here would rather die than let you succeed. The druids know our histories, our stories, and our laws. They receive visitations from our gods. By erasing the druids, you erase us!'

Decimus paled. The veins on his neck tautened. 'Don't you dare turn on me now, princess.'

'Is that supposed to be a…?' She caught sight of something over Decimus's shoulder, and her eyes widened. Suddenly, she screamed and sank to the ground, throwing her arms over her face.

Decimus looked on in confusion as other warriors around the clearing followed suit. Taraghlan and two of Morcant's warriors stood in the middle of the clearing, holding a wrinkled old crone in a shroud. 'What's going on?' He murmured.

'Keep your eyes down!' Luciana yanked on Decimus's arm, drawing him down beside her. She shook her head. 'I knew they had visited her, but I never thought Morcant would *stoop*…'

Decimus listened to the old woman's voice ring a chant across the clearing. He frowned. 'What has Morcant done, exactly?'

'It's the Ancient One!' Luciana gasped. 'The oracle of Danu, mother goddess of us all and patron of the sidhe! As Celts, we are not even permitted to look at her. To remove her from her temple…' She shook her head. 'Morcant has committed a terrible dishonour!'

Decimus narrowed his eyes. 'Wait. You mean the sidhe are real?'

'Of course, they're real!' Luciana glared at him. 'They are the children of Danu, the hill people, the builders of the great stone circles! They were here long before any Roman or Celt walked this land, and they will still be here long after both our races have gone!'

Decimus shrugged. 'I just thought they were another one of your faerie stories.'

'Have some respect!' She wrenched his head away when he tried to catch another glimpse of the woman. She gazed at the grass and mumbled a prayer in her native tongue.

Decimus shook his head. 'If it's such a sacrilege, then why did Morcant even bring the hag out here?'

'She's speaking the Andraste prophecy,' Luciana breathed in between her British cant. *'Andraste's wrath springs from the flood and all she knows shall bathe in blood.* Morcant says her words ensure our triumph. With the Ancient One at our side, he says our warriors will draw all the strength they need to crush the Romans.' She turned to Decimus. 'Little does he know what harm he's done.'

'Like what?'

'She can no longer speak the wisdom of the gods. She has been removed from her temple before her time.' Luciana cautiously lifted her head, searching the tops of the trees. 'The sidhe will have already elected her replacement from the cult of Danu. But to force such things from the hands of the gods invites a terrible wrath upon us, no matter what Andraste might bring.'

'Andraste?' Decimus wrinkled his nose. 'Luci, what are you talking about?'

'The goddess of war. She destroys all in her path and heralds victory.'

Suddenly, the warriors in the clearing gasped at something overhead. Luciana pointed. 'Look!'

Decimus squinted in the gloom. The moon had disappeared below the horizon with dawn just about to break. In the flickering flames of the druid's fires, he could just make out a murder of crows silently soaring over the clearing.

'Her messengers!' Luciana smiled in awe. 'The Ancient One spoke the truth. Rome's mission is doomed.'

They both turned to the centre of the circle where a cacophony of voices converged. The male and female chieftains were on their feet, shouting at each other, as Taraghlan quickly shepherded the Ancient One and her bodyguards away. The druids and other warriors looked on as the leaders quarrelled, filling the space with their threatening and heated invective.

Decimus stood. 'What's happened?'

'The other chieftains are displeased with Morcant's actions,' Luciana murmured. She listened to the argument. 'They say even though we have the favour of Andraste, it is not enough to undo the crime Morcant has committed. There must be a reprisal to satiate the gods. Andraste must have blood.'

Decimus's expression hardened. 'And what does Morcant say?'

'That he is prepared to offer a sacrifice. One that will symbolise the coming destruction of our enemies.' She frowned and stood on tiptoe. 'He is telling Muireach…that's the chieftain of the Ordovices…to bring forth the captive entrusted to his safekeeping.'

'Captive?' A cold shudder rippled down his spine. 'As in…a human?'

Luciana caught sight of a cage as the Ordovices parted to tote the prisoner forth. She lifted a hand to her mouth. 'Not just a human. A Roman.'

Decimus squinted at the filthy figure cowering inside his wicker prison. He was covered head to toe in dirt and his own excrement. What must have once been his undertunic had dissolved into filthy rags. He shrieked at the sight of the druids with their avian hoods, his bony frame curled against the far corner of his cage. His cry in Latin turned Decimus's stomach.

'Leave me alone, you evil bastards!'

'Unimanus,' he breathed.

Luciana turned to him, frowning.

'I thought he'd died when Morcant's men attacked us on the moor…' Decimus's mind crawled back to that day, when he'd been practicing battle formations with his century. Vulso's journey to retrieve Unimanus from his shit in the woods had led to him stumbling on Morcant's hunting party. The Silures must have taken Unimanus captive before attacking the century. Decimus gritted his teeth and clenched his fists at his sides.

'That's one of my men!' He stepped forward, eyes locked on the warriors' prisoner.

'What are you *doing?!*' Luciana grabbed his arm and yanked him back. She stood between him and the centre of the clearing. Behind her, the Britons pulled the sobbing soldier out for all to see. 'You are blowing our cover!'

'I am Unimanus's centurion.' A muscle twitched near his clenched jaw. 'I swore an oath to do my duty by my men.'

'Your men?! What about your legion?! What about us?!' Luciana shook his shoulders. 'Decimus, you stand to fail more than just one man!'

'I cannot stand by when something can be done for him!' He tried to shoulder past her.

'Stop!' Luciana brusquely pushed back. 'Nothing can be done for him! The druids will grant him a swift death. You cannot prevent this, Decimus!' Tears burned in the corners of her eyes. She sank her fingernails into his skin. 'I will not let you sacrifice your own life so stupidly!'

'You fucking savages,' he whispered, glaring down his nose at her.

Luciana slowly released him and stepped back. 'What?'

'You'll throw human lives away to your gods so quickly? Just like that?' He pointed over her shoulder. The druids were hauling Unimanus onto the stone altar. The council erupted in excited shouts. 'Just like you will in this war you're about to wage?! If your gods are so steeped in human blood, if you're so slavishly devoted to them that you'll consign your own lives to these tortures, then you're better off without your fucking druids!'

'How dare you?!' She scowled, thrusting her chin towards his. Decimus's face was white with rage in the gleam of the fires, his angry scar burning bright. Luciana's eyes traced its lines. 'You're no better than us, with your slavish devotion to your stupid, greedy, brutish emperor and his shining city on a hill! If Rome's so great, why must you enslave us? We don't want you here!'

He bellowed, fists trembling. He moved to swat her aside when the action beyond her arrested his attention.

The antlered druid stood over a group of men armed with clubs. One, holding a wire, perched directly behind Unimanus. The chief druid lifted his staff high, focussed on the east. The kneeling legionary lifted his filthy, tearstained face to the sky. 'Somebody, please, help me!' He sobbed.

Luciana stepped towards him. 'Decimus, don't-,'

'I'm sorry,' he breathed, roughly shoving Luciana to the ground. He marched through the ranks of Silure warriors, paying no heed to their disgruntled looks. He stared directly at the stone altar, watching his soldier's face until the birdmen with clubs closed around him.

The antlered druid lowered his staff, striking the rock as the first purple streak appeared over the horizon.

Luciana scrabbled to her feet, grabbing a fist-sized stone from the grass. She darted after Decimus, heart throbbing in her throat. He'd very nearly pushed through to the centre of the circle when she saw the back of his head. Frowning, she collided into his back and smashed the stone over his crown.

Decimus crumpled facedown on the grass.

Luciana stooped, gathering him in her arms. She felt along the bloodied bump she'd created in his sticky, lime-stiffened hair. At the curious glances from other warriors, she smiled weakly. 'Leucus's blood is up. He wanted to kill the Roman himself. I had to stop him interrupting the sacrifice.'

The warriors tutted and turned away, murmuring about the vigour of the Belgae stranger. She curled her arms under Decimus's shoulders and dragged him away, just as the lower Druids parted. The Elder sliced open the garrotted Roman's neck with a golden dagger.

The warriors around the circle cheered. The soldier's dark blood pulsed down the sides of the altar and into wooden collection bowls held by more birdmen. The antlered Elder raised both his staff and the gory dagger high, stretching them towards the skull nailed to the oak trunk. 'Gods and goddesses! Pay witness to our tribute! We consecrate the first of these hated Romans to you, Andraste, so that you may forgive our trespasses and grant us more dead!'

The druids poured the bowls of blood on the grass, chanting a prayer for the blessing and forgiveness of Andraste. Above them, the Elder had opened the victim's body down the middle. His antlered head bent over the form, studying and prodding at the man's innards. He lifted his head and announced to the crowd: 'Andraste has blessed us with her favour! The sacrifice augurs untold suffering for the Romans!' He pulled out lengths of slimy intestines and held them high, exposing a trapped, distended passage. As the warriors whooped, he handed them to Taraghlan at the base of the stone. 'Esus! We commit to you the Roman's guts!'

Taraghlan strode to one edge of the clearing and looped the gassy entrails around an oak branch.

After much struggling, the Elder finally managed to cut free Unimanus's heart and held it up to the crowd. 'Taranis! We consecrate to you the heart of our most hated enemy!' The warriors beat their chests as he threw the pulpy organ into the bonfire.

Luciana cleared the last of the warriors ringing the circle and stretched Decimus out on the grass. She shook her head and grabbed one arm, motioning to the druid guarding the weapons to take his other. Together, they managed to heave Decimus facedown over Aquila's back.

'Thank you.' She nodded to the hooded druid, who stepped away. She mounted Belena and took Aquila's reins, slowly leading them down the path. She watched Decimus's prone form. *Please, don't fall.* She winced as a rivulet of blood streaked down his neck.

'You stupid, brave fool,' she muttered in British.

She reached the end of the path and swung towards the south. The first fingers of dawn were beginning to brighten the sky; she figured she could follow the river to the Silure settlement without issue. They needed to saddle their horses and leave the village before the war council returned. And before Decimus did something else he might regret.

She glanced over her shoulder as the elated cries and chants of her countrymen filled the clearing. There, atop the altar, the antlered Druid had cut the Roman's head free from his body and held it up for all to see.

'To Teutates, we pledge our sacrificial soul! We consign him to you in the rushing depths of the Sabrina!'

He clambered down from the altar and made for the river, the rest of the group crowding around him. Holding the poor soldier's gaping head high, they marched past her to toss it into the sacred waters.

Luciana shook her head. 'Oh, Decimus,' she gasped, 'what's to become of us?'

XXII

Decimus groggily awoke. A purplish sky swayed before his vision, in time with the gentle rhythm of Aquila's footsteps. He tried to lift his head. A sharp pain shot out from behind his eyes. He cried out, wincing.

'Be quiet. Don't draw attention to us.'

As soon as Decimus's wave of nausea passed, he focussed on Luciana's leg. Her knee was even with his head, gripping her ugly little mare beside him. He frowned. 'Where are we? What's happened?'

'We've left the war council. We need to move quickly and leave the Silure capital before Morcant catches up to us.'

'Where's Unimanus?'

He frowned as a tense silence reigned. Finally, Luciana quietly said, 'with your gods.'

'You let him die?!' Decimus tried to sit up. He howled when his headache throbbed anew.

'I had to. He was destined to die, regardless.'

Decimus, clutching his head, straightened and willed the world to stop spinning. He tried to see Luciana's face, but the hood of her wolfskin cloak hid her features. 'He wouldn't have died if you hadn't stopped me!'

'Yes, he would have.' She whirled on him, scowling. 'You are not a god, Decimus. You are one single man. A Roman, no less. A Roman invading the sanctuary of our grove, filled with our warriors and our druids. There's nothing you could have done. Nothing!'

He gritted his teeth. 'I swore an oath…'

'To whom, Decimus?! Who first? To your emperor? Your legate? Your precious city? How about Tullius? Or the rest of your legion?!'

Decimus looked down at his hands. He fumbled with Aquila's reins, refusing to meet her gaze.

'Would *they* have wanted you to uselessly sacrifice yourself?'

He closed his eyes. The truth of her words prickled at his heart. He frowned, refusing to acknowledge her point.

'Fine, choke on your pride. You can thank me for your sorry life later.' Luciana halted her mare at the edge of the path. 'We're far from safe yet. If we travel without stop, we should gain perhaps a day on Morcant. Can you ride?'

He silently nodded.

'Good.' Luciana chirped to her mare, who picked up a bouncing trot. 'Try to keep up. There's no time to rest.'

The following evening, Decimus adjusted the rough bandage tied about his head. The bump behind his ear had swollen and blackened, though it seemed to throb less than it had the day before. His eyes, blurry with exhaustion, followed Belena's bouncing rump. Aquila, breathing heavily beneath him, struggled to keep pace. He'd already had to slow to a walk several times to keep the stallion from blowing out. He only managed to catch up when Luciana stopped to water and graze her mare.

They hadn't spoken since he'd come to. There was nothing to say.

Suddenly, Belena came to a halt. Luciana waited for Decimus to catch up. She turned to him, uttering her first words in nearly a day. 'We're nearing the Silure capital. I don't want the village to know we've returned before the rest. We need to get Cassia and leave. Immediately.'

Decimus followed her silently through the trees. When she stopped at the edge of the wood, he drew Aquila up beside her. He watched Luciana dismount, slide between fence rails, and stalk through the pasture belonging to their Silure host. Her thin form radiated anger and purpose as she headed for Saibh's pigsty.

Silence settled around Decimus. Only the heavy panting of Aquila's breath disturbed him. Cautiously, Decimus slid to the ground and pulled out his waterskin. He dribbled water over the stallion's steaming hide, currying him with his fingers.

The work cleared his mind, allowing intrusive thoughts to set in. His bruise twinged as memories of the war council flooded him.

Mithras god, forgive me. He tilted his head back, closing his eyes. *Unimanus, please forgive me. If you've crossed the Styx, you've no doubt learned what a lousy centurion you ended up with. You join so many shades…*

Tears burned at the corners of his eyes. He still saw their faces, men who'd placed their unearned trust in him, only to be led to their own slaughter. They pressed on his conscious, fracturing his stony resolve.

I can't take this anymore. How many more? How many more lives must I hand to Dis before Victoria is sated? Before Roma is sated?

The answer whispered through his heart. He clutched his head. With trembling hands, he tore at his hair, hating himself and everything he meant. He leant against Aquila's shoulder and vomited into the grass.

'Lovely.'

He turned to see Luciana wriggling through the fence with two heavy pails, a bundled Cassia in tow. She set one pail of sloshing water in front of Aquila and pushed Belena's nose away, leading her to her own bucket. Cassia hung back awkwardly and watched the horses drink. The three stood quietly until Aquila and Belena lifted their dripping heads.

'Mount up.' Luciana glared at Decimus. 'We have no time to waste.'

Luciana watched him slowly lumber into the saddle. He frowned, picking up Aquila's reins with exaggerated care. Sighing, she moved to Aquila's rump and laced her fingers together. 'Come on. We need to head out as soon as we can.'

Cassia placed her foot in Luciana's hold and launched onto Aquila with her thrust. She scrabbled for a purchase on the horse's rump, awkwardly sliding her leg over his other side. Her shaking fingers linked around Decimus's waist.

'Will he be okay with two of you on board?'

Decimus felt Aquila settle under the new weight, lazily mouthing his bit. He nodded. 'I can't push him like I did, but he should be fine at a slower pace.'

'Sorry, we can't afford a slower pace. We'll be riding hard to Glevum. From there, we can take the Londinium road to Viroconium. Morcant will avoid the Roman roads, so we'll be safe from him there.'

Decimus scowled at Luciana. 'I'm not going to risk breaking Aquila's wind.'

'Too bad.' Luciana vaulted onto her mare. Belena jerked her head up, rolling her eyes. 'I'd prefer a broken horse to a dead one.'

Decimus closed his eyes as a fresh wave of nausea hit him. He inhaled deeply, willing the feeling to pass. He glanced over his shoulder at Cassia and frowned at her trembling form. 'You all right?'

'You can talk later, once we're clear of Silure territory.' Luciana spun Belena to the east. 'We can't use any roads until Glevum. Stay close.'

Cassia slid from Aquila's back. Her feet sank into the damp mud lining either side of the vicus's street. She hovered uncertainly for a moment, wondering if she could even walk. She'd long since lost all feeling from the waist down. She tentatively took one step, then another. She moved haltingly for a few paces before steadily gaining momentum.

Decimus and Luciana watched as she slowly wandered off in the direction of Antiope's lodging.

'Cassia.' Decimus frowned, nodding at Charis's brothel in front of them. 'Where are you going?'

She didn't answer, numbly moving towards the only person who could make sense of what she saw three nights ago.

The pair lingered behind her for a few moments before silently riding off to the fort.

Cassia stumbled as she rounded the dingy, puddled alleyway that led to Antiope's door. She hadn't said much in the three days since they'd left the village, though none of the trio had seemed in a very talkative mood.

Bile rose in the back of her throat when she remembered the rites she'd witnessed. She'd seen them in her dreams every night since. Though Decimus had looked at her with concern, she couldn't bring herself to tell him. He wouldn't understand. She didn't understand. And she needed answers.

She pounded on Antiope's door.

'Enter!'

The phallus chimes tinkled as Cassia shuffled inside. She coughed and squinted in the dim, hazy light to see Antiope seated at her table. The Greek woman looked up from an array of counters before her. She took in Cassia's dishevelled appearance. 'I've been expecting you.'

'Who's Palug?'

Antiope frowned. 'Who?'

Cassia collapsed into the seat opposite her. 'I don't…I don't know… what I've seen…'

'There are dark magicks at work in this land.'

Cassia met the woman's fierce gaze. 'You…know their power?'

'Are the natives invoking Palug?' Antiope leant forward, an apprehensive frown on her face.

Cassia nodded.

'Your worries aren't misplaced, child. When that demon is summoned, destruction, death, and devastation will follow. Of a scale you cannot imagine.' Antiope sat back. 'They must be very desperate to unleash such a curse.'

An icy shudder travelled down Cassia's spine. 'What…' She swallowed, trying to form words from her dry mouth, 'what is Palug?'

'Oh, Palug is monstrous. A fiend from Hades. A devourer of men.'

She paled, remembering the offering given by the women. 'Is there… anything you can do?'

'To stop Palug?' Antiope shook her head. 'I cannot match the powers of the native deities in their own lands. I can only look to the Parcae for protection and seek shelter from the coming storm. It is inevitable.' She met Cassia's gaze. 'Those touched by Palug's claws cannot escape their doom.'

A frightened tear escaped the corner of Cassia's eyes. She looked down, wringing her hands in her lap. Had Palug touched her? Had he cancelled all her prayers? 'Then…I suppose Nemesis won't…'

'Oh, don't worry about that. Your work hasn't been in vain.' Antiope selected tokens from a carved urn and placed them next to each other on the table. 'Everything you've done has worked to the goddess's end.'

'But…I didn't…'

'Oh, but you did.' Antiope looked up. 'Did I not tell you to wait for the first moon after Proserpina's return?'

She frowned at the table. 'Well, yes, but…'

'Nemesis has seen fit to grant your vengeance. The pendulum has swung; your murderer's fate is doomed.'

'But…' Cassia picked at a scab on her palm. 'I didn't get to use any of your…'

'You don't need spells or potions to enact change.' Antiope pulled another token from her urn and placed it in front of Cassia.

She fingered the round clay tablet, tracing her fingers over the letters, 'AEN.II.LXXVI.' 'What's this supposed to mean?'

'"The Dardanians clamour in wrath for the forfeit of my blood."' Antiope nodded sagely when Cassia still looked confused. 'Nemesis has cast her judgment, child. Morcant is destined to fall. Just you see…'

Luciana sat straighter as they neared the fort. Belena, scenting the familiar pastures of home, eagerly quickened her steps. Beside her, Decimus relaxed his shoulders, face turned expectantly towards the east gate. Luciana bit her lip. Why, when they were so close to home, did she shudder with growing dread?

The horses emerged onto a mist-draped moor. Somewhere, beyond the fog, lurked the fort's wooden palisade. Decimus frowned up at the dark, clouded sky. 'Might be the second watch or the third.'

Luciana said nothing, hunching her shoulders. The tension travelled down her arms and clenched her hands, drawing Belena to a faltering halt. She reluctantly clapped her heels against the mare's barrel, urging her back into a measured walk.

A crow cawed from the inky forest behind them, calling her back. Tears brimmed in Luciana's eyes. She fought the urge to wheel Belena around and gallop back into its embrace. Back to the land of her ancestors, unsullied by Roman hands. Back to a world that accorded her equal status. Back to a time when she was *free*.

Belena, sensing her hesitation, threw her head up and veered in an awkward circle. Luciana groaned and fought for control, steering her towards Aquila's rump. 'Stop it,' she muttered, as much to herself as to Belena.

When Decimus turned in his saddle to look at her, Luciana felt an icy hand tighten her chest. His questioning gaze had softened, the lines on his face creasing into a hopeful grin. He was happy to return. He belonged to the fort, to the Romans. To the legions that viewed her race as irritating fleas needing eradication. To the world where he was master and she was slave.

You believed too much in your own lies, she thought as she gave him a tight-lipped smile. *This was never anything more than a disguise for him.*

The moon momentarily peeked from behind a cloud, revealing the gate towers only a few hundred paces away. Helmeted sentries, illuminated by their braziers, stood alertly along the palisade. Almost as quickly as it dissipated, the fog closed in again as the moon hid its face.

A lit faggot arched from the palisade walls, briefly illuminating them both before landing a few paces in front of them. The weak flame extinguished the moment it hit the ground.

'They've spotted us. Come on.' Decimus sat forward, pushing Aquila into a more animated walk. Luciana reluctantly urged Belena into a matching pace. Instead of obeying, Belena pricked her ears and came to an abrupt halt. Luciana lurched forward, smashing her nose against the mare's lifted neck.

'Belena!' She sat back, gathering her reins. She prodded with her heels, but the mare stood firm, weight shifted to her hind end. Belena dug into the ground like a recalcitrant mule.

'Stop it!' She pulled Belena's head around with her reins, forcing her to turn in a tight circle. 'Don't be such a mare,' she grumbled, lowering her voice. 'I don't like this any more than you do. Stop making it worse.'

'Luci?' Decimus had halted, frowning over his shoulder.

Suddenly, two pila sang through the fog. Decimus ducked as one narrowly missed him. The other impaled the ground directly in front of Luci and Belena.

'Shit!' Decimus clucked to Aquila, galloping towards the fort. 'Hold your fucking fire! We are friends!'

Luciana gazed numbly at the still-quivering pilum shaft. She relaxed her reins and gently clapped Belena's withers. 'Thank you, girl.'

Belena snorted and ambled forward, arcing out to give the weapon a wide berth.

'Halt!' A distant voice commanded. 'Halt right there and advance no further! Where do you come from?'

Luciana halted beside Decimus, who'd drawn up about fifty paces from the gate. Brows furrowed, he muttered, 'Mithras god, what was that line from Plautus again?'

Luciana shrugged. Perhaps he'd forgotten and they could abandon the fort forever.

'Something about wine…wine and…roses. That's it.' Decimus lifted his head and called out, 'Where roses are red – and where the rose wine is mellow.'

'Approach!'

Biting back her disappointment, Luciana followed Decimus into the glow of the wall's braziers. She slowly ran her gaze up the sturdy towers and solid, oaken doors. The only thing that made her smile was the sight of a tawney dog beside the officer peering down at them. Tor, meeting her gaze, barked a welcome.

'Centurion Maximus! I didn't recognise you, sir!'

'Centurion Fortunatus.' Decimus smirked at Luci as he bowed his lime-streaked head. 'Your vigilance is as admirable as it is hasty. Have your men admit us and report to the legate. We need to speak with him forthwith.'

Luciana sadly regarded Decimus's frame in the fire's flickering glow. The dark woad swirling over his skin, the checked wool covering his legs and cutting across his torso, the long British sword hanging at his side. Had they really been enough to make her forget the treachery she'd committed?

Run. Before you face the legate and betray your kind. Before the chains of servitude ensnare you again.

'Luci?'

She unfroze, turning towards Decimus. He regarded her from the cracked-open gates, Aquila halted beneath him. The affectionate concern in his eyes pierced her resolve. 'Come on.'

She swallowed a painful lump in her throat. If she ran now, she'd destroy everything between them. She'd prove right all his misconceptions about her and her kind. She would lose not only his love, but his respect.

It shouldn't have mattered to her. What did the esteem of one Roman matter?

But when she met his blue-grey eyes, she didn't see a Roman. She saw the one man who could match her passion, the one man who could match and thwart her wits, the one man who owned her heart.

Hanging her head, she followed him through the gate.

'…and this council occurred three nights ago, you said?'

Decimus nodded. He sat opposite the legate around a large table in the middle of the war room. Luciana perched mutely in a chair beside him, eyes drawn to the floor. A clay oil lamp glowed in the middle of the table, just illuminating a map of Britannia stretched across it. The room stood empty besides, rows of benches normally occupied by the fort's officers shrouded in shadow.

Regulus folded his hands together and sighed. 'How many effectives attended, would you say?'

'At a guess, one hundred and fifty to two hundred,' Decimus replied after thinking for a moment. 'Not including the druids. And these are nowhere near full strength counts. The tribes merely brought a selection of warriors to the council. Their field returns will be much higher.'

'And the Silures know our intended route of march?'

Decimus glanced at Luciana and nodded. 'It would appear so, sir. While I personally didn't witness the exchange of information, the man described fits the description of Tribune Cincinnatus. Who, according to you, has attended campaign meetings and studied our intended route. Long enough, in fact, to have created a copy of the maps, which he was then seen handing over to Morcant. I personally saw his freedman arranging the meeting earlier in the camp. I didn't recognise him because he was disguised as a merchant, but his voice sounded familiar.'

Regulus pursed his lips. 'It's rather circumstantial evidence. I'd have preferred more concrete proof of something so high as treason.'

'I'm sorry we couldn't produce that, sir.' Decimus cocked his head. 'We *were* instructed not to take any unnecessary risks. Perhaps an interview between the legion's interrogator and the tribune's man could be arranged. That might elicit your concrete proof.'

Regulus frowned. 'I don't like it. The tribune came from the imperial palace with a recommendation from Seneca himself. Why would he give such valuable information to the enemy for nothing in return?'

'Perhaps you should ask Tribune Cincinnatus, sir.'

'Quite.' Regulus placed the oil lamp aside. 'Now, where do you think the Silures are planning this advance attack?'

Decimus stood and bent over the campaign map. He squinted in the dim light, surveying the lines for a long moment. 'If I had to hazard a guess, sir, it would be here.' He pointed to a spot on the far side of one of the mountain ranges. 'This narrow pass into the valley creates a choke point that will make slow going for the baggage train. The Silures can secret themselves on the high ground and attack us from both the valley floor and above. They don't mean to halt us, sir, but cripple us. If they can seize our wagons and sever us from our supply lines while hitting us with a shock assault, it's going to demoralise our men and significantly hinder our progress.'

Regulus nodded. 'If that's their intention, then it must be there. Smart work.'

'Just thinking about what I'd do from the enemy's perspective, sir.'

Regulus scowled at Decimus. 'Yes, you've been doing a lot of thinking like a savage, lately, haven't you?'

Decimus gazed at the fading blue woad on his chest and reddened.

'Never mind, I'll be able to confirm your suspicions soon enough.' Regulus straightened and linked his arms behind his back. 'I'll have the interrogator work on his man, first. Might save us having to besmirch the palace boy's reputation beyond repair.'

'That won't be necessary.'

The group turned to see Tribune Cincinnatus step out of the shadows, chestnut curls gleaming in the dim glow of the sconces. He folded his arms as a smug smile curled across his lips. 'You won't blacken my reputation at all. Because you won't be able to find him.'

'Why wouldn't I?' Regulus glared at the tribune. 'What have you done?!'

Cincinnatus shrugged. 'Arrest me if you want. Search my quarters. But you won't find Lucius. And you have absolutely nothing to implicate me in this without him.'

Decimus paled.

'Nonsense! I'll send Catullus to have your quarters searched immediately!' Regulus moved towards the door.

Decimus watched Cincinnatus's eyes light up. He stayed the legate's arm, sighing. 'We're too late, sir. I'm sure the tribune's hearth is already blazing.'

'Damn it all to Hades!' Regulus whirled on Cincinnatus. '*Why*, Tribune? Why jeopardize the entire army's campaign?!'

'Money. An enormous amount of money.' Cincinnatus shrugged, baring his teeth. 'Why else?'

Regulus purpled. 'You were sent here with the highest of recommendations. You're the emperor's most trusted man!'

'That's where you're wrong, sir. I don't answer to Nero, but Seneca.'

Cincinnatus studied his nails. 'And the cut he's offered me to disappear from Rome if I can recoup his investments far exceeds the things you short skirts seem to value, like valour and honour.' He chuckled. 'I've already earned back the lion's share of it by getting the Silures to sign away their mining rights.'

Decimus scowled. 'You'd sell your own countryman for an old fool's money?'

'Come now, you're hardly being fair. That makes it sound so sordid.' Cincinnatus sighed.

'But it is. There is nothing so sordid as a traitor to one's own kind.' Luciana sat very straight, staring at the tribune. Her eyes glittered, her face fixed in a rigid frown. She trembled, pale with a fury that seemed directed at herself as much as Cincinnatus.

'I'm no traitor. Nor can you prove I am.' Cincinnatus leant against the wall. 'Arrest me if you like. I've got enough friends in high places to ensure any allegations of treason will only hurt the governor and his little men.' He waved a hand at Regulus and Decimus. 'My conscience rests easy.'

Decimus turned to Regulus, brows raised. The legate nodded. In two steps, Decimus pinned Cincinnatus against the wall.

'Catullus!' Regulus shouted through the opened door. His legionary aide arrived moments later, anxious and panting.

'Seneca will be furious when he hears how you've treated me, Legate! You can consider your career as good as ruined!' Cincinnatus whined.

'Shut up,' Decimus growled, shoving him harder against the wall.

Regulus slowly approached him. 'I don't care what you say. We will find your man. And we will get a confession under torture. You have destroyed your own career.' He motioned to his aide. 'Catullus, take the tribune to the guardhouse and place him in an empty cell. Tell the men on duty he is to remain there and receive no visitors until further notice.'

'Yes, sir.' Catullus unsheathed his pugio and cautiously assumed Decimus's place. Decimus made sure Catullus had a good hold on the tribune.

Cincinnatus sneered at Decimus. 'You're all going to regret this. You'll never find him!'

'Enough!' Regulus pointed to the peristyle hall. Catullus exited with Cincinnatus. He whistled, summoning guards posted along the corridor. Surrounded by legionaries, the tribune disappeared into the night.

Regulus turned back to the table, shaking his head. 'I wish we'd the time to find his freedman, but we have more pressing matters.' He frowned at the map. 'If they know our route, we'll have to accelerate preparations. I'll meet with the governor forthwith.'

Decimus nodded and turned to Luciana. She still looked wan, staring blankly ahead. He frowned. He'd never seen her so quiet and still.

'You are dismissed.'

'Yes, sir.' Decimus motioned to Luciana as he moved to the door. 'I'll have my formal report on your desk by first light tomorrow.'

'As far as this mission is concerned, this is your formal report. I can't risk any of what's said here committed to writing.' Regulus lifted his chin. 'We've gathered everything we need to know from our meeting here tonight. That is, if there isn't anything else you've failed to tell me?'

Decimus glanced at Luciana. She slowly shook her head, avoiding his gaze. He turned to the legate. 'No, sir.'

'Then consider your task complete. And do not breathe a word of this to the other men, do you understand? No one. Not even your second in command.'

'Understood, sir.' Decimus brought a fist to his chest. He looked down at the tartan swathing his bare torso and immediately felt silly saluting the legate.

Regulus narrowed his eyes. 'Right. Go get yourself cleaned up and report to the hospital so a surgeon can tend your injuries. I'm sure I needn't remark upon the odiousness of your appearance.'

'Yes, sir. Right away, sir.' Decimus nodded.

'See to it.'

Decimus marched between the empty benches to the door. Luciana, eyes trained on her feet, silently followed.

'And you, my dear,' Regulus placed one hand on her shoulder, halting her. 'Thank you for your service to the empire.'

She gruffly shook his hand away. 'Fuck off.'

She stalked after Decimus, leaving Regulus chuckling softly in the darkened room.

XXIII

Nicomedes tugged on the traces. 'Whoa, whoa, whoa…'

The pair of plodding ponies slowed to an obedient standstill.

He sighed, slightly relaxing his grip. A relieved smile spread across his face.

'Not bad, not bad.' Tirintius, leaning against a post, nodded. 'Still a bit shaky, but I'd say that was your best corner yet.'

'I'm getting the hang of it!' Nicomedes clucked to the ponies, squeezing the reins gently. His creaking chariot trundled towards the fence. He thought for a moment, wrenching his tongue in the corner of his mouth, before tightening one line and letting slack through the other. He held his hands high, wrenching them about, and the ponies turned at his bidding. He frantically straightened his reins, easing the ponies to a nice, easy halt near the Thracian.

He sighed and wiped away the sweat collecting beneath his helmet. 'I'm not going to win any races just yet, but at least I won't shipwreck!'

'Nicomedes!'

The pair turned in the direction of the fort. There, they saw Luciana darting across the parade ground. 'You didn't tell me you'd learnt to drive!'

'You're back!' Nicomedes flung his reins at Tirintius and hopped down from the chariot. He clambered onto the fence and waited for Luciana to join them. 'I knew you didn't disappear forever!'

'Of course not.' She drew in long breaths, planting her hands on her hips. 'Who ever suggested that?'

Nicomedes shrugged. 'The optio wasn't so sure. Where were you? What were you and the centurion doing? Why didn't you say?'

'I can see you've been busy since I left!' She ran her eyes over the boy's vehicle, ignoring his questions. 'Not the nicest bit of kit I've seen, but it looks like you can handle it!' She ran her hand over the chariot's roughly painted rim.

'If she's bad-mouthing my lads' cart, you can just tell her she won't find a fleeter Roman chariot this side of the Rubicon!' Tirintius called to the boy in Greek. He stroked the neck of the seal bay pony, holding the pair's reins.

'The Thracian cavalry had it imported all the way from Rome.' Nicomedes followed, stooping beside her as she examined the wheel rims and axles. 'He says it's the best you can get around here.'

Luciana threw her head back as she straightened. Peals of laughter erupted from her core. Nicomedes and Tirintius shared a look and shrugged.

'I'm sorry, Nicomedes,' she gasped when she could finally speak. 'I've never heard anything so silly…' She gripped the rim of the chariot with white knuckles as a fresh fit overtook her.

'Has she gone daft?' Tirintius frowned.

'Who knows? She won't say where she and the centurion have been.'

'If this…' she pounded her fist against the cart, '…is the best…Rome can do, our chariots put theirs to utter shame!'

Nicomedes's brows lifted. 'You can drive, too?'

'Oh, dear.' Luciana extended her hand to Tirintius. 'May I?'

Tirintius slowly handed the reins over.

'Get in!' Luciana hopped into the chariot. Nicomedes had hardly followed before she slapped the traces over the ponies' backs, throwing them into a gallop.

The force of their start threw him back and he nearly fell right out again. He gripped both sides of the chariot, desperate to regain his balance. The ends of Luciana's hair licked at his face as she bent forward, leaning into the force of the ponies' trajectory.

He waited a few beats, feeling the shudder and rumble of the wheels beneath him, before chancing a lurch up to the front of the cart. Luciana edged over to make room as Nicomedes transferred his death grip to the front rim. They neared the end of the field at a speed far too fast for the teen's liking.

'What are you doing?! We're going to wreck!' He cried.

Her hands moved ever so slightly. The ponies swept into an elegant arc, swiftly turning away from the fence and straightening without checking stride.

His eyes widened. He continued to watch her hands, which seemed to be quivering extensions of the horses' lines. 'How did you do that?'

'You are your horse. Especially when you're behind it.' She glanced at his whitened face and laughed. 'Try it!'

She held the traces to him. He reluctantly let her shove them into his fists. He immediately assumed the power of the galloping pair and lifted his hands. Every nerve within his body told him to haul them to a stop.

'Don't fight them! Go with them!' Luciana placed her fingers over his. 'Feel their energy. Feel their drive. You are a part of them!'

He focussed, trying to ignore the looming corner ahead. He felt his heart race, beating frantically in time with the pounding of the ponies' hooves. He eased the nervous tension in his grip and felt the living mouths on the other end of the lines. The reins slipped and slid minute fractions through his fingers; he felt their confusion. 'They want me to steer!'

Luciana pressed some of his fingers and loosened a few of the others. To his wonderment, the ponies swerved almost as cleanly as they'd done for her.

'Now straighten!' She pressed and rearranged his fingers. 'Driving is like riding. You mustn't lose contact, or you sever communication with your horses.' She let go and watched Nicomedes's hands.

He felt the grey pony falter to a canter. The brown followed suit, his rocking gait jilting the cart as he fell out of rhythm with his partner's cadence.

'They sense your uncertainty. You must guide them!'

Nicomedes bit down on the inside of his lip until he tasted blood. 'Yah!' He flicked the reins decisively over the ponies' backs and they broke into a smooth gallop.

'Now you're getting the hang of it!' She watched him guide the chariot around another corner and smiled as they straightened. 'Now, watch this!'

'Luciana!' Nicomedes's eyes widened as she vaulted over the front of the chariot. She placed one foot and then the other on the wooden yoke suspended between the ponies.

'Watch where you're going, Nicomedes! Remember, you are your horses!' She slowly turned around and rocked with the motion of the chariot for a few strides. Then she raised her arms out at either side and stepped confidently down to the end of the yoke.

His fingers worked the turn out of fright, his eyes never straying from Luciana perched between the galloping ponies. 'What are you doing?!'

She grabbed the yoke and placed one foot on the back of the grey and the other on the back of the brown. She moved with them at a low crouch for still more strides before straightening into a triumphant, fearsome stand. She punched the air. 'Divine Epona! You ride with me!'

To his relief, she lowered back to a crouch. Holding the yoke, she flipped herself around to face Nicomedes. He kept glancing at her, dumbfounded, as she stepped onto the juddering wooden beam and made her way effortlessly back to the chariot.

'Are you trying to kill yourself?!' He pulled the tired ponies down to a walk, face red with furious disbelief.

'Only the ablest warriors can master all parts of their weapon.' She patted Nicomedes on the back. 'You Romans and Greeks just stick to your driver's seat.'

'Nicomedes!'

They all looked to see a plump form approaching from the brook. Nicomedes's face lit up as she neared. Without thinking, he shoved his reins into one hand and lifted the other to wave. 'Hi, Metella!'

'Oh?'

Nicomedes ignored Luciana's smirk. He guided the chariot to where Tirintius stood wide-eyed. Metella climbed the fence, looping one arm through the top board.

'Oh, my Jove!' Her beaming smile dimpled her cheeks, making Nicomedes's heart flutter.

He pulled the ponies to a halt and wrenched his helmet off. One hand raked through his damp curls. He looked down, willing his tongue to work. 'I…er…didn't…expect to see you here. North of the fort.'

'I was making my monthly visit to Mater.' She pointed to a modest cemetery by the brook. 'I hitched a ride with Lucius out here. He often takes me past it when he drives.'

Nicomedes scowled. 'I've seen you two go by. Heading north.'

'Normally, he takes me back to the vicus, but today he said he couldn't. Strange, he still had the amphorae he said he took to Londinium.'

'The ones that he tossed around as if they were empty?' Nicomedes glowered.

'As if they were empty?' Luciana glanced between the two youngsters.

'He used to. But he was struggling to put one in the wagon before I rode out with him.' Metella frowned. 'It's odd. I thought he was much stronger than that.'

Luciana's eyes widened. 'What does this Lucius look like?'

'He's short, dark-haired. Nice clothes.' Metella offered, studying the fence.

'He has a tongue that can charm.' Nicomedes's gaze hardened. 'But I don't like the look in his eyes. Something mean there.'

Luciana turned to him. 'Do you happen to know if he speaks Greek?'

He nodded.

'Where is this man?'

'He's staying in the room Pater rents upstairs.' Metella cocked her head. 'Why?'

Luciana slipped through the fence and took off for the fort. 'I need to go. Thank you both!'

They watched her frantic steps as she disappeared across the parade ground. Tirintius coughed in the silence and shrugged. 'Whatever you two told her seemed to matter an awful lot.'

Nicomedes translated his words for Metella. She smiled. 'You're the observant one, Nicomedes. I should have noticed Lucius being strange.'

'It's not your fault.' He nodded to the bangles on her arm. 'It's not every day someone comes out here with treasures from the east.'

She brushed her fingers over the bracelets. 'Even still, I should have seen…' A blush crept into her cheeks as she turned to Nicomedes. 'You, um…seem to be quite handy with your chariot.'

'I…er…' He reddened, studying his feet. *Why* couldn't he just talk to her?

'Would you ever consider driving me around sometime?' She shrugged. 'Just…because?'

Nicomedes's throat suddenly went dry. His jaw dropped as he stared at her. Had this worked? Had his wild plan to win Metella actually *worked?*

Tirintius clapped him on the back, making him cough and splutter. 'I would,' he managed to croak between fits.

'Great. How about Saturn's day, at the fifth hour? Outside Pater's caupona?' She twisted a strand of black hair about her finger, her face hopeful. 'I'll pack a meal.'

His throat constricted. A small squeak rasped from the back of his tongue.

'That is, of course, if your master allows it?' Metella bit her lip.

Nicomedes mutely nodded.

She jumped down from the fence. 'I'll hope to see you then!'

They watched her saunter towards the fort. Once she was out of earshot, Tirintius started giggling. 'Congratulations, lad.' He extended his arm. 'I'd say you've won that battle.'

Luciana pounded up The Aurochs' stairs. Metellus stood at their bottom, shouting up at her indignantly.

Ignoring his cries, she tried the first room she came to. The door easily fell open at her touch. She stumbled into the chamber, looking around.

While a rumpled blanket on the mattress attested to the room's recent occupation, nothing else remained. Cleared patches of dust revealed where a trunk had recently sat.

'You can't just run up here without…' Metellus's voice trailed off as he stepped into the room.

Luciana whirled on him. 'Where's your lodger?'

'I didn't even know he'd left!' The proprietor's face slowly turned red.

'The bastard's skipped without paying!'

Luciana ignored him, pacing the room. Where would Lucius likely go? To Rutupiae, surely, to leave Britannia. But that would be too obvious. There's no way he could make it to the coast without passing many armed checkpoints along the road. All the legions had instructions to arrest any man matching Lucius's description.

'Unless he didn't have the amphora…' Luciana stopped. What had Nicomedes told her? That he'd seen Lucius pass…

'If I ever see that dirty little Greek again, I'll-,'

'The cemetery!' Luciana leapt past him, clattering down the stairs. 'He's taken it to the cemetery!'

She leapt aboard Belena and clapped her heels around her barrel. Belena tossed her head and took off along the via principalis. Before long, they passed the fort's wooden walls in a blur. A couple of alarmed sentries on the palisade stood to, unsure if the Briton on horseback was cause for concern.

Luciana leant low, fists buried in Belena's whipping black mane. She pointed her across the deserted parade ground, focussed on the small collection of stones lining the path to the brook.

Belena slowed her furious, thrusting steps as Luciana sat up. She scanned either side of the road as the first wooden and stone tombs hove into view. Nothing looked out of place. Birds perched on the simple graves. Painted portraits of mounted warriors stood out above smaller columbaria with text etched across them. A few spouted libation tubes, inviting visitors to make an offering. A legionary slowly lowered a small, shrouded form into a freshly dug grave. A faint scent of incense hung about the air.

Luciana scanned the premises, frowning. She was so sure she'd been right! Belena trotted on, snorting and shaking her head.

They reached the gentle banks of the Bell Brook and Luciana halted her mare. 'Strange. I could have sworn…' She suddenly gasped. Romans didn't bury their dead, they burned them! And that shroud! She'd seen Lucius wearing it when he told the ghost story at Saturnalia!

She spun Belena around and threw herself forward. The mare pricked her ears, happy to go at her favourite gait. Luciana rested her head against Belena's neck, concentrating on the back of the rather portly-looking legionary.

Belena's choppy hoofbeats came upon him suddenly. He hardly had time to turn around before Luciana launched herself at him. The pair fell into his shallow grave.

'Get off!' Lucius yelped, furiously trying to throw her aside.

Luciana dug her nails in his throat, making him howl. She whipped out the hilt of her blade from her hair and held it to his neck. Lucius immediately stilled.

She lifted her head and smiled. They'd fallen on top of the shrouded amphora. Its broken sherds poked out beneath Lucius's bulk, revealing bright silver coins in the dirt.

She smiled coldly at him. Lucius had shaved his beard; his face, pocked with bright cuts from a razor, quivered above her dagger. His beady eyes silently beseeched her.

'I'm not going to kill you.' She sat up, dragging him with her. 'You've got a date with the legion's torturer.'

Lucius squeaked. Luciana held the knife tighter against his throat.

'And I will start his work for him if you don't come quietly.'

As the sun dipped below the horizon, Decimus stepped out of the legionary bathhouse. He smiled, breathing in a long draught of the cool evening air. He carefully reached past the newly stitched cut across his forehead to riffle his damp, dark ringlets. After spending a few hours with a strigil, he'd managed to wash away all remnants of his woad. Donning a dark red tunic and his military belt had felt like a homecoming of sorts. As his hand fell to his side, his fingers brushed against the hilt of his pugio sheathed against his hip. He hitched the belt higher and straightened, frowning out at the distant lights of the vicus.

He passed through the western gate and marched through the fort. He turned and followed the via principalis, ignoring any men who stopped to salute him. He followed the road through the south gate and down the bank towards the vicus.

The shadows grew longer at his side, throwing the land into an eerie half-light. The utter silence of the spring evening, save for the odd caw of a crow or a grumbled curse from the parapet, forced Decimus to be alone with his thoughts. Thoughts he'd rather left him alone.

His eyes narrowed, focussed on the growing buildings. The scar on his cheek burned hotter as Unimanus's screams replayed in his head. Tears gathered in his eyes. He tried not to blink, for every time he did, he saw the grove.

Failed. I've failed. How many more…?

He stopped and leant against the side of a wattle-and-daub structure. Gripping the wall, he abruptly doubled over and gazed at the road's rough cobbles. He fought the wave of nausea rising in his throat as the shades of his men pressed around him, suffocating. He closed his eyes, gasping through his gaping mouth. His forehead rested against his propped hand. He stood there for a long while, waiting for the ghosts to grow quiet. Finally, he pushed back onto his feet.

Further down the street, teasing laughter erupted from Charis's brothel. Raised voices issued from the doors of a taberna. A mule brayed and kicked at his hitching post outside a closed shop, angry at being roused by his shuffling owner.

'Sir?'

Decimus turned towards the voice. Its owner had paused just behind him, shrouded in shadows. Decimus smirked. He didn't have to see the man's face. He'd have known that voice in the darkest recesses of a cave. '*Salve*, Tullius.'

'Decimus!' Tullius hastened to him. In the glow of a lit sconce, Decimus saw faint bruising about one of Tullius's eyes. It marred his otherwise surprised, smiling face. He struggled for words. 'I didn't think…I just…it…it's great to see you, sir.'

He extended his arm. Decimus heartily clasped it and pulled him close, slapping him across the back. He tried to kiss him in greeting, but Tullius turned his head to take it on the cheek. 'Well met, Tullius. Well met.'

They smiled fondly at each other as they stepped back. Tullius sighed. 'I have to say, when I read the letter Nicomedes brought me…I didn't know what to think.'

Decimus chuckled. 'If truth be told, neither did I.'

'I feared I'd…well,' Tullius scuffed the toe of his boot. 'I feared my post to the centurionate would be made permanent.'

Decimus's face creased, his laughter ringing in the evening air. 'I sure dropped you in it, didn't I?' He bent forward, clapping his hands around his sides.

'I did the best I could, sir, circumstances permitting.' Tullius nodded towards the fort. 'Fortunatus stepped in when it proved to be too much. I have all the reports detailing the men's training and the acquisition of provisions, per your instructions. They're sitting on my desk if you'd like to read through them.'

'Oh, bollocks to that!' Decimus threw his arm around his friend's shoulders and guided him down the street. 'You can fill me in on all the particulars over a jar of Falernian at Bakari's.'

'As long as you're paying, sir.' Tullius chuckled.

Decimus sobered. 'There's something else I need to tell you…'

'Please.' Tullius held up a hand. 'There's no need. After all these years, you don't have to tell me anything, especially if you've been instructed otherwise. You left me a job to do. I did it, or at least tried to, and there's an end to it.'

Decimus smiled at Tullius. 'It's a shame I have to demote you to second in command.'

'With all due respect, sir, you can have it. I'm well shot of that responsibility.'

They paused outside the door to Bakari's noisy wine shop. Decimus turned to face him. 'It's not about that. It's Unimanus. He's dead.'

'Well, of course he's dead.' Tullius shrugged. 'We absorbed his pension into the century's funerary fund with the others who were killed in that skirmish last November.'

'But he wasn't killed in that skirmish last November.' Decimus's gaze hardened. 'The fucking druids got him. They kept him for a sacrifice, then cut him up and served him to their gods.'

'Mithras preserve us,' Tullius murmured softly.

Decimus bowed his head, fists trembling at his sides. He fought to contain the rage and disgust roiling inside him. *I could have saved him. I had the chance, and I failed. One more death on my head...*

Tullius threw the door open. Decimus looked up. The flickering lamplights, bright uniforms, and cacophonous voices of the patrons cast their rowdy glow on the pair outside.

Tullius took Decimus's arm and stepped over the threshold. 'Come on, sir. The first round's on me.'

Luciana followed Legate Regulus to the guardhouse, smirking. Ahead of them, two legionaries marched a bound Lucius between them. With Decimus nowhere to be found, she'd taken the initiative and brought the errant merchant to Regulus. Her steps lightened as they entered the building, anxious to see Cincinnatus's reaction.

They stopped at the first of three iron lattices sunk into the floor. Regulus pointed. 'In there.' The guard on duty unlocked the cell and the legionaries dropped Lucius through the opening.

Cincinnatus, clad in a white tunic with broad purple clavi, scrambled to his feet. His normally oiled curls spiralled about his head in wild disarray. Clenching his fists, he kicked Lucius. 'The fuck are you doing here?! You're supposed to be on a ship to Gaul!'

'The money...' Lucius moaned, covering his face with his bound hands.

'It's over, Cincinnatus.' Regulus linked his hands behind his back. 'The torturer will take his testimony first thing tomorrow morning. The dispatch will be on its way to the emperor by the sixth hour.' He scowled. 'I doubt he'll take the news well.'

Cincinnatus paled, eyes widening. He lifted a trembling finger at Regulus. 'You have no idea who you're messing with. I'll get the best lawyer in Rome!' His voice cracked, belying the conviction of his words. 'I'll get off with exile and loss of property. As soon as Nero's gone, I'll be back in the Senate as if this never happened!'

Regulus lifted his chin. 'You're very sure you'll outlive the emperor. Does your treachery extend deeper than you've let on?'

Cincinnatus's face crumpled. He slowly lowered his hand, dropping his gaze to Lucius at his feet. 'You pumpkin!' He snarled. 'You've ruined everything!'

Luciana, standing on Regulus's right, concentrated on the cell before her. She dared not turn her head towards the furthest grate housing the Cornovii prisoners. She couldn't think about them now, about every other time she visited this place. It felt wrong, standing here with a Roman officer, instead of crouching over her mother's prison.

'Don't blame him, Cincinnatus.' Regulus placed a hand on Luciana's shoulder. 'He would have slipped away were it not for the centurion's woman.'

The tribune lifted his head. His piercing gaze met Luciana's eyes. She stilled, her soft grin slowly fading from her face.

'You sell yourself cheaply, fellow traitor.' He bared his teeth. 'How many of your people will die now, thanks to your betrayal? My price was wealth beyond my wildest dreams. You…' He chuckled. 'The affection of the man who will destroy everything you hold dear. What a good little Roman lapdog!'

A chill coursed down Luciana's spine. Her breath caught in her throat, choking her. Her mind spun back to the grove. The druids, repositories of all the tribes' collective knowledge, their arbitrators and diviners. The tribes only wanted to preserve them against Rome's persecution. The druids were their heritage, *her* heritage. Doomed by her hand.

'The primus pilus's cock must be exquisite!' Cincinnatus cackled, grinning wickedly.

Tears prickled at Luciana's eyes. She ducked away from Regulus's touch and hurried out of the guardhouse. The tribune's cruel laughter rang in her ears.

By the gods, what had she done?

Decimus crashed through the door of his chamber, yawning. He squinted around the darkened room, his hearth fire long since extinguished. He looked past the ends of his sandals as he swayed for a moment. Then, blinking to gather himself, he slammed the door and stumbled to his basin.

Through the window, the hazy glow of the waning moon cast just enough light for Decimus to make out a few shadowy shapes. He fumbled around with jars and vials, accidentally knocking some tweezers and ear scoops to the floor. Finally, after reaching around an unlit clay lamp, his fingers closed around the object he sought. He grasped the basin's ledge while he held his intaglio close to his face, turning it about. Smiling, he slipped the ring bearing his equestrian seal back onto his left finger. He flexed the hand a couple of times and studied it with satisfaction.

He frowned and clamped a fist to his chest as he let out a loud belch. From the bed, Luciana stirred, softly moaning.

He whirled about and his gaze softened at the sight of her prone form curled beneath his blankets. Pausing only to unbuckle his belt, he weaved over to the bed and collapsed on the mattress beside her.

He buried his nose in her soft golden hair and threw an arm around her torso. He pressed against her backside. The heat from her small form warmed him immediately and he relaxed against the bolster. He pressed his lips to her neck, a low growl rumbling in his throat. The semi rising beneath his tunic came to rest just below the base of her spine. With a small smirk, he tightened his grasp and prodded her gently.

She stiffened, scooting away from his invitation. 'You're cold.' She wrinkled her nose. 'And you stink of wine.'

'It's safe,' he slurred, pressing his nose against her ear. 'No more… fucking…headhunters.'

She hunched her shoulders, further freezing him out. 'You forget I am one.'

His giddy chuckle was cut short by a long yawn. 'You don't…want my head.'

Luciana gazed out the window. The moors and forests of her childhood lurked behind that high wooden wall, shut away and hidden from sight. Tears brimmed in her eyes. 'Don't I?'

He answered her with a loud, slack jawed snore.

She released a shaky sigh. She'd turned on everything she knew, everything she was, for *this*. Luciana let the tears streak down her cheeks, her sight of the wall blurring into nothingness.

XXIV

Decimus groggily awoke to the feeling of someone pulling on his legs. He blinked and turned to the window. Fingers of pinkish purple had begun to tinge the blackened sky. At any moment, the cornu would call the legion to rise.

He lifted his head to see Luciana unlacing the sandals he hadn't bothered to remove the night before. He struggled into a sitting position, groaning, as she pulled the last shoe away.

'You'll be late for morning assembly, sir.' She handed him a pair of socks and his calf-length boots. As he took them, she turned to his armour rack in the corner.

'I've fallen away from my morning routine.' He laced the boots up and sighed, shaking his head. 'It's astonishing, what a lack of discipline can do to you.'

Luciana froze at the sound of his words, her spine stiffening. With deliberate slowness, she lifted his cuirass from the rack.

Decimus took it from her, lifting the heavy apparatus over his head and settling it on his shoulders. Luciana ducked behind him and laced it in place.

'Thanks for getting me up in time,' he murmured, glancing over his shoulder.

'I live to serve, *sir.*' She consciously studied her fingers. Kneeling, she scooped his belt from the floor and fastened it about his waist.

Decimus ran a hand through his unruly ringlets before clapping a felt skullcap over them. Then, after checking to make sure his horsehair crest was securely fastened, he slipped on his heavy bronze helmet.

Luciana finished fastening his shin greaves and stood to see him settle the baldric holding his gladius over his shoulder. Her heart thudded in her throat at the sight of Decimus clad in his uniform. He had again become Centurion Decimus Maximus, primus pilus of the Fourteenth Gemina, noble equestrian and faithful servant of Rome. His stony, whiskered face gazed at her from beneath his helmet, his eyes piercingly clear. His appearance was maddeningly handsome and just as remote as when she'd first laid eyes on him.

Words of love bubbled up her throat, only to die on her lips. Her face fell. What business had *she*, a barbarian princess, with this Roman soldier? He would never betray his own cause. He would command his men to murder every last one of her people if he were instructed to do so, and he wouldn't give it another thought. He could never be anything more than her enemy, despite her attraction to him. The chasm between them was too great.

When heart and home are torn in two…

Her fingers tenderly danced along the lines of his muscled cuirass before falling to her side. She turned away, choking back a sob. 'I…I must go and see to your horse.'

'Luci…'

She raced down the corridor and slammed his door behind her.

'What's the meaning of this, soldier?'

The legionary winced, drawing back from Decimus's frighteningly close face. 'What's the meaning of what, sir?'

'This!' Decimus pinched a helmet strap dangling from the legionary's cheek guard. He held the leather before the soldier's eyes. 'This tear is so large I'm surprised it hasn't fallen right off!' He gave it a sharp yank. The thong snapped off in his hand. 'In fact, it just did! Do you mean to go into battle without your helmet securely fastened?'

'I-I'm sorry, sir,' the legionary stammered, 'I've been meaning to have it replaced. Just haven't gotten the coppers together, like.'

'Well, if you'd kept your kit in better repair, you wouldn't need to replace it to begin with!' Decimus threw the leather on the ground and glanced over his shoulder. 'Optio! Take this man's name down. He's to be assigned latrine duty for the duration of our summer campaign.'

'Yes, sir,' Tullius mumbled, scribbling on his tablet.

'I don't care how you do it, but I expect to see your strap replaced by morning assembly tomorrow.' Decimus jabbed a finger at the quailing legionary. 'Understood?'

'Yes, sir. Perfectly, sir.'

Decimus nodded and stepped away, continuing down the row he'd selected for inspection.

'Name, soldier?' Tullius sighed, stylus poised over his growing list.

'Spinther, sir. Julius Leander Spinther, third century, second cohort.' The legionary tentatively nodded at Decimus. 'What's gotten into the centurion, sir? I thought he'd been on personal leave for the last few days, like.'

Tullius shook his head, lowering his voice. 'You know what the old ballbusters are like once they're back to it. I'd get that strap sorted out sharpish if I were you. We're leaving on campaign shortly and the primus pilus is in a right snit.'

Spinther nodded. 'Yes, sir.'

'What do you mean, you honed it all afternoon?! This blade's duller than an orator's twaddle!'

Tullius glanced down the row to where Decimus had paused, holding up a legionary's blade. He clapped his tablet shut and gave Spinther a harried nod before trotting over to Decimus's next victim.

'This couldn't nick a fucking twig!' Decimus threw down the legionary's gladius. Instead of embedding itself in the dirt, the blade's tip pinged off a small stone and bounced awkwardly onto the grass. Decimus pointed at the weapon. 'It's useless!'

'I apologise, sir.'

'Apologies aren't going to fucking cut it when the enemy's giving battle!' Decimus turned to Tullius. 'Optio! Write this man up on a charge for ill maintained equipment. And assign him to barley rations for one month.'

'Yes, sir. Just, if I might suggest…' Tullius led Decimus a few paces away from the men, his voice muted. 'We haven't much time left and there's a lot of preparation to see to. Perhaps it would be best if you'd…' He nodded towards the small tribunal erected at the head of the assembly ground.

The lines on Decimus's face furrowed. He glanced away, breathing a long sigh. 'Yes, I suppose you're right.'

He spun on his heel and marched over to the stand. Before he could ascend its short ladder, Tullius fumbled for something tucked in his belt. 'Sir!'

Decimus paused, heaving an exasperated sigh. 'Yes, Tullius, what is it now?'

'I couldn't help but notice your old one was damaged.' He flourished a vine staff and held it out to Decimus. 'So, I got you this.'

Decimus took the vitis from Tullius's outstretched hand. He ran his fingers over the knotted wood. Waves had been carved into the looping shaft, while the top resembled a horse's head. Decimus's calloused palms closed around the staff. He lifted his gaze to Tullius, eyes shining. 'Thanks, brother.'

Tullius bit back a smile and nodded.

With a flourish, Decimus scaled the platform. 'All right, you sorry sacks of shit!' He strolled to the centre of the tribunal, swinging his new vitis about. 'As you've no doubt heard by now, we are shortly to begin the summer's campaign. Governor Paulinus will tell you more of the particulars when he arrives from Glevum with the Twentieth Valeria. But I will tell you this right now: this summer, the druids' reign of terror on this isle comes to an end.' He swept a finger across the parade ground. 'And *you lot* are going to make it happen!'

A hoarse cheer rippled through the ranks. From beside the platform, Tullius looked on with an approving nod.

Decimus's face shone with a ruddy glow. Every step, every gesture he made conveyed a measured power. 'We shall avenge our fallen brothers! We shall secure the safety of our colonies, and at last bring peace to the people of Britannia!'

The legion roared back enthusiastically.

Decimus brandished his gladius and punched it towards the sky. 'Roma Victrix!'

'Roma Victrix! Roma Victrix!'

As the assembled ranks rattled their weapons, Tullius frowned, eyeing the centurion carefully.

Decimus's expression had softened, a tear streaking down his cheek. He gazed into the distance, remembering Unimanus and the other men lost to the druids' cruelty. This round of vengeance would only create another butcher's bill for the Britons. *Peace. Do they really think we're going to create peace?!*

Even with another victory, the violence wouldn't end. It never would.

'The optio's approved my meeting with Metella, so long as he accompanies me. Do you think I could borrow your mare?' Nicomedes popped his head over the stall divider and smiled at Luciana.

'Of course.' Luciana freed a particularly tough tangle from Aquila's tail. 'Anything for you and your little girlfriend.' She dropped her comb into a bucket and picked up a body brush.

He stuck his tongue out. 'Now you know my secret, it's only fair you tell me yours. Where were you? I was beginning to think you'd convinced the centurion to run away with you.'

Luciana's brush strokes faltered for a moment. 'Don't be ridiculous,' she scorned. 'The centurion would never do a thing like that.'

Nicomedes hauled himself onto the partition and hugged his knees.

'What's happened? Did you two have a falling out again?'

She frowned. 'You know, you really do ask the most impertinent questions.'

'Right.' The boy jumped back into Nero's stall. 'I didn't mean to bother you or anything.'

Luciana sighed. She dropped the brush and shuffled over, folding her arms on the divider. 'I'm sorry, Nicomedes. I just…I have a lot of things on my mind right now.'

He shrugged. 'Ok.' Grabbing a rag, he turned and rubbed it across Nero's shiny hide.

She studied him for a moment. 'Nicomedes, do you ever…?' She frowned and shook her head. 'Never mind.'

The boy's shoulders slumped. He whirled around. 'Oh, *please* ask me! I want to know everything!'

'That's just it.' She dropped her chin in her hands as Nicomedes strolled over to the partition. 'Especially now you have a girl you're interested in. Don't you ever wonder about how much *more* you could know if you weren't just…you know…'

'A slave?' He prompted gently.

Luciana nodded.

Nicomedes slumped against Nero's stall, idly twisting the rag. 'I suppose, if I'd been born to a chieftain like you, I'd feel differently. But I wasn't.'

Luciana arched a brow. 'Weren't you born in Greece?'

He nodded. 'I was, but I don't remember it. All I really knew was life in the Subura.' A small smile spread across his face. 'It was just me, my siblings, and my Mama. I don't really remember Papa. He disappeared right after my sister Laodice was born and Mama would never tell us where he went. Philonikos, he was my hero.'

'Your brother?'

'Yes.' He chuckled. 'Philonikos wasn't afraid of anything. He showed me how to beg and steal food from the vendors. And we snuck into the Circus Maximus all the time. If we hid ourselves well enough, we could watch an entire race. It was thrilling. Philonikos was convinced he'd be a chariot driver someday.' Nicomedes nodded at Nero's rump. 'He's the one who taught me what I know about horses. He'd gotten a job tending a costermonger's mule right outside the track for an *as* a day. He was so sure one of the drivers would notice him and he'd get a job in the stables.'

Luciana cocked her head. 'And did he?'

'No.' Nicomedes's face fell. 'He…developed a fever. And got really sick.' Tears burned in the corners of his eyes. 'Mama tried the best she could. She went without food so she could purchase cures from the apothecaries. But none of them worked. She was just a foreign woman who couldn't speak very much Latin. I guess she was asking to be fleeced.' He sniffed, resting his chin on his knees. 'She wouldn't let us near his room. She was afraid we'd catch whatever he had. I can remember standing in the doorway, looking at him there in bed. He was all red and he wouldn't stop coughing. And I thought, "that can't be Philonikos. It can't be." And I just wanted him to jump up and take me back to the races and teach me how to survive. Because I didn't know enough. And I was scared.'

'So, he died?'

Nicomedes nodded, staring past the ends of his feet. 'I don't even know where his remains are. Philonikos went in a mass grave with thousands of other people who die in the Subura every day.' He sat up, palming at his eyes. 'Laodice, she was so skinny. We hadn't eaten much after Philonikos got sick. All our money had been spent on what the optio calls quack cures. And Mama…Mama sold me to the slave trader so she could feed my sister.'

Luciana straightened, her face falling. 'Oh, Nicomedes…'

'What else could she have done? She couldn't afford us both, and I had a chance of a better life if I went to someone else. And that's exactly what happened. Optio Servius is the best thing that's ever happened to me.' He brightened, smiling at Luciana. 'The optio liked my curiosity. And he answered my questions. And he doesn't treat me poorly at all. I have a clean place to live, and nice food to eat, and I've learned so much. I can read Greek and a little bit of Latin. I'm doing all right with my figures. And the optio has just started to teach me how to write in the evenings, if it isn't too late.'

'Do you want to write to your mother and sister?'

He shrugged. 'What would be the point? They couldn't write back. And they couldn't read my letters if I did. Thanks to the optio, I'll be free one day, and when I am, I'll be educated.' He beamed. 'And I've already gotten a start on my skills as a charioteer, thanks to meeting you and the decurion. Optio Servius has given me something my family will never have: a future.'

'But you were just as likely to end up with a poor owner as you were with Optio Servius.' Luciana tapped her fingers against the partition. 'Your life could have ended up just as bleak.'

'But it couldn't have been any worse.' He stood, tossing the rag aside. 'I will earn my freedom someday, Luciana. And when I do, I will have the skills and the connections to become what my brother could only dream of being. Yes, slavery was a gamble. But it was a way out. My only way out.' He came to stand opposite her, his dark eyes strangely bright. 'I was one of the lucky ones. I've never known true freedom like you have, Luciana. Of course, I dream of tasting it. But if I took it now?' He shook his head. 'I've got a good thing going, and I'm not going to spoil it. It's coming, and I will be ready and able to enjoy it when it comes. My sister, though she might never be a slave, shall never be truly free.'

Luciana bit her lip. 'I…yes, I…I see.'

'There's no cost too high for escaping the Subura.' Nicomedes gestured to her. 'Why do you think the centurion has spent more than half his life on the other side of the world from the city he loves? He knows. He knows you have to take whatever chance you get to leave the Subura behind. No matter the cost.' He slowly shook his head. 'No matter the cost.'

XXV

Decimus looked over the ballistae packed onto waggons and nodded. 'Good. And Valeria's messenger said they're providing another seven siege weapons from their stores?'

'You can confirm with the governor when he arrives tomorrow, but that is what his man reported, yes.' Tullius, flanked by the legion's quartermaster, trailed Decimus along the length of the airy storehouse. He checked the list on one of his tablets and gestured to the next hulking item beyond the waggons. 'Here's the meat you've requested.'

'Ah.' Decimus slapped one of the carcasses approvingly. 'Dried beef and mutton. As many pounds as I requested?'

'To the last ounce, sir.' Tullius jerked his thumb at the quartermaster. 'Fortunatus made sure he made sure of it.' He cleared his throat. 'Are you positive it's enough for the entire legion, though?'

Decimus nodded. 'Yes. Each man will be provided with ten days' rations. Including our drivers, colour parties, and those useless tribunes. After that, everyone shall have to forage. Myself included.'

Tullius frowned. 'Are you sure that's wise, sir?'

'Governor Paulinus has insisted we travel light. If we're to have any hope of passing through those ranges with minimal losses, we must.' He turned to Tullius. 'Make a note so I don't forget. During our briefing with the officers tonight, I must ensure they understand no man in their century marches with anything but the essentials. Waterskins, cloaks, the provided rations, and weaponry. One cooking pot per contubernium. The vanguard is to carry entrenching equipment and palisade stakes. Everything else remains behind. No exceptions. Any man carrying or stowing prohibited gear shall be punished by sleeping outside marching fortifications. That extends to all the officers and their creature comforts. Governor Paulinus was quite clear about that.' Decimus folded his hands behind his back and nodded as Tullius made the notation.

'But...sir?' Tullius pointed his stylus at the waggons. 'Won't our progress be hampered by the siege train?'

'Ordinarily, yes. But the waggons won't be travelling with the main column.' Decimus paced along the floor. 'After we join forces with Valeria and begin our march west, a detached cohort will accompany the siege train south, to Isca and the Second Augusta. It is my understanding that Paulinus has repositioned most of our fleet from Gesoriacum there. They're responsible for taking the ballistae on board and transporting them via sea to meet us at Mona.'

Tullius sucked in a breath. 'Quite a risk. The governor isn't playing around, is he?'

'No. And the governor's campaign will succeed.' Decimus grimaced. 'Even if most of the siege train is lost, we *will* take Mona. I'm sure of it.'

The quartermaster cleared his throat. 'What's this about supplying empty waggons and tarpaulins for the main column if there's to be no baggage, sir?'

Decimus tapped his nose. '*That* is precisely why we're going to succeed. We know exactly where the western tribes plan to strike our trains and cut us off. Won't they be in for a surprise when they find our waggons full of armed soldiers instead?'

Tullius's eyes widened. 'Er…quite.'

'All to the good, sir. And the trader is arriving tomorrow to take what's left of those rotten prisoners at last.' The quartermaster smirked.

Decimus turned to him. 'The prisoners?'

'Yeah, that lot of Cornovii that's been stinking up the guardhouse since last summer. You've been holding off on getting rid of them for nearly a year, now.'

Decimus frowned. 'Only because I was under the impression that your office didn't have the men to spare to accompany the slaves to Londinium.'

'Like Hades I haven't!' The quartermaster folded his arms. 'I've been dying to get those prisoners off me hands for *months!*'

Tullius hummed. 'It seems there's been a bit of a miscommunication between you. Though it hardly matters now. During your absence, sir, we received one of the quartermaster's requests to dispense with the Cornovii. I took the liberty of contracting a slave trader for their removal. He should arrive tomorrow.'

Decimus gazed at him for a moment, a curious gleam in his eyes. He abruptly turned away with a dismissive wave. 'That's settled, then.'

'Yes.' Tullius gestured to the pile of pickaxes stored further along the way. 'If you'd like to continue with the inventory…'

Decimus nodded.

The quartermaster blathered on about the size of the stores available, as well as the relative conditions of the equipment. As they walked along, Tullius gradually noticed that Decimus had grown quieter, his questions more perfunctory. He cast sporadic glances at the door, clearly preoccupied. Tullius made to question him before thinking better of it. He bit his tongue and stared down at the notes on his tablet.

'Centurion Maximus!' Catullus burst through the door, dashing towards them.

All three men turned. Tullius furrowed his brow. Regulus's aide looked unusually pale.

'Yes?' Decimus murmured.

'You're needed at the guardhouse.' Catullus heaved, his expression haunted. 'Immediately.'

Decimus gazed down into Cincinnatus's cell. His clenched fists trembled at his sides. 'How in the name of Dis did this happen?'

'I-I don't know, sir.' The legionary standing behind him stuttered. 'I just came on for my shift, like, and…I didn't see until I just took a peek down there…'

Decimus's nostrils flared. His lip curled as he took in the gruesome tableau below. Tribune Cincinnatus sat huddled on his knees, slumped forward in a pool of dark blood. His pale hands limply curled at his sides, face hidden from view. The tip of a legionary gladius protruded from his spine, staining the back of his white tunic. Intestinal fluid mingled with the congealed blood, emitting a pungent odour so powerful it watered Decimus's eyes. A few flies hovered about, alighting on the tribune's still form.

He steeled himself and turned to the legionary surgeon. 'How long has he been dead?'

The medicus ascended the ladder from the cell and wiped his hands on his bloodstained tunic. He shook his head. 'Body's only beginning to stiffen. No more than two or three hours, I'd say.'

Decimus whirled on the legionary. 'Who did you relieve?'

'Acidinus, sir.' The legionary glanced at the cell, eyes wide. 'We're the third century, fifth cohort.'

Decimus pointed at Catullus. 'Get Acidinus and his centurion.'

As the aide scurried away, Decimus angrily paced the narrow walkway above the cells. 'He never should have gotten his hands on a weapon! Never!' He glared at the medicus. 'Where's the freedman?'

'At the hospital.' The surgeon's face fell. 'He…unfortunately…didn't last long after delivering his testimony.'

'Mithras god!' Decimus threw himself against the wall, arms crossed. He glowered at the open cell. 'That confession's good as useless, now!'

The legionary held up his hands. 'I-I didn't have anything to do with this, sir! I swear!'

'But your bunkmate probably did. Whatever bribe he took, it wasn't enough.' Decimus shook his head. It seemed the tribune had gotten the last laugh, after all.

He looked away, disgusted. His eyes fell on the farthest cell. He stiffened, Tullius's words echoing through his head. *I took the liberty of contracting a slave trader for their removal. He should arrive tomorrow...*

He slowly strolled over to look through the bars. His eyes widened, taking in the emaciated wraiths lying listlessly below. Skeletal children huddled beside naked women, whose skin hung in withered folds. Their matted, wiry hair had turned the colour of dirt. The cell stank worse than an open sewer. One grey-haired woman slowly lifted her vacant gaze. She seemed to stare through him, resignation writ plainly on her hollow face.

His stomach turned. This was what remained of Luciana's tribe. One of those sad shades was her mother. He doubted most of them would even make it to Londinium, let alone the mines that would serve as their grave.

It was little wonder Luci had done what she did.

He tore his gaze away, face flushed in fury.

Luciana whirled around as the front door banged open. Decimus stormed into his quarters and paused, seeing her in the kitchen doorway. He fiddled his new vitis uneasily. Luciana dropped the bowl she'd been cleaning. Its clatter rang against the floor.

With a sigh, he gruffly pushed past her into his office. He laid down his staff and glanced through the scrolls and tablets delivered to his desk. 'And how many of these have you read?'

'Sorry?' She leant against the doorframe and frowned.

'Stop playing games with me, Luci.' He shook his head and ambled towards his armour rack. 'You've been changing my orders about the removal of the prisoners. I knew a literate slave was a bad idea.'

'Then why did you agree to take me?' Luciana followed him into the bedroom. She clutched her crossed arms with white fingers, tears glistening in her eyes.

Decimus gazed at her for a long moment. Her petite, angular face, backlit by the flames, seemed to glow with her rage. Her green eyes glimmered with the spirit he found so irresistible. She was beautiful in her fury, a falcon whose wings had been clipped.

'You should have murdered me in my bed,' he croaked, turning to his armour rack.

Luciana watched him replace each element of his kit. No further words passed between them. Once he'd stripped down to his tunic, he grabbed a small jug from a shelf and poured himself a cup of wine. Luciana wrinkled her nose and faced the fire.

Decimus sipped his drink, moodily staring out the window. He hardly saw the men moving about, nor heard their shouts and songs as day gradually faded into night. He pressed his knuckles against his knee. His eyes glared over the top of Luciana's bowed head, fixated on some point along the horizon.

Sighing, Luciana stood and grabbed his helmet from the armour rack. She whipped out a rag, beginning the arduous task of polishing his equipment.

'You don't have to do that.'

She glanced at him, eyes widening. 'I thought you were leaving for war soon.'

Decimus winced. 'Please, Luci.'

'What? I'm correct, am I not?'

He shrugged and looked away. 'You know I can't talk about such things.'

'Because I am not trustworthy.' She frowned at the metal neck guard, rubbing vigorous circles against its surface. 'Because I am a slimy, sneaky *Brittunculus* who cannot be confided in, even though I just betrayed my own kind for your stupid legate.'

Decimus slammed his cup down with a pained moan. 'Don't you understand?! Thanks to you, that Western horde have faces now. They're *your* people. Your ancestors, your compatriots. The people who helped us. Like Saibh. And they're doomed. All of them. Doomed.' He lowered his head and massaged his temple with thumb and index finger. 'For all I know, your own brother will be lying in wait for us out there.'

She laughed. *Now*, after everything they'd done, he had the gall to show remorse? 'That's hardly likely. Timoteo is far beyond your reach. He's found refuge amongst the druids.'

Decimus sat up, his face stricken. 'Are you saying he's at Mona?'

She nodded. She buried her growing unease as he dolefully regarded her, disguising it with a contemptuous smirk.

He stood and took her arm. 'Luciana, listen to me. Your brother isn't safe. Paulinus knows the druids are gathered at Mona and has made it our target. That's exactly where our army's preparing to attack. Our plans have been accelerated because of Cincinnatus's treachery. We march in just a few days.'

Luciana pulled away from him. 'So you're going to kill even more of my family? Why am I not surprised?!'

He grabbed her shoulders. 'You must send word to him before we march. If he doesn't escape before we get there, he's as sure as dead.'

She trembled, taken aback. Did…did he actually care? She brushed his hands away and shook her head. She took a deep breath, recovering her composure. 'And just where could he go?'

He thought for a moment. 'Tell him to run east. To the land of the Brigantes. Queen Cartimandua is a friend of Rome. He will be safe there.'

'With that traitress?' She spat. 'I'd rather he die at Mona!'

Decimus's face hardened. 'You don't mean that.'

'Don't I?' She rounded on him. 'You have taken everything else from me, Centurion. You may own my body, but you shall never own my mind.'

His flinty gaze never wavered from her, his stance firm. When he spoke, his words were so low that he surprised himself: 'We can send your mother to warn him.'

She froze. They regarded each other silently for several moments before she finally recovered her voice. 'H-how?'

'I can arrange for Tullius to be placed on prison guard this evening. He'll release her in the middle of the night. We can't free all your people, but given how many have died in that cell, the legion will never miss one.'

Luciana's gaze softened. Was this as far as he'd go to betray his own kind? Did it matter if it meant her mother could go free? She considered his words and frowned. 'But can we trust him?'

Decimus folded his arms. 'Tullius has served by my side for twenty-five years. I have and will always trust him with my life.'

Luciana wavered. Decimus watched the indecision play across her face and sighed. 'Please. The trader is arriving tomorrow to march the remaining prisoners to Londinium, where they'll be sold and scattered across the province. Your mother and Timoteo are the only family you have left. This is your last and only chance to save them both.'

Luciana closed her eyes and turned away. 'Fine. I suppose if I can crawl into bed with the enemy, then so can my brother.'

Tullius Servius walked down the length of the guardhouse and nodded to the sentry on duty. 'You're dismissed, soldier. I'm here to relieve you.'

The legionary stood down from his post, frowning. 'Optio? What are you doing on sentry duty, sir?'

'I'm wondering the same thing myself,' he grumbled. Sighing, he rested his pilum against the wall and smiled at the legionary. 'It seems Centurion Maximus's foul temper has extended to me as well. Punishment for something I suggested to him at morning assembly.'

The legionary relaxed his shoulders. 'Oh, sir. I'm so glad he didn't choose to come down my row. Centurion Lactuca's a right cunt, but I'll chance him over the primus pilus any day.'

'Too right,' Tullius murmured. 'He's a great soldier, a great officer, and a great pain in the arse.'

The legionary laughed and saluted. 'Good night, Optio.'

Tullius nodded. He watched the soldier's retreating form until he'd disappeared through the guardhouse door. He waited several long moments, standing rigidly at attention. Then, after observing the quiet of his surroundings, he crouched by the cell and whispered through the bars, 'Gwenfrewi?'

A shadow alongside one of the walls slowly shuffled to its feet. It swayed in the darkness, hanging back uncertainly.

Tullius beckoned with his finger.

The figure slowly crept into the light of the guardhouse torches. As she stepped into view, Tullius noted her thin, leathery limbs, her long, matted grey hair, her sunken face, and doleful eyes. Her clothes had all but disintegrated, leaving her pitiful naked form exposed to the world. She hugged her bony shoulders, shivering.

Tullius pulled out a key and inserted it in the door's heavy lock. 'You are to follow me,' he said slowly, pointing between them. The old woman muttered something in her native tongue but nodded, indicating she understood.

The optio opened the door of the cell and thrust his arm down. He braced himself against the floor, preparing to absorb her weight. When she clasped him with both hands, he grunted in surprise at her lightness. He carefully hauled her up to the floor of the guardhouse. There was a frightened, hunted look to her eyes that aroused his compassion. She did as she was told, accepting the cloak he proffered her and wrapping it around her trembling body.

After relocking the door, Tullius took Gwenfrewi by the shoulders and ushered her into the night air.

She stumbled while leaving the guardhouse, her limbs stiff from disuse. Tullius lifted her in his arms, guiding her across the shadowy fort. He felt her fluttering pulse quicken as they neared the impressive gate facing the vicus.

'Eyes down.' Tullius pointed in front of her face. 'Say nothing.'

Gwenfrewi gulped. She studied the grass swiftly parting past her floating feet.

'Good evening, soldier.' Tullius stopped before one of the sentries manning the gate. The legionary saluted him and nodded. 'Mind if I escort my little visitor back to her home before it grows much later?'

'Yes, sir.' The legionary turned and opened the gate ajar. He stood aside to let Tullius and Gwenfrewi pass through. As the torchlight revealed her shiny grey head, he frowned a little.

Tullius paused and shot the legionary an abashed smile. 'A bit of a granny lover, me.'

The sentry shook his head. 'It takes all sorts, sir.'

Tullius cleared his throat and ducked down the road to the vicus, towing Gwenfrewi in his arms.

Gwenfrewi tilted her head, gazing about the bright lights and tightly tucked buildings. It had been so long since she'd ventured beyond the walls of her cell that moving around a settlement, even a Roman one, felt strangely refreshing. The officer toted her along the Roman path. They turned and stormed down narrow alleys until they came upon a shuttered building with a white bull on its sign. Her feet skipped over the cobbles and hardly alit on the building's wooden stoop before her captor flung open the door and hauled her inside.

He nodded to a grey-haired Roman standing behind a counter. The man looked up from his whittling to return the optio's greeting. Gwenfrewi blinked, cautiously turning her head. What in the name of the gods was she doing here?

As the men exchanged words, the proprietor jerked a thumb at the staircase. He lowered his voice and rasped an unpleasant chuckle.

The optio yanked Gwenfrewi to the staircase, murmuring a stiff reply.

The room blurred past Gwenfrewi's vision as she was swiftly whisked to a chamber at the top of the stairs. Suddenly, the door fell away. Her eyes watered at the familiar figure who greeted her.

'Mother!'

'Luigsech!' The cloak fell away as she opened her arms wide to hug her daughter. She saw nothing more than a blur of green and gold before feeling Luigsech's thin, strong arms squeeze her tight. 'Oh, Luigsech!' She cried, stroking her hair. Her daughter's warmth radiated through her, giving new life to her tired bones. Her eyes watered. 'My precious girl. I thought I would never hold you again!'

The optio brushed past them and made his way over to converse with the centurion seated in a corner of the room. Luigsech glanced over her shoulder at them before turning to her mother. 'Come, I've prepared a bath for you.' She took Gwenfrewi's arm and gestured to a small basin filled with water. A plate of barley bread, turnips, and hazelnuts sat just beside it. 'The night's too short. There's too much I need to tell you.'

At the opposite end of the room, Tullius warmed his hands by the open flame of a clay lamp. 'We're going to have to escape detection sending her off. Any ideas?' He raised an eyebrow at Decimus.

The centurion nodded. 'I purchased one of those native ponies from a trader and tied it up around back. I had Metellus lead me in through the kitchen, so I know the way.' He gazed out the opened window. 'We need to be out of here well before first light.'

Tullius looked at the two women excitedly chatting to each other in British as the old woman sank into the basin. He blew a soft sigh through his nose. 'Good luck with that.'

Luciana cupped her hand. She boosted Gwenfrewi's foot up and over the back of her shaggy bay pony. 'The horse is yours,' she murmured, passing a bundle of food and clothing up to her. 'As well as everything here. It's the least I could do for you.'

Gwenfrewi, clad in a new dress and a warm, fur-lined green cloak, leant over the horse's neck. 'Are you sure Tiernan isn't safe?'

Luciana bit back a smile. She would miss her mother's refusal to use either of her children's Romanised names, her own tiny act of rebellion. She glanced over her shoulder at the officers stood a respectful distance away and nodded. 'I'm sure. It's imperative you travel as quickly as possible so that you both may be in Brigantia before the Roman army arrives.'

Gwenfrewi trembled, hesitant.

'Please, Mother.' Luciana laid her hand over Gwenfrewi's. 'You remember what happened at the Viricos. There will be more of them this time. Mona's too dangerous for either of you to stay.'

'I'll try.' Worry puckered Gwenfrewi's face. 'How I wish you were going with me!'

'I know.' Luciana glanced behind her, face stony. 'But I can't. It's up to you to save him.'

Gwenfrewi wound her bony fingers around Luciana's hand and squeezed it.

Luciana sighed, turning to her mother. 'Travel as swiftly as you can but stay safe. I know you're still weak, so don't push yourself too hard. And take this,' she pulled the small bronze dagger from her hair and handed it up to Gwenfrewi, 'in case you encounter any trouble. You won't be any good to Timoteo or me if you're dead.'

'I understand.' Gwenfrewi tucked the weapon in her belt and nodded. 'But what about the others?'

'Leave them to me. I haven't forgotten my vow.' Luciana reluctantly disentangled herself and took a step back. 'May the gods go with you, Mother. And may the shades of our ancestors keep you and my brother safe.'

Gwenfrewi gathered the reins and regarded her sadly. 'I love you, Luigsech.'

Luciana's lower lip trembled. 'I love you too, Mother.'

Wordlessly, Gwenfrewi prodded the pony and trotted west across the moonlit moors. Luciana stood and watched her diminishing form as it gradually disappeared into the trees.

Decimus's hand fell on her shoulder. 'Come. We must go.'

Luciana reached a hand back and let him take it. She squinted at the distant forest, desperately trying to keep her mother in sight. He tugged her towards the fort, but she didn't turn around. Her feet stumbled over each other as Decimus dragged her in the opposite direction. She sobbed in anguish as Gwenfrewi vanished from sight.

Luciana tromped inside the cramped confines of the centurion's quarters. She sniffed, wiping her nose against her sleeve. Decimus released her but she didn't stop until she reached their mattress. She collapsed across it, folding her arms and burying her head in them. She swallowed her burning tears, trying to stem the misery that threatened to overwhelm her.

Decimus stood before the cold hearth, regarding her sadly.

'I'm sorry, sir.' She slowly rose to her feet. She grabbed a flint and a poker to relight the hearth. Decimus remained rooted to the spot, watching her as she worked. Her shoulders were stooped, her expression drawn. Every step she took, every finger she lifted was a deliberate effort. Her hunched form reproached him, as if she'd been entirely deflated of spirit.

Decimus set his jaw and marched down the hall. With a grunt, he flung himself into his desk chair. Wordlessly, he lit the clay lamp on his table and grabbed a blank sheet of papyrus.

Flames flickered before Luciana's eyes. She gazed into them, absently stirring the coals with her poker. Their heat warmed her body. Sweat beaded her skin and ran down her arms. She hardly noticed. Time seemed suspended, an endless void that felt like a Herculean effort to fill.

'Here.'

She felt something prod at her back and she slowly turned. Decimus had reappeared soundlessly. She frowned down at the scroll he extended towards her. 'What is that?'

'Your manumission.'

Her eyes widened. She cautiously took the paper between her fingers and lifted her gaze his.

Decimus's stormy eyes glimmered grey in the darkness; a roiling mass of emotions fought for precedence within them. 'I've changed your status to *libertus* for the purpose of the legion's recordkeepers and I've prepared copies to hand to the Principia tomorrow. You belong to no one,' he murmured, his usually firm voice wavering. 'And you shall never belong to anyone again.'

'What...?' She stood, suddenly unsure of herself.

'Go where you like. Do what you like. Keep your papers close, so no one, Briton or Roman, may ever control or own you.' Decimus tipped her chin towards him, regarding her in the dim firelight. 'As if anyone ever could.'

'I-I thank you,' she stammered. Fresh tears prickled her eyes.

He shook his head. 'I can never give back what I've taken from you.' He lifted her hand and shoved a plump coin pouch into it. 'Take this. Use it to go wherever and buy whatever you like. Belena, your clothes, your baubles, they're yours. Follow your mother. Join up with Saibh. Do as you wish. I shan't hold you back any longer.'

'Decimus!' She curled her fingers around the money and stood on tiptoe to place a parting kiss on his lips. His hands remained infuriatingly at his sides.

She broke away, frowning.

'You'd better go,' he whispered.

Luciana nodded and dashed down the corridor. As much as he commanded her heart, she belonged to the wilderness he'd been tasked to tame. Tears burned in her eyes as she stuffed her clothes in a pack. She couldn't stay, and he couldn't leave. She knew that now. *When heart and home are torn in two...*

Decimus shuffled down the corridor and seated himself at his desk, brooding at the low flame of the lamp before him. As much as he knew she needed to leave, he hadn't been prepared for the tight pain throbbing in his chest.

She stopped in the kitchen to give Tor a bone and kiss his wet nose. She made her way to the front door and paused, hand hovering over the handle. She closed her eyes, trying to silence the tiny voice calling out to Decimus. She couldn't stay here with her captor, her former master. She couldn't remain Rome's lapdog. She needed to leave before that voice conquered by the invader consumed her completely.

She still turned, gazing at the open doorway to his study immediately to her right. She smiled sadly at his solemn, comely form, thrown into half-shadow by the lamplight. 'I'll never forget you.'

'Nor I you.' He nodded and turned his back on her.

Luciana gazed at him for a moment more, admiring his sharp profile and bristled chin. He hunched his broad shoulders, obscuring it from view. She stepped out into her newfound freedom, still turned towards him. She saw a mighty shudder ripple up his spine before the door closed behind her.

PART THREE
SAMOS

XXVI

Tullius frowned as Porcius clipped his neat grey locks, staring at the street beyond his shopfront. Plancus, who'd just been conversing with him in the doorway, had disappeared into the milling traffic outside. Red tunics flashed up and down the cobbles with hurried steps; the vicus had become palpably energised.

Inside the tonstrina, however, a strained silence had settled. Tullius felt sweat bead across his brow. Damn Plancus to Hades for leaving him here! Porcius, ever the professional, didn't tremble or hesitate. He worked his shears with his same sure, skilled confidence. Tullius closed his eyes, silently willing Porcius to remain silent.

'So, you march on the morrow?' Porcius finally murmured in a disinterested tone.

Damn him! Tullius gulped. He reluctantly grunted his assent.

'It won't be the same, not having the legion around.' A wan smile pulled at Porcius's mouth. 'I've had a copy of *The Suppliants* sitting by my bed for a while, waiting to be aired.'

A trembling sigh escaped Tullius's lips. He winced. 'You'll have…plenty of time to read it in the interim.'

Porcius paused. He gazed down at his head for a long moment. 'I understand, Tullius.' He finally said.

He turned to Porcius, unable to read the bland expression on the man's face. 'I'm…sure I don't know what you mean…'

'Come off it, man!' Porcius finished trimming his hair and brusquely whisked the towel away from his shoulders. 'Aren't things bad enough without you keeping this pretence?'

'What pretence?' Tullius stood, studying the floor.

'That this…*I*…never really meant anything to you.'

He winced. Porcius's words cut deeper than a bracing winter wind. He cautiously lifted his eyes and found himself trapped in Porcius's stern gaze. The tonsor coolly regarded him as he straightened his tools. Tullius's cheeks burned.

'I…wish we could part…on better terms.' He fumbled with the coins clanking in his pouch. He pulled out a sestertius and extended it to Porcius.

Porcius froze, eyeing the proffered payment. 'Keep it.'

Tullius faced the door, struggling to maintain his composure. 'I'm paying for the service you-,'

'And I refuse it!' Porcius slammed his shears on a shelf and stormed up his ladder.

Tullius tensed, listening to his sure, heavy steps ascend to the loft. His eyes traced the profile of young Nero on the coin. Above him, Porcius's footsteps ceased. He could almost hear the groan of the bedframe as his bulk no doubt settled against his sheets. He focussed on the coin, not daring to look at the ladder in the corner of his vision. Every fibre within him burned to follow Porcius upstairs.

Before his thoughts could torment him further, he threw the coin on the chair. Grabbing his helmet, he joined the throng of soldiers milling along the vicus street.

'I'll take it.'

Luciana counted several silver denarii from her coin purse and stacked them on the apartment's small table. She double-checked her sums before pushing them towards an aged Roman gentleman clad in a dark green tunic. 'This should cover the first month's rent?'

The man's brown eyes narrowed suspiciously. He grabbed one of the coins from the top of the pile and tapped it against the table, testing its weight.

'My money is just as good as any Roman's.' Luciana balled her fists at her sides.

'Mmm.' He frowned, mulling over the pile of money before casting a disparaging glance at her. 'I'm not sure the neighbours would take kindly to a *Brittunculus* living nearby.' He wrinkled his nose. 'To say nothing of my associates.'

Luciana growled and tossed her head. 'Then I'm sure one of your associates would be happier to take my money.' She reached out to gather the denarii. 'Even if it comes from a filthy *Brittunculus*.'

He grabbed her wrist. 'I didn't say I wouldn't take you on.' He tossed the denarius in his palm. 'But you have to understand I'm taking a bit of a risk here. And besides,' he scowled, 'as I'm sure any other landlord will tell you, your silver feels a bit…lightweight.'

'It comes from your Roman mints!' She pointed a trembling finger at his bald dome across the table. 'Is that not the face of your Emperor Nero on those coins?'

'It is. Which is exactly the problem.' He sat back, still fingering the denarius. 'Nero's currency isn't worth half what the imperial mint's passing it off for. Hasn't for the last few years, now. Real coin is tough to come by in Britannia. So, if you want my rooms, miss, you're going to have to pay the difference. Or stop wasting my time.'

Luciana blanched, jaw dropping. 'You want double…?'

The landlord shrugged, folding his arms.

She reached for her braid, anxious to launch herself at the smug businessman. How dare he? How dare he try to use his prejudices and his emperor's excesses to demand more? Feeling for the hilt, she grasped at air. She sighed, feeling her rage deflate. Her dagger, with any luck, was halfway to Mona with her mother.

She reluctantly opened the purse and counted out seven more coins. She flung them carelessly across the table. 'There. And not an *as* more!'

The landlord gathered the rent. 'You'd better watch it, miss,' he muttered, counting the denarii. 'If there's any sort of complaint, you'll find yourself out on your ear!' He scrambled off, pausing in the doorway to point at her. 'I won't have my business ruined by the likes of native trash such as yourself!'

He slammed the door, leaving her in silence. Luciana spat at the floor and drew in a long breath. She straightened to gaze about the space she'd just haggled for.

Behind her, the wall housed barren shelves directly above the table. A bare, modestly sized bed, albeit larger than Decimus's cot, lay beside the window. A hearth stood across the bed, jutting out from the notched wall. Like most of the more temporary structures in town, the insula had been constructed from timber. Its dark lumber stood in stark contrast to the cold stone lining Decimus's barracks. Luciana walked across the floorboards and clambered onto her stiff, barren mattress.

There, on the other side of the bed, heavy shutters opened upon the bustling buildings lining the via praetoria. Other flats crowded in on either side of Luciana's door, while shopfronts lined the streets below. Colourful waves of people, British and Roman, passed along the streets. Waggons and mounted horsemen rose above the people on foot, carefully threading their way down the road. And there, at its end, perfectly framed by Luciana's window, stood the southern gates of Viroconium's fort.

Gathering her skirts about her, Luciana folded her elbows on the wide sill. Wrinkling her nose at the pungent, salty odour of a shellfish vendor below, she rested her chin on her arms and gazed at the Roman stronghold.

'We all regret the loss of Tribune Cincinnatus, I am sure.' Regulus gazed at his core staff, meeting the bored looks and scowls of his tribunes. 'However, I am sure the new *Tribunus Laticlavius*, Lucius Cornelius Pusio, will prove more than an adequate successor.'

A bland, nut-brown face bowed from the edge of the gathering.

'Now, then.' Regulus coughed. 'It is essential we present campaign plans to the junior centurions as clearly as possible. We have to move swiftly, before we lose the momentum of surprise. Instructions must be clear, the shared objective apparent.' Regulus pointed to Decimus. 'And it's up to you, Primus Pilus, to ensure they communicate that to their men.'

'Aye, sir,' Decimus replied.

'Ready, sir?' Regulus gazed over their heads at a powerful presence looming in the back of the room.

'Right, men. Let's present our campaign to the legion.' Governor Paulinus stood aside and allowed Regulus's retinue to file out.

'Centurion Maximus, a word.' Regulus gestured to Decimus. He fell into step with Regulus and Paulinus at the back of the crowd.

'I'm afraid we've got a bit to follow up on regarding that report you left me earlier.'

Decimus adjusted the strap of his polished medal harness. The legion's officers had been arrayed in full parade regalia to receive the governor and the Twentieth Valeria earlier that afternoon. 'The…er…one I didn't write, sir?'

'Correct.'

'I understand the recent role you've played regarding the intelligence gathered,' Paulinus murmured. He passed a hand over his silver head. 'And the need to rapidly accelerate our plans. I wanted to go over your estimates regarding the Silures' attack.' He held up a rolled map in his other hand. 'You may be asked to provide those numbers at the officers' meeting shortly.'

'Yes, sir.' Decimus nodded. 'You may depend on it.'

'Good.' Paulinus glanced over his shoulder at the legate.

Regulus coughed. 'I wanted to share what we've gathered from the late tribune, in case it sheds any new light on what you or your wench observed.'

Decimus nodded. The man's slick escape from justice still rankled in his gut. 'Got to hand it to the palace boy, he managed to take the noble way out. I didn't think he had it in him.'

'It seems that wise old Seneca has invested heavily in our new province, granting generous loans to the placated tribes and claiming shares in new silver mines to the north and west.' Paulinus's expression darkened. 'The lack of slaves and product, as well as the volatility of the mining regions, has made him a bit jumpy. Pleas to the emperor to expand Rome's presence here is continually falling on deaf ears.'

Decimus frowned. 'We aren't to abandon Britannia, surely?'

Paulinus shook his head. 'Such an outcome is highly doubtful. Rome is too much involved here as it is. But it's safe to say that Britannia has ceased to become…useful, or…lucrative, in the eyes of the imperial court. So, Seneca began calling in his loans. The whole misbegotten lot of them.'

'Pardon, sir. How does this involve the Silures and Cincinnatus?'

Regulus folded his arms, slowing his steps. 'Seneca handpicked Tribune Titianus's replacement and sent him here under the express instructions to recoup his stake in the silver mines at any cost. That meant charging the Brigantes hand over fist to buy him out. Turns out they were willing to do so, for a price.'

'The army's intelligence,' Decimus breathed.

Regulus nodded. 'The Silures caught word and wanted in on what Cincinnatus was selling. While the sharing of information with the allied Brigantes isn't ideal, sharing with the Silures is nothing short of disastrous. The greedy bastard was out for what he could get, too. He handed over our campaign plans to the enemy in return for a hefty donative to his personal coppers.'

Decimus stared at his toe, thinking over the events in Siluria. 'His man, Lucius, was the go-between. He showed up as a merchant intending to smuggle the payment out in his amphorae, only Morcant wanted the information first. That's what he and the translator were arguing about in Greek when I saw them.'

'It would appear so.' Regulus nodded. 'The Silures never paid up, either. The denarii in that amphora were silver-plated tin. I went through the tribune's accounts, and the only money he sent back to Rome accounted for Seneca's mine shares. That idiot sold us out for a song.'

'Is there anything else significant to you, in the light of this information?' Paulinus's piercing gaze met Decimus's. 'Any words or actions from those cunts, or their wretched holy men?'

Decimus slowly shook his head. 'Their chieftain seemed very sure he knew, or would shortly know, our plan of attack. And it would appear he was correct.' He frowned down the end of his nose. 'There was some nonsense about a prophecy, and the chieftain's druid advisor had a strange habit of disappearing into the trees. But I was told that all that had something to do with the hill people.'

'Hill people?' Paulinus recoiled. 'What in Hades are you on about?'

'Our enemy thinks faerie people dwell in the hills, sir. The druids defer even to them in the matters of their gods.'

Paulinus shook his head and threw open the legate's door. 'The sooner we eradicate these vile, twisted beliefs of theirs, the better.'

'I couldn't agree more, sir.' Decimus shuddered, remembering the night in the grove. He fell into step with Regulus behind the governor as they strode down the peristyle to the war room. He clapped his helmet on and fastened its leather chin straps.

'Governor Paulinus!'

The sound of hurried steps down the colonnade made the trio turn. Decimus's shoulders slumped. An unfamiliar junior tribune raced towards them, a sealed tablet tucked under his arm.

'Yes, Vespasianus, what is it?' Paulinus sighed, extending his hand.

Decimus narrowed his eyes at the young man hastening to a stop before them. He was far too young to be the Vespasianus he knew of, yet the set of his square jaw and the angle of his sizable, patrician nose evoked memories of the former legate of the Second Augusta.

He shot a questioning glance at Regulus, who nodded. 'The former legate's son,' he whispered. 'Arrived with reinforcements from Germania for the summer's campaign.'

Decimus closed his eyes as the lad threw up a hasty salute, feeling the weight of his medal-harness pulling him towards the ground. Nothing made him feel older than seeing the sons of men he'd served with in uniform.

'Urgent communication from the tax office in Colonia Camulodunum, regarding one of the local tribes.' The gasping tribune held out the missive, which Paulinus broke open and read.

With a grunt, he thrust it back at young Vespasianus. 'Send this to Londinium with a note from myself referring the matter to Procurator Decianus. Finances are his domain.'

'Sir.' The tribune clapped another salute and scuttled back down the corridor.

The governor met the studiedly uncurious looks of Decimus and Regulus. He shook his head. 'The colonia's officer is in a dither about what to do regarding the Iceni, now their chieftain's died. Seems the client-king's wife has declared her daughters his heirs and is ruling as queen regent in their stead. With no word about the debt they owe to the imperial coffers.'

'But sir…' Decimus frowned. 'Aren't tribal matters your concern?'

'Ordinarily, yes. But moving the campaign this far forward means I haven't got the time or the resources. Besides, the Iceni haven't been a problem for years. Decianus can handle matters there.' Paulinus looked at the war room door. 'It's best to move ahead with the campaign on Mona and strike quickly, before fresh strife arises from a new quarter.'

Decimus grimaced. 'Isn't retaliation in the east a foregone conclusion?'

Paulinus shook his head. 'Likely, but weak. Nothing that Decianus and the Londinium garrison can't handle. If he needs assistance, Legate Cerialis and the Ninth can be sent down from Lindum.'

'What might or might not happen to our rear isn't our problem.' Regulus frowned. 'We have to push forward to Mona, before the western tribes have time to lay traps and fortify their defences. The faster we move, the more Roman lives we can spare.'

Decimus paled. *Roman lives.* The deaths of Britons, Luciana's kin, the women and children belonging to those warriors and druids, mattered not. They never had. But *Roman lives…?*

The faces of legionaries, centurions, decurions, optios, and prefects crowded his mind. Unimanus's howls as he perished on the druids' altar backed their haunted looks. Too many Roman lives had already been sacrificed in the taking of Britannia. How many more would be lost this summer? The scar on his cheek throbbed.

A throat cleared and Decimus blinked. He saw the eyes of the two officers upon him. Regulus gestured impatiently towards the door.

'Sorry, Governor, sir.' Decimus assumed a bland look, ignoring the nausea swirling in his gut. He brushed past them both through the doorway. He found himself at the front of rowed benches, now filled with centurions and optios loudly conversing with one another. He stiffened, tapping his vine staff against a shin greave to be heard above the clamour. 'Commanding officer present!'

The rows of men alertly hopped to attention as Governor Paulinus and Legate Regulus swept into the room.

Luciana sat up with a start, leaning forward to peer through the window. *Was it?*

She saw a mass of forms emerge from the fortress's gate. The column wound its gradual way down the street. Their progress was painfully slow.

She shifted from foot to foot, elbows propped on the window ledge. Her procurement of the space, her hours of vigilance, were finally going to pay off. She looked over the soldiers, scanning their faces for one in particular.

There! A figure emerged from the fortress, surrounded by a stately entourage and borne aloft from grunts on the ground. She watched his cool, arrogant gaze sweep across the vicus and a smile curled her lips. 'How little you know, Roman. How little you know.'

She pulled the shutters closed. Pausing only to scoop her wolfskin cloak from the mattress, she skipped out the door.

At the sight of the procession making its way towards her, Luciana ducked around the side of the tenement house. She wrapped her cloak about her. Pulling the cowl over her head, she stole between the buildings, ducking stray children and discarded refuse.

After making steady progress, she finally passed small farms situated on the outskirts of the vicus. Pausing to glance at the soldiers' receding backs, she ducked her head and darted off the iron-lined road. She slipped into a paddock and whistled for Belena. She grinned as the mare answered her, galloping to her side. She swung onto Belena's back and circled around. They jumped the fence and made for the open moors. Her rapidly beating heart, synced with Belena's jerky cadence, carried her closer to Siluria.

XXVII

'Sir?' Tullius rapped at Decimus's door. 'Are you there?'

Silence.

He frowned at the door's threshold. No light shone from within. Behind him, men from the Twentieth Valeria lighted cookfires along the intervallum. Tullius pressed his ear to the door, trying to hear something over the noise they generated. He could detect nothing from Decimus's quarters.

Tullius sighed at the black evening skies and pounded more insistently. 'Sir, I bear a missive from the governor. There's business of a matter most urgent I must discuss!'

He stared at the mute barrier for a moment longer. Then, just as he sighed and turned away, a low voice murmured from within:

'Come in, Tullius.'

Tullius clenched his fists, pausing a moment before he stormed inside.

'Sir…' He slowed to a halt, letting his eyes adjust to the darkness. Decimus's lamps sconced along the hall remained unlit. As he slowly neared a flickering light from the bed chamber, Tullius tripped on a discarded sandal. He pushed the door open and grimaced at the sight of his friend's armour scattered haphazardly about the room. Decimus's hound whined, thumping his tail from a pile of furs beside the bed. A low, dying fire glowed in the hearth, providing barely enough illumination to see the centurion.

Decimus sat on his bed, staring at an object he idly turned over in his fingers. Tullius frowned; it looked to be a dull yellow blanket or scarf. He hadn't stirred when Tullius entered, his gaze fixed on the fabric.

'Decimus,' Tullius murmured, shifting from foot to foot. He frowned at his friend. 'Are you all right, brother?'

'She left this,' Decimus said, his voice distant. 'It was the first garment I ever gave her. She wasn't pleased with it by half.' A strangled laugh caught at the back of his throat. 'I suppose that's why she didn't want it.'

Tullius frowned. Decimus's rumpled tunic and bloodshot eyes betrayed his lack of sleep. A jar of olives sat by his elbow, untouched. The lees of an emptied wine amphora dripped onto the tile floor. He looked as terrible as Tullius had felt of late. *Get yourself together, Decimus!* He thought. *You are better than this!*

He gently laid a hand on his shoulder. 'You did the right thing, you know.'

'Yes.' Decimus slowly lifted the tunic to his nose and drew a long breath. A small, anguished cry escaped his lips.

'Come on, Decimus.' Tullius dug in his fingers. 'We've got one last campaign ahead of us. The governor needs you. The men need you. *I* need you.'

Decimus lowered the tunic to his lap. His shoulders drooped. 'You're right,' he croaked. He shook his head at the pooled fabric. 'This is all over now.'

He stood and tossed the tunic into the fire. Tor barked in alarm.

'Come.' Decimus whisked his cloak about his shoulders and walked to the door. 'It's our final night in anything remotely approaching civilisation. Let's make the most of what little time we have left.'

He stormed outside, not waiting for Tullius. Tullius hadn't followed; he stood watching the flames engulf the tunic, mouth agape. It seemed they'd both resigned themselves to misery's clutches.

'Oh…oh!'

Cassia panted, rocking violently on her bed. Decimus loomed at its end, thrusting into her with a force that shook her to her core. She could hardly draw breath as he met her again and again. It was all she could do to cling on for the ride, wincing between gasps.

She opened her eyes to focus on Decimus's handsome face. His features had contorted in an enraged scowl, his whiskered lips pulled back to bare his teeth. Sweat poured profusely down his brow, dripping off the tip of his nose to the skirts cast above Cassia's shuddering freckled legs. His frighteningly stormy gaze bore through her. He roared like a man possessed.

In a matter of heartbeats, it was over. Decimus's snarl petered into a low whine as he withdrew, collapsing facedown on the bed beside her.

Cassia clasped her torso, drawing ragged breaths as she gazed at the ceiling. Her walls throbbed with an intensity she only felt from the roughest of customers. She tried to close her legs and gasped. She might not be walking or sitting properly for the next couple of days.

She turned to him, trying to glimpse his brow through her pillowed halo of curls. She stretched out a hand and stroked his short, greying ringlets. 'I'm glad you came back to me, Decimus.'

'I needed to say goodbye,' he rasped. 'And…I needed to release something else.'

'I could tell.' She grimaced. 'Never matter. One last time before you leave.'

He clutched her wrist, face still buried in the sheets. 'I have provided for you in my will. You should go back to Rome.'

Cassia's eyes widened. She propped herself on an elbow. 'You aren't coming with me?'

'This is my final campaign, Cassia.' He released her arm, curling his fingers under him. 'My time has come. I can feel it.'

'Nonsense.' She shoved his shoulder, laughing shakily. 'It's all that creepy native mysticism getting to you. I know it's gotten to me.' She shuddered. 'I can't wait until we're both miles from here and can enjoy the peace of retirement.' She caressed his cheek with the back of her hand. 'You'll be well shut of this place, believe you me. And I don't mind telling you so. I knew that little British slave girl was trouble from the start.'

She lifted her palm and frowned at damp droplets shining on her knuckles. 'Decimus?'

A low growl issued from his throat. His fingers snatched at the silken sheets before he lurched onto his side, facing away from her. He scowled at the wall, trying to quell his rage as tears streaked down his wizened cheeks.

'Death is all around me…' he whispered, the scar on his cheek burning. He felt the ghosts from his past hover close, taking him to task for his failures.

Unimanus…

Every time he closed his eyes, he saw Unimanus screeching for help on the druids' altar. The poor lad had become just one more in a long list of soldiers he'd failed…

'You aren't yourself, Decimus.' Cassia reached around and clung to his shoulders, jolting him out of his reverie. Her nails dug into his skin with a fervour that chilled him. Did she feel his impending doom, too? The odour of her cloying perfume rankled in his throat, threatening to choke him, as she nestled her head against his neck. 'How can you speak of dying when there's still so much life within you? Think about Rome, about your future and the farm you always wanted. It's right there, Decimus. You'll make it. I know it.' She squeezed him tighter. 'Once you're back on the boat, sailing far away from this horrible place and its horrible people, you'll become the happy young man I grew up with. You'll see.'

He frowned at the wall until it blurred. Cassia's words fell on deaf ears. He knew he was about to die, and he didn't fear it. He could imagine no future more apt, more comforting, than that of his body following his heart into the grave.

XXVIII

Luciana parted the bushes, peering at the slave train moving down the road. Roman legionaries marched along the path to Londinium, prodding the chained women and children whenever they faltered. The sight of her people naked, malnourished, covered head to toe in dirt and grime, made her snap the branches in her hands.

Above them all, borne by a cadre of manservants, a slave trader scowled down at them from his wicker chair. His bejewelled fingers, twitching on the staff of a long-handled flay, sparkled in the dim summer sun. His beady eyes saw everything as he sat barking orders, flicking his whip whenever their progress displeased him.

Luciana drew back from the shrubbery, turning to the woad-painted woman crouched beside her. 'Well? What do you think?'

Saibh narrowed her eyes at the train shuffling past and shook her head. 'Just a moment longer. We can't risk the big one getting away.' She nodded at the trader's chair bringing up the rear.

She cautiously withdrew from the brush and glanced up and down the line of women. They crouched with swords drawn, awaiting her order to attack. Saibh turned to Luciana and smiled. 'I'm hoping Deoiridh is ready with her half on the other side of the road.'

'She's ready.' Luciana fidgeted, every muscle primed for action. She glanced at a young Silure woman beside her, whose eyes were trained on the passing Roman soldiers. Bloodlust gleamed in her gaze. Luciana turned to Saibh. 'Trust me, we all are.'

'Not long now.' Saibh set her sights on the target.

Luciana held her blade steady, pulse roaring in her head. She felt surprisingly calm. At long last, she was delivering justice for the evils done to her people. At long last, she'd fulfil the promise she'd made to her mother. Lugh long-spear was on her side. She would not fail.

As she watched the legionaries pass, her resolve faltered. These men assigned to the slave train belonged to Decimus's legion. Even if she hadn't seen or spoken to them, she knew who they were: homesick, fresh-faced boys and grizzled veterans anxious for retirement. They didn't want to be here any more than Decimus did, she knew that now. They prodded her manacled people along the path because they had no choice. And now, some of them would die merely for being assigned to the wrong duty.

The trader's entourage trundled slowly up the path. Saibh watched its movements, judging its distance from the end of their offensive line. As soon as they'd closed the trap, she waited a heartbeat longer. Then she stood, punching her sword in the air and letting loose an ear-splitting cry.

Luciana and the others immediately followed suit, leaping from the brush onto the forested path. The Roman pickets stood to in alarm and hurled their spears at the charging horde. The pila soared over the thin Silure lines before falling harmlessly into the trees behind them.

Luciana only glimpsed the bright colours of Deoiridh's horde attacking from the other side of the road before hurling herself against a large Roman shield. The familiar winged thunderbolt of Decimus's legion obscured her vision. She wildly swung her sword, jabbing the point over the top of the shield. The legionary ducked low, evading her stroke. She immediately stepped back, throwing up her own shield to parry the short jab of the gladius she knew was coming. As soon as she'd deflected his thrust, she came on again, swinging out at his sword arm before it disappeared behind the thunderbolt.

She heard him cry and saw a bright crimson stain on her blade; she'd managed to draw first blood. Trying not to look at her opponent's face, she struck out again, shoving with her iron shield boss.

The legionary stumbled, knocking over some chained prisoners caught in the melee. Luciana drew away, fearful of accidentally harming one or more of her people. The space allowed her to see the precarious dance the soldier performed to maintain his footing. With quick reflexes, she snaked her sword down on his sandaled foot. The large toe severed with a sickening crack.

The legionary sank onto one knee, yowling in pain. A puddle of bright blood pooled in the dirt around his wounded foot. Luciana swung just close enough to deliver a sharp blow to his head with the hilt of her sword. The clang dented his metal helmet. He slumped over, unconscious.

Luciana drew a couple of deep breaths. Perhaps that had been enough to spare at least one of Decimus's men. She turned to glance over the dirty prisoners, ensuring they were unharmed. 'Stay still and keep down,' she barked. 'We've come to rescue you.'

The mouth of one of the muddy figures gaped, revealing several missing teeth. 'Luigsech…?'

The cries of the Silure girl beside her drew Luci away. She saw a Roman legionary holding firm against his diminutive attacker, stabbing his gladius into her shield arm. Luciana thrust her own shield at his sword hand, crushing it between them.

The Silure girl nimbly spun her sword high and sent the blade overtop the Roman's shield. It pierced him through his throat and his head snapped back. A dark fountain gushed from his gaping mouth as she withdrew her blade. He collapsed to the ground.

'Nice swordsmanship!' Luciana cried, darting behind the wounded Silure girl for the thickest and fiercest of the action: where the trader's bodyguards fought the female horde.

The chair had been placed on the ground to free the guards' hands. One man had been felled by the Silure mob; the other three ducked behind gathering legionaries, barely maintaining their hold against the enemy. The trader stood from his seat and shrieked at his men, flinging his whip at any attacker who drew too close.

Luciana ducked through the press of bodies, striking out to deflect any blow that glanced her way. To her right, one of the men cried as he went to his knees. She glimpsed a face she'd often seen when visiting the prisoners, a rather kindly soldier who'd often turned a blind eye to her passing them food. The horde closed around him for the kill, and he was gone.

The remaining guards at the rear of the chair had been absorbed behind two legionaries' linked shields. The men covered each other to stave off the women. Farther along the line, the remaining legionaries had followed suit, closing to form a shield wall. One soldier barked a count as they beat a steady retreat from the massacre.

'You cowards! Get back here!' The trader, red-faced, flailed about, cursing the legionaries in Latin. The Silures slunk away from him, desperate to avoid the iron-studded tips. 'How dare you?! The governor shall be hearing of this!' He lunged at the growing line backing past him, trying to duck behind the protection of the shield wall. A legionary shook him off, continuing without pause.

Luciana took advantage of the moment to push through the crowd and lunge forward, striking at the trader's shoulder. Her sword sliced through robes and pierced the flesh, stopping just at the bone. The man screamed and whirled about, striking out with his whip.

Luci ducked behind her shield. Two of the studded flays curled around her oblong boss and embedded in her side. She yowled, doubling over in pain. The whip quickly snaked away. She passed her shield to her sword hand, gripping her side. The skin had been stripped away from the fresh hole in her dress. Pinpricks of blood dotted the raised grazes, so tender to the touch they stole her breath. She stumbled back, anxious to recover.

The trader, meanwhile, had clambered onto his chair, screaming and striking out at any warrior in range. Luciana straightened, wincing, and hefted her shield. Her eyes locked on the trader. This man, the one profiting from selling Britons into slavery, must die. This man, she wished to die. This man, she would not mourn.

She dashed behind the chair, face furious as she recalled the dank conditions of her mother's prison. The shield wall continued retreating just a few feet away. Gathering her breath, she let loose a fierce war cry and hefted her sword round, slitting the trader's throat.

He released his whip and swung his arms up, trying to stem the gouts of blood spilling down his chest. Luciana dropped her shield and squeezed his neck in a headlock, her arm impervious to his clawing fingers. The stench of his loosened bowels curled her nostrils. She looked down into his frightened gaze and sneered. 'Bleed, Roman.'

His eyes widened at the sound of her Latin tongue.

'Bleed out like the pig you are.' She tightened her hold, delighting in his choking squirms.

The trader's hands stiffened and fell away. His gaze, still locked on hers, glassed over as the life slowly ebbed from his pathetic frame. She dropped him, watching the body slump into his chair. She wiped her blade on his dark robes, feeling her bloodlust fade.

'Luigsech!'

She turned to see Saibh coming up the road. Behind her, the Silure women had fallen to breaking the prisoners' chains and seeing to the wounded. The bodies of the fallen legionaries they disregarded, walking and standing on top of them as they gathered the Cornovii.

Luciana sheathed her sword. 'How did we fare?'

'Better than expected.' Saibh blew a wayward red strand from her eyes, face flushed with exhilaration. 'A few wounded, none lost.'

'The same can't be said for the enemy.' Luciana grimaced at the butchered legionaries, feeling a twinge of remorse.

'Yes.' Saibh's face fell. 'How fast do you think your people can move?'

'Not very.' Luciana frowned. 'Why?'

'We need to get away from here, and quickly.' She nodded to the soldiers disappearing up the road. 'We had surprise on our side this time. That lot will be back, and next time, they'll bring the cavalry.'

Luciana stood sentinel on the ridge of a hill. She narrowed her eyes, scanning the dense forest below. Satisfied no foot traffic headed their way, she turned and walked down the far side. She clutched at her roughly bandaged torso as a fresh twinge spasmed along her body. Hunching forward to curl away from the pain, she picked her way through the Silures and Cornovii huddled out of the enemy's sight.

As she stumbled down the ridge, she passed a cluster of children accepting bowlful after bowlful of stew as quickly as the Silures could stir a fresh batch up. At the hill's base, women stooped over a small pond and scrubbed the mud from their bodies. Those that had finished cleaning themselves sat near a small, carefully maintained fire, wrapped in blankets. Luciana stopped beside them and straightened. She fished at her belt and pulled out strips of dried beef. 'Is anyone hungry?'

The nearest woman reached out to take one, then paused as recognition lit up her face. 'Luigsech! It *is* you! As I live and breathe!'

'Greetings, Catraoine.' Luci sat next to her, passing some beef to another grasping hand.

'This was your doing, wasn't it?' Catraoine shook her head.

'I said I was going to get you out, didn't I?' Luciana gazed at her feet. 'I'm just sorry it came too late for some.'

'Ah, love.' Catraoine's face fell. She was quiet for a long time, until the sudden laugh of a boy beside a soup cauldron grabbed her attention. Her lips twitched and she breathed a deep sigh. 'You're a woman, not a god. It was a fine thing all the same. Your mother would be proud.' A shadow passed over Catraoine's face. 'Wherever she might be.'

'Mmm.' Luciana nodded.

'You know,' Catraoine tore off a piece of the beef, chuckling a little, 'she was worried you'd actually taken to your stiff-backed Roman officer. I told her from the off she had it wrong! I said to her, "Gwen, don't you fret a moment over your girl. She knows what she's about. She knows more than any one of us you can't trust a Roman after that business with her Latin tutor. She knows who her people are. Just you see."'

'Y-yes!' Luci laughed stiffly.

Catraoine elbowed her. 'I will say, you waited so long that even I was coming round to her point of view. But you came through, after all. You'd never turn your back on your own home!'

Luciana shook her head, softly rubbing her side. *When heart and home are torn in two…*

'And which home would that be?'

Luciana lifted her head to see Saibh drop to the ground beside her. Saibh hugged her knees, the unpainted areas of her skin flushed with energy. 'You Cornovii can hardly go back to your old homes, now that the Romans know you've gone. Ours are too close by. The Roman army sprawls every which way, from the west to the south to the east. Just where is it safe to call home?'

'I've been thinking about that.' Luciana nodded. 'And I think their best chance is north, to Brigantia.'

'Brigantia?' Saibh spat out her words. 'With that Roman-loving cow Cartimandua and her cronies?!'

Catraoine sat back, regarding Luciana warily.

'Yes. For precisely that reason.' Luciana sighed. 'Don't you see? The Brigantes are allies of Rome. In Brigantia, you'll be mistaken for friends and left alone. You won't have to cower and hide every time a Roman turns up. Bar leaving Britannia altogether, I don't see any other choice. Rome is inescapable. The best chance you have is hiding in plain sight.'

Catraoine frowned at her feet, nodding. 'You're right, love. It's the only way to go from here.'

'I can send the younger girls and wounded warriors with them to ensure everyone makes it safely to Brigantia.' Saibh chuckled. 'Their wounds are quite minor, but you wouldn't think so from the way some of them carry on. One girl, Mordag, received a cut all the way down the side of her face, forehead to chin.' Saibh traced a snaking line over her own features. 'She's fretting the scar will chase suitors away. I told her not to worry. A strong warrior loves a mark of courage. She should bear it proudly.'

Luciana coloured slightly, remembering her own fascination with another warrior's scars. 'Oh, yes. There shan't be a shortage of men wanting a place at her side.'

Saibh nodded. 'And Mordag got the worst of it. Most earned no more than scratches, but they'll better serve your people seeing them off to Brigantia than following me.'

'You?' Luciana cocked her head. 'Where are you going? Back to Siluria?'

'Hardly!' Saibh snorted. 'Morcant has no use for female warriors, so I shan't tag along to save his sorry arse. I'm heading east, to the Iceni.'

'The Iceni?'

'Their Roman-loving chieftain just died, and his widow is ruling in his stead. His daughters have been designated heirs to the tribe.' Saibh's eyes glowed. 'That is tribal leadership I can get behind.'

Luciana nodded, brows knitted in recollection.

'I've heard tell their chieftain managed to cancel the Iceni's debts to the Romans before he died, so they should be free of Rome's presence.' Saibh gazed at the hills. 'Given what you've told me, it would seem that defending Mona is a lost cause.'

Luciana thought for a moment. She laid a hand on Catraoine's arm and squeezed it. 'I trust you in the hands of the young Silures. Boudicca is an old friend. I would appreciate the chance to pass my condolences on to her.' She lifted her eyes to Saibh. 'If you wouldn't mind my accompaniment?'

A smile spread across Saibh's face.

Decimus stroked Aquila's nose and gave him a warm, final pat on his shoulder. 'I thank you, Nicomedes, for caring for him in my absence.'

The optio's slave nodded. 'Aquila doesn't make much fuss. Not like Nero. It will be easy caring for them both.' A shy grin spread across his face. 'And I'm glad to stay at the caupona with Tor. And Metella.'

Decimus smiled at Nicomedes. 'The dog should be fed well, given what I'm paying Metellus. And I've ensured the optio sees you rewarded properly for your services.'

'You are generous, sir.' Nicomedes ducked one of Nero's flying hooves, flattening himself against the partition. The stud's foot clattered against the stall wall.

Decimus ran his eyes over Aquila's wide poll, long nose, and broad nostril. He gazed at Aquila's soulful eye and shook his head. 'You are a fine creature,' he whispered, running his hand along the horse's velvety ears. 'You more than deserve all the best mares the empire has to offer. I am sorry I couldn't secure them for you.'

Aquila lowered his head to grab a mouthful of hay.

Decimus exited the stall. He gazed at Tor sitting in the corridor. 'And you…' He raked his hands along the dog's fur. 'Thank you for preserving my life.'

Tor barked, curly tail thumping enthusiastically.

'Metellus isn't a hard man. You'll crack him.' He smiled as the dog licked his palm. 'He'll see you never starve. Thank you for your undeserved loyalty.'

He blinked as he stood, tearing his gaze away from Tor's beseeching eyes. 'Stay,' he commanded, to which the dog whined. He sighed and glanced at Nicomedes. 'Take care.' He waved and, squaring his shoulders, strode out of the stable.

'You as well, sir!' Nicomedes called. Letting himself out of Nero's stall, he paused and frowned at Decimus's lengthening shadow. Aquila pushed his head over the half door, gently nudging Nicomedes's shoulder. He stroked the horse's face, puzzled by Decimus's peculiar mood.

Outside, Decimus clapped his helmet on. The dawn chorus of birdsong tittered at him from the tile roofs of the barrack blocks. Along the ramparts, the shadowy figures of Prefect Corvus and the auxiliary garrison had convened to see the column off. Just ahead, Decimus caught sight of Flaminius and Plancus filing out of the principia, standards hefted above their shoulders. He nodded at them, joining the trickle of officers making their way to the main gate. Gemina's heavy golden eagle, propped against Flaminius's shoulder, winked against the pale grey skies. Its impressive wings stretched up to the heavens. The bird's eyes pierced through Decimus as Flaminius shifted. He shuddered, striding away from its haunting gaze.

Just beyond the fort's gates, the combined Twentieth and Fourteenth legions had assembled for march. Soldiers gathered by cohort and officers dressed their lines. Decimus found his gaze running along the rows. The weapons of Valeria's legionaries gleamed just as brightly as those of his own legion. But, to Decimus's eye, the men of Gemina stood a little taller, their lines more uniform. The confident laughter and jocularity of his cohorts drowned out the quiet preparations of the Twentieth's men. Decimus scowled as he stalked to the head of his legion. 'Silence! What is this, a fucking dinner party?! Look to your kits! Eyes forward! If you aren't a fucking officer, shut it!'

The legionaries closest to him sulkily complied.

Decimus lifted his chin and made for the mounted officers. The governor, legate, and coterie of tribunes sat tall on their horses, coldly surveying the troops from the head of the parade ground. They would assume the vanguard of the column as the army left Viroconium. Then, once the eyes of the vicus were no longer upon them, they'd take their customary place in the middle of the marching men. Decimus curled his nostrils and swallowed a contemptuous sigh. *Senators: always the first to coat themselves in glory while leaving the grunts to do the actual work.* He came to a stop before them, standing squarely. He was proud of his lofty position and the privileges he had earned, but he would never trade his rightful place alongside his men.

'Decimus!'

He looked over his shoulder to see Tullius jogging up to him. He scowled. 'Your haste is unprofessional, Optio Servius.'

Tullius halted and straightened to attention. 'Aye, sir. I apologise.'

Decimus waved a dismissive hand. 'Dress the lines.' As Tullius moved away, Decimus caught the gazes of young Vespasianus and another square-faced tribune mounted beside Governor Paulinus. Nodding once to the young senators, Decimus saluted the governor. 'At your leisure, sir.'

Paulinus cleared his throat and motioned to his bucinator. Drawing a deep breath, the staffer raised the curled horn to his lips and blew several long, resonant notes across the parade ground. Immediately, thousands of men stiffened to attention.

At the governor's orders, Decimus began counting time, leading the first row of his legion into the line of march. Plancus and Flaminius took up their places on either side of him, standards held aloft. Just ahead of him strode the advance guard, entrenching tools slung over their backs. In front of them loomed the rumps of the officers' horses, cutting their way off the parade ground and swinging south to the vicus.

As soon as he'd cleared the fields looming between the fort and the vicus, Decimus found his vision clouded by the pressing faces and hands of civilians. Merchants, veterans, and families alike lined the path of the soldiers' march to see them off. He gave them no more than a cursory look from the corner of his eye, ensuring they didn't interrupt the column's progress. His gaze passed right over Cassia's face, barely registering her.

Many of the civilians called and waved to loved ones within the ranks, entreating them to return home safely at summer's end. Common law wives held their Romano-British children aloft, anxious to catch one last glimpse of their husbands and fathers. These passing sights raised a lump in his throat. His voice faltered a beat. Flaminius shot a concerned glance his way.

Blinking back tears, Decimus trained his sight on the forests looming beyond the vicus. His disciplined attention refocussed on the task ahead. His fists clenched, nails digging into the calloused flesh of his palms. His hobnailed boots ground against the cobbled path with each purposeful stride. He could not afford to dwell on what was, what wasn't, and what could never be; the menacing wilds of Britannia were beckoning him with a siren-like urgency to his doom.

XXIX

'Luigsech, wait!'

Luciana glanced over her shoulder, shifting effortlessly in time with Belena's quick, bouncy trot. She halted and laughed as Saibh, leading her Silure warriors, struggled to keep up on her own short, dark pony.

'How does your mare still have the energy?' Saibh panted as she finally drew within earshot, slumped over her mount's sweaty neck. 'Every day we ride, and every day she seems to quicken instead of slow!'

'She can go for as long as she must.' Luciana proudly tousled Belena's thick black mane. 'I told you, she's the strongest, fastest, toughest horse there is. Even the Iceni can't breed better.'

'You'd better watch out, then.' Saibh nodded at the mare. 'If Queen Boudicca gets a look at what you've brought, she may never let her leave.'

'Queen Boudicca is well acquainted with Belena.' Luciana stroked the mare's neck. 'And she knows that Belena and I can never be parted.'

The mare snorted, tossing her head as if in agreement.

'Have we crossed into Iceni lands, yet?' Saibh shielded her eyes, gazing out across the rolling brown landscape.

'Aye. That wooded pass we traversed this morning marks the traditional border of Iceni lands with the Catuvellauni.' She pointed to a rise several miles distant. 'That might be a herd of their horses grazing there.'

'We're close, then?'

Luciana shook her head. 'The tribal seat is on the other side of their sacred bogs. It's been many years since I last visited, but Belena is clever enough to pick her way. You'll need to keep the women close and follow the tracks I make.'

Saibh nodded, surveying the grassy hilltops. 'We're a long way from any wetlands.'

'If you've had enough of a breather, we might make it before darkness falls.' Luciana pulled back on the reins, sitting low as Belena impatiently pranced in place.

'I will try my best. Don't lose sight of us!' Saibh gestured over her shoulder for the other warriors to catch up. Luciana, grinning, released

Belena's head and let her extend into a quick, jerky canter.

How I've missed this! Her heart sang, racing in time with Belena's sure-footed beats. The wind whipped around the pair, isolating them in their sojourn through the countryside.

The horses in the distance startled and began racing parallel to them. Luciana glanced at the line stretching out beside them and laughed. 'You are no match for us, Iceni nags!'

Lugh's rays broke free of the clouds and shone across the land, bathing Luciana and Belena in warmth. The pair streaked along in the summer haze, weightless, boundless, *free*.

'Halt!'

Luciana sat deep, willing her tired mare to a shuffling stop. A broad figure stepped out from a pair of trees, holding a sharpened spear at the ready. She held up a hand, signalling Saibh to stop the trail of riders behind her.

The man strode closer, eyeing her. 'Who dares to cross our sacred bog?'

'Luigsech of the Cornovii and friends. Send word of my name to your queen, who will gladly receive us.' Luciana's eyes glistened. 'We have come to pay our condolences.'

The man nodded to a young messenger waiting in the trees, who scurried off. He gestured for her to follow at a far slower pace.

'What a pleasant welcoming committee,' Saibh grumbled behind her.

Luciana shushed her. 'The Iceni borders have always been volatile. The Trinovantes and the Catuvellauni aren't the most peaceable of neighbours.'

Saibh nodded, casting her eyes down.

The mounted women traversed in tandem for some time, staying behind their hulking guard. At long last, the trees parted to reveal a vast sprawl of farmsteads stretched across the flatlands. Parched fields dotted the landscape. A large, impressive roundhouse towered above the sparse collection.

Before the great house stood a tall woman in a checked cloak. A fierce collection of warriors, bedecked in gold torcs and armlets, ringed her. Her red plaits had been bound up in a simple knot at the back of her head. Deep circles ringed her eyes, giving her a haunted look. Her pale, ashen complexion stood out against the bright, golden glow of the twisted torc at her neck. Her eyes darkened as she met Luciana's gaze.

'Luigsech. We meet again.'

Luciana swiftly dismounted and threw her reins to the guard. 'I am sorry it isn't under happier circumstances.' She took Boudicca's pale, cool hand and studied it before brushing her lips against the knuckles. It was so white and papery as to be almost translucent. Her eyes followed the course of the blue veins running along her slender fingers. 'Please accept my condolences for the loss of your husband. Prasutagus was a fine warrior and an even finer ruler. Brave, wise, and kind.'

Boudicca withdrew her hand and turned, signalling all to follow her. 'We're still under the same moon that witnessed his departure to the Otherworld.' She squared her shoulders, biting her colourless lip. 'And yet… it might as well have been years.'

'You haven't caught his wasting disease?' Luciana's voice rose in alarm.

Boudicca shook her head. 'The lack of food or sleep is entirely my own doing. There are many matters to attend to, not the least of which involves securing my daughters' legacy.'

'What do you mean?' Luciana frowned. 'I was there when Prasutagus changed his will. Half the Iceni lands go to them. The other half goes to Rome. He intended your girls to be his heirs.'

'Try telling that to Aedicus,' Boudicca muttered, 'my husband's cousin. He seems to think Prasutagus made a terrible mistake, and that the chieftainship is his by right. But he cannot take what belongs to my girls. I will see to that!'

A cough at Luciana's elbow made her turn. She saw that Saibh now dogged their steps, anxiously awaiting her chance to meet the queen. Luciana stayed Boudicca's arm and turned her to face Saibh. 'I'm sorry, I meant to introduce you earlier. I have come with warrior women from Siluria seeking shelter amongst your tribe. This is their leader, Saibh.'

Saibh knelt before Boudicca. She ducked her head and offered her sheathed sword with both hands. 'Queen Boudicca of the Iceni, our tribe no longer has a place for female warriors. It would be an honour to serve one that does. May your causes be our causes.'

Boudicca took the proffered sword and pulled it from its sheath. She hefted the blade, studying the craftsmanship of the steel. 'It is true what they say. Silure weapons are among the finest in the land.' She wielded it, testing its heft, before returning it to its scabbard. She gazed at the mounted women ranged behind them, then placed the weapon back in Saibh's hands. 'The Iceni haven't enough grain to feed their own, but many hands make light work. If your warriors are willing to cultivate the land as well as fight, then you are welcome to stay.'

'Yes, my queen.' Saibh stood, beaming.

'Come.' Boudicca gestured for Luciana and Saibh to accompany her to the largest of the roundhouses. 'Seanus will see that your warriors turn the horses out in our pastures.'

Luciana blew a kiss to Belena, who bobbed her head as the guard led her to a field. The other Silures dismounted and followed suit.

She stepped through a colonnaded portico into a large, impressive structure. She had thought her father's house had been big, but it could have been entirely engulfed by Boudicca's quarters. The thatched ceiling soared high above their heads before diminishing to its central hole. Wattle and daub walls separated the many chambers from each other, giving the dwelling a more structured appearance. The walls had been painted with a bright, pale floral design that repeated itself with precise regularity. Brightly dyed blankets hung beside shields, shelves, and amphorae. Furniture that wouldn't have looked out of place in the governor's villa stood tastefully arranged over red tile floors. Luciana slowly shook her head.

'So, this is what an alliance with Rome gets you,' Saibh breathed beside her.

'This, and the most ornate set of chains.' Boudicca led them through the maze of walls to a room situated near the central hearth. 'Emer! Rioghnach! We have guests!'

Shuffling sounded from another room. Luciana and Saibh took their seats on couches that sat at angles to Boudicca's, encouraging conversation. Luciana watched the regal woman unclasp and fold her cloak, revealing a rather frayed, oft-mended blue gown. She frowned. Boudicca was only a few winters older than herself. Why did she suddenly look as old as Gwenfrewi?

The girls appeared, bearing a black pottery bowl containing some rather wan-looking olives. They set the dish on a low table in the centre of the couches and stood on either side of their mother's seat.

Luciana glanced from one to the other. Emer's dark, neatly coiled hair looked dull and there was a sad tint to her washed-out eyes. Despite that, a faint, rosy glow remained on her cheeks. She was dressed in a gown too short for her, falling to midway along her shins. She'd grown as tall as her parents. The soft baby fat about her face had fallen away since Luciana had last seen her. She was of more than marriageable age, she estimated. The younger daughter, Rioghnach, hadn't yet hit the growth spurt her sister had. Her cream gown, neatly embroidered with gold braid, fit her well. Her dark auburn locks fell neatly down her back and her round black eyes held a soft twinkle above her dimpled cheeks.

'How grown your children are,' Luciana said, taking one of the shrivelled olives.

Boudicca inclined her head. 'Their strength has been admirable. One of the last things my husband managed before his passing was the arrangement of Emer's marriage to Mandusedos, a young nobleman of the Trinovantes. They're to be wed before the coming of Samhain and take up residence here, where they may reign jointly with Rioghnach.'

'My congratulations,' Luciana murmured to the eldest daughter. Emer nodded.

Boudicca tilted her chin. 'And you, Luigsech? Am I right in assuming you've freed yourself of your Roman master since we last met?'

Luciana dropped her olive and watched it roll across the red tesserae floor. 'Yes…yes, you would.'

Saibh turned to her, frowning. 'Was this before you met Leucus?'

She tucked a blonde strand behind her ear and nodded.

'Freedom *and* a new suitor?' Boudicca arched a brow. 'You have been busy since midwinter.'

'Sorry, midwinter?' Saibh raised a finger.

Luciana's heart pounded. She wrung her hands on her lap, forcing a shaky laugh between her lips. 'Yes…yes, Leucus and I…'

'My queen!'

All eyes turned to a young messenger, appearing breathless in the doorway. The muffled toots of carnyxes sounded outside. 'Romans… coming to the settlement!'

'How many?'

'Perhaps fifty? They're military. Armed.'

'Number of crests?' Boudicca calmly stood, brushing wrinkles from her worn gown.

'Four.'

'And who is leading them?'

'A bald man in a purple cloak.'

'I expected as much.' She gestured for her daughters to follow. 'Come. The procurator has arrived to take what's his.'

Luciana closed her eyes, swallowing her relief as Saibh rose to accompany them. The thought of Decimus was enough to constrict her chest. She didn't think she could talk, or even lie, about him. She slowly brought up the rear of the party, holding a hand to her breast.

Her fingers brushed against the raised form of Capricorn beneath her dress. She traced its outline. *Decimus.* Was he a former master or a former lover? The warring identities swirled in her head, one morphing into the other. She frowned, trying to banish him from her thoughts.

It matters not. He is behind me now.

And yet, the cool metal of the charm beneath her throat refused to let her forget.

She exited the house to see Boudicca, flanked by her daughters, facing the imperious look of a mounted Catus Decianus. He was flanked by a rather weedy-looking agent, four centurions, and the better part of two centuries at his back.

'…seize this property in the name of Emperor Nero,' Decianus's smarmy voice concluded as Luciana joined the rear of Boudicca's throng.

'I am sorry, Procurator, but I'm afraid you are mistaken.' Boudicca placed a hand on each of her daughters' shoulders. She cleared her throat and continued in her shaky Latin, 'My husband's will clearly states that my personal property, the tribal settlement, and the fens all belong to my daughters.'

'Ah, yes.' A cruel smile curled the corners of his mouth. 'The will. Which was written while Iceni land still fell under suzerainty. I believe, with his passing, that condition is null and void. After the trouble your lot have caused us, all imperial contracts made very clear that our agreements were with the late Prasutagus and Prasutagus alone; *not* his issue, *not* the Iceni.'

The regional tax man, mounted on an ass beside Decianus, unfurled a roll of parchment. 'In lieu of back taxes owed to the imperial state, accrued interest, and unrepaid loans, Emperor Nero hereby claims the totality of Iceni land and all properties therein as his own.'

'You can't do that.' Boudicca's eyes widened. 'My husband made an agreement. You *said* the terms of his will cancelled our debts. You're only entitled to half!'

She glanced over her shoulder at Luciana. 'Luigsech, you were there! Tell him!'

'That…that is correct.' Luciana stuttered. She glanced at the disgruntled Iceni tribespeople gathering around them. 'Queen Boudicca speaks the truth. I was made to understand your debts no longer stand.'

'But that was under the suzerainty clause Rome contracted with Prasutagus.' Decianus unfurled the will. 'All oral agreements made with Prasutagus no longer stand, and all properties revert to the empire upon Prasutagus's demise. It's right here.' He tapped the cramped writing on the will. 'Like I said before, dearie, it's plain for you to read.'

Boudicca grabbed the document, frowned at it, and thrust it at Luciana. 'Tell me what it says.'

Luciana ran her eyes over the small legalese. Her heart dropped at the mention of the suzerainty clause, and she lowered the paper. The sight of Decimus's intaglio on the document made it all the harder to bear.

Boudicca, reading Luciana's face, whirled back to Decianus. 'You *knew!* You *knew* he was dying, and you took advantage of us!'

Decianus shrugged. 'I wasn't the one who made the deal.' He nodded to one of the centurions, who started dispersing legionaries throughout the settlement. 'Round up everything that can be liquified upon our return to Londinium.'

'Stop!' Boudicca darted to the entrance of her home, blocking the doorway. 'Everything here belongs to my daughters!'

'And your daughters belong to Rome!' Decianus pointed to the girls, who were roughly seized by two centurions. The girls screamed, struggling against their captors' grip.

'Unhand them!' Boudicca abandoned her post and scrabbled towards them. One of the centurions shoved her to the ground.

'Deal with her,' Decianus curtly ordered, urging his horse to follow Emer and Rioghnach. The girls screeched as the soldiers carried them off.

'Mother! Mother, please! Stop this! Let me go! I need my mother! Mother!' Rioghnach's plaintive calls dwindled from earshot.

The man from Colonia Camulodunum slid from his donkey and regarded Boudicca sadly. 'Please, don't make this any more difficult than it needs to be.'

'You tricked us!' She struggled to her feet, her gown muddied and torn. 'You Roman scum! Give me back my girls!'

She lunged at the tax man, who hid behind a centurion's shield. The officer grabbed Boudicca, who shrieked and wrestled against him.

'Tie her up,' the regional agent murmured, 'and make sure she stays out of the way until we've finished.' He met her hateful gaze and shook his head. 'I tried to warn you.'

'Luigsech!' Boudicca cried as the centurion dragged her past Luciana. 'Take your warriors and find the girls! Quickly! Save them! Please!'

Luciana glanced at Saibh, who turned to the pastures. 'Daughters of Palug! On me!' She cried to the Silure women, waving.

Luciana hardly felt the tax man slide the will from her loosened fingers. She gazed at the chaotic scene enveloping her, feeling as though time hadn't moved. The sight of Roman legionaries shoving tribespeople to the ground, storming their homes, herding livestock from their pens, and torching buildings, sent her hurtling back in time. She was again at the top of the Viricos, witnessing the destruction of her own people.

'Luigsech!' Saibh shook her shoulder. 'You heard the queen. Let's go!'

Luciana followed Saibh, melting into the Silure horde. They came upon a round pen near the edge of the settlement. Decianus, still mounted on his grey steed, headed a ring of soldiers inside the slotted boards. He nodded to the centurion who'd bound Boudicca's hands and feet, pointing to a hitching post just outside the pen. 'Tie her there. She won't want to miss this.'

'Fuck you!' Boudicca spat. Her bright red locks had come free from their knot, hanging about her face in scraggly wisps. 'How *dare* you treat the free heirs of Prasutagus so?!'

'Insolent woman.' Decianus scowled. 'You haven't been free since the moment Antedios of the Iceni surrendered to the Divine Claudius!' He nodded to the centurion. 'Shut her up.'

The officer yanked his kerchief from around his neck and stuffed it into Boudicca's mouth.

Saibh unsheathed her sword. Luciana and the others followed suit.

'Release the queen at once!'

'Oh, for Jupiter's sake!' Decianus nodded to the ranged legionaries, who pulled their gladii from their scabbards. 'Drop your weapons or be killed. The choice is yours.'

Saibh silently counted the legionaries before turning to Luciana. 'I like our odds. What say you?'

Luciana glanced more legionaries marching behind them, led by a centurion. They drew weapons and held their shields at the ready, prepared to crush the women between them. 'I like them less than you do.'

A centurion knocked the sword from one warrior's grasp with the hilt of his gladius. 'Drop it now!' He commanded.

'They won't kill us if we comply. We're more use to Boudicca alive than dead.' Luciana threw her weapon at her feet. The others reluctantly complied. Saibh looked furious before throwing hers into the dirt, accepting defeat.

One legionary gathered the weapons at his feet as the rest kept their gladii trained on the women. At the sound of cheers and laughter, they craned their heads to see.

'Get in line, boys!' Decianus cackled. 'Might as well help yourselves to some royal cunny while it's on offer!' He frowned and gestured to the troops. 'Stand aside to let them see!'

The scarlet-clad bodies parted to reveal Emer and Rioghnach bound and gagged in the dirt, their skirts flung up about their waists. Each was being raped by rough-faced legionaries who knelt above them.

Boudicca shrieked behind her gag and ran to the end of her tether. She dropped to her knees when the tension stopped her short of her daughters' ravishment. She lifted her eyes to the sky and moaned in despair.

Luciana gasped sharply and darted towards the girls. A legionary roughly grabbed her and held her back. Tears blurred Luciana's vision. She burned with the shameful memory of her lascivious Latin tutor on her, just a girl, not understanding what he'd done. She hadn't deserved it; Boudicca's girls didn't deserve it. Her rage erupted into a howl as she clawed the legionary's arms.

'People of the Iceni,' Decianus commanded. He gazed at the disarmed female warriors, battered men, and crying children flanking the pen. 'You are now subjects of Rome. Look upon Rome's conquest of your tribe.'

The legionaries grinned, rocking the girls violently until they climaxed. They breathlessly rolled aside and two of their comrades took up their places.

'This is what happens when you dare to defy your Emperor's command!'

The legionary shoved Luciana back into the Silure throng. Saibh held her as she swayed, averting her eyes. 'They can't…' she panted, 'they just can't…'

Boudicca sobbed impotently. Her voice rose to a desolate wail as she rocked back and forth, watching the next pair of men rape her daughters.

'Flog her,' Decianus curtly ordered the centurion, pointing to Boudicca. The officer took a studded flay from one of Decianus's saddlebags and stepped behind her.

Luciana gasped as the centurion tore the tattered remains of the queen's dress from her shoulders, exposing her freckled back. He cracked the flay overhead and brought it down on her exposed flesh, leaving bright red lines along it.

Boudicca twisted at the blow, screeching behind her gag.

Luciana yelped, hiding her face in Saibh's shoulder.

She flinched with each crack of the whip. Saibh shuddered, gripping her tighter. She lifted her head once to see bloody, criss-crossing gashes across the queen's spine. At some point, Boudicca fell silent. Luciana hoped she'd passed out from the pain.

Luciana turned. *Danu on high, please don't let Boudicca be dead.* She could no longer see the queen; her torturer blocked her view. From behind, the centurion's dark red uniform, mail lorica, and transverse-crested helmet made him look exactly like Decimus. Luciana's face contorted. Her heart wrenched.

As pair after pair of soldiers stepped up to take their turns on the sobbing girls, Decianus watched from his seat, his face cold and remote. Luciana narrowed her eyes at him. She'd known he was a worm from the moment she'd met him in Londinium, but this wanton cruelty was monstrous. 'I curse you,' she whispered, glaring at the procurator. 'By the Morrigan, I curse you from the ends of your toes to the tip of your egg-shaped head. May your genitals turn black and shrivel into your skin; may your entrails inflate and twist you with pain; may your teeth fall from your mouth and your eyes become feasts for the crows; may you suffer a thousand agonies before the goddess claims your pathetic life.' She knelt in the dirt by the soldier who'd collected their swords and cut three of her fingers on the edge of a dropped blade. Blood pooled from the soft flesh and dripped onto the rough, dried grass. 'I make this solemn sacrifice to you, goddess of fate, harbinger of war, destroyer of worlds, that you may heed my words.'

Above the sounds of the grunting legionaries, she thought she heard the caw of a raven. She smiled; the Morrigan had heard and accepted her vow.

'Sir!' The fourth centurion dashed up to Decianus and clapped a fist to his chest. 'The livestock and valuables have been gathered. We're ready to depart for Camulodunum.'

'Detail an armed guard for the train and ensure none of this scum gets in your way.' Decianus scowled over his shoulder at the settlement. 'Torch the rest.'

'As you command.' The centurion stalked off, barking orders to some of the men.

Saibh crouched beside Luciana in the dirt. 'Rome must learn who they are dealing with,' she seethed. 'Every time our kind have tried to make peace, the Romans have thrown our friendship away!' She hawked up a wad of phlegm and spat it at her feet. 'A lot of good it did Prasutagus, cosying up to them.' She shuddered. 'It makes me sick!'

'All right, men.' Decianus clucked to his horse and followed the laden carts. 'Move out!'

One of the legionaries tucked himself back into his loincloth and delivered a parting kick between Rioghnach's legs. Beside her, Emer had closed her eyes, assuming a lifeless pose. Their silent mother, her back raw and bleeding, lay facedown in the mud a few feet away, hands still bound to the hitching post.

'May this be a lesson to you all, next time you consider defying Roman law.' Decianus smirked, casting his eyes over the sullen-faced people of the Iceni.

Luciana watched him leave, glaring daggers into his back. Suddenly, the milling bodies of Iceni horses captured her attention. Her eyes widened. 'Belena!'

She leapt to her feet and raced after a herd of horses the freshly mounted legionaries drove between them. She whistled, slowing to a stop when she saw her mare's jug-shaped head lift above the throng. Soon, Belena's chubby form broke free of the herd and galloped back to where she stood.

'Leave it!' One of the centurions barked when another soldier made to follow. 'We've got more than enough to take to Camulodunum.'

Luciana stroked Belena's mealy muzzle, glaring at the disappearing herd. The Romans faded into a cloud of dust, carting all the Iceni owned between them. She knew the bulk of the tribe's wealth resided in their horses, even if not one of them could match her own mare's power.

'Remember what Decimus said,' Luciana breathed into Belena's fuzzy ear. 'We belong to no one.'

The mare snorted hot air onto Luciana's palm. She kissed Belena's shaggy cheek.

'Luigsech! Help us, if you please!'

She made her way back to the pen, Belena trailing at her shoulder. They found Saibh and several of the Silures gathered about Boudicca, dumping canteens of water over her bleeding back. 'Great thinking,' Saibh breathed, glancing her way. 'Do you think your horse can carry the queen to her house?'

Luciana turned to the roundhouses. Men attempted to beat out the flames engulfing their homes with blankets, while women and children had formed a bucket chain to the nearest stream. She sadly shook her head. Even with the entire tribe at work, they'd struggle to salvage half of the burning homes.

'She won't object.' Luciana stroked Belena's neck and cooed to her as the women picked Boudicca up and carefully draped her across the mare's withers.

The remaining Silures had picked up Emer and Rioghnach. They carried them behind Belena. The group made slow progress to the chieftain's home, which had become a smouldering, blackened husk of its former self.

Luciana halted Belena by the entrance. The once-proud colonnade had shattered and collapsed across the portico. Luciana kicked aside some of the rubble and helped Saibh lift Boudicca down.

Boudicca's head moved when she touched her. A long groan issued from her throat. 'My girls…' she croaked.

'They live, my queen.' Saibh took one of Boudicca's arms and toted her inside. 'My warriors are seeing to them now.'

Boudicca's green eyes flickered before rolling back into her head. Her neck swung forward as she drifted into unconsciousness.

'Deoiridh, you have some skill as a healer. See what you can forage to treat them.' Saibh nodded to one of the women, who disappeared from the ruined hall.

'This is a nightmare.' Luciana sadly regarded the soot-stained tiles, her gaze trailing along charred, crumbling screens.

'It's what we've been waiting for.'

Luciana turned to Saibh, brow furrowed.

'Don't you see?' Saibh looked at the insensible queen. '*She's* the one the prophecy spoke of! The wrath of Andraste!'

'She's hardly in a fit state to act as Andraste's messenger.' Luciana considered Boudicca, who'd been stretched out on her stomach across one of the torn couches.

A mumble arose from Boudicca's mouth as she stirred. Her pale, veiny finger extended towards the floor.

Luciana looked down. For the first time, she noticed a crease between the row of tiles, hidden beneath the furniture. She pushed a table aside and knelt on the floor, running her fingers over the groove. With a grunt, she lifted a slab of the tesserae and shifted it aside. There, beneath the floor, lay a collection of spears and swords.

'What did I tell you?' Saibh's eyes glowed. 'It's her!'

Luciana considered Boudicca's insistent, pointing hand. She slowly nodded. 'Yes, I think I see.'

'Look at what they did, in just a few hours!' Saibh gestured to the room and its occupants. 'What they did to her tribe! Remember what they did to yours!' She pointed at Luciana. 'Prasutagus is proof. It doesn't matter what we say or do, we are all scum to them! Scum to be used and abused for their own purposes! Nothing more.' Her expression hardened. 'It is past time Rome learned that the tribes of Britannia shan't abide such treatment any longer.'

She pulled one of the swords from beneath the floor and pressed it into the queen's white hand. Boudicca tightened her grasp on the hilt, her arm suddenly pulsing with power and purpose. Luciana regarded her, eyes wide. The mere act of hefting the sword had seemed to transform the wan, colourless widow into the Boudicca of old.

'There are many injustices to be righted, and she's the one to lead us. The gods are on our side.' Saibh's ruddy face glowed. 'No Roman shall escape my blade. I'm ready to follow Boudicca wherever she leads.' She cocked her head at Luciana. 'The question is, are you?'

XXX

Clouds danced across a startlingly blue sky. Decimus frowned, scanning the trees surrounding the vale. The air was still; nary a leaf stirred in the sweltering summer heat. Even the birds had fallen eerily silent.

Twenty or so paces ahead of him, the backmost row of the fourth cohort continued their steady pace between the steep hills. The Parcae, he grimly thought, had arranged for his cohort to guard the 'supply train' and its hidden human cargo on the very day they marched through the mountain pass he'd identified to the legate. So far, as his men had helped the muleteers down the steep ridge, there'd been no sign of any Britons, Silure or otherwise. But all Decimus's muscles remained tense, his eyes vigilant. He sensed their presence, even if they remained hidden.

He groaned, rolling his head to ease the pressure along his shoulders. He did not know how long they'd already marched; he'd soon lost all track of time as days became weeks. Had it been a month since they left Viroconium? He hardly knew. He did know, however, that the enemy was close. His entire body braced for the coming conflict.

'Sir.'

He glanced over his shoulder to see Tullius trotting up from the rear of the century. He sighed and slowed his pace so Tullius could fall into step beside him. 'Yes, Servius, what is it?'

Tullius frowned. 'I was just wondering, sir, about the report the scout ran forward to the governor. I take it the men are in position?'

'I didn't delay him long, but it would seem so, yes.' Decimus nodded. Earlier, he'd caught sight of a scout racing by. The man had been sent to ensure two centuries, detached to climb the hills on either side of the vale, had picked the correct paths to the top. When the scout had come abreast of his own line, Decimus had questioned him briefly. While he didn't know whether the soldiers had made it all the way to the top or not, he had replied in the affirmative when Decimus asked if they'd scouted evidence of the enemy nearby. An attack was imminent; it was only a matter of time before the Silures struck.

'It's a comfort to know we'll be ready for them, then.' Tullius studied Decimus.

He mutely nodded.

'We can't be far from the Ordovices' own settlement. Rather strange choice of ground to pitch a battle.'

'I doubt they're particularly worried about their homes now. They're fighting for something more,' Decimus grunted. 'As are we.'

Chastened, Tullius strode beside his friend in awkward silence. Much seemed to hang in the air between them, none of it intelligible.

Decimus coughed, clearing his throat. He opened his mouth, ready to dispel the tension, when Tullius suddenly blurted out, 'I'm sorry.'

He frowned at him. 'Whatever for?'

'For…for judging you too harshly.' Tullius stared at his boots, avoiding Decimus's gaze. 'I'm the last person fit to appraise someone's proclivities. I think I'm…that is to say…I might…I'm a…'

Decimus's face softened. 'I know.'

Tullius stopped, whipping his head up. 'You do? How…?'

He smiled, turning to Tullius. 'I knew from the day I met you.' He chuckled at the confused frown contorting Tullius's face. 'You were a lad who hated women and loved Greek. What else could you be?'

'And…' Tullius's eyes lit up beneath his furrowed brow. 'You didn't mind?'

Decimus shook his head. 'It mattered not. You've always had my back. I couldn't run this legion without you.'

Tullius looked away, brushing at his eyes. 'I thought…when Cincinnatus asked us about finding men…'

'Cincinnatus was a tit. You know how I feel about patricians, and he was a prime example. I didn't respect anything about the man. You have always had my respect.'

Tullius stood rigidly for a long moment. He drew long, shaky breaths, trying to compose himself. Clearing his throat, he finally turned to Decimus. 'Remember, sir, that whatever comes this afternoon, I and the rest of the men are at your back. *Sanguinem fratres.*'

Decimus smiled sadly. Melancholy played across his face before it hardened into its customary stern lines. The men bore little resemblance to the young soldiers who'd met in Moguntiacum a lifetime ago. Back then, they'd had everything to prove. Now, it seemed, they had nothing to lose.

He placed a hand on Tullius's shoulder. Their years in the legion together travelled through the soft squeeze he gave him. When he leant close to give Tullius a brotherly kiss, Tullius didn't turn his cheek. Instead, he accepted the chaste peck on the mouth.

'You are a fine officer, and a finer friend,' Decimus murmured softly.

Tullius gruffly nodded, turning to fall back. 'I'll stay right where you need me, sir.'

Decimus watched his friend's fading form and heaved a long sigh. 'Centurion Maximus!'

Tullius brushed pashed Centurion Persius on his way back to his line, giving the officer no more than a passing glance. The anxious centurion hardly noticed, scrambling as quickly as he could to Decimus.

Decimus stepped aside from the marching column and awaited the new arrival. 'Well, Persius?'

'Beg to report, sir,' the centurion panted, drawing a salute across his breast, 'the rearmost of the wagon trains have run into difficulties clearing the pass. Some rockslides from the mountain walls came down about them, killing a couple of the drivers. The rest of the mules bolted, upending themselves on the decline. It's a terrible mess, sir. My men are going to be delayed helping the fourth century deal with the fallout.'

Decimus, who'd lifted his head at the word "rockslides," immediately began scanning the surrounding hills. To his alarm, he saw boulders lined along the ridges beginning to shift. 'Forget about the wagon train, Persius, and get back to your men! On the double!' He roughly shoved the officer away and picked up his shield, darting to the column. 'We're under attack! Form testudo!'

A stone brushed the back of his helmet just as he ducked into the formation. Wincing, he wheeled and threw his shield up. More small stones hailed against the wall, denting the men's shields with a startling alacrity. Legionary Vulso, hunkered just behind him, cried out when a particularly large rock jerked his shield arm back. 'This is worse than slingshot, sir!'

'Hold firm!' Decimus called. 'Our men up top should be dealing with this lot soon enough.'

Galloping hooves approached through the rock shower. 'Paulinus orders all units to the front! The enemy's engaged the advance guard!'

'As if we aren't already under attack ourselves,' Vulso muttered.

'Units to the front! Paulinus-,' the messenger's shout was cut short by a brief cry as the threat from above overwhelmed him. The men heard no more aside from the muffled grunts of a distressed horse.

'That was extremely helpful,' Plancus snorted.

'Indeed,' Decimus mumbled. He listened to the horse, calculating the distance in his head. 'It tells us we're within earshot of falling out of our rock-throwing foes' range. Two hundred paces or so, no further, by his reckoning. He felt another large stone slam into the shield boss directly above his head. He turned to Vulso. 'Send the word down the line that we're preparing to move. Maintain formation. With any luck, we'll clear the bastards in the hills and get stuck into the bastards on the ground.'

The legionary turned. Decimus waited several tense moments as he allowed the order to be relayed. The sizable hail pelting all around them had startled the men closest to him, who shook with each fresh salvo that dented their shields. Yet Decimus felt surprisingly calm. It was with a sense of equanimity that, nodding to Vulso, he called the men to their feet. Slowly, like a long, cumbersome snake, the testudo shifted up in a wave. Then, after a final warning shout, Decimus made the first stride forward, calling the count.

It felt as though he were being rattled in a cage as the stones crashed about him from all sides. Small pebbles and debris threw up dust as they fell, clouding his restricted vision. Holding his battered shield, he gazed at the ground as he placed one boot in front of the other. His voice stridently rang down the line, keeping the formation marching as one. A stone severely dented his shield and behind him, Vulso cursed. Decimus gritted his teeth and kept pushing forward. Twenty paces, fifty…

A roar slowly grew overhead, a lowering thunderclap directly above them. The rumble grew closer as the testudo lumbered forward. Suddenly, a large crash sounded somewhere behind him. Several cries of panic and agony went up, drowning Decimus out. 'What's happened?!' He called to Vulso in between hollered steps.

It didn't take long for news to travel up the column. 'Massive boulders coming down the hills, sir! The avalanche rolled right through an entire line! They've severed the testudo!'

'Reform! Hut! And keep moving! Hut!' Decimus shook his head, pressing on. The thought of Tullius somewhere behind him arose in his mind before he quickly banished the thought. It was kill or be killed now. Letting the formation fall into utter chaos would spell the end for them all.

Several paces later, the hail became infrequent. Then, at long last, it stopped altogether. The new, reigning silence was almost deafening. Decimus continued, maintaining the shape, until he was certain that at least two centuries were clear of the stones. He called the men to a halt and rested his shield against the ground, winded. He remained crouched, hands resting on his knees. Rivulets of sweat collecting at his helmet brim streaked into his dusty beard. As he looked at the dirt, head weighed down by his cumbersome kit, he became aware of the aching spasms along his back, the tension in his calves, the stiffness in his knees. It was just as well he'd met his final battle; his body had suffered about all it could take of this life.

'Is the column clear?' He barked over his shoulder, still trying to regain his breath.

'Yes, sir.' Vulso replied.

'What do you mean, "yes, sir?" Send it down the line!' He gestured angrily.

'I can see the end of the column, sir. We're well clear.'

Decimus slowly turned about. The sight made his face blanch. A mere nine rows of legionaries stretched behind his own. Only half of the first century had made it. The rest had become lost in the dusty hail of stones raining down from the ridges behind them. Atop the hills, some of the assailants had become embattled with Roman troops that had finally made their way to the top. The remaining few tried to keep up the barrage, but the strength and energy of their assault was rapidly failing. Decimus could just see the shapes of men running or cowering on the ground amongst many crushed and felled bodies. A lump suddenly rose in his throat. Tullius was back there somewhere.

'Sir?' Vulso gently prodded. 'What do you want us to do?'

Shaking his head, Decimus straightened, breaking the formation. 'Shields down!'

No sooner had the hazy sunlight assaulted his eyes than he became aware of a tribune, the companion of young Vespasianus, galloping in his direction. The officer's helmet plume whipped behind him. 'Centurion!' He drew the horse up and wheeled on his haunches, pointing. 'The governor requests all available units on the rightmost flank! We're beating them back, but the enemy's holding strong there. We have to break them!'

Decimus nodded and glanced over his shoulder at the eighty or so men remaining to him. He unsheathed his gladius and punched it in the air for all to see. 'Draw weapons and follow me! For the glory of Rome!'

'For the glory of Rome!' They rejoined as a chorus of swords scraped free of their scabbards.

After dressing the men in lines of eight, Decimus jogged beside them to the indicated position. They crested a small rise before heading down into the field. Ahead, Decimus saw a sea of legionaries and officers surrounding an unruly Silure horde. Despite fielding fewer warriors, they were holding their own surprisingly well against the far larger Roman force. He narrowed his eyes, taking in as much of the sight as possible.

With a start, Decimus realised the genius of the enemy's position. Morcant's ragtag band were maintaining a narrow front, with the dense forest at their backs. Only a small faction of the Roman army could engage the Silures at a time, and the dark trees provided the perfect cover for an effective retreat. The Romans weren't beating the Silures back; the Silures were holding the Romans back. They could bottle them up at the mouth of the valley for as long as they pleased. Once the Silures had done as much damage as they could, they'd scatter and melt into the forest, where the Romans couldn't hunt them down. Decimus gritted his teeth. Morcant was far smarter than he'd thought.

'Wedge! On me!' Decimus beckoned with his gladius. Shields linked up on either side of his as the men fell into formation. Plancus, holding the cohort standard aloft, walked behind him. To his right, Vulso took up a rallying yell: 'Gemina!' The rest of the men added their voices, turning heads as they marched. They engulfed their beleaguered comrades on the right flank, investing the Romans with fresh energy.

Decimus didn't stop until his gladius crashed against an enemy sword. He quickly brought his shield up, blocking the brute's parry. He sought his next thrust. The large Briton overcorrected, throwing his sword up to steady himself. Decimus snaked forward, plunging his blade deep in his enemy's armpit. The warrior howled as Decimus twisted the gladius away. His skin parted with a horrible sucking noise, dark blood spouting from the wound. As the man tumbled away, Decimus's eyes widened in recognition. It was the wiry fellow from the Silure capital, the friend of the warrior who'd nearly revealed Decimus's true identity.

An icy finger of dread pierced his heart. He squeezed his eyes shut. *Mithras god,* he silently prayed, *please don't let Luciana be here.* The very thought of facing the woman he loved on a battlefield was enough to make his stomach churn.

As the warrior staggered off, clutching his haemorrhaging wound, Decimus lifted his eyes. He glimpsed two men bearing the old crone Luciana had called the Ancient One. The trio surveyed the scene from the safety of the treeline. The woman's wrinkled old face gazed expressionlessly at the violence. Her long white hair melded with her shroud, enveloping her in an otherworldly cocoon. Just before her, Taraghlan the druid waved his staff about, chanting angry curses.

Then these sights were lost to him as another warrior charged, poised to strike. The smaller, lither figure rushed up in a blue whirl, his long ponytail flying behind him. He lifted his sword high and knocked the butt against Decimus's helmet, momentarily stunning him. Decimus came to before he planted his face against the warrior's woad-painted chest, the aroma of sweat heavy in his nostrils. He lifted his shield, catching the warrior on the chin. The Briton yowled as he stepped back, sword arm brushing Decimus's shoulder. The blade harmlessly grazed his cuirass and kerchief, nicking only the leather ties securing his helmet, before falling away.

Decimus retracted behind his shield, awaiting the warrior's next attack. When the screaming Silure charged at him, Decimus jabbed it up at just the right moment. The shield's iron boss crushed the Silure's nose. The man swung his weapon wildly over Decimus's shield rim, his war cry petering into a whine. Decimus curtly knocked the blade aside with his gladius and pressed forward. The warrior toppled onto his back. Pausing only to stab the man's groin, Decimus stepped back into the protection of the wedge.

He didn't see the threat hurtling towards him until it was too late.

'Sir!'

Decimus turned to see Morcant nearly upon him, dark eyes feverishly bright. The chieftain charged, sword whirling aloft. He was too close when Decimus finally saw him, swinging towards his unguarded neck before he could react. Just as Morcant's blade sang for his throat, Vulso's shield punched its way between them.

Decimus stumbled aside at the shove, his crested helmet toppling off in the grass. He recovered his balance and turned to see Morcant had nearly cleaved Vulso's shield in twain, rendering it useless. As he wrestled his sword free of the twisted wood and metal, Vulso jabbed with his gladius. The short blade disappeared into Morcant's shoulder, and he roared. He stepped back with such force that Vulso lost his grip on the hilt before he could recover his gladius.

Vulso fumbled frantically for his dagger. Decimus watched in growing horror as the chieftain rallied again for his next assault. He lurched towards them, knowing he was already too late.

'Vulso! No!'

Vulso helplessly lifted his busted shield to repulse Morcant's charge. The chieftain's sword passed directly through its gaping tear and impaled Vulso through the throat.

Decimus watched Vulso's head snap back. The pointed edge of Morcant's blade emerged from the nape of his neck. His eyes rolled sightlessly towards the sky, his gaping mouth spewing blood.

'Bastard!' Decimus screamed, pummelling his shield into Morcant's side. The chieftain backed up with the force of the blow and neatly recovered, turning his attention to the helmetless centurion.

Decimus crouched behind his shield, panting. His trembling hand gripped his gladius at the ready.

The Silure chieftain frowned slightly, taking in the distinctive scar along Decimus's cheek. His eyes roved up to the recently stitched line over Decimus's brow. His gaze widened with shock. 'Leucus!' He growled.

His low, rasping voice curdled Decimus's blood. It was a shade from the mouth of Hades, calling him home. Gathering himself, Decimus thrust forward, lifting the tip of his gladius to Morcant.

The weapons rang with a deafening clang as they met, blades glinting in the sun. They fell away and met again, each man thrusting his shield at the other. The blackened stumps of Morcant's fingers, curled round the gilded hilt of his sword, hauntingly reminded Decimus of their confrontation last winter. Here they were again, back to finish what they'd started so many months ago. This time, he knew, at least one of them would die.

Morcant parried Decimus's thrusts, always anticipating his next move. Decimus, guarded by his scutum, deflected Morcant's offensive blows. He danced on his toes, peering just over the top of his shield at Morcant. The chieftain, gladius still embedded in his shoulder, swung furiously at his head. With each failed stab, Decimus felt his sword arm beginning to flag. Were his responses slowing?

Old Amyntas's voice echoed through his head: *'Stay alert now, lad! Don't slip!'*

He bobbed down to avoid Morcant's swinging blade, stepping into the arc of his weapon. The two men came face to face as their shield bosses locked, pressing tightly against the other. Hatred gleamed in their eyes.

Decimus jabbed his gladius forward, smirking as he felt it part Morcant's fur-lined cloak. He watched his face closely, so closely he didn't feel the iron laying his own flesh bare until Morcant returned the smile. Decimus looked down just in time to see Morcant's sword slide away from his shield arm, severing his skin all the way to the bone.

He stumbled back, dropping his shield. Blood poured from the deep wound. He lifted his gaze to the sky in confusion as dark spots began to blot out the sun. A dizziness numbed his senses. Morcant's cruel laughter echoed around his head.

His heel tripped over a corpse, and he collapsed onto his back. His head smashed against something sharp, sending fresh shockwaves of pain through his body. Morcant leant close, grabbing a fistful of Decimus's ringlets. He cackled in triumph and nicked Decimus just above the collarbone. A dark, wide line appeared. He angled his sword against Decimus's throat, ready to claim his prize.

A high-pitched scream sounded somewhere overhead. Decimus's weakening eyes saw a whirling blue figure smash into Morcant. The chieftain violently released his head, falling over in a fresh tousle with his new assailant. A golden braid whipped past his nose before the world went dark.

'Luciana,' he murmured, imagining the sweet scent of her hair filling his lungs as he slipped into oblivion.

XXXI

Tullius blinked, wincing at the blinding beams of sunlight directly overhead.

'I think he's coming round…Sir, are you awake? Optio Servius?'

He grunted, wrenching his face away from Apollo's glare. He scrabbled in the dirt with his left hand, wondering vaguely why it was covered in a fine white powder. He rolled onto his side, groaning as a thousand scrapes and bruises made their presence known. He tried to push himself up with his right hand, but it flopped uselessly on the ground. His elbow smacked against his side, sending a terrible, agonising pang through his entire body. He cried out, his vision blurring.

'Oh, gods, what are we going to do? He's injured!'

Tullius heard a familiar, wheezing hitch somewhere just above him. He forced his eyes to focus and finally saw the ghostly white face of his century's tesserarius. The man's pinched, anxious expression made him look even more haunted. Tullius frowned in recognition. 'Is this…Elysium?'

'Sir, the column's been severed.' The tesserarius looked up at some legionaries hovering just behind him, hovering behind their dented shields. 'Those bastards have finally stopped throwing rocks at us, but our century's been buried in the assault. We've been counting the casualties, but we can't find the centurion. We thought we'd lost both our officers until we found you.'

Tullius frowned. 'Decimus…' A chill gripped his heart. He shook his head, forcing the terrible idea to the back of his mind. 'What about the signifer?'

'Gone, too.'

Gritting his teeth, Tullius scrabbled to his feet. One of the men touched his right shoulder and he screamed, toppling forward into the tesserarius's arms.

'Please, sir. Just rest with the wounded until the medical wagons make their way out of…that mess.' The tesserarius nodded over his shoulder.

Tullius turned to see a heap of boulders blocking the narrow pass. Mules tangled in harness and trapped underneath waggons were strewn about, stoically silent in their distress. Rations scattered the pass, littering the rocky outcrop with strips of dried meat and porridge oats. Tents, entrenching tools, pails, and cookpots lay scattered among other sundry items. Legionaries moved through the haze, dressing their own decimated ranks and stumbling to help other men with the waggons.

He turned back to his own men. 'Fortunatus? The second century?'

The tesserarius shrugged. 'Back there, I suppose.'

'What do you want us to do, sir?'

Tullius surveyed the bodies strewn at his feet. The men, *his men,* lay crushed beneath the rocks. Some stirred, moaning for their comrades' attention. Others lay silent, never to stir again. Shields, broken pila, and dusty swords surrounded the corpses. He watched a trickle of blood slowly seep from the cracked skull of a legionary by his boot. He shook his head. 'I don't…I don't know.'

'Told you! I knew you was going to have to lead us!' One of the men smacked the side of the tesserarius's helmet.

He shrank away, his wheeze growing heavier. 'What do you mean, lead us?! I've never given an order in my entire life! I take care of our finances and passwords, not our tactics!'

'Then why get promoted in the first place?!' Another legionary shoved him. 'Useless sack of shit!'

Tullius glowered, watching the hapless young man absorb his comrades' blows. His teeth ground together furiously. 'Enough!'

The men stilled, turning towards him.

Tullius panted, eyes wide. For once, he couldn't hear his father's voice, berating his uselessness. He didn't hear his wife lamenting his household management. He didn't hear Decimus teasing his lack of initiative. The blood surging through his veins amplified the sound of his racing heart. He swept his gaze over the ragged collection of men. They lacked organisation, something he knew all too well.

It's a process. Be methodical. Dress your lines until they're in fighting order again. One step at a time.

Grunting, he fumbled with the hilt of his gladius, tucked against his numb right side. He bit his tongue, trying to fit his non-dominant fingers around the weapon. Finally, with an uneasy groan, he managed to slide the blade free. He pointed it at the tesserarius. 'Gather every man in the century who can hold a sword and form up in rows of four. Don't worry about contubernia. Leave the walking wounded to finish finding each other. All of you…' He swept his gladius at the legionaries, 'shields up and on me.'

The soldiers picked up their shields and mutely complied. The tesserarius frowned at Tullius. 'But sir, your arm…you can't…'

'I don't seem to have much choice, do I?' He nodded as the tesserarius scrambled off. He held his gladius high, wielding it uncertainly in his left hand. The men began to link shields behind him, and Tullius turned to watch. The two rows of legionaries grew to four, then seven, then ten. The men's eyes, blinking at him from ashen faces, regarded him expectantly.

He gulped. *They're relying on me.*

'First century…forward!' He called, turning about. He marched carefully through the rock-strewn debris, picking his way around the fallen legionaries. The familiar boom of many hobnailed sandals tramping the ground sounded behind him.

Tullius straightened. His form grew taller at the front of his column, his steps more assured. He focussed on the end of the vale, still obscured by the boulder attack's dust cloud. Slowly, shapes began to materialise out of the haze. Distant shield walls appeared, linking together across a narrow front. The cavalry stood back with Flaminius and the bucinators, awaiting an opportunity to engage. The governor's mounted staff clustered even further back. Every so often, one of the tribunes broke off from the group and galloped up or down the vale.

Almost there. Someone will have orders for me! Tullius pumped his gladius. 'At the double march!'

He broke into a jog. The column rattled into pace behind him. He made for the knot of staff officers. A couple of aides lifted a head at his approach. The rest kept their backs to him, obscuring the governor and legates from view.

'Fourteenth Gemina, first century, first cohort!' Tullius shouted at the nearest tribune.

The man merely waved him on, not even turning in the saddle. 'Right flank! Right flank! All reserves to the right!'

Tullius gulped. *Lead them? Into battle? Decimus, what would you do? Why aren't you here instead of me?*

'You heard the tribune!' He called over his shoulder, wincing at the quiver in his voice. 'Maintain your lines. We'll link up with the shield wall on the right flank!'

The men sent a cheer along the column. A few beat their gladii against their shields. 'Ge-min-a! Ge-min-a! Ge-min-a!'

Tullius felt his heart lift at their words. These men were his brothers, ready to die for him and each other if necessary. It didn't matter if he lacked confidence in himself; their trust in him was all that truly mattered. He joined their chant, drawing circles with his gladius.

As he approached, he noted the rapidly thinning lines along the right flank. The shield wall was buckling before a solid mass of Britons, threatening to give way and turn the skirmish into a rout.

'This way!' Tullius pointed, heading for the weakened centre of the flank. 'Into eight! Shields up! Swords over the top! Pass the wounded back and keep your lines secure!' He broke into a run, ready to throw his undefended self into the action. 'For Gemina!'

The century roared with Tullius as they followed him into the fray.

Luciana gritted her teeth. She threw up her shield to parry Morcant's weakened blow. Sweat dripped down her nose to mingle with a growing puddle of Morcant's blood. His wounds were mortal, yet he continued to fight. 'Just die!' she screamed.

Morcant lunged at her, wildly swinging both sword and shield.

Luciana stepped aside, whacking him between the shoulders as he passed. Sapped of breath, Morcant immediately went down.

Luciana, panting, pushed him onto his back with her toe. She gazed down at the man her father had betrothed her to, the man responsible for turning the Romans on her people, the man who'd laughed in the face of their gods, mistakenly thinking them on his side.

He blinked at her, lips curling. 'I may go to Annwn…but I've won the battle.'

Luciana knelt beside him in the grass. She ripped the torc from his throat and looped it around her own. Her expression blackened. 'Are you ready to face the gods' wrath? Are you so sure they approve? I know my father is ready to meet you in the Otherworld. He will make you wish for life.'

'Traitorous whore!' Morcant spat in her face.

Luciana grabbed him by the hair and swung her blade down, severing his head from his trunk. She stood, backing away from the gout of blood rushing from his neck. She smirked at Morcant's sightless eyes and gaping maw. 'Fuck you.' Her gob of phlegm spattered his cheek.

She swiftly tied the head to her belt, knotting thick locks of hair together at her waist. She twisted about, taking stock of her surroundings. The Silures had seen their chieftain go down; they streamed through the trees, disengaging from the Romans in piecemeal fashion. The Romans roared, waving gladii from behind their fractured shield wall. A party of cavalry galloped up from the flank and chased the fleeing Britons into the woods. Luciana held her ground, watching the auxiliaries careen past.

As soon as they'd gone, she stooped to the grass. She grabbed a Gallic helmet from a Silure corpse, glancing anxiously at the nearing Roman lines. She tucked her long skirts up about her knees and folded her braid beneath the helmet. She stood, eyeing the dispersing centuries. With any luck, they'd mistake her for an auxiliary just long enough to let her through.

'Hold your lines! The enemy's in retreat!'

She heard the hoarse, familiar voice croaking above the throng and turned. She squinted at an officer, white with caked dust, pushing legionaries back into line with his sword.

'Let the bastards go! Form by contubernium and gather pila!' He watched the men comply before sheathing his own weapon. It was awkwardly done; for the first time, she noticed he held the gladius in his left hand. His right arm hung uselessly at his side. He finally stowed the weapon and swiped some dust from his face, revealing a familiar pair of brown eyes.

Luciana gaped. 'Tullius?'

He turned to her, regarding her for a long moment. A shadow of contempt twitched at his lips. 'The fuck are you doing here?' He finally rasped.

'Decimus is down. Help me find him.' Luciana studied the heaped bodies in the grass, wandering a few steps along. She picked her way through the fallen Silures and finally saw a line of Roman casualties to the legionaries' rear. She clutched at her helmet and darted towards them.

'So you can finish him off?!' Tullius staggered over and pushed her aside. 'Stay away from him!'

'Stop it!' Luciana hauled on his injured arm, eliciting a yowl of pain. She whirled to face him and tugged on the head at her waist. 'I killed the Silure chieftain. I am on your side!'

Tullius narrowed his eyes. 'I know what you did to those men on the Londinium Road.'

She quailed, loosening her grip as shame burned her cheeks.

He shrugged her off and lurched towards Plancus. The signifer stood with lowered standard a few paces away. 'The primus pilus?'

Plancus mutely indicated farther down the neat line of bodies. Beneath his fierce bear pelt, his brown skin had taken on a sallow hue.

Luciana darted past them both, nimbly moving past stinking, groaning forms in the grass. She slowed every time she passed a man in greaves. *Not him. Not him. Not him.*

'No, you don't!' Tullius struggled behind her, gripping his injured arm tightly.

She ignored him, anxiously scanning faces. Her steps grew slower. Orderlies jogged past her, heading for the men she'd already seen. The bodies were motionless here, eyes gazing sightlessly at the sky. The faces of some had started to grey. Luciana dreaded every centurion she passed. *Please, don't be him. Please, don't be him. Please, don't be him.*

She stopped, gasping as she caught sight of Decimus's bloody, bearded face. Her heart sank with her body to the ground. He lay still, one arm draped across his chest. She teared up as she took in his closed eyes and still, serene expression. 'No!' With a sob, she cradled his head. *Too late.*

The tears bubbled over, flooding her vision. She huddled over him, rocking his head in her arms. 'Decimus, you can't! You can't leave me!' She sobbed. She traced her finger over his scarred cheek, cursing her stupidity. *You made the wrong choice. Again.*

Footsteps slowed behind her. She sat up, ready to snap at Tullius as he approached. She lifted her hand from the back of Decimus's head and stopped short. She frowned at it curiously. There was fresh blood on it, as if his wound still throbbed…

Luciana gasped, lowering her head to Decimus's chest. Tullius stopped before her, growling. She held up a finger to silence him. She nestled her ear closer, frowning. *Please.*

There! It was faint. It was slow. But she heard Decimus's pulse.

'He's still alive!' She sat up. 'Quickly! We need help!'

Tullius's eyes widened. 'He's…'

'Yes!' Luciana pulled Decimus's kerchief from his throat and wound it about his head. 'Take yours off and make a tourniquet. We can't let him bleed out!' She nodded to Decimus's arm.

Tullius fumbled with one hand at his knot. Luciana sighed and helped him slip it loose before fastening it snugly at Decimus's elbow. She moved to grab his shoulders, then shook her head. With Tullius down to one arm, there was no way they could carry him. She leapt to her feet, scanning the orderlies moving along the line. 'The primus pilus lives!'

Her words echoed through the valley. One of the purple-plumed riders wheeled his horse around and galloped towards the dumbstruck orderlies. Luciana watched him go, then glanced down at Decimus. *Please, hold on…*

She noticed a patch of clover not far from Decimus's head. She kicked herself internally for not learning her mother's knowledge of medicinal plants. If he died because she'd been reading Cicero instead of picking herbs with her mother…

She looked up at the sound of approaching hoofbeats. The tribune galloped towards her, dodging scattered legionaries. He drew up as he approached. 'Only a few of our waggons survived the wreckage at the pass. I have two orderlies coming with a makeshift stretcher. They have strict instructions to get him to a medicus immediately.'

'Take the optio as well.' Luciana nodded to Tullius. 'He can walk on his own power, but he's lost the use of an arm.'

Tullius gaped silently at Luciana.

'Very well.' The tribune narrowed his eyes at her. 'You're not a soldier. Just who are you?'

'I am…' She lifted the head at her side. '…an agent of vengeance.' She fingered Morcant's torc before pointing to the head's tattooed brow. 'The Silure chieftain is no more.'

'Good work.' The tribune nodded, looking impressed. He glanced over his shoulder. Luciana followed his gaze to see a pair of orderlies racing towards them, bearing a scutum lashed to palisade stakes.

'Sir…' A centurion approached Tullius and coughed. 'I've got the first numbers from the eighth cohort.' He extended a tablet towards him.

Tullius took it, nodding. 'Form up by century and detail a burial party. Tell the other cohort commanders they can find me in the hospital tent.'

The centurion saluted and trudged off.

Luciana regarded Tullius curiously. Where had this confident, commanding personality come from?

The orderlies knelt in the grass and hauled Decimus's unconscious body onto the shield.

'Careful!' Luciana folded his injured arm across his chest and anxiously watched the men lift him up. As they set off down the valley, she and Tullius followed.

'Halt! Where do you think you're going?' The tribune turned his horse.

Luciana paused, letting Tullius shoulder past her. 'I'm not leaving the primus pilus's side. And I don't answer to you, your legate, or your governor.' Her face softened. 'I'm a free agent.'

XXXII

Luciana knelt beside Decimus, holding his torso still as the cart jolted. He lolled his head, moaning. She frowned at the medicus, who crouched near his feet. 'Can't you do anything more?'

The medicus shook his head, examining the bandaged leg of another officer stretched beside Decimus. 'He's had enough poppy, as it is. Nothing to do until it's time to drain his arm.' He lifted the folds of the other man's bandage and winced. 'Hopefully, it won't putrefy like this one has.'

Luciana glanced at Decimus's bound forearm. She hadn't liked the greenish tint to his sutures when the medicus had last drained it.

She gingerly turned his head, fingering the herb-stuffed bandage over the contusion behind his ear. The swollen bump had shrunken considerably overnight, to Luciana's relief. The medicus mentioned trepanation, which she'd been staunchly opposed to, a lot less frequently now. She frowned as she felt the hot throbbing of his temple. 'He's far too warm.'

'It's high summer.' The medicus glanced absently at the sun overhead. 'We're all warm.'

She scowled. 'He's feverish! Even I know a fever brings one closer to death!'

'Here.'

She turned to see a proffered wet rag. She took it from Tullius's outstretched hand and nodded her thanks.

'How is he?' Tullius, broken arm encased in a sling, turned about from the driver's bench. His face, washed clean and rinsed with vinegar, sported several abrasions he insisted looked worse than they felt. They weren't enough to mask the concern etched across his features.

'Much the same,' she murmured, sponging Decimus's brow. She gripped him and hissed as the waggon jolted over another rut. 'Can't the driver see where he's going?!'

'That boulder attack completely blocked the mountain pass. There's no choice but to use the native tracks around the range. No Roman roads here, yet.'

Luciana wrung out the rag and draped it over Decimus's forehead.

'More's the pity.'

'Excuse me?' Tullius smiled uncertainly. 'Are you *sorry* we haven't paved any roads out here?'

'I'm sorry for his sake!' She glared at him. 'This detour may cost Decimus his arm! Every stone in the road is another agony! The longer he travels like this, the worse he'll be!'

Tullius's eyes softened. 'I know.' His gaze flickered over his prone friend. She noticed his withheld tears and hunched shoulders. His lips parted as he reached down to tenderly stroke Decimus's ringlets. 'But you won't let him go without a fight,' he choked.

'No.' She took Tullius's fingers and squeezed them. When he lifted his eyes to hers, she smiled thinly. '*We* won't.'

Tullius turned crimson and withdrew his hand.

Luciana smiled softly. 'You love him, don't you?'

She watched Tullius's shoulders heave an enormous sob. An uneasy silence fell over the travellers.

Luciana tried to shade Decimus with her shadow. Still cradling his head, she studied his lined, weatherbeaten face. She ran her finger down his pointed, patrician nose. There wasn't anyone else like him. She didn't know what she'd do if she lost him now.

The waggon hit another rut and Decimus cried out. Luciana pulled his shoulders onto her lap. 'I'm sorry, *carissime,*' she whispered.

Tullius thrust a waterskin at her. 'Make sure you keep him hydrated.'

'I am.' She glared at him, snatching the skin. Still cradling him in her arms, she propped him up enough to hold the spout to his lips. 'Drink up.'

Decimus complied. His bristled throat pulsed with each long gulp. When he'd had enough, he turned his face away and let out a distressed moan.

Tullius sat up. 'Is he coming round?'

'He's still insensible. His fever's too high.' Luciana felt Decimus's brow and soaked her rag with the remaining water. She sponged his face, shushing him.

Tullius watched the medicus pass her some poppy-laced posca. She carefully administered a few drops on Decimus's tongue. She murmured softly to him until he drifted back into unconsciousness. He studied her pressing the rag along Decimus's arms.

Luciana felt his gaze and frowned self-consciously. 'It's rude to stare.'

'Why did you come back?'

'Fuck off.' She waited until he'd turned back around to sigh and gaze at the passing scenery. It was a question she'd frequently asked herself.

When heart and home are torn in two…

The goddess's words had haunted her every waking moment. She'd watched Boudicca make sacrifices at the temple of Andraste and lead the Iceni nobles in ritually burying their torcs. They had cast off their riches and burned their seeds of grain, committing themselves as warriors to Andraste's charge. Luciana had known, then, that she could not follow Boudicca. Killing Decimus's men had been trying enough; she wasn't prepared to put strange Roman civilians to the sword. She'd entrusted Catus Decianus to the Morrigan's care, and that was an end of it. Boudicca's fight wasn't her own.

She'd left the Iceni capital heading west. She wasn't quite sure where she was going until she found herself halted before her father's deserted roundhouse. Belena had grazed patiently in her familiar pasture while Luciana moved through the screened rooms, touching a bowl here, a blanket there. She'd lit a fire in the hearth and prayed to see the wisdom in Danu's words. After a restless night's sleep, she'd mounted Belena and ridden away. It was no longer home.

She'd struck out north, with the idea that she'd try to find her mother and brother in Brigantia. But as soon as the Ordovician ranges had appeared to her left, she found herself pointing Belena their way. Had she disobeyed the goddess? Had she succumbed to the pull of her heart?

She felt Decimus's warm, heavy presence in her lap. The sound of his troubled breaths pulled her back into the present moment. Gazing down at him, she knew she had done as Danu advised. Her heart longed to ride across northern British lands, free from the constraints of Roman occupation. But she felt incomplete without Decimus at her side. Decimus, the Roman who was in so many ways her opposite, and in others so frustratingly alike. In his presence, she felt whole. With Decimus, she was at home.

Decimus shook, mumbling incoherently, as the medicus slowly unwound the bandage from his arm. Luciana leant over to inspect the stitched wound, hovering just behind the medicus's head.

'Mmm.' The medicus made a small incision near the stitches and pinched his skin.

Luciana watched greenish liquid seep out from Decimus's arm. 'Well? What do his humours tell you?'

'Just as I feared.' He frowned at the hemp stitches, swabbing them with vinegar. He wound a clean bandage around them. 'Infection is beginning to set in.'

'Infection?!' Luciana sat up, her heart sinking into her stomach. Tullius wrenched around. She saw her fear mirrored in his eyes.

'Which he's going to have to fight.' The medicus sat back. 'He might lose his arm, if it worsens and I'm forced to amputate. He might die. Perhaps both.'

'There must be something you can do!' Luciana tightened her hold on Decimus's shoulders. 'Can't you reopen the wound? Stuff it with salve or flush it out?!'

'The infection isn't so severe.' The medicus patted the unconscious officer lying beside Decimus. 'I can't, given how short we are on staff and time. My men and I will have our hands full taking the leg off this one once we make camp. I'd suggest you make a sacrifice to your gods. His fate's in their hands, now.'

Decimus's head rocked uneasily in her lap. Luciana blinked away her tears and mopped his sweat with the drying rag. She'd done so much, had come so far. She was *not* about to lose him now!

Tullius frowned down at Decimus. His friend lay stretched on a tattered bedroll, convulsing with shivers. Decimus's teeth chattered, sweat streaking from his every pore. He flung his bandaged arm back and forth. Luciana, kneeling beside him, caught his wrist and pinned it to his side. She tried to wipe away the sweat with her cool, damp rag, but every patch of skin she touched seemed to sweat anew. She soaked the cloth in a bucket of cool water by her side and slapped it across his brow.

The veins in Decimus's neck had grown taut. Laboured grunts escaped his throat. He struggled in place, turning his head one way and another. The bandaged lump behind its ear lost some of its herbs to the damp ringlets clinging to his skull. An unnatural, greenish pallor had set in beneath his tan skin. His chest heaved, struggling for every breath.

Tullius's eyes watered. Never, not even on the day Decimus had received the scar on his cheek, had he looked so near death.

He turned and abruptly stormed out of the tent. An orderly carrying bloodstained cloths scurried around him, making for the stream running past their campsite. He slowly followed, stopping only at the head of the bank. His nostrils curled at the acrid stench of gore emanating from the orderly, walking several feet upwind. He carefully lowered himself to the grass and frowned at the gently flowing current.

He might die. Tullius felt his lips tremble as a tear streaked down his cheek. Before him, a hare crept out of the bushes and timidly lapped at the stream. A leaf blown free of an elm swirled in the water past it, letting the current take it where it would. Tullius frowned. It didn't seem right that the world got on with its business, as if the tenuous thread of Decimus's life made no difference.

He kicked a stone down the bank and watched the rabbit scurry away. He pulled his legs up and cried out when his knee brushed his shattered elbow.

Tullius squeezed his eyes shut and cradled his sling, willing the pain to pass. When the agony released its grip on him, he found himself staring down at his injured arm.

I nearly died. Dis spared me in that boulder attack, only for me to throw myself into battle without a shield. I shouldn't be here now. I nearly died, without ever telling the two men I love how I really felt.

He lifted his head, staring at the undulating hills above the far bank. He sat with the thought and slowly nodded. Yes, he realised, he *did* love Porcius. It wasn't the same love he felt for Decimus; it was a newer, revealing, affectionate sort. He missed Porcius's soothing voice, his gentle laughter, his thoughtful conversation. He missed the warmth and security that coursed through him whenever he'd cuddle up against Porcius's sturdy bulk and read a scroll with him. Porcius was more than touches, kisses, or sex. He was a companion of mind and heart.

And I threw him away. Because I couldn't let go of...the shame. The wrongness. The disappointment. He shook his head, banishing the thought. He refused to let the expectations of his father haunt his conscience any longer.

There were Antonia and Jacobus to contend with, but they felt as though they belonged to a different life. Antonia, he'd never felt anything but pity for. She didn't deserve the loveless marriage foisted upon her any more than he did. She probably resented Tullius as much as he resented her. Jacobus he couldn't help but love, though he found it hard to picture his son's face. He hardly even knew his child, and his child hardly knew him. They would be waiting for him back in Rome, where he'd face them later. For now, the distance suited them all.

'The medicus wants to see you.'

He jumped as Luciana brushed past him. He watched her take her pail to the stream and refill it.

She glanced at him over her shoulder. 'He wants to check the splint. If I were you, I'd do it now, before he gets embroiled in that amputation again. You don't want to end up like Decimus.'

Tullius stilled. He felt his heart sink to the bottom of his chest. His mouth went dry. 'Is he...?'

'Unchanged.' Luciana carefully hauled her brimming pail up the bank. She paused in front of Tullius. 'Don't worry. I'm not going to let him go without a fight.'

Tullius sighed. He haltingly lumbered to his feet as she moved past him. 'You know, he is lucky to have you.'

Luciana stopped and turned, regarding him incredulously.

Tullius felt a smile tugging at the corner of his lips. 'You're both lucky…to have each other.'

To his surprise, Luciana stepped towards him and gently took his shoulder. He quailed at the intensity of her gaze. She regarded him for a long moment, as if searching his face. Finally, she said, 'Danu has seen fit to grant you a rebirth. Do not spoil this second chance.'

A warm shudder coursed down his spine. He fervently nodded. 'Believe me, I don't intend to.'

XXXIII

Voices. Decimus heard a chorus of voices swirling around him. He blinked and saw a dark press of bodies shuffling past him. Odours of blood, sweat, fish, and urine wrinkled his nostrils. As the world increasingly came into focus, he realised he stood in the middle of the Subura. The voices crystallised into merchants hawking their wares, women conversing in doorways, children shrieking as they darted around puddles, and the low murmur of men conducting business in hushed tones. A prostitute curled around the side of an alley and beckoned to him. Above, he saw the fluttering form of a blanket airing from a dingy insula window. A cart laden with amphorae creaked past his nose, clattering over the cobbled streets. Decimus frowned. He opened his mouth to reprimand the driver for congesting the street after sunrise, but no words came.

'Decimus!'

He gasped, whirling about in place. His eyes searched the teeming crowd, desperate to find the source of the voice. 'Mother?'

'Decimus!'

He turned in the direction of the call and pushed through the crowd. 'Mother, I'm coming!'

He saw a tall woman in the middle of a crush of people, her back to him. He raced to catch up to her, but no matter how hard he tried, she remained the same distance away. When she rounded a corner onto another street, he ducked down a side alley in the hopes of heading her off.

The darkened lane stretched before him, zigging and zagging every which way. He bravely darted along his twisted path, impervious to a cat howling by his feet or children cowering in doorways. From above, someone tipped a slop bucket out of a window. Decimus stopped short as a foul deluge of human waste spilled onto the ground before him. The strong, pungent odours of urine and faeces made his eyes water. He sucked in a deep breath and passed on to the end of the alley.

Gradually, its opening onto the street grew closer. Hazy sunlight falling on the open square beckoned him from the dank, darkened side street. Decimus nearly tripped over his own sandals in his haste to reach his target.

He saw the crowd he'd been following pass by the mouth of the alley and nearly cried out in dismay. Scrambling into the light, tight on their heels, he clawed his way through the mob. 'Mother!'

The woman stopped and turned round, halting Decimus in his tracks. The laughing green eyes of Luciana bore into him. Her teasing smile shocked him as her sensuous form swayed against the crowd.

As he stood there, stupefied, her mocking laughter rang in his ears. He cringed, clapping his hands over his face. To his dismay, her taunting voice grew louder and louder, echoing inside his head. He moaned, his own voice joining the growing crescendo as the world darkened around him…

He stirred uncomfortably, wondering where he now was. A suffocating weight seemed to press down on him, a discomfort that would not release him from its clutches.

Hades, I'm in Hades, he thought, trying to make out anything in the darkness.

Death did not look the way the poets described it. There was no river, no ferry, no skeletal Charon waiting to shepherd souls across the water. There were no trees, no rocks. Nothing. Just a terrible, smothering darkness. And a delirious, heady warmth.

Slowly, a form began to take shape in the darkness. Not something natural, with its graceful lines, but square and manmade. A desk. A desk and a stool? He frowned. What sort of Hades was this? With a start, he realised the desk looked almost exactly like his own.

His barracks block? *This* was Hades? He opened his mouth to cry out, but no sound issued forth. Instead, he gazed past the edge of the desk. The light illuminating it began to pulse brighter…

Flames emerged in long tendrils. The blaze yawned larger and larger before him. He twisted and writhed about, trying to escape their force, but he remained in place. It was as if he possessed no earthly form, as though he were nothing but a consciousness. A consciousness that could still feel pain, fear, and immense discomfort. This really *was* Hades.

A small figure crouching before the fire gently stoked the flames, making them rise higher still. As the body took form, he found to his shock that it looked startlingly, once again, like Luciana. She fed the fire with a stack of tablets and scrolls, throwing them into the heart of the conflagration. When they'd disappeared, she picked the phalerae off his medal harness and tossed them into the flames. Everything that made up his life, his service, his career, she slowly fed into the fire.

He squirmed as the heat overwhelmed him. He struggled to form words. *Stop, Luciana! For the love of the gods, stop!* He silently fumed.

She did not listen, continuing her steadfast destruction.

To his growing horror, the flames burned hotter and hotter. He twisted in place, screaming noiselessly into the void, as their searing heat consumed him.

The next thing he knew, he found himself resting against something hard and cool. The profound darkness had returned. Slowly, his consciousness awakened to the cool drip of water echoing somewhere above him. He felt as though he were stranded in the darkest recesses of an underground cave. Perhaps Virgil had gotten something right, after all.

He rested against the rocks, languishing in their chilly embrace. The reigning silence enveloped him. He finally felt at peace.

Then, distantly, the eerie echoes of a song began to whisper within the chamber. Decimus started, ill at ease. Though her siren's call sounded far away, he knew in an instant it was Luciana's memory back to haunt him.

He turned over, trying to shut it out. But it continued to softly flow through his mind, stoking his sadness, impotence, and rage into a mad cocktail of anguish.

'Stop!' He cried out in the blackness. 'Please leave me alone!'

The singing carried on, unabated.

He fumbled through the dampness, seeking the source of the sound. As he entered another blackened chamber, he again beseeched Luciana's voice. The singing didn't stop. She sounded just as far away as she had before.

He stumbled into another part of the cavern, and another, blindly feeling his path. He begged Luciana to leave him be. But no matter how far he travelled, no matter how fervently he pled, her voice remained distant, untouchable.

A heaviness befell him. He sank against the rocks, exhausted. The drips of the cavern melded with his tears as he gave up, succumbing to Luciana's torturous song.

Luciana walked down the dank corridor, a kerchief to her nose. The sickly, sweet odour of poppy commingled with the rot of putrefied flesh, turning her stomach far more than any battlefield could. She brushed past an orderly emerging from a ward and entered the doorway of a far smaller room.

She stopped short and hovered there, eyeing the chamber's single occupant suspiciously. 'You sent for me?'

'Aye.' Tullius Servius's heavily scraped face looked up from the bed. His bandaged left arm rested in a neatly knotted sling from his shoulder. The thin, undyed linen undertunic he wore made him look far less officious. To her surprise, a small, tight smile appeared on his lips. 'Come in.'

Frowning, Luciana perched on a stool by the side of his bed. She gazed around the thinly plastered wattle and daub walls, the scattered instruments left sitting by a basin, the flickering light of far too many tripods along the perimeter. 'So, this is what being the primus pilus's optio gets you.'

A lone, pained chuckle forced its way between his teeth. 'It has its perks.'

She considered him for a long moment. Before she could stop herself, she asked, 'Why didn't you like me?'

His face fell. 'You're an enemy of Rome. I'm not supposed to like you. And neither, I thought, should Decimus.'

'You've hated that.' She shook her head. 'You could never be happy for him. You didn't trust me with him.'

'And for good reason.' He met her gaze and held it. 'Was I wrong?'

She coloured and looked away. The difficult betrayals she'd made, both to Decimus and her own kind, rankled within her. 'Why did you ask me here?' She mumbled.

He sighed. A long silence settled between them. Just as she rose from her seat, he finally said, 'Because I believe you love him.'

She slowly sat down, eyes wide.

'No one would do what you've done if they didn't.' Tullius fiddled with the blanket pulled midway up his torso. 'Even I can't deny that.'

She nodded, for once dumbstruck.

'It's hard…' He lifted his gaze to the tiled roof. 'I made a vow to him, the very first day we met, that I would always look out for him. I've known Decimus for far longer than you have. I know…I know more about him than you will ever know.'

She cocked her head, clearing her throat. 'Are you so sure about that?'

He regarded her, sitting as tall as her diminutive stature would allow. His eyes ran over the bone pins she'd bought in the vicus to keep her wayward braids behind her shoulders. Her neat, green tunica had been laundered and mended, with just the lightest whiff of urine about it. His gaze fell to her throat and her fingers lifted to the Capricorn charm, hanging outside her clothing for all the world to see.

'The crown you found in Londinium.'

Her hand dropped. 'How did you know about that?'

Tullius grinned. 'Take a wild guess.'

She sighed. *Nicomedes.* 'What about it, then?'

'That crown is the Corona Civica.' Tullius's face fell. 'It is Decimus's greatest honour. And his greatest shame.' He settled against the propped bolster on his bed. 'I don't think you quite understand just how excellent an officer Decimus is.'

Luciana snorted. 'I know exactly how "excellent" an officer he is. He is a loyal servant of Rome, who knows how to bully his men and win battles in the name of your precious emperor and his eagles. He is so dedicated to his job that nothing anyone might say or do could ever entice him away from it, away from this fort. Not even me.' She studied one of her chipped nails, picking around the cuticle. 'Why else do you think I'd ever come back?'

Tullius slowly shook his head. 'He's much more than that. Decimus knows the names of his men. He knows their strengths, their weaknesses. He knows who to rely on in the heat of the moment, and he knows who is best for each job. Decimus and I have spent many a night by our men's campfires. We've passed around the wineskin and shared stories, jokes, fears. The men confide in Decimus, they trust Decimus. He takes that to heart. He is more than their brother in arms; he is their father, their uncle, their role model, and their protector. The men in his century would follow him to the ends of the earth because they know he's one of them. He has their best interests at heart.'

She stared at the floorboards, remembering the haunted, determined look in his eyes when he'd tried to rescue his soldier from the sacred grove. A shudder coursed down her spine. 'And the emperor gave him a chaplet for that?'

'In a sense.' Tullius winced and shifted his shoulder. 'The chaplet was meant to honour that commitment. You see, the emperor only awards the Corona Civica to a man who saves the life of another Roman citizen in enemy held territory. It is not, you understand, an honour many men achieve. Fewer still live to receive it.' He ran a finger along the length of his sling. 'And Decimus uses that chaplet to torture himself.'

She waited silently for him to continue.

'He can't...' Tullius scratched at white stubble peppering his cut chin. 'He doesn't understand that he can't save everybody. Least of all the man who gave him that award.' His gaze fell. 'I remember that day clearly. I swore to Decimus I'd never talk about it.' He glanced at Luciana. 'But…'

'Please.' She leant forward. 'I want to know.'

'It was during the battle for the Medway River.' Tullius settled against his bolster, considering the far wall. 'He'd detailed one of our men, Caecus, to relay an important message to our extreme flank, only your lot ended up capturing him.'

'You mean, the Trinovantes and the Catuvellauni.'

'Exactly.' He regarded her coolly. 'Your lot.'

She frowned as he continued.

'We took the lad's contubernium to retrieve him. I'm still not sure how Decimus managed it, but he got Caecus out of there. It was a suicide mission. I covered his arse while he went in and took Caecus's torturers out. We managed to escape their defences by Fortuna's good graces. The rest of the contubernium didn't make it. I don't…' Tullius looked away and sighed. 'I don't know what it was about that day, but something in him broke. It… scarred him. And I don't just mean physically.'

Luciana shuddered. 'How could it hurt him so much?'

'Ask Decimus. It's his story to tell.' Tullius picked at his blanket. 'I took down Caecus's report and gave it to the legate. I had no idea what the consequence would be at the time. Emperor Claudius awarded Decimus the Corona Civica himself when he handed out campaign decorations in Camulodunum. Marcus Vinicius also promoted him to *hastatus posterior* of the first cohort at the same time.' Tullius wagged his head. 'It was quite an honour. The men of the Fourteenth chanted his name. But I have never seen Decimus angrier in my entire life. He told me to never mention it again.' Tullius looked down at his hands. 'He said he felt like an imposter.'

Luciana inhaled sharply. 'I…I had no idea.'

'It's not your fault.' He turned to her, smiling sadly. 'You weren't to know.'

She looked away, biting her lip. 'If…if that's how he feels…why would he keep it? Why travel with it?'

'Roman law requires a recipient of the Corona Civica wear it to all public gatherings. Such as…'

'…the governor's Saturnalia banquet.' She paled. 'I wasn't permitted to attend. I stayed behind and helped Hilaria prepare the legate's Saturnalia party.'

Tullius nodded.

A cough sounded in the doorway. She turned to see a hulking, bearded man with kind dark eyes hovering by the entrance. She stood. 'I…I thank you for telling me, Optio.'

He caught one of her hands and clasped it. 'It's not as if he could stop me, now. After everything…you deserved to know.'

'Yes.' She smiled grimly and returned his squeeze.

They shared a long, understanding look before she withdrew her hand and bustled down the corridor.

Tullius turned to his new visitor, a bright flush creeping up his cheeks. 'How did you find me here?'

'Easily. I asked one of the orderlies which room was yours.' Porcius plonked onto the vacated stool and scooted close.

'I mean, how did you know I was invalided back to the fort?'

Porcius cocked his head, grinning at him. 'I'm a legionary barber. I hear about everything that goes on in these parts.'

Tullius rapidly blinked his watering eyes. 'That's right. Not many are willing to discuss *The Suppliants* while in your chair.'

'Speaking of which…' Porcius laid a scroll next to him on the bed. 'I thought you might need something to pass the time.'

Tullius gazed at the book and chuckled softly. 'I appreciate your provision of entertainment.'

'It wasn't the only reason I came.' Porcius met Tullius's eyes and tentatively cupped his scraped chin in his palm. 'I had to see how you were.'

Tullius finally let his tears fall as Porcius scanned his many bruises and abrasions. 'I…I'm so sorry!' He whispered.

'And I was so worried I'd never see you again.' Porcius leant close and tenderly kissed Tullius's lips. 'Thanks be to Aesculapius, who heard my prayers. You'll heal.'

Tullius's unbandaged arm snaked out and trapped Porcius's hand. He locked his fingers through his and gripped it fast, trembling. 'I…was just so…frightened…that…'

'And you needn't be.' Porcius kissed him again. This time, Tullius returned his kiss, capturing his whiskered mouth with an unchecked passion.

'Ah, Porcius! Doing a round of dental inspections, I see?'

Tullius broke off and turned to a tall, dark surgeon who'd bustled into the room. When he saw the gentle smile on the surgeon's face, he relaxed against the bolster.

'No, Philosir. I'm very much off duty for the day.' Porcius ran his free hand through his receding curls and smiled at Tullius, who still squeezed his fingers. 'Visiting your patient here is purely for pleasure.'

Tullius chuckled, slowly relaxing in his lover's affectionate gaze. 'You could always give me a shave while you're here.'

Porcius appraised him for a moment. 'No, I don't think I will.' He ran his eyes along the week-old bristles. 'I'd rather you try growing that out. The white beard is quite handsome.'

Tullius blushed and lowered his gaze. 'Then how about you start in on *The Suppliants?* It'll take my mind off what Philosir's doing.' He hissed as the surgeon eased his injured arm out of its sling.

Porcius brushed his lips against Tullius's brow and picked up the scroll. 'I thought you'd never ask.'

XXXIV

An odour of raw shellfish wrinkled Decimus's nostrils. He frowned, moaning, as he blinked his eyes open.

The sunshine bathing his face lent a form to his surroundings that he'd grown unaccustomed to. The end of the silken bolster he rested against came into focus first. As he gazed at it, the rest of the room slowly took shape. His eyes travelled along the length of the bed, at his limp arms and prone form rising beneath a woollen blanket. A sizable, pristine white bandage had been wound tightly about his left forearm, which looked all the more alien in the morning light. Beside the bed, a shutter hung open. He could hear birds singing, feet bustling, and voices calling to one another outside.

He slowly moved his head. For the first time, he felt the heaviness of his body as muscle and bone swung to follow his eyes. He focussed on a neatly thatched ceiling. Wattle siding extended down from the flat roof, giving way to a clean, freshly swept floor. A wolfskin stretched across the middle of the room, lending the space a rather savage warmth. Along the wall, just beyond the foot of the bed, loomed a desk and chair. He squinted, frowning. The articles looked suspiciously like his own desk and chair, with scrolls and tablets neatly stacked to one side. The other side of the desk contained small cosmetic pots and scents. A brass hand mirror lay nestled among them.

His gaze moved beyond the edge of the desk. With a start, he recognised his own armour rack looming in the corner. His cuirass and medal harness shone with a dull sheen. His helmet perched just above, sporting a vibrant horsehair crest and intact chin laces. At the foot of the stand, his calfskin boots leant against the wall, radiating a well-oiled glow. Decimus's brow furrowed. What had happened? Why were these things here? Where *was* he?

Slowly, his gaze roamed along the wall. Not far from the armour rack sat his worn leather trunk. Just beside it, a newer trunk he didn't recognise. Beside that, a chamber pot skirted along the edge of a sizable hearth. Blackened remains of old fires lurked within the hearth's depths. Above its centre perched a cooking pole. The casements were simple: mere wood instead of the sturdy stone structure of his quarters. The bronze fire dogs flanking it curled into stylised horse heads. Before the hearth, a rather plain wooden chair sat at an angle, a discarded fur pelt draped over its back. Tor lay curled at its feet, dozing. Decimus craned his head to examine the room's furthest corner.

A wicker screen had been erected further along the wall, creating a tiny partition. A dark blanket had been thrown over its top. The screen was tall, its length just skirting the floorboards. A small wash basin atop a cabinet sat in the space's cosy recesses. An expanse of floor and blank wall separated the partition from a door, which Decimus assumed exited to the outside world. Beside the door, wooden shelves cluttered with jars, bottles, sacks, and amphorae lined the wall. Below the shelves sat a simple table with two empty stools perched on either side. Just beyond the table, skirting the wall beside the bed, stood what must be a household altar, crowded with strange effigies and votive trinkets. Bone white antlers crowned the display. Decimus recoiled as soon as he recognised them, drawing his attention closer to the bed. Before his gaze could fall on the stand beside him, a hand bearing a waterskin clouded his vision.

'Drink.'

He frowned and opened his mouth to speak. Only a weak rasping noise issued forth.

'I imagined you'd find yourself at a loss for words.' Luciana's entrancing green eyes shone down at him. 'Don't worry. This isn't the poppy-laced concoction the surgeon sent you home with. Come on, drink.'

He cautiously wrapped his lips around the skin as Luci tilted it up. The rich, dark warmth of an Alban vintage alighted his senses at once. His bristled throat pulsed as he gulped drink after drink of the restorative wine.

Luci obligingly held the skin up. To Decimus's eyes, there were new lines on her brow, a pallor to her creamy skin, a weariness to her gentle smile. She'd gathered her long golden tresses back with a leather thong. Her off-white tunic looked a bit rumpled. One hand checked his bandaged arm. He felt a small tremor down his spine as her fingers brushed his skin. However tired she looked, the obdurate energy radiating from her small, powerful form still marked her every touch.

'There you are.' She lowered the skin and stoppered it. 'Tullius said it wasn't the best wine in the world, but Bakari told him it was the finest he could get at the moment.'

'Tullius?' He rasped. 'Where?'

'Up the road, at the fort, of course.' She shrugged, turning to stow the wine. 'The surgeon keeps a close eye on him, but he's come round to check on you a couple of times. I dare say you don't remember.'

He winced, struggling to work his disused vocal cords. 'Where…am…I?'

'Viroconium.' Luciana grabbed one of the stools and sat down beside the bed. She took his right hand in hers and smiled softly. 'You are home.'

He stared at her, mouth agape. She returned his steady look, caressing his hand with her fingers. When he tried to lift his head, a jolt of pain issued from somewhere behind. He sucked in a sharp breath, grimacing.

'Easy, there!' Almost immediately, he felt Luci's hands on his shoulders, firmly pressing him against the pillow. 'Stay still. You've got quite the bump on the back of your head. I promised the surgeon I'd keep you quiet until the swelling goes down.' As soon as she'd settled him against the bolster, she took her seat. 'Another move like that and I'll have no choice but to put you under again.'

'Again?' He frowned. 'What…what's happened?'

'I suppose the last thing you remember was knocking yourself out on your own helmet. Banged the back of your head up quite fiercely.' She tenderly stroked his limp ringlets. Her fingers carefully avoided the matted hair covering his swollen contusion. 'It's just a massive bump now. The surgeon says you should feel better once that shrinks. But it's best not to rattle your head around before then.'

He grunted. The feeling of her fingers gently wending through his hair seemed to soothe the throbbing pangs in his skull.

'Truth be told, we were far more worried if you'd keep your arm.' She nodded to his white bandage.

'Hmm?'

'That landslide at the pass blocked our way to Viroconium.' She stood and reached into a pail sitting beside the bed. She wrang out a washcloth and dabbed it across Decimus's brow. 'It took us six days to bring the wounded around the hills. By that time, your arm had become infected.'

He gazed at her silently, watching her wipe the perspiration from his face.

'You were in a fever for days.' She lifted his uninjured arm and deftly sponged along his elbow. 'I worked day and night to break it. You're still much too warm, as it is. At least your wound has turned a corner. The surgeon's been over every day to drain it and change the dressing. He thinks you're going to be fine.'

Decimus watched her make her way around the bandage and noticed a yellowish tinge to his fingers. He wiggled them and breathed a long sigh at the ease of movement.

She caught sight of his expression and smiled. 'You'll live to fight another day.' She whisked back the blanket and bent to resoak her towel.

He looked down the end of his nose. His eyes widened slightly. 'I'm… nude.'

'How else am I supposed to keep you cool and clean?' Luciana dabbed along his scarred shoulders. 'It's not as if I haven't seen you like this before.'

He reddened.

'I was quite surprised to find you still wearing this,' she murmured as she brushed against the wheel of Taranis.

He grunted, his eyes following her hands. 'Said…I'd wear it…always.'

Luci paused. She leant forward and pecked him on the cheek before continuing her sponge bath down his legs.

He caught a glint of his armour behind Luciana. 'Where's…here?'

'My home, of course.' She didn't pause, working her way along one shin. 'Or tenement, rather. I rented this place when I left the fort because it's not far. It wasn't much to look at when I got it, and it hardly came cheap. Your camp prefect? The unpleasant man with the crooked nose who once told you to muzzle me? He was reluctant to let me move your things over here. But once I'd explained you were my lover and had provided the down payment for our domestic quarters, he released them to me without another word.'

'I'm…your lover?'

She straightened, her expression bland. 'Are you not?'

A delighted grin crept across his face. Luci threw the blanket over him, squeezing his shoulder as she stowed the bucket and towel.

'I must say, the landlord has been considerably politer to me. Now he knows I'm attached to the primus pilus of the Fourteenth legion.' She drew her seat up to the bed, snorting. 'The racist pig.'

'But…why?' He frowned, struggling to articulate. His surroundings felt too idyllic to be true. It had to be another hallucination, or his arrival in Elysium. It couldn't be all it seemed. His puzzled eyes settled on Luci. 'Why…are you…here?'

She shrugged. 'Why not? You granted me the freedom to go where I pleased, and I pleased to go here. My choices and actions are my own.' She jutted her chin.

He lifted a finger and tapped it weakly against her arm. 'Should… have…gone…home.'

'You silly man.' She giggled, enveloping his calloused palm in both her own. 'I am home. This room, this bed is my home.' Her gaze met his. '*You*, Decimus, are my home.'

Something inside him, some rigid inner barrier broke. His fingers weakly squeezed her back. He gazed incredulously at her as a lone tear streaked down his wizened cheek.

When he tried to speak, she slowly shook her head. Gripping his hand, she snuggled her head against his shoulder.

'There.' She emphatically released his arm and moved away. 'If you think you can handle it, I'll get you something to eat.'

He nodded.

She mixed a slurry of ingredients together in a small pot. Tor wandered over to her, wagging his tail. Decimus gazed at the ceiling, slowly mulling over everything she'd told him. He frowned in concentration, trying to make sense of his muddled thoughts. The dull throbbing in the back of his head steadily increased, forcing him to close his eyes.

He heard Luciana pad across the room and suspend her pot over the hearth. He cautiously opened his eyes to see her bent form lighting a fire. Her bound golden hair glimmered in a long line down her back, flashing in the rays of the morning sun. It triggered a memory. His frown deepened. 'You…'

'Yes?' Luci stoked the low flames and turned to face him, brushing sooty hands along the sides of her tunic.

'You…were there. At…the bottleneck.'

'Lucky for you, I was. You'd hardly be lying there now if I hadn't arrived when I did.' Her tired face suddenly brightened. 'That reminds me. I've got something for you…'

He watched her stoop beside the cot. She pulled a dull wooden box from beneath the frame and placed it on her stool. To his growing puzzlement, she carefully unlatched it and submerged her hand in a dark, ominous cavity. When she proudly lifted out the object inside, he cringed. Morcant's lifeless, gaping maw glared at him, suspended by thick tendrils of dark hair. His shrivelled, embalmed visage looked even more fearsome than the last time Decimus had seen it. Haunting black sockets had replaced the Silure's eyes. The dark blue woad lining his leathery skin, converging into the rectangle on his forehead, looked even more gruesome and twisted in death. Decimus's stomach lurched.

'Put…that thing…away,' he gasped, squeezing his eyes shut.

She slowly lowered the head. 'Are you not pleased?'

'You…mad?' The strong stench of cedar assaulted his nostrils. With a concerted effort, he slowly turned his face away. 'It's…sick.'

She returned her prize to its resinous compartment. 'It's quite an honour to possess the head of a chieftain, you know.'

'Fucking…savage,' he mumbled.

Luciana tucked the container under the bed and picked up an object from the desk. She held it to the sunlight, where it gleamed so brightly that

Decimus shut his eyes again. 'I also brought you *this* for your uniform. I suppose you're just going to spurn that, too?'

He peeked one eye open and saw Morcant's torc resting in her grip. Bright amber beads gleamed along its thick golden band. The two knobbed ends had been intricately detailed, their swirls reminiscent of the sacred triskelion spiral. He laid a trembling hand over hers. 'I…can't.'

'Fine, then.' She drew away, letting the torc clatter to the floor. 'I suppose I should have let him kill you, too, for all you seem to care!'

'No…' He groaned, frustrated that he couldn't raise his voice. 'I can't wear that…because…only soldiers who kill a chieftain…may wear their torcs.'

She turned, brows furrowed.

He pointed to the floor. 'Your kill…your honour…your torc.'

She hugged her shoulders, biting her lip. She saw the pride radiating in his eyes and her own began to water. A bright blush suffused her cheeks as she retrieved the ornament. Gripping it in her fingers, she swallowed her tears and smiled. 'Well, when you put it like that…'

He nodded. She stowed the torc with a measured, stately grace. He paled, however, when she turned back around with the Corona Civica in her hands. Gently, she set it on his lap in place of the torc.

He frowned. 'Put…that…'

'No.'

He gaped at her cold expression.

'I won't. You can't make me, physically or otherwise.' She nodded to the chaplet. 'Tullius told me a little about it, but I still don't understand. Why does this hurt you so much that you need hurt those around you?'

He closed his eyes. 'I…can't…'

'If you don't, I'm leaving. Now.'

She opened the newer trunk and tossed some of her cosmetic bottles inside.

He scowled. 'You…wouldn't…'

'Wouldn't I?' She whirled on him, holding a bird-shaped perfume bottle aloft. 'Decimus, I love you. I am here because I choose to be here, with you. And I can choose to go elsewhere any time I want! There is nothing stopping me!'

His jaw dropped. Another searing pain behind his ear forced him to close his eyes.

'I saved your life, Decimus.' She slowly approached his bed. Decimus heard the contained rage trembling beneath her words. 'You owe me an explanation.'

He whimpered. A couple of hot tears escaped down his cheeks. 'Put it away…I'll tell you.'

She silently complied. He opened his eyes to see her waiting, arms crossed.

'I…can't…forget…' He felt the scar on his cheek burn. He lifted his uninjured arm to brush at it. 'The torturer…tried to…skin me. Split my face open. I didn't care. I just…needed…to do right…by my men.' His lips trembled. 'And I failed.'

Luciana sat down at the end of his bed, silently imploring him to continue.

'I didn't…get the lads out safe. Only Caecus.' He sniffed. 'What sort… of survival rate…one in eight…and their centurion still lived.'

He turned to gaze out the window. 'It was…the day after the first battle for Medway River. The lads were tired. Tough fighting. I was tired. No excuse.' He inhaled sharply and sighed. 'The Second Augusta…got pummelled…in opening attack. My century reinforced them. The Ninth Hispana…still needed to cross. Geta…legate of the Ninth…wanted the scrappiest century in Gemina. Our legate chose mine. Geta needed a lad… to deliver…message to our flank…before next morning's attack.'

He gazed beyond the sky, his mind snatching at the memories of that terrible evening…

River Medway, AD 43

Gnaeus Hosidius Geta's pinched, squat face frowned up at Decimus. 'I need *you* to send a man across the river to inform Valeria of tomorrow's plan. He *must* get through, and he *must* go undetected, so Valeria's in position by dawn. Without the Brits' knowledge. If those bastards get the wind up about our plans, it'll jeopardise the entire operation. Got that?'

He remembered Legionary Caecus's lean face grinning up at him. He took Geta's signet ring and nodded at Decimus, eyes shining. 'I won't let you down, sir. I'll outrun Mercury himself.'

A few hours later, they'd swapped the legionary camp for tall reeds lining the Medway's banks. The dark waters shimmered in the moon's soft glow. Decimus turned, seeing Tullius and the other men of Caecus's contubernium at his back. All held their breaths as they watched Caecus slowly wade into the water. Decimus started when a patrol of Britons emerged from the trees. He unsheathed his gladius, ready to parry the charging enemy.

When the dust had settled, two of Decimus's men lay dead. He gasped through his mouth, his nose a bloody pulp. He impotently regrouped his men, watching the Britons drag Caecus away to their camp.

After dispatching another man to swim the message across, Decimus had no choice but to lead the party to the enemy fortifications. The Britons would find the general's signet and torture Caecus for information, information they *must* not get.

More time passed before they finally found the shadowy parapet surrounding the Britons' high ground. Caecus's agonised wails travelled on the wind, chilling Decimus's blood. He silently willed the lad to hold firm as he slowly paced the perimeter, Tullius and Caecus's remaining three tentmates in tow.

They ventured too far from the shadows and drew the ire of slingers on the ramparts. Another man down. He and his men had taken more damage, including a well-aimed blow to his right arm that left it numb.

After pacing the perimeter, they found a way into the fort. They ascended a steep hill containing the Britons' livestock pen. Decimus reluctantly took off his helmet and armour, laying them in a heap beside the other men's heavy trappings. Holding his breath, he tucked his injured arm close and wriggled through the small hole his men had dug under the fence.

Once inside the enemy's defences, they carefully kept to the shadows of the Britons' campfires. Low voices muttered in their inscrutable tongue, mixed with tired sighs and the patter of piss. Decimus and Tullius fell facedown in the mud and held their breaths when a warrior ventured too close.

They left the pen behind. Decimus darted from shadow to shadow beside Tullius, nearing the source of the tortured screams. His heart leapt in his throat. With every step, he grew less certain that he'd ever make it out alive.

Then he was inside the hut, gazing at the horrors that greeted him. A nobleman in Gallic armour, capable of only barking a little mangled Latin, stood to one side. A tall brute hulked beside him, cruel eyes glittering from a blood-spattered face. Caecus lay on the other side of the hearth, sobbing in his own puddle of vomit and shit. His gangling legs were twisted and purpled, lying at unnatural angles. Neat strips of flesh had been carved from his calves. His face was bruised beyond recognition. Three fingers remained on his bloodied left hand. A cauterised stump where the right hand should have been. Decimus would never forget the suffocating, acrid stench of burnt flesh, the haunted terror in Caecus's eyes.

Tullius had gone for the nobleman. The giant filled Decimus's vision, slamming him to the floor. He remembered losing his gladius in the tumble, helpless to defend himself from the torturer. Hard fingers pressed against his throat, crushing his windpipe. The man above him dimmed into darkness. He heard distant laughter as a blade sliced his chin open. It made a slow, torturous path up the side of his face. He felt his skin parting to reveal the bone beneath. He couldn't make himself care, waiting for the darkness to claim him.

Screams echoed above his head. The torturer's knife suddenly cut a jagged path across his cheek before falling away. The darkness receded, revealing Tullius gripping the giant's arm, thrusting his hand into the fire.

Decimus's fingers fumbled at his belt for his pugio. He sank the blade into the fleshy gut above him and sawed it open. He didn't remember crawling out from under the torturer, but he did remember gathering a trembling Caecus in his arms. Remembered emerging from the hut, feeling the cool evening air against his severed, flapping cheek. Caecus's tentmates had readied four native ponies for their escape. He threw Caecus over the shoulders of one, clambering up behind him. They galloped for the nearest gate as the camp slowly came alive. Bare-chested men began to surround them, swinging long swords.

The legionaries peeled off from Decimus and Tullius, drawing the attackers to them. Their diversion saved the officers and Caecus but came at the cost of their lives. He saw one pulled from his mount and butchered on the ground as the other swung futilely at the horde enclosing him.

Fortuna smiled on their escape. Decimus and Tullius reached the gate just as it opened to admit a returning mounted patrol. They galloped through the confused men before they could realise what happened. Too soon, the Britons were in pursuit. He heard them draw nearer as his pony tired beneath him. He hunched low, clutching Caecus's prone form to him. He raised his eyes to Tullius aboard his own flagging mount and reflected his friend's despair. *We are already dead men.*

Suddenly, the Britons drew up, letting them escape. Decimus couldn't understand it until he saw the red banner of Legio XX Valeria fluttering between the trees, announcing the vanguard of the flank as it shifted into position.

'Hold still, please, sir.'

Decimus growled and steeled himself. An orderly gently cleaned his freshly stitched wounds with vinegar. The application of the liquid to his face felt like licks of flame penetrating all the way to the bone. He closed his eyes at the orderly's touch and winced. '*Fuck*, that hurts!'

'Sorry, sir. Can't be helped.' The orderly pressed a linen dressing against the centurion's cheek. He held it in place as he wound a bandage around his head. 'That one'll leave a rather nasty scar. You shan't be prized for your beauty, but you'll cut quite the rakish figure with the ladies, sir.'

Decimus grunted. His nose had already been roughly sutured over and encased in a waxed bandage. His right arm, neatly bound, rested against his knee. The fingers of his opposite hand drummed impatiently at his side.

'The surgeon wants you to report every other day so he can change the dressings and check on your progress.' The orderly tucked in the ends of the bandage and stepped back.

Decimus sighed. 'Is that really necessary?'

'Oh, yes, sir. The surgeon will need to drain off any pus that issues from the sutures.'

He stood from the camp stool and smiled. 'Then let's hope there's none of that, hey?'

'No, sir!' The orderly looked aghast. 'On the contrary, you'd better hope there is! No pus is a sure sign of mortified flesh. That's a short road to amputation or death.'

Decimus frowned. 'Forget I said anything, then.'

He ducked, exiting the tent into the predawn gloom. The prone forms of wounded legionaries lay to his left and right, moaning, as they waited for transport across the river. Decimus picked his way over to a larger medical tent erected across the track. Even worse cases lined the walls of the goatskin structure: men missing limbs, parts of their faces; men who writhed in agony and called on the gods to ease their suffering from punctured vitals; men who'd had their hamstrings cut lying crippled on the ground; men who stared at the canvas ceiling and silently prayed for death to come.

Orderlies in white tunics moved between them, winding bandages, making notations, and administering tonics to the soldiers at their feet. The heady odour of poppies mingled with the sharp, acidic notes of vinegar and the metallic tang of blood. Flies buzzed around the densely packed soldiers, enhancing their torment.

Decimus didn't stop until he reached the Greek duty surgeon. He was still bent over Caecus, cautiously examining him. His touch, though featherlight, elicited howls and groans from his patient. In between cries of pain, Caecus murmured to Tullius, who crouched by his side scribbling notes in a wax tablet.

'How is he, Aristides?'

The surgeon straightened and turned to Decimus. He glanced at the patient before shaking his head. 'I'm not going to lie, the lad's in a bad way.' He ran a hand through his tight, greying curls. 'Both of the legs are crushed beyond repair, and I'd have to take more from his arms to correct the botched job those savages did. There's damage to his ribs, and I'm worried from the looks of his contusions that he's got internal bleeding. I'll do what I can for him, but even with the best of recoveries, he'll always be a helpless cripple.'

Decimus gulped. To be invalided out of the army was a soldier's worst nightmare. Most of the men's families relied on their army income to survive; they could ill afford to look after them in kind. Living on the streets of the Subura, surviving off the grain dole and having to endure the pity of strangers and friends alike…it was no way to live. Decimus closed his eyes and shuddered.

'I'm sorry, sir.' Aristides laid a hand on his shoulder. 'You did well to get the boy out alive. I'm not sure he would've lasted much longer with those blasted *Brittunculi.*'

Decimus nodded numbly.

'Let's pray to Aesculapius that he makes the best recovery possible, eh?' The surgeon pulled a tight smile before brushing past Decimus. Wearily, he trudged down the row, calling to an orderly for his equipment.

Decimus stepped over to Caecus and gazed down at the young man. Caecus had crossed his mutilated arms on his stomach. The remaining fingers of his left hand pressed tightly against his flesh as shudders racked his body. His hooked beak still lay in a mangled pulp in the centre of his face, the rest of which had swollen. Green tinged the dark bruises marring his face. His dark hair lay plastered to his head with sweat. His tongue darted out to wet his cracked, dry lips as he quietly dictated to Tullius.

'…I swear by the almighty Jupiter, best and greatest, that I kept my oath to Legate Geta. The Britons never learned what message I carried. I fulfilled my duty to the plan and was prepared to die with my knowledge. But I would not be alive to affirm so without the intervention of my centurion, Decimus Maximus. He entered the enemy camp and saved my life, at great personal risk to his own. It is thanks to his ingenuity and courage that I was spared an ignominious death at the hands of a torturer. To him I forever owe my gratitude.'

Tullius finished taking down his words. 'Shall I make a mark for you?'

Caecus lifted his left hand. 'I want to sign it myself.'

'But Caecus-,'

'Let me do it.'

Tullius worked the stylus between two of Caecus's fingers. With a sigh, he held the tablet in front of him.

Caecus struggled, awkwardly wielding the tool in his only hand. Fresh beads of sweat broke out on his forehead. His face contorted as he struggled to form the letters. He glared at Tullius whenever he opened his mouth to speak. Long, painful moments passed while he struggled with the task. Then, with a final, concerted grunt, he dropped his arm.

Tullius glanced at the malformed signature before clapping the tablet shut. 'Right, then.' He plucked the stylus from between Caecus's fingers. 'I'll see that these messages are relayed to the appropriate avenues.'

'Thank you, sir.' Caecus smiled weakly. He looked at Decimus. 'I'd like to speak to the centurion now, if you please.'

Tullius moved back, allowing Decimus to take his place at the legionary's side.

Decimus hunched down beside Caecus. He gazed at him for a long moment before slowly shaking his head. 'I'm so, so sorry, lad.'

'For what, sir? You gave an order, and I obeyed.' Caecus swallowed. 'Didn't I say I'd do you proud?'

'You did more than that.' Decimus glanced at his stump before tearing his eyes away. A lump rose in his bruised throat. 'Cerberus's teeth, son, but you've had a rough time of it.'

'If you'll excuse my saying, sir, you don't look so good yourself.'

Decimus met his gaze and saw a faint, laughing twinkle in Caecus's eyes. He suppressed a choking laugh and sighed. 'You'd have made centurion if Fortuna had been kinder. You're the best soldier I've ever had.'

'Fortuna's an ugly old cunt. Let her go hang.' Caecus tittered. He laid his mutilated hand on top of Decimus's bandaged arm, his expression sobering. 'Before you go…there's one last thing you can do for me, sir.'

Decimus smiled at the lad. His fortitude here, in the tent, inspired him more than Caecus would ever know. His heart swelled with pride. 'Name it.'

'Finish me.'

Decimus frowned, eyes widening. 'What?'

'Finish…me.' He nodded to the hilt of Decimus's sheathed pugio. 'You saved my life. Now I'm asking you to take it. Don't send me back to Rome a cripple, sir. I couldn't stand it. If I was as good a soldier as you say, then I deserve a soldier's death. A dignified death.'

Decimus sat back. 'I couldn't!'

'Please, sir!' Caecus curled his fingers about Decimus's hand, trembling violently.

Decimus sadly regarded the legionary. When Caecus first joined up, he hadn't been expected to last a month. The lanky, beak-nosed recruit was slow, ungainly, uncoordinated, and physically weak. But Decimus, seeing too much of himself in the lad, hadn't given up on him. Under Decimus's tutelage, Caecus had grown into an enthusiastic, capable soldier. And no one, in Decimus's estimation, was braver. For that reason, he'd chosen Caecus to run the message. For that reason, he'd been reduced to such a sorry state.

The threat of forever enduring the contemptuous and pitying stares of people who would never lift a weapon for their empire, of living in the gutters of the Subura, reflected in Caecus's eyes. Decimus, in flight from the Subura himself, understood the lad's desperation. He, too, would be begging for the same.

He sighed, swallowing tears. 'All right.'

'Thank you, sir.' Caecus released him and fell limp. A relieved smile twitched across his chapped lips.

Decimus held the tip of his dagger at Caecus's throat. His bound arm wobbled. He drew a deep breath and blinked several times. 'I'll see you in Hades, brother.'

Caecus closed his eyes and nodded contentedly.

'On three. One…' He thrust the pugio through the top of Caecus's throat, angling it up to pierce his brain. Gritting his teeth, he twisted the blade. Caecus's eyes opened wide. His mouth gaped in shock, but no sound came. Dark blood bubbled from his lips. With a violent shudder, his rigid body finally relaxed.

Decimus withdrew his dagger and gently closed the lad's sightless eyes. He fumbled at his belt for a sestertius to pay Charon and slipped it into Caecus's mouth. 'Rest easy, soldier.' He sheathed the blade without pausing to clean it and abruptly strode out of the tent. Tullius followed.

Decimus did not stop until he'd reached a spot along the riverbank, away from the medical tents, transports, and reserve forces stirring about the camp. Once he was finally alone, he sank into the mud, lowered his head to his knees, and wept.

Viroconium, British Frontier, AD 60

Decimus startled out of his reverie as Luciana took his hand. He slowly turned to meet her gaze.

A war of words seemed to form on her lips. She silently struggled, face contorting, before swallowing them back with a tight smile. 'Thank you.' She squeezed his fingers.

He nodded.

She rose from the bed and unpacked her trunk.

'You'll…stay?'

'You can hardly care for yourself. Too many ghosts.'

He frowned. 'But…'

'No buts, Decimus.' She pointed a hairpin at him. 'Understanding is only half the battle. And I never run from a fight. Neither will you.'

He cowed as she approached the bed. 'You must learn to live with your pain. I don't know how, but you can't keep treating me like shit every time your past returns to haunt you. If you don't, I *will* leave you. I am here by choice, and you need to remember that.'

Decimus slowly nodded.

He watched her replace her things and walk to the kitchen. He couldn't help but admire her cold fury: the proud carriage of her spine, the gentle swish of her hair, the measured power of her stride. She was formidable. She had brought him back from the bank of the Styx. And all because she had chosen him. Decimus felt like his heart would burst out of his chest.

XXXV

Nicomedes gazed down at the rather simple stone embedded in the earth. On it, the vacant stare of a female face with two flowing braids looked back at him, flanked by roughly carved words detailing her name and age at time of death. The letters 'DM' headed the inscription, followed by the words, 'Metellus, late decanus of Legio XIIII and devoted husband, erected this altar in memory of his wife. Though not a Roman, her virtue made her so.'

Beside him, Metella knelt and poured wine into a flute on top of the stone. Her dark head, covered by her palla, bent over the altar. 'Mater, please accept this offering. Look upon Pater and I with your kind counsel and loving grace.'

Nicomedes likewise hung his head, waiting for Metella to finish.

She straightened, holding the pitcher in front of her. 'Forgive me for not following your direction earlier. I should know better than to fall for shiny presents.' She turned to Nicomedes, eyes bright. 'You always told me that the best gifts are those we cannot wear.'

He blushed, running a hand through his tousled curls. 'Your…your mother wasn't a Roman?'

'Dobunni.' Metella fingered the bulla she wore about her neck. 'But I am a Roman. Pater's citizenship makes me so.'

'I'm not a Roman, either, but I'm freeborn.' He tentatively took her hand. 'And I will be a citizen one day.'

'I'm glad, but it isn't everything.' Metella faced him. 'You are kind. You are skilled. You are curious, and you love adventure as much as I do.' She smiled. 'You don't have to travel far, either, to find it.'

Nicomedes laughed. 'I don't think the optio shares your appreciation.'

Metella cocked her head. One black curl fell free from its pin to dangle enticingly over her ear. 'Pater speaks well of your master. He says the optio is a good man, and you'll do well to learn from him.'

'I am.' Nicomedes nodded, then made a face. 'Even if the sight of an abacus fills me with dread.'

She giggled, displaying the high dimples he found so enchanting.

'You're so funny, Nico!'

He shuffled his feet, feeling his heart flutter in his throat. He glanced at the altar. 'Do you think your mother approves?'

'I'm sure she does.' Metella touched her brow to his. 'You have all the qualities she told me mattered most.' Her eyes flickered. 'It doesn't hurt that you're cute, too.'

She closed her eyes and planted a soft, featherlight kiss on his mouth. Nicomedes curled his arm about her plump waist. He held her close to keep his knees from buckling. She placed her hand over his. 'That feels nice.'

Nicomedes's mouth opened and closed, unable to find words. She felt as soft and warm as she appeared. The round form of her rapidly maturing body absorbed his slight frame in a way that filled him with longing. He found his eyes fixed on her breasts, unable to look away.

She coloured and reluctantly broke their embrace. 'Come on.' She linked her hand in his and strolled along the row of tombstones. 'We've been gone long enough. I'd hate for Pater to think any less of you.'

Nicomedes wordlessly fell into step beside her. They passed Optio Servius, Luciana, and Centurion Maximus, who stood about a newly erected stone for a man named Vulso. Nicomedes waved to his master and gestured to Metella. The optio nodded and shooed them on.

'I'll take you home.' Nicomedes helped her into the chariot and took the reins. A Thracian horse and Luciana's mare obediently picked up a sedate walk in response to his subtle cue.

'You don't have to hurry.' Metella clasped his elbow, pressing her fleshy form against his. 'I love this, riding with you.'

'Me too,' he managed to say, his mind's eye dazzling with the light of a thousand stars. He stood even straighter as she rested her head on his shoulder.

In the traces, Belena snorted. She slowed her steps to an uncharacteristically stately pace as the chariot creaked away from the cemetery, as if to lengthen their time together.

Cassia moved along a line of flats on the insula's first landing, counting the doors. She stopped before an entrance sitting directly above the fishmonger and pulled a bronze hairpin from her head. She pressed close, looking either way, as she worked the door's lock with her pin.

She was beginning to get annoyed with Antiope, who'd insisted that her work had been completed. How could Antiope know? Cassia had done nothing!

'The gods have their own methods and heed our pleas as they see fit. I tell you, Nemesis has fulfilled her part of the bargain and binds you to yours.'

'Nemesis, you bitch,' she muttered under her breath, 'I gave up my son for this. Let me share in the spoils!'

Antiope had studied her tokens when Cassia insisted for proof of Nemesis's favour. Her only words had been, 'You may find it where your only love becomes your only hate.'

With a click, the door's latch finally gave way. She stepped into Luciana's apartment and glanced around the sparse furnishings with distaste. She closed her eyes, stilling her mind and heart. *Where my only love…* She smiled as she pictured Decimus, *…becomes my only hate.* The sight of him kissing his British whore in the woods wrenched at her gut. A warmth suffused her, travelling down her spine.

When she opened her eyes, they focussed on a square casquet situated near the end of the bed. The bed Decimus shared with *her.* She strode directly to the wooden box and knelt beside it. With trembling hands, she lifted the lid and peered at its contents.

She reached inside and pulled out Morcant's head. Its gruesome, abhorrent appearance and resinous odour didn't phase her. She turned the leathery flesh this way and that, holding it aloft. The chieftain's dark hair and moustache hung in matted clumps. His black, sightless eye sockets gaped as impotently as his slack-jawed mouth. The woad markings, including the rectangle he'd taken such pride in, had shrivelled, pinching his puckered skin.

She held the head up to the light. A broad smile slowly spread across her face.

Epilogue

Boudicca stood at the front of her bronze-encrusted chariot, leaning on her spear. Emer crouched beside her, ably driving the ponies in their red-and-blue enamelled harness, just as her mother had taught her to do. Rioghnach stood solemnly at her back, gazing at the darkened path before them.

Boudicca flicked her long, flowing red locks over her shoulder and glanced at her youngest daughter. Rioghnach worried her; she hadn't spoken a single word since her rape at the Romans' hands. She'd refused to stand before the Trinovantes as Boudicca rallied them to her cause, slapping her mother's hand away with a shriek when Boudicca tried to encourage her.

She straightened and looked at Mandusedos, standing in the chariot at her flank. Thankfully, she hadn't needed to parade her youngest daughter's trauma before the Trinovantes. The insult to Mandusedos's bride had been more than enough.

'Look you upon the might of Rome!' she'd cried, lifting stony-faced Emer's skirts. The Trinovantes had gazed at her bruises. 'This is how they treat our daughters!'

She'd then turned around and gathered up her hair, motioning for Emer to unfasten the back of her gown. Her badly scabbed lash marks screamed at the tribesmen and women in their black and purple agony. 'I am a client queen of Rome! I have passed many winters obeying their laws, suffering my tribe's injustices, bargaining for the Roman peace. This is what I get for being a friend to Rome!'

She'd turned about to see only Mandusedos's kinspeople outraged. The remaining Trinovantes had worn various guises of shock and dismay, but no anger. The wrath of Andraste hadn't yet infected them.

'Do you not see what they do to us?' She'd swept her drawn sword over the throng. 'They tell you that we, the Iceni, are your enemy. That you must take land from us because we have more than you, that you deserve it more. They want you to forget the real reason you feel the constraint of your borders! Because their retired veterans keep building on your land! The land of your Trinovantian ancestors! The land that is rightfully yours!'

An outraged cheer had risen through the tribe's ranks. A glow had suffused Boudicca's cheeks. 'They take your sons and conscript them into the priesthood of their emperor! The emperor that made both your father and mine kiss his feet when he stole their freedom! It wasn't enough for Rome to take your tribal seat and use your labour until your backs broke building their enormous temple! No, now they make you serve its dead emperor, all the while telling you this is what you really wanted! You are nothing but Roman slaves!'

Men and women had begun to bang on shields, angrily conversing and cheering, just as the Catuvellauni had done when she'd spoken to them.

'The governor has turned his armies on Mona, because the thread of our very ways threatens him. It isn't enough to pay their taxes and work their temples. No, we must revoke the very people who decide our laws, sing of our past, and commune directly with our gods. He thinks that, by killing the druids, he can kill our ability to resist. How little the Roman knows!'

She'd motioned to a rabbit darting around the corner of Mandusedos's roundhouse. 'Look upon the sign of Andraste! She speaks! She tells me it is time, time to unleash her wrath! If you come with me, you do not fight for the queen of the Iceni. You fight for Andraste! You fight for retribution! You fight for yourselves!'

By then, every head was rapt, nodding enthusiastically.

'Now is the time to take back our lands and throw off the yoke of Roman servitude!' Boudicca had then thrust her sword aloft. 'Who is with me?!'

The thousands of Trinovante warriors fanning out behind Mandusedos's chariot was answer enough. They commingled with the Catuvellauni carts and the Gaesatae warriors trotting behind the chariots. She knew not how many had answered Andraste's call, only that the better part of three tribes marched with her.

She gazed over her opposite shoulder and caught the eye of Saibh, riding in a chariot at the head of her Silure women. Boudicca coolly acknowledged Saibh's nod and lifted her head. She had more than three tribes on her side. Andraste had gifted her warriors from as far away as Siluria. Everything had worked to point her down this road: the dirt track leading her host to the gates of Camulodunum.

She rested a hand on Emer's shoulder as they crested a small hill. The triangular roof of the Temple of Claudius appeared on the horizon, rising above the collected buildings making up the Roman capital. She glanced to the left and right. Fields populated by healthy-looking crops and herds of sheep stretched away on either side.

She held up a hand, bringing her incensed army to a rippling halt. Several had already broken away from the host, helping themselves to the bounty surrounding them. Boudicca punched her spear skywards, demonstrating her approval. A cheer went up and still more warriors fanned out, falling on the fast-disappearing barley.

'Take what you can, burn what you can't!' She called in a deep, booming clarion. 'Kill every man you see and bring the women to me! Andraste must be sated!'

Chariots wheeled off, spinning in the direction of distant farm buildings. Others whooped, driving livestock to the main body of the host.

With bright eyes, blackened by woad, she gestured for Emer to drive on. These provincials would merely be the first of the goddess's victims. Their cries of alarm would come too late for the urban dwellers of Camulodunum, who'd been stupid enough to dismantle their city walls. How complacent the Romans had become, taking their subjects' friendship for granted!

She glowered, remembering the procurator's imperious scowl and the regional agent's apologetic grimace. Their faces haunted her every moment, waking and sleeping. When she closed her eyes, she still saw the horrors visited on her daughters. Every ache and twinge from her disfigured back returned her to her humiliation in the mud. She lowered her gaze to the rutted path, willing it to give way to Roman cobbles.

Prasutagus's sad eyes floated up to her out of the dust. She grimly shook her head. *I am sorry, my love. You did what you thought was best. Now, I must do what I think is best.*

The acrid smoke of freshly lit fires assaulted her nostrils. The skies darkened behind her, lengthening the shadows of her warriors fanning out across manicured fields. Distant screams travelled on the still, summer air. She focussed on the distant temple roof and smirked.

The Romans would pay for what they'd done. This was only the beginning.

GLOSSARY

Aesculapius (ai-skool-AH-pee-oos): in Greek and Roman mythology, the deity associated with medicine and healing

Ala (literally, 'wing'): a unit of auxiliary cavalry roughly composed of 500 mounted warriors during the early principate

Amphora (am-fer-uh; pl. amphorae): a large, double-handled container with a narrow or squat body; usually contained liquid goods like wine and garum

Andraste (ahn-DRAH-stay): an ancient British goddess of war, vengeance, victory, and sovereignty; associated with rabbits and ravens as symbols/messengers

Annwn (AHN-un): the Otherworld

Apollo: in Greek and Roman mythology, the god of music, prophecy, the sun, healing, and archery

Aquilifer (ah-KWE-lih-fer): the legionary bearer of the eagle standard

As (AHS; pl. asses): a copper coin, ancient Roman equivalent of a penny; held the lowest monetary value of all Roman coins

Atrium: in ancient Roman buildings, an open-air entry and central room that acted as a social and political hub. Closed rooms and chambers were accessible behind doors surrounding the atrium. It featured an impluvium, or small pool, in the centre to collect rainwater descending from the skies overhead.

Aureus (OW-ree-us; pl. aurei): ancient Roman gold coin equal to 25 denarii or 100 sestertii

Aurochs (AW-ROCKS): a now-extinct wild ox, larger than modern oxen, which used to inhabit ancient Europe

Auxiliary (AWK-zee-lee-aree): in the Roman army, a noncitizen of the Roman empire serving in the Roman legions, either in an infantry or cavalry unit, typically alongside fellows from the same region. Auxiliary units were attached to Roman legions and soldiers were paid less than Roman legionaries. Upon successful completion of their twenty-five-year enlistment, auxiliaries were granted full Roman citizenship alongside their pensions

Ballista (BAH-lee-stah; pl. ballistae): an ancient Roman artillery weapon in the form of a large crossbow; often used in siege action

Balteus (BALL-tay-us; pl. baltea): an ancient Roman legionary belt, often featuring leather strips with metal studs that fell over the groin area

Bireme (bye-reem): an ancient warship that featured two rows of oars on either side; traditionally used in ancient warfare through the time of the early principate

Braccae (brach-kai): a pair of trousers, typically of wool, fastened about the waist with a cord and associated with ancient Celtic races

Brittunculi (brih-TUN-cyoo-lai; sin. brittunculus): a Latin derogatory term for the native Britons

Bucina (boo-KEE-nuh): a curved brass horn used by bucinators in the Roman army; also referred to as a cornu

Bucinator (boo-KEE-nay-tor): a player of the brass horn in the Roman legions; categorised as a signifer

Bulla (BOO-lah): a clay or metal pendant suspended from a child's neck, marking them as free citizens of Rome; the bulla was gifted by the father upon birth and cast aside when the child either reached adulthood (male) or married (female)

Caligae (KAH-lee-guy): ancient military sandals worn by Roman legionaries

Carissime (kah-REE-see-MAY): Latin term for 'my dearest' when addressing a singular male

Carnyx (car-nix): an ancient war horn associated with Celtic and Germanic races; a long instrument that typically ended in an animal shaped bell, featuring a rattle that vibrated when blown into; the instrument could create low, ominous tones

Caupona (COW-poh-nuh): an ancient Roman food stall that served hot meals quickly and provided lodging for travellers

Centurion (sen-TUR-ee-on): an ancient Roman army officer who commanded a century; the centurion commanding the first century of a cohort doubled as cohort commander

Centurionate: the collective term for the rank of Roman centurion

Century: a unit within a Roman legion, usually consisting of 80 men, commanded by a centurion. Six centuries would typically comprise a cohort. The first cohort of a legion contained five centuries of double strength, or 160 men each.

Cerberus (kir-bur-oos): the giant three-headed dog of Greek and Latin myth that guarded the entrance to Hades

Cryf (creef): Welsh word for 'strong'

Cohort: A unit in a Roman legion, typically consisting of six centuries (except for the first cohort, which contained five centuries of double strength). Ten cohorts made up a Roman legion

Contubernium (con-too-BEAR-nee-um; pl. contubernia): a sub-unit within a century consisting of eight legionaries. These men shared sleeping quarters in a barracks and a tent when on campaign. Ten contubernia made up a typical century (there would have been 20 contubernia in a double-strength century)

Cornu (KOR-noo): a curved brass horn used by bucinators in the Roman army; also referred to as a bucina

Cunus lingere (coo-nus LEEN-gur-ay): a derogatory term for a man that partakes in cunnilingus; literally, 'cunt licker'

Cuirass (queer-ASS): a piece of armour encasing the torso of a Roman soldier, sometimes referred to as a jerkin; typically worn underneath the lorica

Decanus (day-KAHN-oos): in the Roman military, the section leader of an eight-man contubernium, the lowest level of organization in the legions.

Decurion (deh-KUR-ee-on): in the ancient auxiliary Roman cavalry, an officer and commander of a 32-man troop (or turma) of cavalrymen. Decurions held a roughly equivalent rank to a centurion in a legion and answered only to their commanding officer, a prefect of the cavalry

Denarius (deh-NAR-ee-oos; pl. denarii): a silver coin equal to four sestertii in Ancient Rome; one of the most traded currencies, as most salaried professions were paid in denarii

Dis: another term for Pluto, the god of the Roman underworld

Elysium (eh-LIZZ-ee-um): in Greek and Roman mythology, the paradise in the afterlife that was the domain of heroes and those blessed in death

Equestrian: in the Roman empire, the middle-class rank, sitting below the senatorial class. Men had to be free citizens, reputable, and hold at least 400,000 sestertii in landed property to be accepted into the equestrian rank. Often denoted by a gold ring worn on the third finger of the left hand and a thin purple stripe on a man's toga; the status was rewarded to military officers upon attainment of a suitably paid rank, such as primus pilus

Equite: another term for the equestrian class

Eros: in Greek mythology, the winged god of love, desire, and sexual attraction; known in Roman mythology as Cupid

Fawr (vow-r): in Welsh, 'great' or 'big'

Fortuna (for-TOO-na): ancient Roman goddess of luck

Garum (GA-room): a sauce/condiment made from rotten, pickled fish guts; quite popular among ancient Romans

Gladius (GLAD-ee-oos; pl. gladii): a short, double-bladed sword carried by Roman legionaries and officers

Gradarius (gra-DAR-ee-oos): a type of horse in the Roman world specialized for combat

Hastatus Posterior: the most junior centurion (6th centurion) in a cohort

Infamia/Infamis: a person of ill-repute in Roman society, thus lacking the rights and privileges accorded to Roman citizens; actors, sex workers, and gladiators all fell within this classification

Intaglio (in-TALL-yo): carved gems used as personal seals; often of intricate miniature design and set into a ring

Intervallum: the open buffer space between the buildings and the palisade inside a Roman fort

Jove: another name for Jupiter, the most important deity of the

Roman pantheon

Kalends: the first day of the month in the Roman calendar

Latrunculi (la-TRUNG-coo-lee): an ancient boardgame thought to be a type of proto-chess

Legate (luh-GAYT): the commander of a Roman legion, always a man of senatorial rank with seasoned military experience

Legion: the largest unit of military organisation, typically consisting of ten legionary cohorts and commanded by a legate

Legionary (pl. legionaries): an infantry soldier in a Roman legion; men had to be Roman citizens to serve as legionaries and an enlistment typically consisted of 25 years

Lemures (lem-oo-res): in Roman mythology, the spirits of the dead; often connoted as restless, wandering spirits that haunted the living

Lorica (law-REE-kah; pl. loricae): metal armour worn over a jerkin or cuirass by ancient Roman soldiers; in the mid-1st century AD, most loricae still consisted of heavy chain mail, though the new 'lorica segmentata' consisting of overlapping steel plates was beginning to emerge and gradually replace chain mail loricae

Lupanar (loo-PAHN-ar): the term for a brothel in ancient Rome; literally 'wolf den'

Miles Gloriosus: a comedic play written by the Roman playwright Plautus and first performed around 206 BCE about a boasting, swaggering, vainglorious soldier

Mithras (MEE-trahs): an ancient Roman god, of Persian origin, that was worshipped by an all-male cult; rites, beliefs, and ceremonies related to the Mithraic religion are little-known, as the cult was shrouded in 'mystery' and secrecy; the cult was extremely popular among Roman soldiers

Morrigan (MOR-uh-gun): ancient shape-shifting Celtic goddess of death, destiny, and battle

Mulsum: a sweet alcoholic drink consisting of wine and honey; a popular drink at banquets

Mustaceus (moo-STAY-cus; pl. mustacei): a must-cake

Nemesis: in Greek and Roman mythology, the goddess of vengeance and retribution

Nones (NO-nays): in the Roman calendar, the ninth day before the Ides (the middle of the month); typically fell on either the 5th or 7th of the month, depending on how many days the month contained

Optio (AWP-tee-oh): second-in-command to a centurion in a Roman legion, often handling more administrative duties and marched at the rear of a century

Palisade (pal-iss-AID): a protective, walled barrier surrounding a Roman fort or marching camp; typically constructed of wooden stakes when attached to a more permanent structure; constructed from earth when attached to a temporary marching camp

Palla (pah-lah): a cloth wrapped over a woman's head and shoulders when outdoors in ancient Rome; the longer the palla, the higher status the woman wearing it

Palug (PAL-ug): a monstrous cat in Welsh medieval legend, thought to be a remnant from an earlier spotted cat god worshipped by Iron Age Welsh peoples

Parcae (par-KAI): Roman term for the three Fates of Greco-Roman myth

Peristylium (para-STY-leeum): an open courtyard within a Roman villa, surrounded by columned walkways on all four sides leading to other rooms within the villa. Often, the peristylium would contain gardens that housed both decorative and edible vegetation

Phalera (fa-ler-uh; pl. phalerae): a military decoration medal awarded to a legionary soldier or officer and worn on the bearer's medal harness on parade

Pilum (pih-lum; pl. pila): a throwing spear used by Roman soldiers; legionaries usually carried 2 pila each while on the march

Praetorian Guard (pree-TAW-ree-uhn): an elite unit of legionaries and centurions stationed just outside the gates of Rome; men of the Praetorian Guard were assigned to guard the emperor, his retinue, and the imperial palace

Praetorium (pree-TAW-ree-um): the headquarters of the commanding legionary legate; his offices, living quarters, and corresponding rooms for members of his staff and personal household existed in this centrally located building

Prefect: in the Roman legions, the camp prefect was the highest-ranking non-senatorial officer, in charge of overseeing the running of a fort but retired from campaigning, a post typically held by a former primus pilus; also the title of the commanding officer of an auxiliary unit (cavalry or infantry), typically a Roman citizen of equestrian or senatorial rank

Primus pilus (PREE-moos PILL-oos): the most senior centurion in a Roman legion, in charge of the first century in the first cohort. A man of equestrian rank and a career soldier, they often held the post for 1-2 years before retiring from the legions or moving into a prefecture; translates as 'first spear'

Principia (preen-KIP-ee-ah): the most centrally located building within a Roman fort that functioned as a legionary headquarters; this is where the legionary temples and standards were located

Pugio (POO-gee-oh): a dagger

Salve (sal-way): a Latin greeting to a singular person
Saturnalia (sah-tur-NAY-lee-uh): the ancient Roman festival held in honour of the god Saturn, typically taking place around 17 December; this time involved feasting, fooling, role reversals (in which masters served their slaves) and gift-giving by masters and heads of household

Scutum (SKOO-tum; pl. scuta): a curved, rectangular shield borne by legionary soldiers; the shield was large enough to protect most of a Roman's body

Sestertius (say-STUR-tee-oos; pl. sestertii): an ancient Roman coin equal to 2 dupondii

Signifer (SING-nih-fer): a legionary standard-bearer; this man would carry a century's standard and accompanying decorations on parade and into battle; they also often handled a century's finances, such as funerary funds

Strigil (STRID-gel): a small, curved metal tool used to scrape dirt, oil, or sweat from the skin

Styx (sticks): in Greek and Roman mythology, the river separating Hades (the underworld inhabited by the dead) from the world of the living

Subura (suh-BOO-rah): a dingy, slum neighbourhood of ancient Rome situated in the valley between the Esquiline, Viminal, and Quirinal hills

Taberna (tah-BEAR-nah): a single shop or stall in ancient Rome, with its front opening onto the street

Tabula (tah-BOO-lah): an ancient Roman board game with rules similar to backgammon

Tali (TAH-lee): knucklebones, usually of sheep or goats, thrown like dice in some ancient board games

Tesserarius (TEH-seh-ar-ee-oos): in the Roman legions, an optio's second-in-command; often tasked with administrative work and legionary security

Tonsor: a barber

Tonstrina: a barber shop

Torc: an intricate gold or silver necklace, usually comprising twisted bands and rounded by decorative knobs, worn by nobles of Celtic tribes

Tribune: in the Roman army, one of 5 administrative assistants to the legionary legate of equestrian rank, except for the *tribunis laticlavius,* (tree-BOO-nuhs lah-tih-KLAH-wee-oos) who came from senatorial rank and was appointed directly by the emperor or senate. These men only served a couple of years in noncombatant roles before continuing their climb up the social ladder, or *cursus honorum*

Triclinium (tree-KLEE-nee-um): a formal Roman dining room, often featuring dining couches surrounding a table on three sides

Typhon (TAI-fon): a monster of Greek and Roman myth; often invoked in curses

Vicus (WIH-kuss): an unofficial settlement located just outside a Roman fort

Virtus (WHIR-toos): the ancient Roman notion of manly ideals; encompassed their ideas of honour and duty

Vitis (WEE-tiss): the vine staff wielded by centurions to instil discipline in their men

353

HISTORICAL NOTES

As I've said before, the ancient historical fiction author has fewer resources to draw from than her fellow historical fiction authors. Therefore, she must take on more of a detective role: critically evaluating what information is available, consulting multiple theories, and filling in the many gaps in the record with her own imagination. While efforts have been made to root the story in the historical record, please keep in mind that this is a work of fiction and certain liberties have been taken. I've tried to bind together many thrilling elements from this era, both to better understand the circumstances that led to Boudicca's infamous revolt and to heighten the dramatic tension of Luciana and Decimus's tale.

Firstly, it is true (as far as we can tell) that Emperor Nero had his mother, Agrippina, murdered in March of 59 CE. As ludicrous as Lucius's ghost story is, the ancient sources (Tacitus and Dio) agree that Nero's clumsily executed matricide played out in that manner: backfiring booby-trapped boat, attempted murder at sea, stab through the womb, and all. The one fact Lucius gets wrong is the Praetorian Guard murdering Agrippina. According to Tacitus and Dio, the Praetorian Guard refused to kill a daughter of Germanicus, so Nero dispatched marines in the employ of the imperial fleet to murder her. Lucius took some dramatic license when recounting his version of events. And all of this was hearsay at the time— the official version of events omitted everything but the fact that the Augusta had perished. While news and mail travelled surprisingly swiftly in the ancient world, Nero certainly didn't put the truth out (in fact, he claimed that Agrippina tried to murder him and, upon failing, killed herself. Typical).

The philosopher Seneca (the Younger), despite championing stoicism and simplicity in his surviving works, was himself an extremely wealthy man. He invested heavily in Britannia's colonial infrastructure, loaning large sums of money to building projects and newly conquered tribes. The amount of interest he expected back on these loans was enormous and is considered a likely reason for the poverty the Iceni and several other tribes living under Rome experienced prior to the rebellion (it didn't help that Nero's excessive spending had already led to a general devaluation of the currency). Seneca was determined to call in his loans, especially in the wake of Nero seriously considering the abandonment of Britannia. His resorting to espionage and slimy tribunes to recoup losses his debtors couldn't pay is a scheme entirely of my own invention.

At this point in history, Nero was beginning to rethink Rome's presence in Britannia (probably because one of his closest advisors, Seneca, couldn't shut up about how much money he'd lost in British investments). The timing of the Boudiccan revolt likely decided Nero against withdrawing the legions. Just when the threat of recall and abandonment seemed a possibility, destruction of such a scale occurred that Rome had to save face. Abandoning the island to its fate would have appeared weak to the rest of the Roman world, and Nero couldn't have that. It is ironic that Boudicca came the closest to forcibly evicting the Romans, but her attempt only ensured their continued presence for the next 350 years.

Not much is known about Prasutagus, Boudicca's husband and chieftain of the Iceni. We do know that he likely didn't have anything to do with the (minor-scale) Iceni rebellion in 47 CE that led to the confiscation of their arms, as Rome resumed business with the tribe through him as client-king. He must have stayed loyal to Rome through the rebellion, likely seeing peacekeeping as the only option for his people's survival. There have been Iceni coins found with 'PRASTO' engraved on them; numismatists have interpreted this word as Prasutagus's name. The minting of coins under his reign plays into the notion of a client-king friendly with Rome. According to the classical sources, he took ill and died around 59 CE, though not before making a will leaving half his kingdom to his two daughters and the other half to emperor Nero. I believe Prasutagus had to have known he was dying, and worried about the future of his tribe once he was gone. He knew how deeply in debt the Iceni were to Rome, and his will smacks of a last-ditch effort to preserve the peace he worked so hard to keep. That is how I have represented his actions in this story. Poor Prasutagus couldn't have known that the Romans never had any intention of honouring his will.

Roman suzerainty was a policy by which the British tribes loyal to Rome could hold 'independence' over their internal affairs while paying taxes, sending troops to the auxiliary, and cooperating with Rome's governance over all Britannia. It was a halfway step to conquering tribal territory. Once the client-king chieftain had perished, Rome moved in before a successor could be named and claimed all tribal territory as now under full control of the provincial government. This was a smooth method of 'legal' subjugation until the policy famously backfired with the Iceni. The ancient sources all agree that Boudicca was beaten and her daughters 'ravaged' for defying this policy. It would provide the spark for Boudicca's terrible rebellion.

When it comes to the Silures, the cat cult might seem ridiculous. However, Eurasian lynx were living (though not abundant) in Britain until their extinction during the dark ages. Iron Age relics depicting a spotted cat approximating a lynx have been excavated in Silure lands, with some of the relics having a religious/votive nature. Later Welsh myths of the medieval era describe a man-eating, monstrous cat named 'Cath Palug,' which heroes like King Arthur must defeat. The Iron Age artifacts offer the terrific suggestion that the 'Cath Palug' of myth might be a transmutation of an earlier pagan god worshipped by people in southern Wales. So, I created the 'Daughters of Palug' to fill that suggestion.

Governor Suetonius Paulinus was no fan of the native Britons. He determined that taking out the druids, who seemed to have retreated to the shores of Anglesey (or, as the Romans called it, Mona), would break British resistance to Rome's occupation. He planned a massive offensive, sending the men of the XIII Gemina and XX Valeria to Mona to eradicate the druids. The result was the so-called 'Battle of Anglesey,' which will take place in Roman Equestrian III. Because Paulinus's attentions were firmly fixed on the west, he left the problem with the Iceni to the imperial procurator, Catus Decianus. Decianus sent a rather small vexillation of garrison troops to force Boudicca into submission, and we know exactly how well that went. With half the legionary troops occupied on the opposite side of the country (and a further fourth mere raw recruits training in Exeter without a legate), conditions were ripe for Boudicca to strike in the east.

Decimus's traumatic memories of the Medway River mark the bloodiest moment of the 43 CE Roman invasion. This conflict has been well studied, with some excellent descriptions and maps drawn up, though the exact location of the battle is still disputed. This action involved the Batavian auxiliary swimming across the Medway to land upriver and hamstring all the British charioteers' ponies, while the future emperor Vespasian's II Augusta established a hard-won beachhead for the rest of the army to cross. The following day, XIII Gemina took part in a diversionary frontal assault while Gnaeus Hosidius Geta, legate of IX Hispana, led a spearhead action from the flank. The plan almost faltered and Geta was nearly captured, though the Romans did manage to succeed and force their way across. The battle ended with the (supposed) death of Togidubnus, while his brother, Caratacus, fled for Wales. The Romans would encounter no more substantial resistance to the first phase of their invasion. I found Geta's role in this interesting, especially considering his near failure. I cooked up the notion of his needing to pass a message along the flank, and Decimus supplying a man for the job. Caecus and his doomed contubernium are inventions.

Now for the fun stuff: did the British really walk along the yokes of their chariots to stand and fight from the backs of their horses? According to Tacitus, they absolutely did (and he ought to know, his father-in-law was Agricola, Titus Vespasianus's fellow square-jawed tribune – you'll meet him properly in Roman Equestrian III). Given the Britons' oft cited impetuosity and fearlessness, it doesn't seem unreasonable. War chariots were handled by a driver, leaving the warrior's hands free to wield weapons. Luciana's antics along the yoke are as described by Tacitus.

When it comes to the sidhe, the idea that some remnant of Neolithic Britons lived in the hills and provided the purest line of communication to the Earth Mother was an invention meant to connect later Welsh/Irish myth of the sidhe (fairy people) to actual people revered by British Celts (and I can't claim credit for this idea, Amanda Cockrell did it first). New research suggests Celtic peoples didn't 'invade' Britain in 800 BCE, but rather gradually integrated with earlier populations through slow cultural adoption and waves of small, non-disruptive migrations. I like the idea that the resulting British Celts didn't forget their Neolithic ancestors and were in fact in awe of them (these were the folks that built Stonehenge, after all). It grounds the reverence their descendants had for magical, mystical beings in an earlier, more concrete, spirituality.

I have Philip Matyszak's *Ancient Magic in Greece and Rome* to thank for the character of Antiope. Romans read a lot into star charts and astrology, but they also practiced divination in some rather interesting ways. One of which was to paint line numbers from Virgil's *The Aeneid* onto tokens and pull them out of a jar or sack, determining significance from the corresponding passage in the poem. Gale was a Greek witch that displeased Hecate, who turned her into a weasel. Hence Antiope's familiar, as weasels were linked to witchcraft in Rome.

Finally, sex. Did the Romans loathe cunnilingus that much, or was Tullius overreacting? Unfortunately, they did. Calling a man a *cunus lingere* (cunt-licker) was the worst possible insult you could hurl at a Roman man of standing. The ancient Romans were obsessed with *dignitas* and *virtus*, and a Roman man's mouth was thought to be irrevocably sullied by taking part in oral sex (similarly, self-love carried out with the dominant hand also dirtied it forever). However, this is what people thought and said in public. While considered profoundly degrading, we know Roman men practiced oral sex – we have the graffito to prove it. Sex with other men wasn't as taboo to the Romans as it was in later eras – it just mattered who was in the dominant position. If the prominent Roman citizen was doing the deed, it didn't matter if he was doing a man, woman, or sheep; it was manly to dominate. Now, if you were the man being dominated, you'd better hope to be a pleb or a slave, because if you were a man of public standing, your reputation was sunk. Again, though, that's only if it became public knowledge. Kinky hypocrites, those Romans.

I had the enormous pleasure of seeing more sights in Roman Britain for this round of research, with some of the most significant coming from Colchester (Camulodunum). The good folks at Colchester Castle host a treasure trove of artifacts from the Iron Age and Roman eras, including evidence of Boudicca's burnt horizon and the lovely Fenwick Treasure. Touring the Roman foundations of the Temple of Claudius, located directly beneath the Norman keep, was awe-inspiring. The Colchester Circus Museum and grounds tickled every single bone in my Horse Girl body, and going there during the King's birthday celebrations meant I had the entire place to myself – thanks a million, Samantha! Repeat visits to London, St. Albans, and Wroxeter continue to throw up new treasures. The Roman Legionary Museum and baths/barracks in Caerleon gave me a sense of Roman occupation in south Wales, along with the topography of Silure lands.

As before, I've included a bibliography of *some* of the books I read to research this novel. I haven't been short of excellent resources to guide my research and answer my questions, and I hope I've done a serviceable job interpreting their information. Any factual accuracies are down to them; the errata you encounter are entirely my own.

SELECTED BIBLIOGRAPHY

Aldhouse-Green, Miranda J. *Celtic Myths: A Guide to the Ancient Gods and Legends*. Thames & Hudson, 2015.

Aldhouse-Green, Miranda J. *Enchanted Wales: Myth and Magic in Welsh Storytelling*. Calon, 2024.

Aldhouse-Green, Miranda J. *The World of the Druids*. Thames and Hudson, 1997.

Allen, Denise, and Mike Bryan. *Roman Britain... and Where to Find It*. Amberley, 2020.

Allen, Stephen, and Wayne Reynolds. *Celtic Warrior: 300 BC - AD 100*.

Osprey, 2006.

Burn, A. R. "The Battle of the Medway, A.D. 43." *History*, vol. 38, no. 133, 1953, pp. 105–15. *JSTOR*, http://www.jstor.org/stable/24403306.

Chittenden, Joseph. *Roman London*. JC3DVIS, 2024.

Chrystal, Paul. *In Bed with the Romans*. Amberley, 2017.

Clarke, John R., and Michael Larvey. *Roman Sex: 100 BC-AD 250*. Echo Point Books & Media, LLC, 2014.

Collingridge, Vanessa. *Boudica*. Ebury, 2005.

de La Bédoyère, Guy. *Gladius: Living, Fighting and Dying in the Roman Army*. Little, Brown, 2020.

Fields, Nic, and Steve Noon. *Britannia AD 43*. Osprey Publishing, 2020.

Howell, Raymond. *Silures: Resistance, Resilience, Revival*. The History Press, 2022.

Matyszak, Philip. *Ancient Magic in Greece and Rome: A Hands-on Guide*. Thames and Hudson, 2023.

Matyszak, Philip. *Legionary: The Roman Soldier's (Unofficial) Manual*. Thames & Hudson, 2011.

Shelton, Jo-Ann. "The Provinces." *As the Romans Did*, Oxford University Press, 1998, pp. 268–288.

Symons, Sarah. *Roman Wales*. Amberley, 2015.

Tacitus, P Cornelius. *Great Books of the Western World: Tacitus*. Translated by Alfred John Church and William Jackson Brodribb, Encyclopaedia Britannica, 1952.

Trafford, L J. *Sex and Sexuality in Ancient Rome*. Pen and Sword History, 2021.

White, Roger H. *Wroxeter Roman City*. English Heritage, 2012.

Webb, Simon. *Life in Roman London*. History Press (SC), 2012.

ACKNOWLEDGEMENTS

I couldn't have delivered the story I wanted to tell into your hands without the invaluable input of many people. Firstly, to my incredible editor, Jenny Quinlan, thank you! You really helped me shape this narrative into its beautiful, coherent form. I am so lucky to have your incredible insight and guidance! Brook – thank you for leading me to Jenny! Your friendship and advice are invaluable! And thank you to Cathie Dunn – without your blog tour, Brook and I might never have connected. My amazing and talented beta readers, Cheryl and Artemisia, identified the blind spots in my writing. I so needed your eagle eyes going over my drafts! My alpha reader, Laura, saw this book in its earliest, roughest form and always provided encouragement when I needed it most. I take so much inspiration from your perseverance. Thank you so much, dear friend. For my English teacher, Renee Wolfe, who encouraged and guided my writing efforts so long ago and provided my model for teaching, I wouldn't be the writer I am today without you!

A huge thank you to the incredible author community and my arc readers! You make this whole process far, far less lonely.

For Dee Marley, thank you for seeing the potential in the Roman Equestrian series and providing the beautiful formatting, cover art, and exposure for my books. I'm so grateful to call Historium Press home for my books.

Finally, the biggest thanks of all belongs to my family: Tanya, Ken, Bettylou, Courtney, and little Chloe. You mean everything to me.

About the Author

A.M. Swink, the author of the award-winning Roman Equestrian series, grew up in Dayton, Ohio, obsessed with two things: books and horses. After a childhood of reading, writing, showing, and riding, she moved to Lexington, Kentucky to complete three degrees and work as a college professor of reading and writing.

She's travelled extensively around Europe, exploring ancient sites and artefacts relating to the Iron Age and Roman era. She is fascinated by our connection to the past and the ancestral tether that draws us back into the mists of time.

*****

If you enjoyed the story, reviews are appreciated
at Amazon or Goodreads.

Follow the author at

www.thehistoricalfictioncompany.com/hp-author/am-swink

or

www.amswink.com

HISTORIUM PRESS

www.historiumpress.com

www.ingramcontent.com/pod-product-compliance
Lightning Source LLC
Chambersburg PA
CBHW021438310726
48971CB00005B/1411